THE OTHER SIDE OF TOMORROW

MICALEA SMELTZER

Cover Design © Copyright Letitia Hasser with R.B.A. Designs

Photo © Copyright Regina Wamba

Edited & Formatted by: Wendi "The Swirl Queen" Temporado with Ready, Set, Edit

For the doctors, nurses, and techs who are there every day for us dialysis patients. Your hard work doesn't go unnoticed. We see you. We appreciate you. Keep rocking it.

AUTHOR'S NOTE

In May 2017, at twenty-three years old, I got some of the worst news imaginable. I walked into an emergency room thinking there was something wrong with my gallbladder and learned my kidneys had shut down. I was literally dying. It was a shock to me to hear the words, "Don't worry, you're not going to die," since it hadn't even crossed my mind that I was *dying. I later found out I had hours left to live and it was a miracle I came when I did.*

The next few days, even months were a whirlwind as my whole life changed forever.

Dialysis is not easy. It's so incredibly hard on your body and so tiring.

When I was in the hospital, Willa's story came to me. It kept nagging at me to write it, but I wanted to wait until I had a transplant so I could describe that part accurately too, but Willa was insistent and kept reminding me this was her story not mine.

While there is a large amount of myself represented in the following pages, it is very much Willa's story. Maybe one day I'll write a non-fiction journal type story chronicling my own journey, but for now, there's this. If it helps give hope to one person who's on dialysis waiting for a transplant it's worth it.

I also want to thank Willa for giving me the strength to switch to peritoneal dialysis. It's something I contemplated months before writing this book to do myself, but I kept hoping transplant would happen. Every week that went by with no news, the more I considered switching. Hemodialysis is extremely tiring on the body and hard on the heart. I want to believe I'm going to live a long life post-transplant, and I want to do everything I can to ensure that.

Thanks, Willa. I think you saved my life.

—Micalea

Life can change in an instant…

For Willa Hansen, this statement couldn't be truer. One minute she was a seemingly normal fourteen-year-old, and the next, her life was turned upside down with only a few words. Three years later, she's receiving a kidney transplant and can start living again, only now she's not sure she knows how.

Life can end in a moment…

Jasper Werth knows this all too well, seeing as a drunk driver killed his little brother. He's always been a carefree guy, never taking life too seriously, but losing his brother is a major blow, and he finds himself lost until Willa walks into his life.

Life can mend the most broken parts of our souls…

Willa and Jasper couldn't be more opposite, but as fate brings them together they'll learn maybe they're not so different after all.

Sometimes what you need comes in a package you least expect.

CHAPTER ONE

I blink up at the sky. It's bright—too bright—and I shouldn't be staring at it, but it reminds me that I'm alive.

I'm still here.

I'm still breathing.

Nothing will knock me down.

I am strong. I am resilient. I will make it through this.

I've repeated this mantra several times a day since I was fourteen.

I remember the day so clearly that everything changed. I'd been sick for weeks, longer, really, but only then did everything come crashing down. The weakness was overwhelming. I could barely place one foot on the floor. My mom had been worried, I knew, but I kept making excuses—I'd been practicing dance too hard, school was exhausting; on and on, I blamed everything else. It was easier that way.

Until it wasn't.

I was at the bowling alley with my friends when I collapsed.

One minute I was upright, forcing a smile, trying not to think about how tired I felt, and the next I was on the ground. I didn't open my eyes until I was being loaded into an ambulance.

The horrified gazes of my friends are something I'll never forget.

The ten-minute ride to the hospital seemed endless.

"What's wrong with me?" I asked over and over, but no one could tell me anything.

"Keep that on," one paramedic scolded, putting the oxygen mask back on my face. I hadn't even realized I'd removed it.

We arrived at the emergency room and they wheeled me back into a room.

My parents were already at the hospital waiting, one of my friends having called them, and they followed the paramedics as I was wheeled back, hospital visitor badges clipped to their shirts.

"Oh, Willa," my mom cried, trying to hug me as the paramedics wheeled me down the hall.

I was put into a room and helped into a gown and ugly blue socks—which was mighty embarrassing as I insisted I could change myself, but since I fainted they wouldn't let me.

When the doctor came to see me, I immediately blurted, "I'm *not* sick. I don't know why I'm here. I'm tired, that's all."

The doctor paused, raised a brow, his lips twitching with the threat of a smile. "How about you let me determine that, okay?"

I sighed but nodded. My mom and dad huddled in the corner, her with her hands clasped at her chin, with him rubbing her shoulders.

"You look awfully pale," the doctor remarked. "Stick out your tongue."

I did.

"Mhmm."

"What? What does that mean?" my mom burst out.

"Nothing yet," the doctor waved away her concern. "I need to listen to your heart and lungs; can you sit up a bit?" he asked me.

I did as he asked, feeling like this was all completely stupid.

He continued to cluck his tongue as he checked my ankles. Finally, he said he was ordering blood work and left.

It didn't take long for someone to come to take my blood, and after that, we sat waiting.

This all felt so silly to me.

I was fine, my blood work would be fine, and then they'd send me home.

But that's not what happened.

The doctor appeared in the doorway of the room. There was something different in his eyes, not quite sad but almost. Maybe he looked a little surprised too.

He cleared his throat and walked over to the stool, sitting down.

My parents stood at my side, waiting for what he had to say.

He didn't look at them. He looked at me. Straight in my eyes as he delivered the news.

"Willa, I have some bad news." My heart stopped. "Your kidneys have failed. Based on your numbers, you have chronic end-stage kidney disease. We will have to get you started on dialysis immediately." My eyes widened in fear. "Don't worry, dialysis isn't scary. You're going to be fine. This isn't a death sentence."

I stopped.

Everything stopped.

Not a death sentence?

I hadn't even considered the fact I could be dying—that this could kill me.

He was right, of course, it wasn't a death sentence, not since it was caught in time. Dialysis also wasn't scary, but that didn't mean it was easy. It sucked. It was exhausting, and most days all I wanted to do was sleep. It made going to school impossible. I was home schooled after that. If it wasn't for my best friend Meredith, I would've completely fallen out of touch with the "real" world. It was easy to shut myself away, but she forced me to get out. Sometimes, for a little while, I could pretend I wasn't sick.

That was another thing. I didn't look sick, not at all, but I was.

The dark shadows beneath my eyes from restless sleep were the only way to tell that something was going on with me.

Other than that, I looked like any other spritely seventeen-year-old now.

I felt more like I was seventy, though. Going through this had aged me—I understood more than most kids my age, and I'd come to terms with my mortality.

Everybody dies, you might as well *live* while you can.

I'd noticed a lot of people "died" before they actually *died*. They went through the motions, unhappy, and that wasn't what I'd call living at all.

You could live without being *alive*, and that was one of the saddest truths I'd learned.

I spread my arms wide, like I'm making snow angels, but it's sand instead.

It's always sand in sunny Santa Monica, California. I love it, though, the warmth, the ocean, the pier. It's magic, and no one can convince me otherwise.

The telltale grinding of the sliding glass door on our deck puts me on alert. But I don't move.

I close my eyes and pretend to be invisible.

"What are you doing out here? You're turning red." There's a shift in the sand beside me as my fifteen-year-old sister, Harlow, drops down next to me.

I crack an eye open and twist my head to face her. I sigh, envious of how effortlessly beautiful she looks. Her blonde hair hangs halfway down her back, way longer than mine, and is stick straight opposed to my slightly wavy hair that doesn't want to be straight but doesn't want to be curly either. She wears a pair of shorts and a loose gray sweater with sneakers. It's a simple outfit but somehow, she makes it work. It looks effortless next to my ripped jeans and baggy as hell T-shirt to hide the tube in my stomach. However, I must admit the belt I wear to hold the catheter does a good job of concealing it as well as securing it. It's not like you want something dangling out of your body to get tugged on something. I practically shudder at the thought.

"Hiding," I answer her.

She glances down at me, stifling a laugh. "From who? Mom? What's she doing? Trying to get you to take those weird vitamins some shaman gave her?"

I snort. "She knows I can't have any of her weird health stuff. And I'm not hiding from anyone."

"Then what?" She blinks against the sun.

I sit up and dust the sand off my back. "Life, I guess. It's hard sometimes. Overwhelming."

She frowns. "I'm sorry."

"It's okay." I force a smile, but it doesn't take away the pain in her eyes.

As hard as my diagnosis is on me, I know it's hard on my family too. No one in my family was a match, not my mom or dad, not my extended family, and my sister is too young to donate. Instead, the last few years I've been waiting for a donor. A deceased donor. I'm literally sitting around waiting for someone to die, and there's something morbid about that. As much as I want and need a kidney, I hate the fact somebody has to *die* for me to get it.

It's been three years since my diagnosis, and most days I'm happy. In fact, a lot of the time I feel relatively normal. But some days it catches up to me, the reality of it all, and I can't help but go to a dark place in my head. Today, unfortunately, is one of those days. I don't like having these days, but I know it's not healthy to not have them, either. But most of the time, I'm able to choose being happy because while my disease has taken a lot from me, I refuse to let it take my happiness too. It won't beat me. I'm stronger than that.

Harlow reaches for my hand. "I low you." She gives it a squeeze. My hand is pale underneath hers. She spends way more time on the beach than I do, and her skin is tanned to a bronze color.

"I low you too," I reply.

When Harlow was little, she couldn't say V, so love always sounded like low, and ever since we've always said it that way to each other. Born two years apart, I can't remember a time without my spunky little sister. I love her to pieces, she's my best friend, besides Meredith, of course, and she's made all this easier. She's *always* here when I need to cry or scream or vent or whatever it is I need to do at that moment.

People on the outside tend to close themselves off when they see something like this happening to someone. They think, "oh, that's not bad," or "it could be worse."

When, really, I think it's best to acknowledge the fact that it freaking blows.

So does cancer.

And Alzheimer's.

Every disease out there, whatever it may be, *sucks*.

Why sweep it under the rug and pretend it doesn't exist?

Just because it's not happening to you, doesn't mean it's not happening.

And yeah, it *could* be worse, I tell myself that all the time, but that doesn't mean it should be brushed under the rug, either.

I feel like we should support our fellow human beings instead of turning a blind eye. Why do people find it easier to turn away from the old lady struggling to reach for something on a high shelf in the grocery store than to take a few seconds to help?

I don't understand this notion many people have of pretending things don't exist.

They do. Stop being a pussy and face the facts.

Harlow pokes her finger into my cheek. "You're thinking too much. Snap out of it."

"Sorry." I shake my head and flash her a smile.

I've always lived in my head way too much. It's easier there, less scary.

"Are you going to sit out here all day?" she asks.

I shrug and pick up some sand, watching it fall through my fingers. "Maybe."

She shakes her head. "Come on, we're going somewhere." She stands up and offers me her hand.

"You can't drive," I remind her.

She rolls her eyes. "*You* can."

"Where are we going?" I reluctantly take her hand and let her lift me up. I shake the sand off my body, but, of course, I can't get rid of all of it. Sand is as dangerous to be around as glitter.

"To get ice cream, of course. Ice cream makes everything better."

"You know I'm not supposed to have ice cream."

Since I do peritoneal dialysis, my diet isn't quite as restricted as it was in the early stages of my diagnosis when I was on hemodialysis. But that doesn't mean I can go crazy and eat whatever I want.

Our kidneys do *a lot* for our bodies.

My fourteen-year-old self thought all they were good for was gathering urine and sending it to my bladder.

Wrong.

Your kidneys clean all the blood in your body—when they fail, toxins build up in your bloodstream and can ultimately kill you. Your kidneys do more than that too. They also tell your body to absorb vitamin D. Therefore, when your kidneys don't work, you could stand in the sun all day and not get any vitamin D.

Honestly, I'm a full-blown kidney expert at this point. It's amazing the things you learn *after* you get sick.

Harlow groans and tilts her head to the sky for a moment before facing me. Sometimes it's jarring looking at her with her one blue and one green eye. It's almost like looking at two people at once.

"Willa, one *teensy-tiny* cup of ice cream isn't going to kill you."

I give her a look.

"Bad joke, I know." She takes my hand. "But come on, let's get out for a while. Mom and Dad won't be home for a while yet, and I hate seeing you sad."

"Why are *you* home?" I ask, suddenly realizing it's the middle of the afternoon and she should be at school. It's May, and her school doesn't end until June.

I finished up my home schooling back in December and graduated. It was nice being done nearly a year and a half early, but it also made me that much more confused.

I wanted to go to college, right? But how did I do that with all the extra baggage I had? It wouldn't exactly be easy, or sanitary, to dialyze in a dorm room. The thought alone made me want to shudder.

It was possible I could enroll at the community college and continue to live at home, but … I wasn't sure that was what I wanted.

Lost, that's the only way I could describe myself at the moment.

It seemed like my whole life was on pause, waiting for the day I got a kidney. For the day when I could really start living again and didn't have to think about dialyzing or anything that goes with it.

There wasn't a day in the last three years where I didn't have to think about something regarding my illness. There was no escaping it. It was there all the time.

While at times, like today, it was hard, most of the time it was such a part of my routine I didn't even think about it.

But for the moment, I was having a major case of the poor me's.

"We got out early today," she supplies. "Parent-teacher conferences are tonight, the teachers need time to prepare. I'm sure they have to give a lot of bad news." She claps her hands together and tilts her head to the side. "I'm sorry, Mr. and Mrs. Jones, but it looks like little Tommy is going to fail," she mocks in a high-pitched voice.

"Is it that bad?" I ask, picking up my flip-flops and heading up the deck steps and into the house.

"You have no idea," she groans. "Half the kids there don't do *anything*. They expect a free ride or Mommy and

Daddy to pay their way. All they talk about is partying, drinking, and sex."

"Sounds like I haven't missed much."

"Eh." She shrugs, sliding onto one of the barstools. "It can be entertaining at times, but it's mostly annoying."

"Let me go change, and then we'll go," I tell her.

There's no way I'm going anywhere with sand in my crotch. I don't know how it always manages to find its way inside my clothes, but it does.

"I'll be here." She kicks her legs up on the counter.

I bound up the steps and push the door open to my room.

It's a mess, like always. My mattress lies on the floor, covered in a million pillows and blankets. String lights hang across an entire wall, making my room glow with a warm golden hue. Pinned to the string of the lights are Polaroid photos. I still have aways to go to fill it all up, it's a work in progress, but it brings me joy to see all the different happy moments I've captured. There are some not happy ones there as well, but I like to be reminded of how far I've come. How no matter what's been thrown at me, I'm still standing tall.

I change quickly into another pair of shorts and a loose tank top, then check my appearance in the floor-length mirror behind my door.

My hair's a wild mess and looks like it hasn't been brushed—even though it has. My eyes are wide, and my cheeks flushed, making my freckles even more prominent.

I have a love/hate relationship with my freckles. Some days I love them and think they're cute, other days I think they look like mud streaked across my face.

"Willa! Are you done yet?" Harlow yells up the steps.

"Yeah, yeah," I chant, grabbing my purse and slinging the strap across my body before reaching for my car keys on my dresser.

I stumble down the steps and find Harlow waiting by the front door.

"I'm starving now," she whines. "Let's grab a bite to eat and then get ice cream."

I open my mouth to argue, but then my stomach decides to rumble.

"Yeah," I agree. "Food first."

As if conjured by our words, our giant golden retriever Perry bounds into the foyer.

"No, Perry, no food for you. Stay here."

"We could take him with us," Harlow suggests.

"The last time we did that he tried to eat a bird."

"He's a puppy. He doesn't know any better."

"Sometimes you make me sound like such an annoying, *boring* mother."

"Uh … because that's what you act like." She laughs and runs down the hall for Perry's leash.

The nice thing about living in Santa Monica is you can take your dog pretty much anywhere.

She returns with the leash and Perry sits, tongue hanging out, waiting for her to put it on him.

Once it's clasped I unlock the door and we head to my car—a mint colored Chevrolet Spark. It's small, the perfect size for me, and a gift from my parents. I didn't want them to spend their hard-earned money on a brand-new car for me, but they insisted so it became my birthday and graduation present.

It's come in handy having my own car; I definitely get out more than before.

Perry climbs in the back, leaning between the two front seats, panting like he's been outside for an hour already. He's barely a year old and gets overly excited about everything.

"Would you want to go to Monsterwiches?" I ask Harlow.

The sandwich shop a couple of miles away is a favorite for locals. Not many tourists know about it, which makes it a nice place to hang out. When tourists start clogging up a place the locals usually clear out.

"Yeah, that's good with me." She clicks her seatbelt into place then proceeds to place her feet on the dashboard and turn the volume on the radio up to a deafening level. I turn it down to a more sensible level and she scoffs. "You're such a fun sucker."

"Yep, that's me. Willa the fun sucker. Tell Mom and Dad to put that on my tombstone for me, m'kay?" I start to back out of the driveway.

"Willa," she gasps, genuinely offended. "Don't even joke about that kind of thing."

I put the car into drive, heading down the street. "I'm sorry."

Sometimes, I forget that I'm weirdly comfortable with my inevitable death. When you come close to dying it's not that scary anymore, it seems easier, more peaceful than this living part. But I'm sure for my sister, who was twelve at the time, the experience was traumatizing.

"I don't want to think about a world in which you don't exist. You're my sister. My best friend." She reaches for my hand and squeezes it.

I glance at her quickly with a smile. "I'm not going anywhere, not for a long time," I vow. "This may have tried to knock me down, but I'm stronger than it."

I'm stronger *because* of it.

She smiles softly, emotion flooding her eyes. "You're the strongest person I know."

Her words squeeze my heart. It's nice to hear them.

She turns the radio up again, and this time I don't change it.

The music quiets the chaos of my mind, as backward as that sounds.

We reach the sandwich shop and I park in the tiny side lot—seriously, there are only three parking spaces, which are frequently fought over since this place is popular.

"I'll go get our food—you take care of Perry."

Before I can protest, my sister is gone, and I'm left with the demon dog.

Not that he's *mean*, he's … a little nuts.

Perry looks at me, tongue hanging out, with this doofus look like he's saying, *"What are you talking about? I'm adorable. I'm a good boy. Me so cute."*

"All right, Perry," I sigh. "Let's do this thing."

I get out of the car, tucking the keys in my pocket and slinging my purse across my body so I don't have to worry about it falling off my shoulder while trying to wrangle the dog.

I close the door and quickly open the back door. Perry tries to dart out, but I quickly grab his collar and then the leash. Bumping the door shut with my butt, I lock it and return the keys to my pocket.

"Come on, Pear."

We start through the small parking lot and onto the sidewalk. Monsterwiches has around ten tables set up outside, with the majority of them taken. It looks like everyone in Santa Monica has decided to come here and eat outside at the exact same time.

Perry jerks on his leash, and I tighten my grip.

"No, Perry!" I scold.

But Perry doesn't give a flying shit what I have to say to him.

He jerks again. This time, his leash goes flying out of my hand, and Perry goes running down the street.

"Perry!" I scream, running after the dog, disaster scenarios of him being run over playing out in my mind—as well as my sister's eventual murder when I kill her for leaving me with the dog.

People watch me run after him but do nothing to help—I can't help but think there's probably someone sitting back videotaping this to post on social media instead of helping me.

"*Perry*," I shout after the dog.

He doesn't care. He's doing what he wants.

He turns the corner and I run faster, nearly tripping as I turn after him.

"Oompf."

I skid to a halt, wincing as I see Perry collide with a guy walking out of Cool Beans coffee shop. The guy's iced coffee drops to the ground, splattering all over his worn sneakers, legs, and the sidewalk.

"I am so, so, *so* sorry." I hesitantly approach him. Perry licks at the coffee on the ground like this was his plan all along.

The guy looks down at the coffee, my dog, and finally, me.

I stop in front of him and suddenly feel very small. He towers over me, at least a foot taller. He's big, too, wide shoulders but a narrow waist, and the way his shirt hugs his chest I can see every indent of his abs. Around here, fit people are the norm, but there's something about this guy that I can't take my eyes off of. It's not just his looks, it's this *aura* he has. He hasn't even opened his mouth and I'm enraptured.

"It's not a big deal," he finally speaks, shielding his eyes from the sun. I notice they're a startling green color, bright against his tanned skin. His brown hair is cut short and there's a light dusting of stubble on his chin like he forgot to shave this morning. "I didn't really want the coffee much anyway." He smiles, and I suddenly understand why girls my age lose their minds over guys. My stomach flips and I can't seem to tell what's right side up anymore.

"He's still a puppy," I explain, not wanting to stand there staring at this guy like a creep. He looks older than me, probably twenty, I'm sure to him I look like a little kid.

He grabs the leash and holds it out to me. "Might want to grab him before you lose him again."

Color floods my cheeks as I reach for the leash. My fingers brush his and my heart skips the beat. It's like all my years of lack of hormones have combusted to this one moment and now I'm drowning in them.

"Right, thank you." I wrap the leash around my hand. "I'm really sorry—can I buy you another coffee?" I offer, feeling bad that Perry has destroyed his drink.

He shakes his head. "I really shouldn't be having one anyway. If I drink that now" —he nods down at the mess— "I won't go to sleep until five in the morning."

I laugh, but it sounds forced and not at all like my natural laugh. I'm nervous, and I'm being weird.

Get it together, Willa. He's only a guy.

"Well, um, thanks for … catching my dog."

He throws his head back and laughs, and that's when I notice one of his ears is pierced. A slender silver hoop rests in his left ear. I've always been irked by guys with pierced ears, but this guy pulls it off.

"I don't know, I think maybe he caught me," he says when he stops laughing.

I blush again. "Right …," I pause. "Well, thanks again." I wave awkwardly and start back down the street.

When I reach the end, I can't help but turn and look behind me.

The guy is still watching me, and when he sees me looking he smiles wide, not at all bothered by me catching him.

I wish I had his confidence. If it'd been the other way around I would've quickly averted my gaze.

"There you are!" Harlow's voice startles me. She's holding two wrapped sandwiches with two water bottles dangling precariously between her fingers. "What happened to you?"

"Perry got loose," I explain, walking up to her.

She sighs and glares down at the dog. "Bad Perry."

Perry wags his tail and sticks his tongue out. "He looks really torn up about his bad behavior," I joke.

We grab a table and I tie Perry's leash to my chair—if he runs this time, he's taking me with him.

"He needs to go to obedience school," I grumble as Harlow hands me my sandwich. I unwrap it and my mouth waters.

"Aw." She pets his head. "He's not that bad. Plus, he's still a baby."

"You're going to be saying he's a baby when he's ten."

She giggles. "Probably."

My phone vibrates in my bag, and I quickly grab it in case it's my mom telling me something important.

Instead, it's a text from Meredith.

Merebitch: Hoe r u home?

Me: Out with H.

Merebitch: Rly? Where?

Me: Monsterwiches.

Merebitch: I'm 2 blocks away. I'm coming over. Don't fucking leave before I get there.

Me: Wouldn't dream of it.

"Who's that?" Harlow asks. "It's not Mom complaining about me forgetting to do the laundry again, right? I mean, she knows I forget it on purpose all the time, so why does she keep bitching about it? She tells me to do it. I tell her I forgot. Wash, rinse, repeat—without the actual washing part, of course."

I snort. "No, it was Mere."

"Should I go get her something?" she asks, wiping her hands on a napkin.

"Yeah probably, or else she'll steal our food."

Harlow snaps her fingers. "I'll be back then. Just make sure *Perry* doesn't try to eat my food."

"I should let him," I call after her as she heads into Monsterwiches.

I take a bite of my sandwich while Perry looks at me with pleading eyes. I steal a piece of overhanging turkey from Harlow's sandwich and give it to him. What she doesn't know won't kill her.

After another bite, I pull my binders from my purse. In the beginning it was weird having to take medicine every time I ate, but now it's second nature.

"Heeeeey," Meredith calls, running down the street with shopping bags flopping in her hands. She honestly looks like she's trying to use them to take flight.

She reaches me and collapses into the chair beside me. Her bags drop to the ground and she lets out a breath that stirs her vibrant red bangs. "Shopping with my mom should be an Olympic sport. I was in school until noon, but from then until now we've managed to hit up ten different stores, and you *know* how long my mom takes in each of them. The good news is, I have five new pairs of shoes and an entirely new wardrobe. I swear my mom sits around thinks to herself *what can I spend money on today that I don't need?* Like, seriously. She's got a problem. Hey, can I have some of that?" She ends her breathless tirade to point to my water. I hand it over and she uncaps it, drinking it down like she hasn't had any water all day.

Harlow comes out with Mere's sandwich and a new water. She sees Meredith with my water and hands me the new one without question.

"Hungry?" she asks Meredith.

"Not really, but I'll take it anyway." She tucks a piece of hair behind her ear and Harlow places the wrapped sandwich on the table, the two of us exchanging a look.

Meredith is super tall and super thin to boot but the girl eats like a college football player preparing to hibernate for the winter. She hates her knobby knees and long legs, but they're *her* so I think they're perfect.

I take a bite of my sandwich and notice Meredith has already devoured almost half of hers. I'm not even shocked anymore. I've learned over the many years of knowing her that she can eat more in one sitting than an entire football team combined.

"Are you guys going home after this?" she asks.

I shake my head. "This one wants ice cream." I point at Harlow, who shrugs unapologetically.

"What can I say? Ice cream is my friend—it's always there for me."

"I wish I could go." Meredith frowns. "But I have to get back to my mom. I told her I was going to the bathroom."

I snort. "You told her you were going to the bathroom but you came here instead?"

"Well, when I texted you I was going to see if we could hang out tonight but since you were close I was like, why don't I head over there, so that's what I did. Don't worry, my mom won't notice I'm still gone for another thirty minutes."

Harlow giggles. "I love your mom."

"She's one of a kind," Meredith agrees. "You guys wanna go to the beach this weekend?" she asks.

"We go to the beach every weekend," I remind her with a laugh.

"Well, I can't help it. The beach has hot guys, and that's where I gravitate. Hot guys feed my soul. I can look but I can't touch—because you know my dad would chop my hands off and feed them to the sharks. He acts like I'm still four years old."

I snort. "Mere, you do act like a four-year-old most of the time, I can't blame him."

She sighs. "*You* right," she exaggerates, stuffing the last of her sandwich into her mouth. "See you this weekend." She wipes her mouth on a napkin, grabs up her bags, and is gone with a swish of her red hair.

"Sometimes I think Meredith is a species of her own," Harlow chortles. "I mean, seriously, I don't know anyone else like her."

"Me either … you know, considering she's the only friend I have left."

It doesn't bother me much anymore, how my friends shied away from me after my diagnosis, but there are moments where it threatens to overwhelm me.

The reality of it all, that is.

"Fuck them," Harlow spits.

"*Harlow*," I scold. "Don't talk like that, you're fifteen."

She tilts her head. "Exactly, I'm fifteen. I've heard worse than the word fuck. And seriously *fuck them*. They showed their true colors. If someone can't acknowledge your illness, or be there for you, or for Christ's sake even say *hi*, then they don't deserve to stay in your life. They don't."

I smile. Harlow makes my heart happy. I hear horror stories about siblings, but mine couldn't be more perfect. Yeah, we fight and disagree at times, but she's always there for me and I'm always there for her.

"When did you get so smart?" I ask her.

She cracks a grin. "I've always been this smart—you're finally starting to notice."

I shake my head. "Nah, I've always noticed, I just can't go out handing you praise all the time or your head will get even bigger."

"Ha-ha," she intones sarcastically, throwing a piece of cucumber at me.

I finish my sandwich and roll up the paper wrapper. Perry harrumphs at my feet, clearly showing his displeasure at not being slipped a treat from my food.

"Do you ever get bored?" Harlow asks me suddenly.

"Bored?" I repeat, my eyes squished together in obvious confusion.

"Yeah, you know—you're home alone a lot, you don't have school anymore or a job. Don't you get bored?"

I play with a corner of the paper wrapper sticking out from the rolled-up ball I'd turned it into. "Yeah, at times. But I have my books and the computer."

She shakes her head. "That's not a life, Willa. You need to be out here *living*." She sweeps a hand.

"It's not that simple."

Don't get me wrong, I'm thankful every day to still be here, but I know my disease holds me back. I see people doing things and being adventurous, but then I think about how tired I can get and I talk myself into staying in the house.

It's a vicious cycle.

I want to be more present. I want to *live* and have fun. I want to learn to surf and go to a bonfire. I want to make more friends.

I want to do things I've always been afraid of, because coming close to death has taught me they're not to be feared. A life unlived is what we should all fear.

And yet, I haven't done any of the things I want to.

I'm grateful that dialysis allows me the ability to live, and there are *lots* of things I can still do while on it, I won't deny that. What holds me back is my own fear.

But one day … One day I'm finally going to get a transplant and that kidney will not only save my life, it'll transform it.

"It's more simple than you think," Harlow says. "I know how you are. You sit around and overthink everything. Sometimes you have to just do it. Just. Do. It."

I tilt my head. "Are you quoting Shia LaBeouf to me?" I crack a smile and she laughs.

"I mean, he *is* my future husband." She winks and takes a sip of water.

"I'm pretty sure he's like double your age."

She stands up with her trash and grabs mine too. "Age is just a number." She swishes her hair over her shoulder and saunters off to throw away the trash.

I stand up and grab Perry's leash. He looks up at me with his lolling tongue, trying to act cute and innocent.

"You're not fooling me," I tell him. I swear he grins.

My mind drifts back to the guy Perry practically mauled and my stomach stirs once more. This giddy feeling bubbling inside me is foreign and slightly strange, but I think I like it.

Harlow returns and takes Perry's leash from me—probably not trusting me not to lose him again—and we head back to my car.

The drive to the ice cream shop is short. It's a small little shack right on the beach. Guilt floods me, knowing ice cream is a no-no with my diet, but it's not like it's something I do every day, or even once a week, therefore I tell my guilt to take a hike. I can indulge now and then.

"You stay with Perry. *I'll* order this time," I tell Harlow.

She laughs, her blonde hair stirring against her shoulders in a slight breeze coming off the ocean. "I want a banana split with extra chocolate syrup."

I nod and head over to the stand. There's a long line of about ten people. I don't think I've ever come to get ice cream here and there's not a line. Being right on the beach gives it access to a plethora of tourists, but this is one place locals refuse to avoid because the ice cream is that good.

The line moves slowly, and I shift my feet back and forth restlessly. I glance over my shoulder and squint, spotting Harlow and Perry in the distance. Perry licks her cheek and she laughs, ruffling the fur at his neck.

I turn back and find that the line has moved forward. I take a step and open my purse, grabbing a wad of cash that's loose. I'm terrible about putting money back in my purse. It drives my mom crazy because she finds money in the laundry all the time since so much of it ends up stuffed in my pockets.

When I finally make it the front, I've been in line for fifteen minutes.

"Um, a banana split with extra chocolate syrup and a small cup of strawberry, please."

The girl working the register gives me the total, and I pay before stepping to the side to wait.

It doesn't take nearly as long to get my order. I grab it, getting chocolate syrup on my finger, and make my way over to where Harlow sits in the sand, all the while praying I don't drop our ice cream.

"Here you go," I tell her, and hold out her dessert.

She takes it, Perry making an immediate dive for it.

"Perry, no," she scolds him, turning her back to him.

I sit down on her other side, digging my feet into the sand. The sun is beginning to show signs of setting. I didn't even realize how much time had passed. For once, I'd been enjoying myself. I guess when I got out of my head time didn't seem to drag so much.

"This is freaking good," she says, digging her spoon in for another bite.

I take a small bite. "Thanks for wanting to get out."

She smiles. "Is that your way of saying you're having fun?"

I laugh. "Yeah, I guess it is." I take another bite, savoring it.

Harlow bumps my shoulder with hers. "I low you."

"I low you more." I lay my head on her shoulder, glancing out at the ocean as it beats against the sand.

It amazes me that something so perfect can exist on Earth when there's so much ugliness in the world.

I believe there's more good, if you take a second to look—the problem is people are constantly going a hundred miles an hour. Everything becomes a blur and nothing seems to matter.

And that's every human's biggest mistake—thinking nothing matters.

But every moment is important.

After all, you never know which one will be your last.

CHAPTER TWO

I love and hate the moment when I first start to wake up from a deep sleep.

There's this brief moment where for a second, only a second, I forget about my kidney failure and the dialysis, where I'm a normal girl who can do normal things.

Then reality hits me, and I realize I'm not normal.

Awareness creeps back in and I feel like I'm going to suffocate.

I lie on my back, my hands on my chest, and stare at my ceiling as the dialysis machine whirs beside me.

Almost every day I tell myself this might not be ideal right now, but one day I'm going to get a kidney, and all those years I'll have with a kidney far outweigh this.

Except the fact I'll have to have another transplant one day.

I try not to think about that—the inevitability of my future donor kidney failing.

You see, the first thing doctors tell you when your kidneys fail is that a transplant is not a cure, it's simply another treatment.

How morbid is that?

It's like they enjoy dousing that small flame of hope in your heart.

I get it, they have to tell you, and it makes sense. The kidney isn't *yours* and eventually your body will do what it's designed to do, which is reject foreign tissue. Immune suppressants can only do so much.

But I refuse to dwell on that, and I'll deal with it when that day comes.

I slowly sit up and rub my eyes. Looking over at my dialysis machine it flashes big green letters that say END OF THERAPY. It sucks on days when I can't sleep and I wake up early with an hour or two left and have to stay here. The lines are long enough for me to go the bathroom if I have to, but most of the time I stay in bed.

But being home and not going in-center makes me much happier. Not to mention I *feel* much better. I swore the hemo-dialysis was sucking the life out of me. PD isn't really so bad, and for me it's the best treatment option.

That's what's nice too; patients have options and you're not stuck with only one treatment type. If something isn't working for you, there are alternatives.

I'm thankful I finally switched over. It was the best decision I ever made, even if it was one of the most difficult of my life.

I close off the lines and grab a mask to put on so I can begin the disconnecting process.

In the beginning, my mom did it for me. I was a panicky fourteen-year-old and I cried every time, even though it didn't hurt. I was terrified I'd do something wrong and pull the tube out—which is entirely unlikely—or contaminate something and it's very important to keep everything sterile.

But I've been doing it myself now for probably two years. Now the whole process of setting up the machine, hooking up, and taking down is a piece of cake.

Once I'm free I pick up my dirty laundry off the floor and stuff it in the hamper. I even try to straighten my bed a bit that way my mom can't yell at me to make it.

Looking around, I decide my room is in the best shape I can get it at the moment and crack open the door. I pause, listening. My mom's voice trickles up the stairs along with Harlow's laughter. Then my dad's deeper voice joins the conversation briefly, followed by the sound of paper rustling.

I stuff my feet into a pair of slippers and head downstairs, finding my dad and Harlow sitting at the counter while my mom makes breakfast.

"Morning," I say softly, stifling a yawn. I pull out an empty barstool and sit down.

"Good moooorning," Harlow beams beside me. She's already dressed for school in a pair of ripped skinny jeans, tee, and Converse.

My dad has his nose buried in the newspaper and won't know anyone else in the house is alive until he finishes it.

"Do you want some scrambled eggs?" My mom asks from the stove.

"Yes, please."

I get up and grab a bottle of water, slightly jealous at the sight of Harlow drinking orange juice. It's not often anymore that I find myself envious of people enjoying the things I can't have, but sometimes the cravings get to me. I'm only human after all.

I sit back down and take the cap off the water bottle. The cap spins on the counter and I flatten my hand on it to stop it. I take a small sip of water, savoring it. Dealing with fluid restrictions makes me appreciate every little bit of water I get to enjoy.

"You're lucky you're done with school," Harlow whines softly under her breath to me.

I snort. "You only have two more years—besides, adulthood is not all it's cracked up to be."

"You sit at home and read—what's not to love about that?"

"You have a point." I laugh. "I really should get a job," I grumble.

"You have time," she assures me.

"I guess." I shrug, spinning the bottle cap under my fingers.

"You know," she begins, "it'd be really cool if you could come talk to the school about your situation. Most people are so dumb when it comes to this kind of thing—and the transplant part. Even the media doesn't talk about it. It's cancer this and cancer that, and yeah that's *bad*, but at least there's awareness, you know? People know to get tested, but you almost *died*, Willa. You could've died, and it could've been easily prevented if we'd known what signs to look for."

"I don't know," I hedge as my mom starts handing us each a breakfast plate. She has to set my dad's down for him since he's still absorbed in the newspaper.

"Think about it," she begs. "The school year is almost over, exams are done in two weeks, so we have a lot of free time. I'm sure the principal would be all for it."

"I'll think about it," I lie.

I spend ninety percent of my time pretending nothing is wrong with me, and most of the time I can believe it since I don't feel sick anymore. The idea of getting up in front of an entire school, some of them kids I went to school with until this happened, makes me feel nauseated.

It's not that I want to completely erase this experience from my life, that's impossible, but it's not something I'm sure I want to advertise.

"Please," she says quietly. "It'd mean a lot to me, and I think it'd mean a lot to you too once you did it."

"I wish I could be more like you," I confess.

She chokes on her egg and pieces come flying out of her mouth. "Why?"

"You're so …" I struggle to find the right word. "Vibrant," I settle on. "And I'm not."

She shakes her head. "Trust me, Willa. You shine brighter than any star in the sky. The thing is, it's a rare person who can see their own brilliance. We're all too blinded by fear."

I take her hand and lace our fingers together. "Regardless, I got really lucky getting you as a sister."

She smiles, her eyes lighting up. "Ditto."

I flop onto my bed staring up at the ceiling. Above me, pages from books are glued to the ceiling.

Yes, I murdered some books, but it was all in the name of love and art.

When I first started doing dialysis at home, I couldn't fall asleep and I'd stare up at my plain white ceiling.

It started making me crazy.

One weekend, my mom, dad, sister, and I tore pages from all my favorite books and glued them to the ceiling.

Every time I look at it makes me smile and I can't help but feel loved.

Words from J.K. Rowling, Sarah Dessen, Sarah J. Maas, and many, many more gaze down at me.

Their words help remind me how small I am and how big the world really is—because with each book yet another world is created.

The door to my room slips open and I turn my head as Perry strolls in. Everyone's left for the day so I knew it had to be him.

Or the cat.

But we *never* see the cat.

When Harlow was six she found this kitten hiding from squirrels, yes squirrels, and he's been with us ever since. Webber spends the majority of his time hiding under Harlow's bed and only comes out once in a blue moon. He's funny looking too. His hair sticks up on end like he's permanently electrocuted.

Since I'm home all the time, occasionally I'll see him slip out of her room. We'll exchange a look in which I know he's telling me with his eyes alone that if I slip the news he's been out of the room he'll murder me in my sleep.

I'll never cross that cat. I'm not convinced he's actually a cat.

Maybe a demon.

Or a gremlin.

Possibly a goblin.

I don't know which would be worse.

"Hey, Perry."

The dog makes his way over to me and plops on my bed, his head resting on my stomach.

I pet the top of his head.

"You're determined to make me like you, aren't you?"

He yawns in reply.

I take that to mean yes.

"I wonder what I should do today?" I ask Perry. "Maybe I should clean?" I hate cleaning, it's the thing I loathe most—I'd rather do laundry—but it's something I try to do since my mom works and I'm here. She has a maid come every two weeks, but I figure if I can pick up on the week in-between it helps.

Perry sticks his tongue out. "Yeah, I agree. No cleaning today."

I swear he smiles at me. He's expressive for a dog.

I stretch, reaching over to the low table beside my mattress, and pick up the book I've been reading. I open it to my bookmarked page and start reading.

Books have saved my life since my diagnosis. Those initial months were difficult. I was weak and tired, and my body had to adjust to dialysis. So, I spent a lot of time in bed, and honestly there's only so much TV one person can watch. But books? I never seem to get tired of those.

After about an hour of reading time, my phone buzzes.

And buzzes again.

And again.

I place my bookmark inside and set the book aside, scrambling to find my phone lost in the tangle of my bed covers as it buzzes again.

I finally find it and the screen is lit up with several different texts.

Harlow: Willa?

Harlow: Please answer

Harlow: It's important!

Harlow: I NEED YOU!

Willa: What?

I'm totally confused as to why my sister is blowing up my phone while she's at school. I mean, she texts me occasionally while she's at school but never like this.

Harlow: Oh thank God

Harlow: I need you to go into my room and get on my computer. I forgot to print off my essay for English and Mr. Slater will MURDER me if I turn it in late. Please, print it out and bring it to the school.

Willa: I can do that.

I head across the hall to her room.

The walls are a vibrant yellow, and her bed covers are a floral monstrosity. Her room is a lot neater than mine. Her violin sits in the corner along with a stand that has sheet music on it. The floor is covered in mismatched rugs—I think it looks silly, but Harlow says it's aesthetic.

I look around, but I don't see Webber hiding anywhere. He's probably under her bed hidden by the bed skirt.

He better not try to sneak attack my feet.

I pull out her swivel chair at her desk and sit down. Lifting the lid of her laptop it wakes up and asks for a password.

Willa: What's your password.

Harlow: …

Harlow: You can't laugh.

Willa: …no promises

Harlow: Ugh

Harlow: It's…

Harlow: TomHiddleston'sWife

I snort.

Willa: Isn't he a little old for you?

Harlow: Age is just a number. Now please print off my essay. It should pop up when you log on.

Sure enough, it does. I print it out and grab up the pages, stapling them together.

Willa: Got it. I'll head to the school right now.

Harlow: Thank you!

Her relief is palpable.

I scurry back to my room and grab my book and purse before slipping my feet into a pair of flip-flops. If I'm going out for this, I might as well stay out for a while.

Perry follows me down the stairs and to the kitchen where I grab my keys from the counter.

"I'm sorry, Perry, but you have to stay home this time."

I can imagine it now—Perry escaping my car and storming into the school. He'd have the time of his life while I'd be hating mine.

I lock the door behind me as I leave, hearing Perry whine from the inside.

Even if the dog drives me crazy, I do feel sorry for leaving him behind.

It's blazing hot outside, and when I open my car door I'm blasted in the face by the heat rolling out. I reluctantly get inside and roll down the windows for some immediate relief.

The parking lot is full when I get to the school. I end up parking against the sidewalk with my flashers on.

My phone buzzes as I get out of the car.

Harlow: I'm in the courtyard. It's to the left of the entrance. You can't miss it.

Willa: I just got here. Be there in a sec.

I double check that I've printed off the right paper; it'd be my luck she had two up and I printed the wrong one, but it looks right. It doesn't take me long to find the courtyard. It has several picnic tables surrounded by palm trees for shade. Several students sit eating while others appear to be working on homework.

I spot Harlow sitting on top of a table looking at her phone.

"Harlow!" I call, and her head pops up, elation taking over her face.

She hops off and runs over to me. "Thank you so freaking much. You're the best sister ever."

"Glad I could help." It feels good to be useful for a change.

"You're seriously a life saver. I can't believe I forgot to print it off. I think I was tired when I finished it last night that it slipped my mind. I wanted to sleep. I have to go or I'll be late, but thank you."

"You're welcome," I say, but she's already dashing away and through the glass double doors into the school.

I hesitate for a moment, looking around. I have a brief flash of what my life could've been like if I hadn't gotten sick. This could be my life. Laughing and chatting with friends. Going to football games. Maybe even being a cheerleader—okay, let's face it, that one would never happen, I don't have enough pep for that shit.

Somehow, I manage to pull myself away and back to my car.

I'm not sure what I should do, there's not much in this town you can do for fun with just yourself. I finally decide to pick up a coffee and go to the beach to read.

I'm clearly the life of the party.

There's nothing wrong with that. Being quiet and liking to keep to yourself.

I drive to Cool Beans and as I walk inside I can't help but think of the guy Perry ran over when we were here yesterday. Heat rushes to my cheeks and I press my hand to them, surprised by the sensation.

Chances are I'll never see the guy again and that, for some stupid reason, makes me sad.

It's not like I'm exactly in a position to start a relationship.

Besides, he was older, and older guys don't want someone like me.

A kid—that's all he could possibly see me as.

I step into line, looking at the menu. They're constantly adding new items, I never know whether I want to get my go-to favorite or try something they've added.

Cool Beans is a local hangout, much like Monsterwiches. It has a unique vibe, with cobalt-blue and lime-green walls. The tile behind the register is a mirrored iridescent that sends rainbows around the entire shop. Many people come here to work and sit clacking at their laptops while sipping a coffee.

Sometimes, Harlow has me bring her here to do her homework. I'll sit with her, drinking coffee and eating a snack. They make the best croissants here.

The person in front of me moves aside and it's finally my time to order.

"What can I get for you?" The barista asks.

"Um …" I sway back and forth on my feet. "I'll have an iced caramel latte, and can I also get a small lavender lemonade?"

"Sure thing." She gives me my total and I pay.

I take a seat while I wait since there are a few people who ordered before me still waiting.

I glance around the shop, watching the people inside.

People watching is one of my favorite things. You can learn so much about someone by paying attention to them.

Like the man in the corner with one hand on his head and spinning his wedding ring in his other is having marriage troubles.

And the woman on her phone scrolling through a dating app is feeling her biological clock ticking.

How can I possibly know that?

I've seen her here before looking at fertility websites.

You can learn a lot about your fellow human beings if you care to look.

But most people don't.

Care, that is.

"Iced caramel and a lavender lemonade?" another barista calls out, and I hop up and scurry to the counter to get my items.

"Thank you." I take the drinks from him and quickly pull out a couple of wadded up bills from my purse to slip into the tip jar.

It doesn't take me long to get to the beach. I grab a towel from the trunk of my car and drape it over my arm. I take off my flip-flops to carry them and not get sand in them—though, I'll inevitably get sand in them anyway—and juggle my drinks. Thankfully, my book is tucked safely in my purse so I don't have to worry about carrying it too.

I could've gone back home and hung out on our beach outside our doors, but it's not the same. It's a private stretch of beach, and always quiet, and today for some reason I'm craving the chaos of a public beach. I want to be surrounded by other people.

I find a spot and set down my stuff before spreading out the towel. My poor towel has definitely seen better days. It's a polka dot design that's faded from the sun and too many washes. The once vibrant hues of pink and orange now look like spilled Kool-Aid.

Plopping down on it, I open my purse and pull out my book. The sand acts as a cup holder for my drinks. I grab the lavender lemonade and take a tentative sip.

"Mmm," I hum, pleasantly surprised by the flavor. It tastes like regular lemonade with the smallest hint of the lavender. I'd worried the lavender would be overwhelming but it's perfect and surprisingly refreshing.

A light breeze stirs my hair around my shoulders, tickling my skin. I look up out toward the water. It sparkles from the sunshine and I squint from the brightness. Surfers hang out in the water, and I watch them with envy as they catch waves, laugh, and joke with each other.

Sometimes I miss my naivety. When I had the ability to block out all the bad things in the world that can happen to you.

I guess, most of all, I miss believing nothing would ever happen to me.

But it can.

And it did.

I look down at my book, blinking the brightness from my eyes, and start reading.

Before I know it, it's after lunch. There are plenty of stands on the beach that serve food, and since I don't feel ready to leave, I opt to do that instead of going home.

I grab my stuff and toss my empty drink cups into a nearby trashcan.

My feet sink into the sand as I walk. I love the feel of it squishing between my toes. I don't think there's anyone on the planet who can say they don't love the feel of sand underneath their feet. It's one of those things that instantly makes you feel happy, even if it is a pain in the ass to get rid of.

The smell emanating from one of the burger stands draws me in. I stand in line, perusing the menu. I don't normally eat out a lot, it's a big no-no since that kind of food is loaded with things I shouldn't have. But sometimes, you have to splurge, and I still try to make the best choices possible even when I'm making the wrong one. If that makes sense.

When it's my turn to order I ask for a hamburger with lettuce and mayonnaise. I don't have to wait long before they hand me a brown paper bag with my hamburger.

There are a couple of picnic tables nearby and I take a seat, laying my stuff down beside me. Pulling out my burger, I unwrap it, and my mouth immediately waters.

If only it was a cheeseburger.

I miss cheese.

Don't get me wrong, every now and then I'll cave and have some, but it's something I try to avoid if I can.

I take a bite and look around. Across from me are a group of guys, about my age and younger, so they're probably ditching school. They're skateboarding—if you can call it that. It looks more like a lot of falling than actual skating to me.

But I can tell they're having a good time, being silly and ... *normal.*

One of them looks up and makes eye contact with me.

I quickly drop my gaze, heat flaming my cheeks at being caught.

People watching might be one of my favorite pastimes, but it has its downsides.

I hear the guy say something to his friends and then it isn't long until a shadow is covering me.

"Hey," he says. His voice has that slightly raspy sound where it hasn't quite turned deep but isn't squeaky either.

I force myself to look up.

He is the quintessential California boy. Floppy brown hair bleached blond from the sun, blue eyes, and freckles speckled across his nose from too much time spent outside.

"Hi," I mumble reluctantly.

"You look familiar," he remarks. "Did we go to school together?"

I shake my head. "I don't think so."

The fact of the matter is, we might have, but if we never shared any of the same classes when I went to public school then I'm not likely to remember him.

"What's your name?" he asks, smiling. I notice his teeth are straight, but his front tooth has a slight chip in it.

"I'm not in the habit of giving my name to strangers," I blurt, and then immediately feel like an idiot. The guy is clearly my age, and I don't get funny vibes from him, plus there'd be no harm in giving my first name.

"I'm Spencer," he chuckles.

"Willa," I reply.

"Willa," he muses. "Willa … yeah, I remember you—"

I hold my breath and wait for him to finish with, "You're the girl who needs a transplant." But that's not what he says.

"You had that cool birthday party at your house when we were in grade school, right? The bouncy house? And you live right on the ocean?"

My mouth pops open in surprise. "Y-Yeah," I stutter. "That's me."

"Harlow is your sister too, yeah?"

I nod.

"I thought so. You guys look alike. I miss seeing you around."

When he doesn't ask me where I've been I know he knows the answer, but I'm thankful for him not saying it.

One of the guys from the group walks up.

"We need to go," he says to Spencer. His eyes drift to me. He wears a baseball cap, shielding most of his face.

"I'll be there in a sec, T.J."

T.J. nods and glances at me. He gives a small wave and awkward smile before going back to the other guys.

"Well, it was good seeing you, Willa. Maybe we'll run into each other again sometime."

"Maybe," I reply, feeling doubtful.

He grins, like he knows exactly what I'm thinking. His eyes sparkle like he's excited at the prospect of proving me wrong.

He joins his friends and they skate away. I watch until they become a speck in the distance.

I finish my lunch and wad up the trash, getting rid of it.

Grabbing my phone, I glance at the time. It's almost time for Harlow to get out of school. I text her that I'll pick her up instead of her getting on the bus like usual. Her excitement is palpable when she texts back, and it makes me feel bad for not doing it more often.

Sometimes I feel like the shittiest person ever.

I walk back to my car and toss my stuff into the backseat.

Traffic, as usual, is a nightmare, and by the time I make it to the school, kids are already walking out to buses and waiting cars. I pull off to the side and Harlow spots me easily. It's not easy to miss my mint colored car.

She tumbles into the car, all awkward legs and flailing arms, and stuffs her backpack into the back.

Sliding her seatbelt into place, she says, "We could make it to Santa Barbara in two hours—maybe make that three with traffic—Mom and Dad probably wouldn't even miss us."

I snort. "What's in Santa Barbara?"

She shrugs as I make a U-turn out of the lot. "No idea, but at least it'd be different scenery."

"Well, we're not doing that. I'm sure it'd be considered kidnapping."

"I'm your sister, not some kid you nabbed out of the parking lot."

"Regardless, it's not happening."

She sighs and kicks her feet up on the dashboard. "You know what you are?"

"No, enlighten me."

"A ruiner of fun."

"Is that even a word?"

"If it's not, I made it one." She smiles beatifically over at me.

"Some days, I'm convinced someone left you on our doorstep and Mom and Dad decided to keep you."

She laughs. "Good one."

"Thank you, I thought so myself. I'm swinging by the grocery store. I need to make dinner and haven't been to the store in over a week, the refrigerator is pretty barren at the moment."

I make dinner most nights. Cooking is something I enjoy, and I love trying new recipes. It makes me feel good, too, that my mom can come home from work and not worry about making a meal—because Lord knows my dad *definitely* isn't going to worry about making dinner. Or breakfast. Or even his lunch. When it comes to anything food related he stays far, far, far away—unless it's popcorn. He loves making homemade popcorn.

"Sounds good to me. It's nice to get out instead of going straight home even if it *is* the grocery store. Are you going to the one with Starbucks in it?"

I nod.

"Sweet. Even better."

The grocery store parking lot is packed. I end up having to park at the very back. Harlow skips and twirls through the lot and into the store, while I shake my head.

As much as I give her shit for it, I love her carefree and happy attitude. She lets things roll off of her and takes nothing to heart.

Inside, she runs straight to the Starbucks at the front while I grab a cart. I stroll through the store and it isn't long until she joins me and hops onto the front of the cart, holding on with one hand, her iced coffee in the other.

I stop the cart in the middle of the aisle. "Harlow," I hiss, "get off of there."

She rolls her eyes. "Fun. Ruiner."

She then swings her leg up and over into the cart and hops inside.

My jaw drops. "Where am I supposed to put my stuff?"

"Around me," she replies, drawing her legs up to her chest.

I laugh and shake my head. "Are you sure you're not five?"

"Nope, fifteen through and through." She wraps her lips around her straw and takes a long sip, eyeing me.

"All right then."

Even before I got sick Harlow was always the spontaneous and carefree one and I was the kid who followed every rule to a T.

I push the cart forward, scanning the shelves for items I might need.

I rarely make a shopping list, instead preferring to pick out items in a spur of the moment decision that sound like they might make a good meal.

As I peruse the aisles, I add in items here and there.

By the time I'm done and heading to the checkout Harlow is covered in items and looks like she's regretting her decision to get in the cart now—especially since she can't get *out* until I unload it.

I find a line that's not as busy and get into it. Self-checkout is an option but every time I do that I always get an error message or the machine malfunctions. I've learned to avoid it at all costs.

It's finally my turn to unload my cart and I do it quickly. As soon as Harlow is free she hops out and stretches, throwing in a couple of squats for good measure.

"Gearing up for a race?" I ask her.

She swings her arms. "Yeah, the race to the kitchen to get some food in my belly."

"You know it'll take time for me to make dinner, right?"

"That's what Oreos are for." And she points to a box that was stuffed behind where she was sitting.

I shake my head and grab it, adding it to the queue.

"You're lucky I like you or I'd make you put them back."

She grins. "You'd never. Oreos are magic. No one gets rid of magic."

I wheel the cart forward and, with Harlow's help, start loading the bags inside.

The checker gives me a total and I pull out the debit card my mom gave me that's linked to her and my dad's account.

I get the receipt and stick it in one of the bags.

Harlow takes control of the cart and treats it like a skateboard. Kicking one foot against the ground and hopping onto the cart to ride it.

I don't bother scolding her. It doesn't do any good anyway. Harlow dances to the beat of her own drum.

We load the car then Harlow returns the cart.

Once home we carry everything inside and I immediately get started on making dinner while putting away the groceries. Harlow sits on the couch in the family room across from the kitchen, eating Oreos, and shouting unhelpful tips at me.

Like, "Don't forget to set the oven to six-hundred degrease. Not only will it cook in seconds it'll degrease your food."

I shake my head at her antics and turn on some music, swaying my hips and dancing slightly as I make a homemade pesto sauce. I slather it across four chicken breasts and stick it in the oven—not at six-hundred degrees, might I add.

I make some mashed potatoes and broccoli to go with it. It's not much, but I know it'll be good.

Once everything is made and the rest of the groceries are put away I sit down with Harlow on the couch.

She's got *One Tree Hill* playing on the DVD. She begged my parents to buy her all the seasons on DVD for Christmas. I bet they regret doing it now since she's been watching it non-stop and had probably already watched the entire thing three times before then.

The alarm beeps and the garage door swings open.

"Hey, girls," my dad says, his voice sounding tired. "Something smells good."

"I made dinner," I say unnecessarily. "Pesto chicken."

"Mmm, sounds delicious. I'm going to go take a shower."

He drops his bag on the floor—he refuses to carry a briefcase and instead has a leather messenger bag—and heads upstairs.

He hasn't been upstairs long when the door opens again and my mom steps inside. She immediately kicks off her heels and comes to join Harlow and me on the couch.

"How was your day?" she asks the two of us.

"Uneventful, if you don't count the part where I had to beg Willa to bring my essay to school because I forgot to print it."

My mom gives her a look.

"What?" She shrugs innocently. "It was an honest mistake."

"And what about you?" Mom looks at me.

"I went to the beach and grocery shopping."

Suddenly, I remember Spencer and I feel blood rush to my cheeks. I'll have to remember to ask Harlow about him. The encounter had completely slipped my mind.

"Well, that's good." She smiles wide. "I'm happy you didn't stay here the whole day."

"Yeah, I'm thinking about getting a job," I blurt.

I don't know where the words come from, but in my gut, it feels right. I'm seventeen, almost eighteen, and I can't mope around here forever. I have to get on with my life—and seriously figure out what the heck I'm going to do about going to college.

"Really?" she asks, her eyes widened with surprise. "You know we don't expect that of you. You have a lot on you. And honestly, Willa, I'm going to advise against it."

"Why?" I ask, surprised by the angry tone to my voice.

"It's … it's been three years of waiting, and … I'd think you'd be getting a call any time now."

I duck my head and play with a thread on the blanket draped over Harlow's legs. "Yeah, I suppose you're right."

It wouldn't make sense to get a job now and a month or two down the road, finally get a kidney, and have to be off of work for weeks on end. It's a major surgery after all, so I wouldn't be able to work right away.

It's one of those things, even after three years, it feels like I'm never going to get that call.

I know that's not true, it has to happen one day, but one day is so ambiguous that I hate even thinking about it.

"But after," she says, snapping me from my thoughts, "I think it's a great idea to get a job. Have you thought about starting dance again?" she asks, and I flinch.

There's no reason why I couldn't dance now. Yes, the tube in my stomach would be an eyesore in the tight leotards but it wouldn't be a hindrance.

I shrug. "It's been so long. I doubt I'd be any good now."

My mom gives me a look that clearly says she thinks I'm being an idiot.

"Willa, you were a brilliant dancer. Talent like that doesn't get up and walk away."

"It …" I stop and look away.

It's hard to describe to someone how that part of myself feels so far away, like an entirely different person altogether. When I look back on who I was then, and things I did, it seems like someone else's life. I couldn't have possibly done those things or been that carefree.

"I can call them for you?" she suggests, not noticing my lag. "I'm sure they'd let you practice on your own. Ulysses loved you, remember him?"

"Of course I do."

Ulysses Gordon was the owner of the studio. He's in his sixties now, but he'd been a brilliant dancer back in the day, traveling the world. His studio was one of the most sought after in all of California to be a part of.

"Do you want me to call?" she asks, her eyes bright with excitement, and I know I can't say no, besides it might be good for me.

"Yeah, go ahead and call," I agree. "But only if there's a time I can practice on my own. I … I'm not ready to join a class." Especially with being so out of practice. I was sure there would be many moves my body wouldn't be fluid enough to do anymore.

Harlow glances at me and I can see a question in her eyes. I shake my head, telling her now is not the time. We'll talk later when it's the two of us.

"Is your dad in the shower?" Mom asks, standing up.

"Yeah," I answer.

"Let's go ahead and get everything on the table then. I'm starving. This smells delicious, honey." She smiles at me gratefully.

"I hope it tastes just as good," I reply.

By the time we have the food and drinks on the table my dad has come downstairs in his pajamas with his hair damp.

Dinner is spent catching up; it's one of the few times of the day we all sit down together. We always make sure to ignore our phones and just be in the moment.

Occasionally we'll watch a movie as a family, but dinner is a must.

After we've eaten, my dad heads straight for the chair in the family room and kicks his feet up on the ottoman. He picks up his book and reading glasses from the side table and flips the pages.

I doubt he'll come up for air until it's time to go to bed.

"Do you girls mind loading the dishwasher?" my mom asks.

We're quick to tell her it's not a problem, and she gives a small, tired smile before disappearing upstairs to shower.

Mom's a middle school teacher, and how she does it is beyond me. The idea of spending a whole day wrangling kids in puberty age doesn't sound appealing to me, and she does it five days a week.

Dad, on the other hand, is a lawyer, so he wrangles a whole different kind of people all day long.

Harlow and I clear the table together, both of us quiet. I want to ask her about Spencer, but I know not to do it yet, not in front of Dad. He might be reading now, but if I mention a boy's name he'll be sure to come to life.

Between the two of us it doesn't take us long to get everything cleaned up. We both make our way upstairs and into our opposite rooms. Perry follows me into mine, tail wagging. I think since I'm home more than anyone else he's attached himself to me and made me his favorite person.

I bustle around my room, straightening it up a little more. I plop unceremoniously into my chair at my desk and lift the lid on my MacBook. I watch some YouTube videos, check Twitter and Buzzfeed, and then get sucked into Pinterest. Finally, I force myself to close it, knowing if I don't I'll be scrolling through for another hour, and I need to get ready for bed.

I shower and change into pajamas before walking across the hall and tapping lightly on Harlow's door.

"Come in," she replies, and I push her door open.

I find her sitting on her bed, under the covers, typing away on her laptop.

She closes it and smiles when she sees me, moving it to the side.

"Sit." She pats her bed, pushing pillows aside to make room for me.

I sit, crossing my legs, and brush my damp hair off my shoulder.

"I ran into someone today," I begin.

"Ooh." She grins from ear to ear. "This sounds interesting. Do tell."

I shake my head. I knew Harlow would be all over this.

"We went to school together … before, you know. His name is Spencer. I can't remember his last name. He knew you were my sister."

"Oh, yeah, I know him," she chimes. "He's a senior but we're in the same cooking elective. He burnt my cookies once." She frowns suddenly like this is the saddest thing that could ever possibly occur.

I realize now that I have no more to say about the encounter and I feel silly for being excited to tell her about it.

"Oh, here, have an Oreo," she says suddenly, grabbing the blue bag buried beneath her covers. "Dad came in, so I hid them—you know he'll eat them all in under a minute." She extends the package to me and I take two, shaking my head when she continues to hold it out for me to take more.

"Spencer's cute." She gets a conspiratorial smile. "You think he's cute, right?"

"Yeah, he's cute," I hedge. "But …"

I pause, not knowing how to explain to her how I didn't feel excited by him or have butterflies in my stomach. Not like I'd experienced with the guy Perry had run over outside Cool Beans—a guy I knew I'd never see again.

"I think it'd be cool to maybe have another friend, you know?"

She looks at me. "A friend?"

"Yeah, someone other than you and Meredith. But, I mean, it's unlikely I'll bump into him again. But it was kind of cool to see someone I used to go to school with. I guess

I thought everyone forgot about me." I take a bite of Oreo.

Harlow leans forward and wraps her arms around me. "No one could forget you, Willa. I know you think you're a wallflower, but you're a wildflower. You grow and sway to your own beat. You leave a mark wherever you go."

I smile and hug her back, dropping Oreo crumbs on her bed in the process, but she doesn't notice.

"You're the best sister ever."

"Duh." She flips her hair dramatically. "You lucked out with me."

I stand up and finish the last of my cookies.

"Good night."

"Night." She picks up her laptop and gets back to work on whatever paper she's currently writing. Smarty-pants Harlow opted to take all honors classes. The little freak. I'm secretly proud of her. I know her courses are hard and I've never, not once, heard her complain this year.

I pad down the stairs, my feet thumping on the carpeted hardwood—my dad insisted it be installed so no one could slip—and into the kitchen. I grab a bottle of water, kiss my dad on the cheek, and reluctantly go back to my room.

It's that time of day, or I guess *evening*, where I have to hook up for dialysis.

I swear the monotony of it all is frying my brain cells.

I try not to think about it as I hook up to the machine. I *have* to do it. The reality is if I don't, I die. It's that simple. There's no point in fighting something that literally means life or death.

If something gave you the opportunity to live, wouldn't you take it?

I settle into bed, grab my book, and begin to read.

Exactly like every other night.

CHAPTER THREE

This morning after breakfast I leave when everybody else does.

Once a month I have to go to my dialysis center to check in and be seen by my nurses and nephrologist.

My mom used to go with me to every appointment, but once I could drive myself I put my foot down and told her she didn't need to anymore.

After all, she wasn't sick, I was—why should she have to suffer?

It only takes me twenty minutes to get there. I sit in the lot and turn the radio up. I'm ten minutes early, and I'm not going into that building until I have to.

Don't get me wrong, they *try* to make it look homey, but they fail miserably.

Thankfully, I'll only be going to a small, closed-off room today.

I haven't had to set foot in the actual center since that first year.

I'll never forget the endless recliners, with attached TVs, and so many people. Before this, I never knew how many people needed dialysis. Heck, I didn't even know what dialysis was. The place always burned my nose too with the harsh smell of bleach used to disinfect everything. And yet, even with that antiseptic smell, it still seemed *dirty*. Not like you could see actual dirt or dust, but there was something about the place that screamed uncleanliness. Maybe it was how unnatural the whole process of dialysis is that made me feel that way.

I tap my fingers against the steering wheel, singing along to the song under my breath. When I glance at the clock again I have a minute to go, with a reluctant groan, I shut off the car and go inside.

The receptionist smiles at me. "They're ready for you, Willa. Room three."

"Thanks, Tanya." I give a little wave with little to no enthusiasm behind it.

I push open the door to room three and find my nurse but no doctor yet.

"Willa," she beams. "How are you, sweetheart?"

My nurse, Nula, is from the South. I asked her once, I think she told me Georgia, but I can't remember now and am too embarrassed to ask. That first year when I was diagnosed is still a blur to me. Sometimes I try to remember a distinct moment, but I can't grasp it. I don't know whether that's a defense mechanism or the brain fog associated with kidney failure.

"I'm good," I reply.

It's my standard answer.

It sounds better than, "I fucking hate this." Or, "I don't want to do this, but I know I'm too young to die." And even, "Bleh, I hate my life, why'd this happen to me?"

"Good, good," she chirps. "Sit down and I'll take your blood pressure and temperature."

I sit down in the recliner, and she slips the thermometer strip in my mouth. I have the same kind at home. They're ones you use once and throw them away.

She puts the cuff on my arm, makes sure it's situated right, and pushes the button so it starts squeezing my arm. Again, I have the same one at home.

I hate having my blood pressure taken now, since it has to be monitored carefully. If I never have to have my arm squeezed again it'd be a miracle.

She takes the strip from my mouth, glances at it, and quickly writes it on my chart.

"Anything new to report, Willa? How are you feeling?"

The blood pressure cuff deflates and she quickly writes down the numbers.

I shrug. "Same as usual."

She sits down on the chair and slides in front of me. She pats my knee and gives me a sympathetic look. "I know this must be hard."

I want to snap at her that no she doesn't. Only other patients know how hard this and what it's like, but I don't stay that; instead, I nod.

"It's not the easiest," I supply, when she continues to stare at me waiting for an answer.

She nods. "No one your age should be in this place."

"No one *any* age should be in this place," I blurt.

I hate how because I'm young they act like I have more of a right to a transplant, to getting out of this place. *Everyone* deserves that but, sadly, many aren't even eligible. It's unfair in so many ways, but I understand why. There aren't enough kidneys to go around, and a lot of people have other health issues that deem them ineligible for transplant.

Once upon a time, there wasn't even enough dialysis for everyone. A committee would pick from the people who needed it, choosing who they thought would benefit society the most and, in the end, deciding the others would have to die.

How would you like having your fate left up to someone else? To decide whether you were a *benefit*?

It makes me sick to my stomach to think about it, but at least things are different now.

President Nixon made it a law that anyone with chronic end-stage kidney disease—or renal disease, depending on who you're speaking to—made you eligible for Medicare.

That's right, I'm seventeen and on Medicare.

I can't complain; it keeps my parents from having to pay for my dialysis, which without insurance can cost anywhere from six to eight thousand dollars.

People are doing dialysis anywhere from three to five days a week on average.

You do the math.

That's a lot of people on dialysis.

A lot of days.

And a whole heck of a lot of money being spent.

"Yes, yes, you're right." She pats my hand but doesn't meet my eyes, and I know she's only placating me. She looks over my chart a moment longer and then stands. "I'll go grab the doctor and let him know he can come see you."

She slides out the door and it clicks into place behind her.

I sit on my hands, swinging my legs as I look around the room.

Taped to the door is the standard "Cover Your Cough" diagram, along with an information sheet on no-nos regarding the renal diet.

There's a light knock on the door and Dr. Keegan pokes his head in.

"Willa!" He smiles, stepping into the room, nurse Nula coming in behind him.

Dr. Keegan is awesome and made me feel at ease from the start. In his forties, he has a daughter my age, and I think that always made him sympathize with my situation. He has dark hair, beginning to gray at the temple, and he almost always has a beard starting to grow like he frequently forgets to shave.

"Hey, Doc," I chime, with a smile I can't hide. He always makes me feel at ease, like I'm a *person* and not a part of a herd of cattle ready to be auctioned off.

He pushes his black-rimmed glasses up his nose and sits down, picking up my chart.

I keep quiet while he and Nula discuss my numbers and a bunch of other things.

Finally, he puts down the chart and listens to my heart and lungs.

After I sit back and he puts his stethoscope around his neck once more, he asks, "How have you been feeling? Everything good?"

"Just dandy—except for the part where, you know, I still don't have a kidney."

I'm joking. Mostly.

He frowns, and I instantly feel bad for what I said. I know it bothers Dr. Keegan that it's been three years and I still don't have a kidney, but it's not like he can do anything to help. It's a waiting game—one we all have to play.

"Well" —he twists his mouth— "it's been three years, I'd say chances are you'll be getting a call soon with that kidney. Have you spoken with your transplant hospital recently?"

I nod. "They call me every month. I'm due to go in person next month for a checkup."

"And you're up to date on everything if they would call with a kidney?" He double checks.

"Yeah, they make sure everything stays up."

He nods and glances back at my chart. "Everything looks great keep doing what you're doing, and maybe by the time I need to see you again you'll have that kidney."

I burst out in laughter. "Yeah, right, but we can hope."

"We definitely can. I'll be thinking about you, kid." He taps my knee with his finger and leaves the room.

"See you next time." Nula smiles and follows him out the door.

I grab my bag and leave. Start to finish, I'd only been in there forty minutes, but it feels longer.

When the warm air hits my face, I stop and take a breath.

Every time I leave that place I always feel like I'm breathing for the first time. Something about it makes me feel like I'm suffocating. I … shut down.

After a breath, I force myself into my car and drive away.

I head home, not in the mood to hang out anywhere on my own.

Today is one of those days where I miss having schoolwork. It'll be hours before I need to make dinner.

It's time to kill with nothing really to do. Maybe my mom was right suggesting I get back into dancing. It'd certainly give me something to do when I don't need to do anything else. I think I've had a hard time going back to dancing because in some ways it feels like that part of me died. My life has been different, and it'll always be different now.

The old Willa is gone, my life where I was *normal* doesn't exist anymore. The new Willa will always have to take immune suppressants and watch the types of food she eats—however, not as closely as it's watched now—and be monitored for the rest of her life by doctors.

Until, inevitably, that kidney fails me too.

I try not to think about that too much, the fact that a transplant won't cure me. I understand why a kidney won't last, especially at my age, but that doesn't make it any easier to deal with the fact that one day this will be my life again.

And I'd be lying if I said I wasn't envious of the naivety other people have about this kind of thing.

Not just kidney disease, but other illnesses in general.

I miss that.

I miss thinking nothing would ever happen.

And it's not that I went around thinking it, but more since I didn't know about this stuff I didn't think about it at all.

I just lived.

Now, that worry hangs like a guillotine over my head. I'm sure, with time, it will lessen. But it'll always be there.

When I get home, I head straight outside and to the expanse of beach outside our door.

The wind carrying off the ocean whips my hair around my shoulders as I stroll along. The water sparkles in the sunlight, looking as if it's covered in glitter.

Eventually, I sit, drawing my knees up to my chest.

I startle when I feel the first tear on my cheek.

It isn't often now that I cry about my situation. What's the point in any of it? Of crying? Of being sad or angry? It doesn't change the situation—it'll still exist, I might as well be as happy as I can.

If I let it rob me of my happiness, I truly have lost everything then.

The tears, however, don't seem to share in my mindset and continue to fall.

This isn't easy, not by a long shot, but I'm thankful to still be here. To have a chance to grow up and get a job, maybe even get married one day.

Sometimes all those things feel like impossible hurdles to overcome, but I know they're not.

What I've been through has been hard, so freaking hard, but the worst of it's behind me and the best lies ahead.

That's what I choose to focus on.

Not the bad.

Why anyone sits around and obsesses over bad things is beyond me. Bad things only have the ability to hurt you, to eat at you, if you give it permission. Sure, we all have days where we can't help but feel down, but I also believe we can choose to make our own sunshine.

Or sometimes you're lucky to have someone who *is* sunshine.

Like Harlow.

She lights up the world with every step she takes.

She's special like that.

My phone buzzes, and I raise up to pull it from my back pocket.

Unknown Number: Hey, this is Willa right?

Willa: Um … yeah. Who is this?

Unknown Number: It's Spencer.

Willa: Ohhhh.

Spencer: I got your number from your sister. I hope that's okay.

Willa: Yeah, of course. I was worried a cereal killer got ahold of it or something.

A serial killer? Really, Willa? Get a grip.

Spencer: Sorry to disappoint you, but I'm not a cereal killer.

I blink. And blink again, then look back at the text I sent.

Willa: Auto correct hates me. You know what I meant.

Spencer: Yeah, I do.

Spencer: What are your plans this weekend? Would you want to go to the beach?

Willa: Well, I have plans with Harlow and my friend Meredith.

Spencer: Oh, well maybe some other time then.

I take a breath and decide to plunge headfirst into uncharted waters—uncharted for me, at least.

Willa: Why don't you join us? I know they wouldn't mind.

Spencer: Are you sure?

Willa: Yeah. It'll be fun.

I feel good about this decision. Spencer seems cool and genuinely nice, he should get along great with Meredith. True, Meredith can be a little … well, *Meredith*, but I think he can handle her.

Spencer: Cool. I will then. Where should I meet you?

Willa: How about Cool Beans Saturday at 11? We usually stop there and then head to the beach.

Spencer: Sounds great. See you then.

I feel this funny fluttery feeling in my chest and I smile, biting down on my lip to try and hide it.

I feel … giddy.

It's a strange feeling.

I don't think I've looked forward to something in a long time but, suddenly, I'm ready for the weekend.

CHAPTER FOUR

"Is he cute?" Meredith asks, wrapping her lips around her Oreo iced coffee—calling it coffee is a stretch, more like a heart attack waiting to happen.

I shrug. "Yeah, he's cute, but I don't feel anything like that toward him. I mean, I only saw him once for like two minutes and before that we only knew each other when we were kids."

"Sometimes I wish I grew up here and knew people when we were little."

"Trust me," Harlow interrupts, coming to the table with her iced vanilla latte, "you don't want that. Then you remember that time Justin Kirk ate a worm on a dare in second grade and you can't get behind everyone's backing that he's the hottest guy in your class." She shrugs as the two of us stare at her. "What?" she asks innocently, blowing her straw wrapper at me. I pull it out of my hair and lay it on the table.

"Nothing," I say. While Meredith says, "Do tell me more."

"*Don't* tell her more," I warn Harlow. "She'll only use it as blackmail against people."

Meredith rolls her eyes and brushes her long, red hair over her shoulder. "Oh, ye of little faith. Blackmail makes the world turn. Without it, no one would ever get what they want."

"I'm sure there are other ways to get what you want."

"Yeah, but they're not as fun," she argues.

"Hey, sorry I'm late," Spencer's voice breaks into our conversation. "I had to help my mom. Let me grab a coffee real quick." He points over his shoulder with a smile before getting in line.

"You didn't tell me he was hot," Meredith hisses, leaning across the table to me.

"You didn't ask," I defend.

She turns and looks at him and I know, without a doubt, she's staring at his ass.

Meredith is shameless.

"How come I've never noticed him before?"

"Probably because he's smart." Harlow hides this slur behind a cough, but Meredith catches it anyway.

"Just because I'm more interested in the art of taking off my clothes doesn't mean I'm not smart," she snaps.

I snort. "Mere, you're as much of a virgin as I am, get off your high horse."

Her cheeks flame. "It's not my fault high school boys *suck* and don't know what they're doing. I'm not losing my virginity to a clueless imp, but that boy" —she looks significantly back at Spencer— "looks like he'd know what to do with his hands." She makes a crude face and cups her breasts.

I dive across the table, swatting at her.

"Stop that," I hiss. "You're embarrassing me."

"You're no fun." She frowns. "You should know by now I don't care what people think of me."

"And that's your problem," I tell her. "It makes you do things no sane person would ever do."

She points her finger at me. "I never claimed to be sane."

I shake my head as Spencer joins us and takes the empty chair beside me.

I hadn't even realized Harlow had purposely sat beside Meredith so this space was empty. If I had, I would've demanded she sit by me. She smiles at me triumphantly from across the table like she knows exactly what I'm thinking.

Little traitor.

"My best friend's parents own this place," he muses, playing with his straw. "You met him. T.J.," he adds to my blank look.

"Oh, right. We love this place."

"Should we head to the beach?" he asks, looking at the three of us. "Hi, I'm Spencer." He holds out his hand to Meredith.

She takes it with a smile like a snake about to devour its prey.

Poor Spencer doesn't know what's coming for him, but he seems like a nice guy, maybe he could tame Meredith.

Harlow glances at me with a worried look and I shake my head.

I'm not interested in Spencer, not like that, at least. But it does feel nice to be around someone new. Harlow doesn't need to get worried about me being jealous. I don't feel anything for Spencer other than a growing fondness.

"I'm Meredith," she says, releasing his hand.

Spencer glances at me with a look that says he knows he's in trouble with this one and I laugh.

We leave our cars parked where they are and walk the mile to the beach.

It's a cooler day, in the high sixties, with a strong breeze making it feel cooler.

"Are you ready for graduation?" I ask Spencer.

He shrugs, his hands shoved deep into his khaki cargo shorts. "Yeah, in a lot of ways I am ready. It's the next step, you know, but it's scary too."

Meredith makes a noise. "I'm shocked to hear a guy say that."

He snorts. "What? We can't have feelings and worry about things too? This is a big thing. College. Work. Adulthood. I don't know about you guys but I feel sorely unprepared. Like, how do I know how to do taxes? Or balance a checkbook? Or … loads of other shit." He ruffles the back of his hair nervously. "There's a lot to think about."

"Have you decided on a college?" Harlow asks him.

"SMC," he answers. "I don't want to leave home. I love it here too much. I can't imagine living somewhere else, even for only a few years. What about you guys?" he asks Meredith and me.

"I'm not sure," I answer honestly. "I got into several places, some here and some where I'd have to leave, but I honestly don't know if I'm cut out for college. I don't know what I want to do with the rest of my life. Going to college scares me. I don't want to be trapped doing something I hate, but I don't want to not get an education, either. I'll have to decide what I'm doing soon."

Spencer shrugs and gives me a sympathetic look. "You could give yourself another year, you know? You don't have to decide anything right now. It's a *big* decision and it should be *your* decision. Do what your heart tells you."

I smile. "Thank you."

"Not a problem." He grins back. "And what about you?" He turns to Meredith.

"I'm planning to go to UCLA."

"Really?" He raises a brow in inquiry.

"What?" she questions a little snappily. "Do I not look smart?"

"No, it's not that. It's … that's a tough school. I'm not surprised, but I am impressed."

Her smile returns at that.

"Do you skateboard a lot?" I ask him. "I don't think I could ever do that. I'd fall flat on my face."

"It's not that hard, I promise you." He laughs. "You might like it. If you guys ever want to try it, my friends and I would be happy to teach you."

Meredith looks stricken at the idea but quickly sobers. "That might be … fun."

He laughs, taking note that *fun* wasn't the word she wanted to use. "We'd go easy on you. No crazy tricks."

"Sounds fun to me," Harlow pipes in.

We reach the beach, and instead of stopping on the sand, we continue on to the pier where there's more to do. It's the weekend, so the pier is busy with locals and tourists. It's nothing compared to how it'll be in only a few short weeks when summer vacation season hits.

It becomes nearly impossible to get around.

The pier boasts small shops, games, food stands, and the Ferris Wheel. It stretches up, up, up into the sky overlooking the ocean.

I've been on it a few times, and each time I swear is better than the last. I feel free up there, like a bird ready to soar across the sky into new horizons.

When I'm up there, I can't think, I only exist in the moment.

"Anyone want to play?" Spencer asks, stopping at one of the games. It's one you toss a basketball and try to score as many points as you can, beating the person next to you.

"I will," Harlow volunteers when neither Meredith or I say anything.

He hands some money to the man working the booth and they both step up.

When it dings, they start throwing the balls into the basket.

Harlow is surprisingly good at it, and in the end beats Spencer by twenty solid points.

She accepts her giant blue stuffed gorilla with a beaming smile.

Spencer can't help but laugh. "Good game."

"I wanted the gorilla." She shrugs. "Or I would have gone easy on you."

He waves his hand and grins. "I'm glad you didn't."

Harlow clutches her gorilla under her arm and we move on to another booth. This one, you shoot water guns at a target.

"I'll meet back up with you guys," I say, spotting my favorite store tucked around the corner.

"Are you sure?" Harlow asks.

"Yeah, I won't be long," I assure her.

I leave them behind and step into the store. It's tiny, with every surface covered in some sort of jewelry made from seashells. From the ceiling, kites made from paper meant for decoration swing merrily. Interspersed throughout the shop are sketches and paintings by local artists.

"Ms. Willa," chimes Julio upon hearing me.

"Julio." I beam back at him.

I met Julio on a very bad day shortly after my diagnosis. My friends had brought me here, it was supposed to be fun, but I found many of their comments to be insensitive instead of understanding. I'd dashed in here to get away, crying my eyes out. Julio had asked me why I was crying and, after a bit of hesitation, I told him.

He held me while I cried, like a grandfather would their grandchild, and told me with total certainty, *"This is one bridge of many you will cross in your life m'dear. But if you don't cross it, you don't get to the next one, and you have to because good lies there—just like some good lies here too. There's good and bad in everything, it's up to us to determine what we make of it. Like me? I went blind at twelve years old. I miss seeing the sun, and my parents' faces—I'll never see my own children's faces. But if I hadn't gone blind, I would've never met my wife—she saved me when I nearly walked into traffic. I wouldn't take this back if it meant I never met her. She not only saved my life, she completed my soul."*

"How is my favorite little flower?"

"I'm doing okay." I touch my finger to a bracelet with turquoise beads and shells.

He clucks his tongue. "That doesn't sound too convincing."

I smile, though he can't see. "You know too much."

"Ah." He taps his forehead. "God might've taken my sight from me, but he gave me much more than I had before, and it's the ability to hear emotions. I don't have to see your face to know you're sad. Now, tell me, what is it?"

I sigh and turn to him. He's seated in a chair that hangs from the ceiling and sways as he moves. His gray hair is cut short and appears almost white next to his dark skin. His eyes stare beyond me, unseeing. In his lap his hands are clasped, his thumbs rubbing back and forth against each other.

I move in front of him and sit down on the floor, crossing my legs.

"Lots of things, Julio. Sometimes this is easy to deal with, and sometimes it's freaking hard. I feel like I'm never going to get a kidney, and I feel horrible for wishing for one, because that means I'm wishing for someone to die so I can live, and what kind of person does that make me?"

"That's quite the conundrum." He swings lazily in the chair. "But you do not *want* someone to die."

"No, of course not. It's, unfortunately, what has to happen."

"You should not dwell on such things that are not in your control."

"I know." I look away. "But I can't help it. I know it'll happen when it happens,."

"My sources tell me it'll be soon." He grins at me.

"Your sources, huh?"

"The spirits whisper to me, you know?"

"How high are you right now?" I ask, laughing.

He laughs back. "On a scale of one to ten? I'm a solid twelve, m'dear."

"Well" —I shrug, suppressing a laugh— "I guess it could be worse."

"I think the word you're looking for is *better.* It could be *better.*"

I shake my head and twiddle with the laces on my sneakers to have something to do with my hands.

"I know you can't help but get down some days, it's natural, but find something that makes you happy and focus your energy on that. The other stuff will fade away."

"Thanks, Julio."

"Anytime." He points at me with a small smile. "You do not visit me enough, Ms. Willa."

"I know, I'm sorry for that."

"It's okay. You have your own life, I know."

I snort. Some life I have.

"Come with me," he says, standing.

I follow him to a small back room where he keeps his new stock. He moves fluidly, not bumping into anything—someone who didn't know wouldn't even realize he's blind.

"Aha," he peals, closing his hand around a bracelet and holding it out for me. "When I got this in, I knew I must give it to Ms. Willa. To bring her sunshine and luck."

I take the bracelet from him and twirl it in my fingers. It boasts yellow beads, interspersed with shells, with a single charm dangling from it—a silver sun.

"It's perfect," I tell him honestly, slipping it on.

"Every time you look at it," he tells me, "think of something happy."

"Thank you, Julio." I hug the man who's shown me nothing but kindness the last three years. He's right, I don't visit him enough, and I feel bad for that.

"You come see me again soon, Ms. Willa."

"I will." And this time, it's not an empty promise, it's a vow.

I leave the store and Harlow, Meredith, and Spencer are no longer at the game. I stroll for a bit and spot Harlow waving to me from a picnic table set up outside a food stand. I weave through the crowd and join them.

"I got you a sandwich, I hope that's okay." There's an apology in her eyes as she and Spencer eat a hot dog—which I'm not allowed to eat. Meredith, however, is eating a sandwich like mine.

"This is fine," I tell my sister. "Thanks for getting it."

"Not a problem." She smiles, clearly relieved.

I sit down beside Spencer and take a bite of my sandwich before digging my pills out of my purse.

In the beginning, it was hard to remember to take them when I ate. Now, it's automatic and half the time I don't remember if I've taken them or not.

After we've finished eating, we play a few more games before the sun starts to set, and then head back to Cool Beans and our cars.

Meredith says goodbye and leaves first.

"I had fun today," Spencer says with a smile, doing that thing where he rubs the back of his head when he gets nervous.

"I did too, it was nice. And, uh, thanks for this." I hold up the stuffed bunny he won and gave to me—he won a turtle also and gave that to Meredith. Harlow won a live goldfish to go with her gorilla and has already named him Fred.

"Don't mention it. Maybe I'll see you this weekend?" he asks, looking between Harlow and me. "We could go to the skate park if you guys want to learn."

"Yeah, sure, maybe. We'll see."

He chuckles. "Um, right. Then … bye." He glances between the two of us and then ducks into his car.

Harlow and I pile into mine and I start it up.

"He likes you," she tells me with a giddy giggle.

"No, he doesn't." I back out and drive toward the exit, getting behind Spencer in his old 90s Mustang.

"Yes, he does," she counters.

"Well, I don't like him like that. Just as a friend," I say, shoulders resolute.

"Are you sure?" she sing-songs.

"Yes, I am," I defend, a bite to my tone.

She shakes her head. "You're weird. He's super cute, and he's *nice*. He's going to college too, clearly he's got his shit together. What's not to like?"

"I won't lie," I begin. "It made me … feel good when he came up to me the other day at the beach. It was nice to have someone notice me for *me* and not because they remembered me as the girl who needs a kidney. But … he doesn't make my stomach explode with butterflies or my heart do back flips. I feel … fond of him."

"Fond," she repeats. "The one word with the potential to kill any budding relationship. Fine," she relinquishes, "you don't like him like that, okay—but tell him that you only want a friend and don't give him false hope. If he's a genuinely good guy, he'll still be your friend after, and if not? Well, you dodged a bullet there."

I laugh. "Thanks for the advice.

"I gotta look out for my big sis," she defends, looking down at Fred in the plastic bowl he came in.

I shake my head. Harlow is way too smart for her age.

We're quiet the rest of the drive. We arrive home and, when we get inside, we find Mom and Dad watching *Scandal* on TV.

Dad pauses it and looks at us from the back of the couch. "How was your day?" he asks.

Perry lifts his head from his paws on the floor.

"Good. I got a bunny." I hold up my stuffed bunny. It's rather cute—the pale purple plushy with floppy ears.

"And I got a gorilla *and* a fish," Harlow beams, juggling both.

He and Mom laugh.

"Sounds like you had a good day then," Mom says with a smile.

"Night, girls," Dad says.

"Night," we echo, heading upstairs to our rooms.

I close my door behind me and flop on my bed. Lifting my wrist to my eyes, I study the bracelet and smile.

Every time you look at it, think of something happy.

My mind immediately goes to green eyes and the smell of salty sea air and my chest most definitely feels lighter than it was before.

CHAPTER FIVE

I dance around the room.

My movements are free and fluid.

The smile never leaves my face.

Riiiiiiing.

I spin. I twirl. I leap.

Riiiiiiiing.

I revel in the sounds of the pads of my ballet slippers touching the floor.

My soul feels ignited, vibrant, alive. I missed this. How could I have possibly stopped?

Riiiiiiiiiiiiiiiiiiiiing.

I jolt awake, shaking off the groggy effects of my dream state.

Riiiiiiing.

I grab my phone, and my heart stutters at the name flashing on the screen.

"H-Hello?" I answer, my voice shaking.

It's the transplant hospital, and they're calling in the middle of the night, which can mean only one of two things.

They have a kidney for me, if I take it after they give me all the information on it, or I'm basically an understudy for someone else if they turn it down or for whatever reason can't make it to the hospital in time.

"Is this Willa Hansen?"

"Yes, it is."

I sit up and rub my eyes with my free hand. Glancing at the clock on my desk, I see it's three in the morning, yet I'm completely alert. In fact, I'm not sure I've ever felt this awake in my life.

"Hi, Willa. This is nurse Amanda. We've had a kidney come in, and the network chose you as the best match."

I can't breathe.

It's like my body has completely forgotten how to do it.

I force myself to breathe before I pass out.

"Are you still there?" she asks at my quiet.

"Y-Yes. I'm here. I'm … this is great."

"The donor is male, seventeen-years-old, no history of drug or alcohol abuse. Medical history is clean. The kidney donor profile index is coming in around eleven percent."

"Is that good or bad?" I blurt. "I can't remember." I begin to panic.

I remember the hospital saying deceased donor kidneys are graded between zero and one-hundred percent but for the life of me I can't remember if a low rating is a good thing or bad.

She laughs lightly over the phone. "The lower the better."

"R-Right."

"You have some time to think about accepting if you want. But we need to hear back by the hour."

"N-No. I'm taking it," I say.

An eleven percent is rare, and someone my age at that. This is an opportunity I can't throw away. I have to jump on it before it's gone.

"Are you sure?" she asks. "It's early in the morning; maybe you should talk to your parents."

"No," I say firmly. "I'm taking it."

"Okay, we'll prep the operating room. How soon can you be here?"

"About an hour? Is that okay?"

"That's perfect."

She then goes over questions like *when was the last time you ate? Drank? Blah, blah, blah.*

She hangs up, and I sit for a moment in stunned silence.

Did that really happen?

I stare down at my glowing phone and know it did.

I quickly go about doing an emergency shut off from my dialysis machine. Once I'm free, I run down to the end of the hall and barge into my mom and dad's room.

"Mom! Dad! Get up!"

My dad sits straight up. "Whashappenin," he slurs, looking from left to right.

"Get up." I beat my hands on the bottom of the bed. "The hospital called. They have a kidney for me. It's a good match. I have to take it."

My mom rolls out of the bed. "We have to hurry, Jake," she tells my dad.

I leave them to get dressed and grab their things, then I wake up Harlow, knowing we can't leave her behind to wake up to an empty house with no clue where we went.

"Are you serious?" she asks, coming awake oddly alert.

"I'm serious."

And then I burst into tears.

My body is a rollercoaster of emotions.

Happy, scared, overwhelmed, completely euphoric. It's a lot to process.

"Oh, my God, Willa, this is amazing." She hugs me tight and I sob into her shoulder.

It *is* amazing.

More than that, it's life changing.

"I have to go change," I tell her, and dash back to my room.

I throw on a pair of my favorite sweats, a jog bra, and a loose T-shirt. I know I'll have to change when I get there, so I don't see the point in trying to look cute.

I dig in my closet for the backpack I packed, probably a year ago now, so I'd be ready at a moment's notice when the hospital finally called with a kidney. Inside, I have several pairs of pajama shorts and tops, my toothbrush and toothpaste, an old hairbrush, and other miscellaneous things I thought it would be important to have with me.

I throw my hair up into a sloppy ponytail to get it out of my way. A light sweat has broken out across my skin as I've rushed around.

I look around my room for anything else I might need.

My bedroom door is nudged open, and Perry wags his tail as he comes inside.

"Hey, boy." I smile from ear to ear. "I'm getting a kidney." I pet him.

I can't keep the giddy tone from my voice. I begin to cry again.

It's impossible to describe the feeling of elation. I'm quite positive nothing in the world could ever make me as happy and grateful as I am now. I've never understood the meaning of the word *blessed* until now, but that's exactly how I feel.

My life is about to change in about an hour.

My life is being *saved.*

Unless you've experienced this, or know someone who has, you can't possibly begin to imagine how life saving it is.

My heart thunders in my ears and Perry looks up at me seemingly confused by my tears but happy tone.

I've waited for this day for so long. I hoped for it and imagined what it'd feel like, but nothing I could've thought up truly compares to what it actually feels like.

Wishing for this day led me to believe it was never going to happen. That I was destined to live my life on dialysis.

But each day, each treatment, has brought me closer to this moment.

To the moment when I finally get to live again.

When I'm free of tubes and wires.

When I don't have to take my blood pressure constantly.

When I don't have to take pills every time I eat.

When I don't have to think about these things all day long.

I get to be *me* again.

Yes, my life will never be the same, but at least it'll be an actual life and not half of one.

I stuff my feet into a pair of flip-flops and nearly trip myself up.

I catch myself against the wall then Perry looks at me with his tongue lolling out of his mouth like he's laughing at me.

Straightening my backpack, I meet everyone else in the hallway. By some miracle, we're all ready at the same time.

We rush downstairs and tumble into my dad's Mercedes SUV.

I sit beside Harlow in the back. She looks as excited as I am but scared too.

Reaching over, I take her hand in mine and squeeze. She smiles back at me.

"I'll be okay," I tell her. "Better than ever."

"I know."

She then hugs me as best she can in the back of the car.

We hold each other all the way to the hospital.

Once there, it's a flurry of excitement, having me change into a gown, putting an IV in, going over the risks and precautions with my family and me.

It's overwhelming, that's for sure. There's even a part of me that begins to panic that I can't do this. What's the point? This kidney won't last forever.

But I remind myself I can't dwell on the promises of the future; I have to focus on the gifts of now.

The room they have me in is small, a temporary space before wheeling me back for surgery. My mom sits on one side holding my hand, while my dad stands by her. Harlow sits on my other side holding that hand.

I'm scared—I can't help it, surgery is daunting. Knowing they're going to be cutting me open and putting someone else's organ in my body feels wrong on so many levels, but I know I'm being overly paranoid.

"What are you thinking about?" Harlow asks beside me.

"Things I shouldn't be," I tell her.

She smiles and reaches up, pushing a piece of hair out of my eyes.

"Do you remember when we were little and I tripped on the Slip n' Slide and broke my ankle?"

I nod. I don't think I can ever forget my sister's cries that day.

"You told me it was okay to be scared—that being scared didn't make me weak. You're not weak, Willa, not at all. You're strong, and brave. You've overcome more than anyone your age should ever have to, and I've watched you do it with dignity. I admire you more than anyone else in this world, and I'm lucky to be your sister."

I cry again, for the umpteenth time tonight.

"I low you."

I let go of my mom's hand and hug my sister.

"I low you too."

She squeezes me tight. I feel a tear leak from my eye onto her shoulder but she doesn't let me go.

"Knock, knock." The surgeon raps his knuckle on the open door.

"Hey, Doc." I smile.

Dr. Marks was one of the first surgeons I met at the transplant hospital and we clicked. He reminded me of Dr. Keegan in a lot of ways. He was in his forties with two sons, twelve and ten years old. He was quirky in a lot of ways—always wearing bright yellow Converse with his suits every time I saw him, and constantly spinning a pen or pencil between his fingers like he had pent-up energy he needed to expunge.

"Are you ready for this, Willa?" he asks, stepping up to my side. My mom and dad scoot out of his way.

I nod. "As ready as I'll ever be." My chin begins to tremble with the threat of tears.

He picks up my hand and pats it gently. "It's okay to be scared," he echoes what Harlow told me. "I'd be more worried about you if you *weren't* scared. This is a big moment for you."

With the back of my other hand, I dry my face. "It's overwhelming," I admit.

He nods and lowers my hand back to the bed.

I notice for the first time since I've seen him he's in scrubs.

This is happening.

This is *really* happening.

"I want you to know how you feel is completely normal. The transplant process is a long, difficult, journey and often times feels like there's no end in sight. But you made it, Willa. You've made it to the end. Is there anything you want to discuss with me before we take you back?"

"How long do you think she'll be in surgery?" my dad asks, his hand on my mom's shoulder. She reaches up and places her hand on his. I can see the worry etched into every line of their faces. This hasn't been easy on them, either.

I'm the one going through the hard stuff, but my family suffers from this too.

It's a hard burden for everyone to bear.

"Typically, it's between three and four hours."

"That long?" my dad asks surprised.

"Yes," Dr. Marks replies. "But don't worry. Willa's in good hands, I promise you. Anything else?"

They shake their heads. I know they're too stunned and overwhelmed to think of anything else.

Dr. Marks turns back to me. "You'll be sedated after surgery, you might not wake up until tomorrow. Once you do wake up, it'll be important that we get you up and walking as soon as possible. We definitely want to see you peeing on your own, okay? And it's important that you drink as much water as you can. No more fluid restrictions. Any questions?" His kind brown eyes sparkle behind his glasses at me.

"Just … take care of me, Doc."

His face turns suddenly serious and he nods. "I will."

Before he leaves, he marks on my body where they've decided to hook up the kidney—he presses on my abdomen feeling the pulses of my bowels or some gibberish like that and decides that my right side will be the best place to put it.

He looks at me as he leaves. "We've got this." He gives me a thumbs up and leaves.

Barely a minute passes before the anesthesiologist comes in and goes over the risks of being put to sleep and on a ventilator and all that jazz.

I have to sign a paper and my parents as well.

Another person comes in and puts a hair net—I guess that's what it's called—on my head.

And then, in a matter of minutes, I'm being wheeled away from my family.

I hold my sister's hand until the last possible second.

Once in the OR, I scoot onto the table and they position me as they need me.

Around me I hear the rustling of paper being spread and the clinking of metal.

Somewhere, I hear someone washing their hands.

"I'm your nurse, Willa. My name's Jessica. I'm going to be right here by your side the whole time monitoring your vitals. I'm going to put this mask on you, and I want you to take deep breaths."

I nod, tears shimmering in my eyes, my chest tight.

Fear is seizing my body and asking, *why me? Why do I have to go through this? Why does anybody have to go through this?*

She places the mask on my face, and I breathe like she says, my eyes darting around.

"Count to ten in your head for me, sweetie," she says.

One. Two. Three. Four.

Five.

… *Six.*

Seven.

Eight …

My eyes close, the bright round lights above me disappear, and I am no more.

CHAPTER SIX

Awareness prickles in slowly.

Muffled voices.

Shuffling of feet.

Beeping outside.

Why is it beeping?

I try to open my eyes but it's like they're caked shut.

I reach up, rubbing at them, and hear an intake of breath.

"Willa?" my mom asks.

"What? W-Where am I?" I ask.

"You don't remember?"

I finally manage to open my eyes and look around, taking in the hospital surroundings and my parents', and sister's, worried faces.

It all comes rushing back to me.

"N-No, I remember," I hasten to assure her. "D-Did everything go okay?"

"It went perfectly." She brushes her fingers through my hair. It feels ratty and matted to my head.

"How long have I been asleep?"

"Well, they wheeled you back to surgery at almost six in the morning. It's almost nine at night now, so you woke up sooner than they hoped, which is good. Honey, can you go tell the nurse?" She looks at my dad over her shoulder.

He leaves the room, but not before grasping my foot under the covers and giving it a shake with an encouraging smile.

"How long did it take?"

"Almost four hours, like they said. I want to hug you," she blurts, "but I'm scared of hurting you."

I open my arms. "You hugging me won't hurt me. I promise."

She smiles and hugs me, her body melting into mine as she releases her worry.

"I love you so much, Willa. I don't tell you enough, but you girls are my entire world."

When she releases me, she quickly wipes tears away as my dad returns with a nurse.

"Hey, sweetie, how are you feeling?" the nurse asks, checking my vitals on the machine.

"Good," I reply. "Sore, of course, but I expected it to be worse."

"Good, good," she croons. "Well, right now we have a catheter in to collect your urine, and so far …" She bends to check the bag. "You're producing the exact amount we want to see. Tomorrow morning I'll come back and you'll need to try to pee on your own. Are you thirsty? Can I get you some water? Ice?"

"Both, please."

I hadn't noticed until she mentioned water, but my mouth feels dry and sticky.

"All right, sweetie. I'll be right back with that."

She sweeps out of the room, the door closing lightly behind her.

"How are you really feeling?" my dad asks, leaning against the railing at the foot of the bed.

"Good," I repeat like I told the nurse.

"You had major surgery—" he begins, but I shut him up.

"Dad," I say in a warning tone. "Sadly, I've been through worse."

He frowns. "I suppose you're right."

"I'm always right," I goad with a laugh and he smiles.

"Only you, Willa, could have major surgery and be making light of it."

Harlow steps up beside me and my mom moves back.

She takes my hand in hers. "I'm so, so, so happy for you."

"Thank you for always being here for me." It's the only thing I can think to say, but it hardly seems to encompass exactly how I feel.

She bends and kisses my forehead. "Your life is going to change after this," she whispers in my ear. "I can't wait to see the amazing life you live."

The nurse comes back in with two Styrofoam cups, a spoon stuck in one, and a bendy straw in the other.

She places the ice cup on the tray and hands me the water.

I sip it slowly, not wanting to get sick by drinking it too fast.

The water is cold on my tongue and the dryness evaporates.

"Are you in any pain?" the nurse asks. "I can get you medicine if you are."

"Right now, I'm okay."

She nods. "What they gave you earlier probably hasn't worn off, but if that changes and you want something push your nurse call button or send out one of your family for me." She smiles kindly and heads back out to tend to more patients.

I continue to sip my water—for once, with no fear of thinking about how much less I can drink later.

"Did you guys get a hotel?" I ask them.

My dad nods. "We thought it'd be best to have somewhere we can go to shower and for breaks."

"Go back and get some sleep," I tell them. "It's late."

"No, no." My mom rushes past Harlow to my side. "We want to stay with you."

"Mom," I say, in the most reassuring tone I can muster. "I'm fine. I feel great, actually, for just having surgery. I'm going to drink my water, have some ice, and go to sleep. You guys should do the same and you can't sleep here." I indicate the three small chairs in the room, just basic chairs not even recliners. This room is much bigger than the holding one they had me in before going into surgery, but it's still not large. There isn't even a small love seat like some rooms have. "I have the nurses and doctors with me. Nothing is going to happen."

She looks over at my dad, biting her lip.

"Willa, are you sure you want to be alone right now?" he asks me.

"Don't get me wrong, I'm happy you guys are here, but I'm going to go to sleep and you guys need to sleep too. It's silly to try to do that here."

The three of them exchange glances.

"Seriously," I laugh. "I'll be fine."

My mom sighs. "Fine, okay. We'll go, but we'll be back early, hopefully before you're awake. Do you need anything before we go?"

I think for a moment.

"Can you grab my book from my bag?" I ask, pointing to my backpack leaning against the wall in the corner.

My sister laughs. "We should've known she'd want her book."

She goes over to my backpack and pulls it out, placing it on the tray beside my ice cup.

I finish my water and my mom takes the cup from me, handing it across the bed to my dad so he can throw it away.

"Go, go," I encourage them. "I'm sure the nurse will call you if I need you."

My mom nods. "Okay. I love you." She kisses my cheek and moves out of the way so I can hug and say goodbye to my sister and dad.

I watch them leave, and I know they don't want to go, and while their presence brings me comfort, I know they need their rest. I'm sure they haven't slept at all since I woke them up this morning.

It's crazy to think that only a matter of hours have passed since I got that phone call.

One phone call has changed my life forever.

I pick up my book and open it to the bookmarked page. I read while I munch on ice and it isn't long until it feels impossible to hold my eyes open.

I put everything back on the tray and adjust the pillow.

My eyes barely close when sleep overtakes me once more.

CHAPTER SEVEN

I'm sitting up, eating French toast with a bowl of fruit when my family returns.

"You're up early," my mom exclaims, and I don't know whether she's merely surprised or happy.

"I was hungry," I admit.

I woke up at five in the morning with my stomach growling. I rang for my nurse and she put in an order for my breakfast but it didn't come until ten minutes ago, a little after seven.

At this point, my head throbs slightly with the need for food. I take small bites and chew them slowly, for fear of getting sick from lack of food and whatever kind of medicine might be in my system. I woke up at another point in the night and they had to give me medicine. I don't remember the episode much, but I know there was crying involved.

"Well, I'm glad you're feeling hungry." She takes the seat nearest me, placing her purse on the floor.

They all look rested, but not well-rested, and freshly showered.

I wish I could shower, but I know my body isn't ready for that yet. I haven't even been up walking yet. They told me the doctor will be by soon to take the catheter out and then they want me to try to walk.

I'm scared it's going to hurt, but I know fighting them will only keep me here longer and I want to go home.

I want to be in my bed, with my things, and I even want Perry. His furry body would provide much-needed, and appreciated, comfort at the moment.

Piercing a piece of cut up French toast, I dip it in the plastic container of syrup. It doesn't taste that bad. I remember eating it almost every morning when I was in the hospital after my diagnosis.

"Did you guys eat?" I ask.

"We had some breakfast at the hotel before coming over," my mom says. "Ours didn't look quite as good as yours," she jokes with a wink.

"Yeah, not much can beat this," I joke back, taking another small bite.

So far, my stomach seems to be handling it well and seems to be rejoicing at the sugar hitting my system.

"How do you feel this morning?" my mom asks, and I can see the concern on her face that she's been trying to hide since she walked in.

"More sore," I admit. "But I mean … they cut me open, I'm supposed to be sore. It's not bad," I hasten to add when she looks even more worried. "But I wanted to be honest. I feel tired too, but not exhausted. I just want to go home."

She nods. "That's understandable. You've been through a lot. I talked to the nurse before we came in and she said the earliest you'd be home is tomorrow afternoon. They want to be able to monitor you closely right now to make sure there's no chance your body is rejecting the kidney."

At her words, I get a visual in my mind of cells in my body wearing punching gloves and attacking my new kidney. I force my fear away, knowing I can't dwell on it.

We grow quiet and I finish my breakfast, lying back and waiting to see if any nausea hits, but it seems like I'm in the clear.

I pick up my book and begin to read to pass the time until the doctor comes. Outside, the sun begins to shine brighter.

Someone comes and takes my breakfast tray away. Two nurses come in, going over everything for shift change. My dad flips through a car magazine, Harlow scrolls on her phone, and my mom taps her foot nervously as her eyes dart around the room.

It isn't long after that and the doctor comes in.

"Willa," Dr. Marks beams, "you look good. How do you feel?"

"Better than I thought I would," I admit.

"No pain?"

"Not right now."

"Good. Well, let's get this catheter out of you and see if we can get you up and walking."

He clears my family out of the room and my new nurse comes in, closing the curtain across the windows overlooking the nurses' station and the door.

I close my eyes while they remove the catheter, whimpering slightly from the pressure of release.

Finally, it's out and I feel like I can breathe.

"You okay?" Dr. Marks asks.

"Y-Yeah." My voice is slightly shaky.

"I know it's not the best feeling," he says in a sympathetic tone. "I'll be back to check on you later. I'm going to leave you with Ashley here" —he glances at the brunette nurse— "and she'll get you up and moving."

He gives me one last smile before leaving.

"Let's try getting out of the bed, sweetie," she says coaxingly.

It doesn't sound like it should be something hard. I mean, it's not like they were operating on my feet or legs.

Unfortunately, that's not the case.

Ashley takes my hands, helping me swing my legs out over the bed. I scoot my butt until my feet touch the floor.

"Apply as much pressure to my hands as you need to," she says soothingly. "I'm here to help."

I press down on my feet and move to stand, but as I do my body starts to collapse under me and I lean heavily into the nurse.

"It's okay, it's okay," she coaxes when I whimper, nearly crying because I thought this would be easy. "Your body is weakened, and you've been through a lot. Take it easy."

I take a deep breath and exhale slowly.

"That's good." She smiles as I take one small step.

I feel like a toddler being praised for making my first steps in the world.

She leads me around the room to the other side of the bed where she lets me climb in once more.

"That was good." She fixes the blankets back over my legs. "I'm going to bring you some water and ice and try to get as much fluids in you as you can. It's very important you start peeing on your own. You did still produce urine while on dialysis, correct?"

"Yeah, I did."

I was considered one of the lucky ones because I still peed. A lot of people with kidney failure don't produce any urine at all. While my body holds on to some fluids, their bodies holds onto *all* of it. They have to be even more watchful of their fluid intake and run a fine line between fluid overload and dehydration.

"That should definitely help you then. I'll let your family back in and bring you water."

She slips from the room, and I lean back on the pillows taking several deep breaths. I still feel overwhelmed, my emotions all over the place. It's a lot to process. I'm sure I'll feel a range of emotions for a while yet.

My family comes back into my room.

"How'd it go?" my mom asks, taking her seat once more at my side.

"Pretty good. It was harder to walk than I thought it'd be, but I did okay."

Granted, it was only from one side of the bed to the other, but baby steps were probably best right now. I knew from prior information during previous hospital visits that many people weren't out of the bed until day two, and this was only a little more than twenty-four hours after surgery. I was sure they were pushing me harder because of my younger age, as they should.

Ashley comes back into the room and places the water and ice on my tray.

"Drink," she says in a playful warning tone.

I smile and pick up the cup taking a dramatic sip. She gives a thumbs up before leaving the room.

"Wanna play a game?" Harlow asks.

"What kind of game?" I hedge—one never knows with Harlow.

"I have LIFE on my phone—an app isn't as fun as the actual board game, but I doubt they'd have let me sneak it out of the house to bring to the hospital."

"And you'd be right," my dad says, peering over the edge of his car magazine.

"That sounds fun," I tell Harlow.

She jumps up and drags her chair around to the empty side of my bed, getting as close as she can. She rests her phone on the thick white blankets and brings up the app.

We pick our colors and she starts the game, the little stick women running to their vehicles.

We take our turns and start making up entire stories for our characters to make it even more interesting. By the end, we can't stop laughing and play two more games—all the while I make sure to drink my water.

An hour passes before I finally, mercifully, feel like I have to pee.

I don't think I've ever, in my entire seventeen years of life, felt thankful to have to go pee.

I press the button for my nurse and tell her. She clears my family out—since I'm still naked under my gown—and helps me walk to the bathroom.

"Pull that when you're done." She points to the string hanging from the wall with the large sign with red letters that declares PULL FOR NURSE ASSISTANCE.

"Okay," I say as she closes the door behind her.

I sit.

And I sit.

And I wait.

"Come on," I beg. "Just pee already."

Nothing.

"Ugh," I groan. "Please."

I reach over and turn on the faucet on the sink. The trickling of the water helps me a little.

I loosen my shoulders and close my eyes.

"Breathe, Willa. Breathe."

I can feel my body tensing up, and I know there's no chance I'll pee if I don't calm down.

It's amazing how something so simple suddenly becomes so complicated when you know you *have* to do it. That people are counting on it to happen.

There's even a collection bowl attached to the toilet so they can measure how much urine I produce.

Like I said, *pressure*.

Finally, a little begins to trickle out.

I squeal with excitement and it stops.

"Well, shit," I mutter to myself.

I sit a few minutes longer and manage to pee a little bit more.

I pull the string and Ashley comes in a moment later and helps me up and over to the sink to wash my hands before guiding me back to the bed.

"I didn't do much," I say, a single tear falling down my cheek.

"It's okay," she replies in an understanding tone. "We don't expect much from the first time you go."

"I think I got stage fright," I admit with a laugh.

She laughs too. "It happens to everyone, believe me."

She helps me into the bed and I groan as I feel pain shoot up from my incision.

"Are you okay?" she asks.

I breathe out, sweat coating my brow. "Mhmm. I'm okay."

The pain subsides and I cover my legs with the blankets.

"Do you need anything right now?"

I shake my head. "I'm fine."

I pick up my cup of ice and use the spoon to scoop some up.

She lets my family back in and the first thing my mom asks is how it went. I begrudgingly admit not well.

I spend the rest of the day walking as much as I can and going to the bathroom every time I get the urge. By the next day I'm walking without help and peeing a normal amount, which is a huge relief. They monitor me closely still, but so far there are no signs of rejection and no need for dialysis to help the new kidney along. By the afternoon on the day after that they finally discharge me and send me home with an appointment to return in three days for a check up.

"Thank you for everything," I tell Ashley who's on duty as I'm released and the one to wheel me to the entrance where my dad has brought the car around to load me.

"No problem." She smiles at me, putting the brakes on the wheelchair so I can't roll away. "Good luck with everything, sweetie."

She leaves me with my mom and sister, who carry my bag and wheel the cart of balloons and flowers that have been delivered over the last couple of days from friends and family.

Meredith's family sent a huge bouquet of sunflowers, my favorite, and a gift card to Barnes and Noble.

Dad hops out of the car and helps my mom and sister load the trunk with everything.

Harlow helps me out of the wheelchair and I manage to get into the car on my own. I'm surprised by how quickly I've recovered but they explained that my body is so overjoyed to have a working kidney that the pain becomes minimal.

Harlow gets into the back beside me and hands me the kidney-shaped pillow the hospital gifted me.

"Thank you," I tell her, and clutch it to my chest.

My mom and dad get in and Dad looks at me in the rearview mirror. "Is there anywhere you want to stop before we go home?" he asks me.

I shake my head. "Nope."

After being in the hospital the last three days I want nothing more than to be home. My home is my safe place, right now it's the place I need to be.

I fall asleep during the drive and wake up when the car pulls into the garage, my head resting on Harlow's shoulder.

"Sorry," I apologize to her as I sit up, rubbing sleep from my eyes. "I didn't mean to fall asleep on you."

"It's okay." She unbuckles her seatbelt. "You know I didn't mind."

My mom opens my car door and offers her hand to help me out. I wave her away. "I can do this."

She gives me a doubtful look. "I'd feel better if I helped." She reaches for my hand.

I swat at it. Not meanly, more in a joking way. "I'm fine, Mom. I have to do this."

She huffs out a breath and mutters, "Always so independent," under her breath before stepping away from me so I can slide out of the car on my own.

"See?" I tell her when I stand on my own two feet. "I've got this."

She shakes her head but her lips twitch with the threat of a smile. "Yes, I suppose you do," she relents, and moves to the trunk of the car to help carry everything inside while I hobble into the mudroom.

Perry barks madly when he spots me, prevented from getting to me by the baby gate that blocks him. One of our neighbors took care of him—and the elusive cat—while we were at the hospital, but Perry still looks delighted to see us.

"Hey, Perry." I pet him over the gate, waiting for him to calm down before I enter. He's large, and if he stood up to love on me he'd be likely to push on my incision which sounds like the least pleasant thing in the world right now.

Dad comes in with a vase of flowers and my bag, setting them down on the bench across from the storage cabinets.

"Perry, wanna come outside, boy?" he asks and the dog jumps and barks.

Dad grabs his leash and clips it on. I stand to the side as Perry enters the mudroom. Like I envisioned, Perry tries to jump on me, but my dad pulls him easily away and out the door. "I'm going to walk him," he tells me over his shoulder as he descends the three steps into the garage. "Hopefully it'll calm him down."

I don't feel like going up to my room, instead I grab a bottle of water from the refrigerator and walk a few laps around the island—not only because I *need* to walk, but to stretch my legs which have grown stiff from the car ride.

Finally, I sit down on the couch in the family room, resting my legs on the leather ottoman. I turn the TV on and flip to a random channel, wanting it on more for the distraction of the sound than to watch something.

Harlow carries in a vase of flowers—a mixed assortment of odd flowers I've never seen before—that my dad's work sent. She sets them on the table beside me.

"Wanna watch a movie?" she asks.

"That would be nice," I agree.

"Let me finish getting everything in and then I'll put something on."

It isn't long before her and my mom have arranged the different bouquets around the house. I noticed Harlow disappear upstairs with the sunflowers and can only assume she's put them in my room.

She comes back down, changed into a pair of sweatpants and tank, her hair gathered up in a messy bun.

"What are you in the mood to watch?" she asks.

"Nothing really," I admit. "Maybe something light and fun."

She grins and dives toward the cabinet that hides the DVDs. "I know the perfect thing," she sing-songs.

She grabs a DVD case and opens it, popping the disc into the player.

It isn't long until the play screen pops up and I smile back at her.

Chasing Liberty is one of our favorite, go to, girly movies. I mean, who wouldn't want to be the President's daughter gallivanting across Europe with Matthew Goode?

She hops onto the couch beside me and grabs a blanket, draping it over the both of us.

"You girls want some popcorn?" Mom calls from behind us in the kitchen.

"Yes!" we squeal together.

Mom laughs and we hear her open the cabinet that houses the boxes of popcorn and other miscellaneous goods.

Harlow rests her head on my shoulder and wiggles around getting comfortable.

"I still think you should come talk to my school," she whispers.

I swallow thickly. "I don't think I can do that. Not yet." I pick at the blanket on my lap.

She sighs. "You could do a lot about this, Willa—to bring awareness to kidney disease and transplant. I know it can't be easy to talk about it, but someone has to raise their voice and create a platform. That could be you."

I press my lips together. "I'll think about it, but I don't think it's something I'll be doing any time soon. Right now I need to learn how to live my life normally again."

My thoughts stray to the dialysis machine that still lives in my room. It's been my constant companion the last three years, and if everything checks out good this first month I'll be saying goodbye to it for good.

Well, until I need another transplant.

But I can't think about that fact right now. I have to focus on *now* and the years I have ahead of me with a healthy kidney.

Already, only days after surgery, I feel better than I have in my entire life. It's weird to look back now to when I was small child and how bad I felt, but I didn't know because it was *normal* for me and I thought everybody felt that way. Now, I know the truth. My kidneys never worked right, and this was inevitable.

My mom brings us each a small bowl of popcorn. She then dims the lights and closes the blinds, making it cozy for us.

The garage door opens, and Dad appears with Perry, who's panting from his walk. Dad unleashes him and he goes straight for his water bowl instead of bounding for me. After he drinks an entire bowl, he wags his tail over to us and lies down on the floor by my feet, resting his head on them.

I smile down at the dog that drives me crazy most of the time but somehow, I share a special bond with.

Harlow sneaks her hand into my popcorn bowl.

"Hey!" I scold playfully pulling my bowl away from her. "You have your own," I say as on-screen Mandy Moore bumps into Matthew Goode on her way into the concert.

Harlow giggles and grabs a handful from her bowl then stuffs it into her mouth, several pieces falling out and onto the blanket.

We grow quiet, getting sucked into the movie like usual. We've probably watched it a hundred times, and it never grows old. The ending always leaves us wishing for more but happy at the same time. I think any good movie or book should be that way. It's always good to love something so much you wish for more but appreciate that it has to end.

I think life is a lot like that—it has to end eventually, work to love it and yourself. It isn't always easy, but that doesn't mean you shouldn't try.

The movie ends, and we decide to watch another—but not before I make a bathroom break and walk around the house for fifteen minutes while Harlow times it to make sure I do said fifteen minutes. She can be a bit of a slave driver when she feels like it.

After the second movie, it's starting to get lateI eat a quick dinner my mom made and head up to bed.

I push open the door and immediately my eyes go straight to the dialysis machine beside my bed. It'll stay there for the next month, to be sure that everything with my donor kidney is, in fact, okay.

As I look at it, I feel a mix of emotions.

Anger—anger that this happened to me, to *anyone*.

Sadness—sadness that my body depended on this to keep me alive instead of working like it should have.

Happiness—happiness because a machine like this exists and *does* keep me alive and gives me the chance at a future I wouldn't otherwise have.

Most of all, I feel relief.

Relief, because I made it.

I did it.

Three years of this.

Three years of dialysis.

Three years of wondering when I'd get a transplant.

Three years, and it's finally here.

Tears burst out of my eyes, and I don't stop them. I let them fall freely down my cheeks.

I earned these tears.

I deserve them.

And I'm going to relish in them.

CHAPTER EIGHT

My mom keeps adjusting her hands on the steering wheel as she drives me to the hospital for my first appointment of the week since coming home. She's nervous, that much is obvious to me, and I can't help but think she's worried we might get bad news the kidney is rejecting. I don't think that's likely. I'm producing a good amount of urine, my incision site looks good, and I feel good.

But she's a mom, and moms worry.

I wish Harlow was with us; her easy energy would help put her at ease, and Harlow always manages to make me laugh, so she'd be good for me too. But she had to go to school, and my dad had to work. My parents decided to take turns with my appointments, since for starters I'm not allowed to drive for almost two months—seems a little extreme to me, but who am I to argue with doctors—plus, transplant hospitals stress how important it is to have a care team, and regardless of age they want someone to come with patients.

Mom takes the exit off the freeway that leads to the hospital.

We've taken this drive many times over the years. For checkups and to keep up to date on all the tests that were needed to keep me listed active on the list.

It's crazy to think I'm no longer on that giant list. They've crossed off my name and moved on to the next person.

I wonder how long it'll be until someone else on that list gets a kidney.

My mom turns into the hospital and drives around until we find the garage that will lead us straight into the transplant department.

We walk inside the double doors and through the hospital. It's not far until we come to the door with the sign labeled KIDNEY AND PANCREAS TRANSPLANT DEPARTMENT. I release a breath and open the door.

The room is painted a cheery yellow with cornflower blue chairs and couches. Several TVs dot the room, playing the news and one in the corner has HGTV on. The receptionists sit behind the counter, checking in patients and answering questions.

For the first time, I don't feel a heavy weight on my chest by stepping into this room.

My mom takes a seat and I check in where they slap a plastic medical bracelet around my wrist. I hate the stupid things and cut them off the moment I'm free of this place.

"Can I have a water?" I ask the receptionist before I join my mom to sit down.

"Sure." She smiles and swivels her chair around to grab a bottle of water from the mini fridge.

"Thanks." I take it from her and twist the lid off as I sit down beside my mom on a loveseat. She flips idly through a *People* magazine, but I'm not sure she's seeing the pages at all.

I pull out my phone and smile when I see a text from Meredith.

Merebitch: Good luck today! Thinking of you sweetie! I'm coming by tonight to see you!

Willa: Love you bitch!

Merebitch: You better ;)

Minutes pass and then one of the assistants steps out and calls, "Willa Hansen."

My mom and I jump up and hurry to the door across the room.

"How are you feeling?" the assistant asks me.

"Really good," I reply honestly. "Better than I ever have." Better, I'm sure, than most people who have had major surgery. There's something about getting an organ your body desperately needs that completely overshadows the healing process. I feel like a whole new person.

"Good," she chimes, leading me down the short hall and into a room. I hop up on the table, the paper crinkling under my butt as I shift.

My mom takes the chair in the corner and the assistant takes my temperature and blood pressure—both of which are great—before leaving us to wait for my surgeon.

The hardest part about all of this is the waiting games you have to play.

Waiting to get seen at a transplant hospital.

Waiting to get put on the deceased donor list.

Waiting, and hoping, and ultimately having your heart broken when no living donors are a match.

Waiting for that perfect match kidney to come along.

And, finally, waiting for doctor approval that everything is, in fact, okay.

My mom lets out a breath in the corner, looking anywhere but at me.

"It'll be okay, Mom," I tell her. "I feel great."

She forces a smile. "I know, but I'm your mom, and I worry."

More minutes tick by until there's a soft knock on the door and then Dr. Marks pushes his head in.

"Willa," he chimes with a beaming smile.

"Hey, Doc," I reply.

He closes the door and uses the Germ-X sitting on the counter.

"How are you feeling? Any soreness?" he asks, approaching me.

"None. I feel really, really great. Better than I have in a long time."

His smile grows wider. "That's what I like to hear. Lie back; I want to look at your incision site."

I do as he says, staring at the ceiling while he inspects. Like a child would make shapes out of clouds, I do the same with the ceiling tiles. There in the corner, a cluster makes a dog. Another looks like the sun.

"Everything looks great here. I'm going to send in someone to take your blood and I'll be back to talk to you after those results come back—give it about thirty minutes. Any questions?"

"Not yet."

"And you?" he asks Mom.

"You think she's okay, right? No signs of rejection?"

"Well," he starts, "I certainly can't guarantee anything, but so far I'd say things look excellent. The surgery went perfect, the kidney came right to life like we hope to see. She started producing urine while on the table, which again we hope to see. Let's get her blood checked and we'll go from there. Okay?" He waits for my mom to nod and then gives her a thumbs up. "I'll be back." He smiles at me and slips from the room.

It isn't long until the phlebotomist comes into the room with her cart and vials. I used to be terrified of getting my blood taken, but once this happened to me I had to get over that fear quickly.

I sit quietly while she puts the tourniquet on and sticks the needle in.

I hate the popping sound the vials make as she uncorks one and applies another.

When she finishes she sticks a piece of gauze around the site and wraps it with medical tape.

While we wait for the results to come back, I read and my mom fiddles on her phone, probably texting my dad.

Reading doesn't do much to distract me in these situations, but I refuse to sit and dwell for thirty minutes, or however long it might take for the doctor to come back. Dwelling gets me nowhere but a one-way ticket to Downersville. It's a real place, trust me.

When there's a knock on the door, Dr. Marks comes in again. I shut my book and stuff it behind me.

He holds sheets of white paper in his hands.

"Everything with your blood work is excellent. It shows us the kidney is working as it should. I warn you it's still early, that's why we check you closely this first month—and once a month for the rest of the year. But so far, we're seeing exactly what we want."

"Thank you," I tell him, fighting back a flood of emotions. "Thank you for saving my life."

"Oh, Willa," he breathes, his face softening.

I open my arms and he lets me hug him. Pulling away, I wipe at my face.

"I'm sorry for crying."

"Don't ever be sorry for feeling how you need to feel. This process isn't easy—even when it's *good* like now, when you've gotten a kidney, it's still not easy. It's very emotional."

I nod. "Seriously, thank you."

He nods back. "You're welcome. I'll see you back here in a few days, okay?"

"Okay."

He hands me a tissue. "You can call the social worker any time you need to talk. I know you have your family and friends, but if you need someone else to speak with I know she'd be happy to talk to you."

"I know." However, I have no intentions of calling her. Spilling my guts to a stranger is not appealing. I've met the social worker a few times but still haven't interacted with her enough to feel comfortable.

"Be good." He points at me with a playful smile and leaves for good this time.

My mom and I gather up our things, check out, and I get rid of my dreaded plastic medical bracelet.

On the way home, we stop and eat since both of us are starving.

By the time we walk in the door at home, I'm exhausted.

Anything emotionally draining makes me far more tired than if I physically ran five miles.

"How'd it go?" Harlow asks, sitting at the kitchen island doing her homework.

"Good. Everything looked great," I tell her, as Mom slips the leash on Perry to take him for a walk.

I slide onto the stool beside Harlow.

"I wasn't sure if you should see this or not," she begins, biting her lip nervously, "but I figured better to find out now, and it might not be … I mean, *he* might not be …"

"What?" I blurt confused.

"Oh, just look."

She slides the local newspaper across the granite countertop to me.

"What am I looking at?" I'm confused as the headline is about nothing important.

"There." She points to the bottom of the front page.

My eyes follow her finger. There's a picture of a boy, a boy I recognize. For a moment my heart stops, thinking it's Spencer—Spencer whom I haven't spoken to since all this happened since it happened so fast, but it's not him. It's another boy, but I know him because I met him, however briefly it was. T.J., Spencer's friend.

The headline reads **LOCAL BOY KILLED BY DRUNK DRIVER**

Below it is a picture of T.J. in a baseball uniform and cap.

I read the article below it.

A local Santa Monica teen, Thomas James Werth, was killed when a drunk driver t-boned the car he was driving home from a late visit at his ailing grandmother's.

His parents, Tessa and John Werth, describe him as a bright, happy young man who had a promising future ahead of him. Thomas, in his senior year of high school, was being scouted by several prestigious colleges to play baseball.

His parents have made the decision to donate his organs in this hopes that while Thomas is gone, others will get to live because of him.

The funeral will be held this Saturday, May the twenty-sixth at Kell's Funeral Home at three o' clock.

His family asks that in lieu of flowers you make a donation to Santa Monica County High School in his name instead.

I lower the paper and blink at my sister.

"You think …?" I pause, and she nods.

"It makes sense, right? I mean, they told you it was a seventeen-year-old and he's eighteen."

I swallow thickly, my heart racing.

It crossed my mind, of course, to wonder who my donor was, and I knew curiosity would eventually get the best of me and I'd look into it more, but seeing it there, right in front of me, makes it more real than anything else could have, and it *hurts.*

While I was happy and celebrating getting a kidney, this family was *mourning* their son. My chest felt tight and my heart hurt for them.

It seemed wrong that I should be happy while they lost their son.

He was a real boy, a guy practically my age since I'd be eighteen in a month, who had a future in front of him. A future that got cut short while mine seemed to be beginning because of him.

He was Spencer's *friend* too.

We didn't know for sure, of course, but I didn't see how the kidney inside me couldn't be T.J.'s.

I stare at his picture, his smiling face, and realize his parents are only ever going to remember him like this.

They'll never see him get to grow old and get married, have kids, and do normal things.

But because of his death, my parents get to watch me do those things.

I look at Harlow, my breathing funny as I fight back tears.

"I shouldn't have shown you," she mutters, trying to take the paper back but I place my hand over it.

"No, I'm glad you did."

"Willa …," she starts, and I shake my head.

I stand and grab a pair of scissors, cutting out the article and picture.

"What are you doing?" she asks.

"I don't know," I answer honestly.

I climb the stairs to my room and clip the newspaper to my lights where my instant photos hang.

I stand there, unable to move.

I stare at the boy who had so much life left to live but doesn't get to now, and I promise myself that I'll live my life to the best of my abilities because he can't.

I might not have gotten his heart, but suddenly mine seems to be beating for the both of us.

CHAPTER NINE

Willa: Hey, I wanted to say I heard about T.J. and I'm sorry.

I bite my lip and read my text ten times over, analyzing it like crazy every single time. I hope it doesn't sound too insensitive but isn't too much at the same time. I also, don't mention that I've gotten a kidney. Not yet, at least. I know Harlow and Meredith wouldn't tell anybody, because they don't feel it's their business to tell, and it's not. But since chances seem likely I got T.J.'s kidney I don't think now is the time to break that potential news to Spencer. Not that I think it'd bother him, but it couldn't possibly be easy to hear days after your friend died.

Minutes tick by and I break out in a sweat.

I flop down on my bed, cover my face with a pillow, and scream.

I shouldn't have said anything.

I sound like an idiot.

He's going to think I'm crazy. It's not like I'm friends with him, why should I be texting him about his dead best friend?

My phone vibrates, and I dive for it on the end of my bed.

Spencer: Thanks. It's … weird. I literally saw him that day and now I'll never see him again.

Willa: I want you to know I'm here to talk.

Spencer: That means a lot … I'm not sure I can. Not yet.

Willa: I understand.

Spencer: Would you want to come with me to his funeral tomorrow?

I hold my breath.

Go to the funeral of my maybe donor? Uh … I might throw up if I do that. I can't imagine having to see his family mourn for him while I sit there knowing I might have his organ inside me.

Willa: I'm sorry, but I…

Willa: I don't think I can.

Spencer: I'm sorry I asked. That was insensitive of me. I'm sure it'd be hard for you seeing someone your age like that when … well, when you've been through what you have.

Willa: Thanks for understanding.

Spencer: I want to see you. I don't think I'll be much company, but we're friends, right?

Willa: I think we are.

Spencer: Good.

I set my phone down, feeling better overall, even if my heart still races at the question he asked me.

How could I possibly face that family?

I flop back on my bed, staring at the pages on my ceiling, all the stories that exist in the world—too many for me to possibly ever read them all, no matter how hard I might try.

Harlow pushes my bedroom door open.

"Come with me."

"Where?" I ask.

She rolls her eyes. "Don't ask questions, just do it."

I stifle a laugh. "All right bossy pants."

She sticks out her tongue. "It's the only way to get you to do anything."

She's right.

I stand up and follow her downstairs and out the back.

She plops into the sand, and I do the same.

"What are we doing?"

"Wait, you'll see." She drapes her arms over her knees and smiles mischievously at me.

I shake my head. Knowing Harlow, there's no telling what's about to happen.

I cross my legs and dig my hands into the sand. It's a warm evening and the salty air slides over my bare arms.

The beach has to be the most calming place to live.

It isn't long until I understand why Harlow brought me out here, as the burnt orange sun begins to sink beneath the ocean, bathing the world in purples and pinks.

"Do you see that?" she asks, looking at the sunset. "The sun rises and sets every day. That's God's promise to everyone on Earth that when darkness comes, the light will always conquer it. Things might get bad, Willa, and that's okay, but goodness will come too. You have to have the patience to wait."

I lay my head on her shoulder. "Thank you," I whisper.

She tilts her head so it rests on mine. "You're welcome."

We continue to sit there, watching the last rays of sunlight sink beneath the midnight-blue ocean.

"I think you might be a little bit wrong," I tell her.

"What do you mean?"

"Maybe the sunset is supposed to serve as a reminder that the darkness isn't scary. You have to face it. It's when you turn your back, when you let fear get the best of you, that the darkness begins to swallow you whole."

She's quiet.

"All that matters to me is knowing the light comes back. Your sunrise is here, Willa, don't let it get away."

I smile to myself because she's right.

My transplant is my sunrise, and I have so much to accomplish before the sun sets again.

CHAPTER TEN

Saturday, I find myself sitting forlornly by the window in my bedroom that overlooks the street below.

I can't help thinking about the family burying their son today.

A beautiful life cut impossibly short.

Am I wrong for not going? It's not like I'd have to tell them, "Hey, I think I got your son's kidney."

A part of me *wants* to meet them, to thank them, but fear of rejection keeps me at bay, especially today.

Perry pushes his nose against my hand, demanding attention.

"Perry," I groan at his persistence, but pet him anyway. Immediately, I feel better. I don't know what it is about pets that make you feel better. They have this calming presence that washes over you.

Downstairs, the doorbell rings and I hear my mom open the door, greeting whoever is there.

Feet thud up the steps and then my door is blasted open.

I look over to find Meredith silhouetted in the doorway, a bag of junk food in her hands and a stack of DVDs under her arm. She kicks my door shut behind her and drops everything onto my bed.

I don't move from the window, but Perry goes to inspect the food.

Meredith puts her hands on her hips, glaring down at me from her impossibly tall height, with her red hair billowing around her shoulders.

"I'm here to save the day. No more moping. We're gonna watch movies *all day long* and talk about hot guys, binge on food that's bad for us, and I'll even braid your hair if you're nice to me."

I shake my head, stifling a laugh. "How'd you know?" I ask.

Her smile falters a little. "Harlow told me what was going on and that you might need a pick-me-up. And who better to do that than me?" She bows dramatically, then crosses the room to me, taking my hands and hauling me up from the bean bag I recline in.

"Now get your tush downstairs, make us some popcorn, and invite your sister in for some girl time. I'll get everything set up."

I felt down only minutes ago, but already Meredith has managed to turn my feelings around. I know I'm lucky to have a friend like her, one who's always willing to drop what she's doing to be by my side.

"Chop, chop." She claps her hands and then smacks my butt, ushering me out of the room.

"Okay, okay, I'm going," I say, holding my hands up in surrender as I leave my bedroom, Perry trailing behind me. I'm shocked he'd leave the food behind, but I guess he decides seeing what I'm up to is more important.

Downstairs I find my mom hefting her massive purse onto her shoulder.

"Oh, good, there you are," she sighs in relief. "Take a look at this and see if I forgot anything."

She hands me the grocery list, and I almost ask why she's going grocery shopping when I always do it during the week, but then I realize that I can't drive and until I can she'll have to unless someone takes me.

I read over the list and then grab a pen off the holder on the counter and add a few items before handing it back.

"That should be good," I tell her.

She reads over the items I added. "I can't believe I was going to forget eggs."

I shrug. "You haven't done this in a while. I'm impressed you remembered everyone's favorite cereal."

She folds the piece of paper and sticks it in her purse. "I'll be back soon. If you girls need anything call me. Your dad went up to see Grandma this morning and won't be back until Sunday evening."

"He didn't say bye?"

"It's a seven-hour drive up to Napa, he left before five this morning so he'd have most of the day with her and tomorrow."

"Right." I shake my head. "How's Grandma doing?"

"Oh, you know, the usual." She waves her hand before swiping up her keys. "Spying on neighbors and calling the cops on loose cattle."

I laugh. "She's something else."

"That she is." She starts for the garage door. "See you in a bit."

Once she's gone I rifle through the pantry for popcorn. I decide to make regular butter popcorn and Kettle corn. After they've both popped I put them in separate bowls and carry them upstairs while Perry, of course, follows.

Pushing the door open to my room I find Meredith has moved my three bean bags in front of my TV as well as dumped all my pillows and blankets onto the floor.

She pushes a DVD into the player as I walk in.

"That smells good." She hops up and takes one of the bowls from me as Harlow comes in behind me.

"What are we watching?" Harlow asks, shoving her hand into the popcorn bowl I hold then taking a bite.

Meredith flops into a beanbag and popcorn bounces out of the bowl and onto the floor. Perry dives for it, devouring all the pieces in seconds.

"Ladies and … gentleman" —she glances at Perry— "first up, we are watching *The Proposal*, because Lord knows my love of Ryan Reynolds is unparalleled, but can only be overshadowed by my love of Betty White, so this movie is the best of both worlds."

Harlow looks at me and shakes her head, stifling a laugh.

Meredith picks up the remote and skips through the previews while Harlow and I get situated in beanbags on either side of her.

I pick up one of the blankets and drape it over me.

My melancholy that's hung like a dark cloud over my head all morning has disappeared. Don't get me wrong, my heart still aches, but it's a little lighter now.

The movie starts, and the three of us being, well, *the three of us*, goof off as we watch the movie. Reciting lines and making up our own as we go.

By the afternoon we've devoured all the popcorn and snacks Meredith brought and have raided the freezer for ice cream.

"Do you feel better?" she asks, putting yet another DVD in.

I smile and nod. "Loads better."

She bites her lip and I can tell she wants to say more, to maybe even talk about why I was down—she knows the reason—but then she decides better of it. I think it's best not to talk about it right now. My emotions are already all over the place from finally getting a transplant; toss in worrying about my donor's family and it's a recipe for disaster. Right now, I have to focus on healing. That's the most important thing of all, because while I feel amazing that doesn't mean my body doesn't have to recover from the trauma.

Meredith lies back into the beanbag once more and presses play when the screen pops up.

I'm thankful that her and Harlow have decided to spend the day with me. Not just distracting me, but truly having fun. I needed this.

The movie has barely started when my mom appears in the doorway of my room. Meredith presses pause so she can speak.

"Meredith, your mom called and wanted to know if it was okay if you spent the night—you know we don't mind."

"Cool, thanks Kate," she thanks my mom.

"No problem. But don't stay up all night," she warns the three of us before heading back downstairs.

"Is your mom trying to get rid of you?" I ask. "When has your mom ever asked for your permission to stay here?" I laugh, because it's true.

Meredith rolls her eyes and lets out a dramatic breath. "The last time I invited myself over here for a sleepover she was livid. She's on this new kick of being like a … punisher parent or something. She told me the next time I wanted to sleepover here I had to ask her permission and she'd speak to your mom. She's been listening to too many podcasts if you ask me. I think they're brainwashing her."

She throws her hands up in the air like she doesn't know what she's going to do.

"That's hilarious." I hide a giggle behind my hand.

"The woman is crazy. She can drink a martini before twelve o' clock but I have to ask permission to stay at my sister from another mister's house. That's nuts."

"Do you have your stuff, or do you need to borrow some of mine?"

"Oh, don't worry, I knew the pushover would give in and let me stay, I already have a bag in my car."

I shake my head, but I'm secretly glad she's staying. I know she'll keep my spirits high and there won't be any crashing of emotions to come over me at night.

She starts the movie once more and our laughter soon fills the room. Sadly, we're far more amused by each other than the movie, but I think that's better.

Meredith lies beside me in my bed, staring up at the ceiling like I often do.

"I still can't believe you defiled your ceiling to glue book pages onto it."

I snort. "You know, most people would be more concerned by the defiling of the books, not the ceiling."

She shrugs. "I don't love books like you do."

"You should give them a chance."

"I don't have the attention span for it."

I look up at the ceiling with her, my hands crossed over my chest. "The next time I go to the bookstore I'm getting you the smuttiest book I can find. *That* you will love. I know it."

"Mmm, *smut*. Now you're talking my language."

We both laugh, and she sobers first.

"I'm sorry I didn't get to see you in the hospital."

She's already apologized numerous times since I've been home. The thing about Meredith is, while she portrays herself as loud-mouthed and without a care in the world, she's one of the most caring people I know. She's soft-hearted and loves fiercely.

"It's okay," I tell her for the umpteenth time. "I didn't feel up for any visitors anyway."

"But still … I feel like I should've been there."

"I don't care if you were there, I care if you're *here*, and I have you. I need my best friend to be by my side to talk to me, to distract me, or even to be a shoulder to cry on if that's what I need, and you do all those things. That's more than enough."

She turns her head to face me, red locks of hair falling over her forehead.

"When I was little I used to beg for a sister. It was all I wanted. But I think God knew I did have a sister out there in the world, and that's you. We might not share the same DNA but we share a heart, and I think that's worth more."

I reach my arms out to hug her and she hugs me back.

I think it's a rare thing to have a friendship like ours, like she says we're more sisters than anything, and it's something to cherish.

CHAPTER ELEVEN

Three weeks pass with doctor's appointment after doctor's appointment.

I begin to feel like I live in the hospital, like I did in the beginning of my diagnosis, but I'm quick to remind myself this isn't forever and for a very good reason.

June comes to a close, school ends, Meredith graduates, and life goes on.

Life goes on, and yet my mind always circles back to the Werth family.

I can't help but think about T.J.'s parents and what losing their son must have done to them.

Every time I've been at the hospital I've done everything I can to learn if he was my donor, but the medical staff is tight lipped, as they should be. All I have to go on is the information they gave me when they called, what was in the newspaper, and my own gut feeling.

My days become obsessive as I spend my whole time thinking about meeting them—for thanking them for their selfless sacrifice to donate their son's organs. I want them to know, to feel relief in their heart, that their son's death managed to bring good to the world.

I pace my room, back and forth. It's a miracle I haven't worn a hole through the floor and fallen straight down into the room below.

I've been warring with myself, and I know I'm about to lose the fight.

Finally, I dive for my desk chair and sit down, lifting my laptop lid.

With a few quick strokes of the keyboard I find the address for Diane and Peter Werth. It's almost scary how easy it is to find someone if you know their name and the relative location of where they live.

I save the address to my phone and look down at it.

"Are you going to do this?" I ask myself softly.

Yes. Yes, I am.

I have to. There's this innate need inside me to meet them and I know it won't go away until I do.

This feels crazy, and it is, but I have to do it.

I change into a pair of jean shorts and an off-the-shoulder top. My hair is a wavy mess, I try my best to make it look decent. I even take time to apply a little makeup. I don't want to show up at their house looking like I rolled out of bed and threw on some shoes.

I stare at my reflection in the mirror.

Wild blonde hair that refuses to be tamed. Freckles dotted across my nose like sprinkles on ice cream. Hazel eyes swaying golden today. Now, post transplant, there's a slight pink hue in my cheeks that wasn't there before.

It's the same face that's stared back at me for seventeen years.

But my eyes?

That's where I see the biggest difference.

My eyes aren't those of a peppy teen, living life to the fullest.

They're the eyes of someone who's lived through more than anyone ever should.

I swallow past the sudden lump in my throat and remind myself I can finally say that all the things that put that look in my eyes are now in the past.

Now's my chance to get my spark back.

I turn the light off in the bathroom and grab my purse.

The house is empty—my parents are at work and Harlow met some of her friends from school at the local pool.

I pad down the stairs, my purse slapping against my leg.

Downstairs, Perry sits by his water bowl, begging for more. I quickly fill it and escape while he's lapping at it.

I haven't been cleared to drive yet, but I know their address is in a neighborhood not far from this one, only two miles, and the walk will do me some good.

It's warm but breezy, perfect beach weather. I love that it never gets sweltering hot here, the ocean breeze always keeps the air feeling fresh.

All around me are signs of summer.

Kids squealing in their yards as they dart through sprinklers. The chiming music of an ice cream truck in the distance. Bees buzzing from flower to flower. A beautiful blue butterfly dancing through the air.

Dancing.

My transplant came upon us so suddenly I haven't even thought about dancing until this moment.

I no longer have to worry about the tube sticking out of my stomach, the area now healed with a raised circle scar all that's left behind.

My shoulders feel lighter at the idea of getting into the studio again. It's something I know I'll have to discuss with my doctor at my next appointment. I'm not sure if a month is enough time for them to think any sort of exercise, especially dance, is okay. Healing is going great, and I feel amazing, but that doesn't mean my body doesn't need longer to recover.

I check my phone and find that I'm one block from their house.

My heart starts to beat a little bit faster.

As I grow closer to the house it thunders in my ears like a mighty drum announcing my approach.

What if they're not happy to see me?

This was a bad idea.

What were you thinking, Willa?

You're such an idiot.

Like, seriously, THE *biggest idiot on the planet.*

Turn around. You still have time.

I CAN'T

I can't.

I can't.

I CAN'T.

I have to do this.

I stop outside the house and double check that it's the right one.

A gate out front opens onto a stone pathway that leads up the Spanish-style home with a stucco outside and long branched trees shadowing the front.

A French door on the second floor opens up to a balcony.

It's a nice home, obviously they have money, because a house like this in Santa Monica costs even more than the home I live in.

I follow the path up to the solid wood front door.

Are you going to do this?

Yes. Yes, I am.

Before I can chicken out I raise my finger to the doorbell and press it. I hear it chime loudly inside the house.

I can barely hear over the whirling of the blood rushing through my veins.

I've never done anything like this before. Put myself *out there* and braced for rejection.

While I desire nothing more than to meet them, I realize they might not want to meet *me.*

And I'll be okay with that.

I might run home and have a good cry over it, but I'll be okay.

Embarrassed, yes, but okay.

I inhale a deep breath and let it out slowly.

"I got it, Mom," a male voice says on the other side.

The door swings open, and before I can brace myself for this meeting I'm standing before the guy I couldn't stop thinking about only a month before.

He stands in front of me, same short hair, earring in his left ear, turquoise green eyes, and tanned skin. His chest is bare this time, displaying a pair of six-pack abs that makes me decide they should be called *sex pack abs*, because the thoughts I'm thinking are wholly sex worthy. He wears a pair of basketball shorts low on his hips, the top of his boxer briefs peeking out. I look further down and note his long bare feet.

I can't breathe.

I can't breathe.

I can't BREATHE.

It's HIM. It's THE guy. The one Perry mowed over and that, up until my transplant, kept slipping into my thoughts unbidden.

I'd never been the kind of girl who obsessed over guys. After my diagnosis, and subsequent enrollment in home schooling, I just hadn't taken an interest in guys. I didn't have the time or energy.

But something about this guy, from the moment I saw him, was different.

And it wasn't just his looks, there was this aura around him that drew me like a moth to a flame.

It feels like I look at him for minutes, but I know in reality it's only seconds.

"I'm sorry," I blurt. "Wrong house."

Before he can do or say anything, I turn and run.

I run straight down the path, through the gate, and down the sidewalk.

"Hey! Wait!" I hear behind me and the gate clinks.

I don't stop. I keep running. After all, he can't chase me on the hot sidewalk with no shoes.

I run, and I run, and I run.

I don't know if I'm even allowed to run, but I keep going, because I'm scared to stop.

If I stop, he might be able to catch up to me if he went back and got shoes, and I can't let him.

I can't face the truth.

I don't want to.

CHAPTER TWELVE

A whole week passes, and I don't tell anyone, especially not Harlow and Meredith, what I attempted to do.

It was a bad idea to begin with and I never should've done it.

July slams into California with a sweltering heat that makes me rethink all my praise for our weather. It's almost impossible to walk outside and not break into a sweat.

"Willa! Harlow! Meredith!" my mom yells up the steps. "You can't hide inside all day!"

"We can, and we will," Meredith says from where she lies on my floor making … well, floor angels.

"Come on." I hold out a hand to haul her up. "If we don't go out there, you know they'll march up here and drag our asses down."

"No," she whines. "It's too hot. Why do we need to celebrate the Fourth of July anyway?"

"I don't know," I hedge. "Maybe because it's the day our country declared it's independence."

"Ugh. Fine." She slaps her hand into mine and I haul her up.

Harlow stands from my mattress. "If we die out there I'm having Mom and Dad put 'Here lies Harlow Jewel Hansen—she melted to death and we let her.'"

I snort. "That's a good one. I'll put on mine, 'Here lies Willa Layne Hansen—she got a transplant, only to die of heatstroke.'"

Meredith snorts. "Funny, mine's going to say, 'Merebitch is here to haunt yo ass.'"

Harlow and I bust out laughing. "You win," I concede.

The three of us reluctantly make our way downstairs.

On the kitchen island is a spread of food. Everything from finger food like chips and mini turkey sandwiches all the way up to hot dogs and burgers. There's anything and everything.

We each grab a plate and pile some food on it before joining everyone outside.

Meredith's parents mingle with mine and even more of their friends. Their friends have brought their children too, but most of them are either older or younger than us, therefore the three of us have always stuck together at these types of gatherings.

We step off the deck, right into the sand, and keep walking until we finally find a spot far enough away from the others to have our own conversation, but close enough that they can see us, lest they think we've snuck back into the house.

"It's like they want us to melt to death or something," Meredith whines. "Even the sand is too hot." She squirms uncomfortably.

"I think it's somewhere in the parenting handbook that it's their job to make our lives miserable," I joke, taking a bite of my burger.

Meredith gathers her hair up off her neck and twists it into a knot, securing it with a hair tie. You *know* Meredith is hot if she's forsaking looking good for getting her hair out of her way.

We eat in silence, too hot to talk much. Meredith finishes her chips and hotdog and tosses her plate to me. I catch it, but glare at her, because she could've gotten ketchup all over me. I don't know why she piles it on her hot dog like she does and then smears it all over the plate. Wouldn't it be easier to put a normal amount on to begin with?

"Forget this," she says, standing. She kicks off her shorts and removes her tank top, revealing her hot pink bikini beneath. "I have to get in the water before I die."

I wish I could join her, but it's too soon post-transplant to be safe. I'm just glad swimming in the ocean isn't on the list of things I won't be able to do, because that would suck. Lakes, however, are out of the question, too much bacteria. Same with public pools—however private ones are okay.

Harlow finishes and joins her. I gather our trash up and take it inside to dispose of it.

They're still in the ocean when I return, and I stick my toes in the water.

I smile to myself as the crystal water swells around my feet. It sparkles as the hot sun shines down on it. The water, which is normally cool, even in the summer, is decent today.

Off in the distance, I see other families out enjoying the day, either on the sand or in the water. A group of three surfers sit in the distance, waiting and hoping for a decent wave that might never come.

The water tickles my toes, bringing me back to the here and now.

Meredith and Harlow wade out of the water, dripping wet and smiling.

"I feel *so* much better," Meredith cries, plopping into the sand.

Harlow drops down beside her and I join them.

Behind us, the party rages on, music blasting out of speakers, kids shrieking and running around, adults standing around with beers in hand.

Meredith looks over her shoulder and must see what I see because she looks back at me and says, "It's sad you'll never be able to drink alcohol. Like … it's a coming of age tradition to steal alcohol from your parents and get so drunk you can't even see the toilet so you throw up in the bathtub instead."

I laugh and shake my head. "Sounds to me like I'm not missing out on much. That's one rule I'm okay to follow."

Alcohol is hard on your kidneys; therefore, I'm not supposed to drink any. I'm sure many transplant recipients *do*, but I think they're dumb. I'm not doing anything to potentially compromise this precious gift I've been given. I want to know I've done everything I can to keep this kidney as healthy as I possibly can. I won't have guilt weighing on my shoulders, wondering if I'd followed certain rules if it would've lasted longer.

Meredith bites her lip. "I've been curious, but I haven't wanted to ask …"

I raise a brow. "That's not like you—you love asking the most uncomfortable questions ever." I laugh and bump her shoulder with mine.

She shields her eyes from the sun and shrugs. "It's just … I mean … I don't want to … ugh, I might as well ..." she stammers. "Can you have kids?"

I grind my teeth together. I should've known this question would come eventually from someone. I guess maybe I didn't expect it to be so soon, or Meredith of all people.

"I *can.* That's why a lot of younger women with kidney disease advocate to get a transplant, but … pregnancy is hard on your kidneys, and I only have one that isn't even mine, and that makes me hesitate to think about having biological children. Do I want to risk going on dialysis again just to have a child that's my blood? I don't think so. I think I'd rather adopt and be healthy and there for my child."

"Whoa … that's deep. I never even thought about it like that."

I pick up sand and watch it sift through my fingers like so many other things I haven't been able to hold on to.

When I was little I dreamed of having my own family, two or three kids of my own that had my blonde hair and maybe my freckles.

But that dream has drifted away like so many others.

Maybe it's selfish of me but keeping my donor kidney healthy and lasting as long as possible is far more important to me than having biological children.

Brushing the sand off my hands, I look out at the ocean. "I've thought about it a lot," I admit. "I've had to."

"You're the strongest, most brave person I know, Willa. I aspire to be more like you," Meredith admits. It's one of the sincerest things she's ever said to me.

"Thanks," I say, but I don't feel strong, nor brave enough, to deserve her praise.

Most days, I feel like I'm just skating by, going through the motions and doing what I have to do.

"What are you going to do for your birthday?" she asks, changing the subject.

"I haven't even thought about it," I admit.

"We should do something big." I open my mouth to rebut that idea, but she continues on before I can say anything. "After all, this is a very big birthday for you. Not only is it your eighteenth, but you got a kidney, that's a big freaking deal."

She's right, it is, but I don't find myself in the mood to celebrate. Maybe I'm still butthurt over my disastrous attempt to meet T.J.'s parents, and instead encountered his brother? Cousin? Who knows, it's not like I hung around to find out, but the fact that he's *the* guy I saw outside Cool Beans is more than a little ironic for my tastes. It's like the fates are mocking me. I finally meet a guy who makes me feel more than just a general feeling of fondness, and he's potentially related to my kidney donor.

I don't know why I'm bothered by it. I don't *know* him. He doesn't know me. It shouldn't matter, and yet it does.

"What do you propose we do then?" I ask her. I have no ideas, I might as well hear what she has to say.

She taps her lip in thought. "We could go to the mall—eat at the Cheesecake Factory, you love that place—maybe get our nails done."

"Maybe . . ." I hedge, it's not a bad idea, but it doesn't excite me either. "What about bowling?" I suggest. The irony is not lost on me that I was bowling when I first collapsed and found out at I had CKD.

"Bowling?" Meredith wrinkles her nose. "Why?"

"That sounds like fun to me," Harlow pipes in. I can always count on my sister to have my back.

"I don't know." I shrug, thinking it over. "It'd keep my mind off things. It might be good for Spencer too."

We've been texting some, but I haven't seen him since before T.J. died. He sounds different now, even through text, almost older like he's experienced too much. I know that all too well.

Meredith tilts her head this way and that. "Okay, okay. If that's what you want to do then you should."

"Yeah, I think it is."

Bowling would be low key and chill. I don't want to do anything at home, I'm already here enough, and while Meredith's suggestion wasn't the worst thing in the world it's just not what I want to do.

Besides, I don't want to make a big deal out of my birthday. For me, it's always been just another day. I'm not one of those people who celebrates the whole week, or heck even the whole month. It's just not my style.

I've always preferred to fade into the background.

The song changes and Meredith grabs my hands, hauling me up.

"Dance with me," she begs, but not giving me a choice as she begins to swing my arms.

I can't help myself and begin to dance with her. Harlow stands and joins us, the three of laughing and dancing the goofiest dance we can muster.

When the sun begins to go down, sparklers are passed around, and I run around like a joyous child, watching the sparks ignite in the air.

Above us, fireworks go off, lighting up the dark and starry sky with red, white, and blue. The fireworks shimmer over the ocean before melting into the nothingness.

With a racketing boom, more and more light the sky.

The three of us stand together, our sparklers extinguished, and watch the show above us.

I grab Meredith's hand on one side and Harlow's on the other.

I give them each a squeeze, thankful to have these two amazing girls in my life. I don't think society puts enough emphasis on friendship and how important it is. But I'll never take having them for granted.

As the last of the fireworks disappear, I make a wish.

Maybe it's not normal to make a wish on fireworks, but I do it anyway.

CHAPTER THIRTEEN

A week later I throw the ball down the lane and watch it soar toward the pins, and then at the last second, fly into the gutter.

July fourteenth marks my eighteenth birthday.

Legally, I'm an adult, which is weird to think about.

In many ways, I feel like I've been an adult for years, and in others, I feel like a child who still needs her mom and dad.

"Ugh!" I groan and swing around to face my small gathering of friends—just Meredith, Harlow, and a forlorn Spencer.

I can tell he's trying to be a good sport and be as upbeat as he can, but he can't hide his sadness completely.

It's hard being a teen and losing a friend. It reminds us that we're not invincible. I learned that a long time ago, unfortunately, and had plenty of time to come to terms with the fact that death is imminent.

You can't avoid it. It's the one uniting factor in all human beings. No matter your color skin, where you're born, your gender, we all die.

I want to say something to him, to try to offer him any comfort I can, but everything I think up sounds too … *blah.* I don't want to sound like I'm trying to write off his friend's death, because that's not what I'm doing, but I wish I could make him understand death isn't the worst thing in the world. In fact, it's the *easiest.* Living is harder. Feeling emotions. Experiencing pain.

"Well, I tried," I mumble, waiting for my shiny purple ball to come back around. I'll be honest, I picked it more for the color instead of paying attention to the weight, so that might be part of my problem.

The ball pops back up and I grab it.

I hold it steady as I walk to the lane. I take a deep breath and let my arm swing.

The ball releases and slides down the lane. I squish my eyes closed but still manage to peek through. There's a crash as the ball collides with the pins and I open my eyes fully, jumping for joy when I see only two pins remaining upright. I'll take that as a definite win.

I skip back to my seat beside Meredith; Spencer and Harlow sit on the outside of the table.

On the screen, it's clear Spencer is kicking all our butts, but today isn't about winning, it's about having fun.

Meredith hops up for her turn.

Every time she's stood for her turn I take time to study Spencer.

Dark circles cling to the skin beneath his eyes. He looks like he hasn't slept since he got the news about T.J. His hair hangs lank, like it doesn't have the energy to keep its normal bounce. His smile is absent, only a small half one poking out every now and then.

"You're kicking our butts," I tell him, for lack of anything else to say.

He glances at me, that half-smile appearing for a moment before disappearing altogether. "What can I say? I'm a natural," he jokes.

My heart hurts badly for him, having lost his friend, but I can't help the tightening of anxiety in my chest I feel wondering what he'd think if he knew T.J.'s kidney was in my body.

I don't think Spencer even knows I've gotten a transplant, I certainly haven't told him, and I doubt Harlow or Meredith would have either.

I bite my lip nervously, my heart thudding a symphony in my ears.

My mouth opens of its own accord and I blurt, "I got a transplant."

Spencer's eyes open wide and his mouth parts. "Really? You're not joking, are you?"

I scoff, mildly offended. "I wouldn't joke about something like that."

"Wow." He shakes his head, gathering himself. "That's amazing. Congratulations. How are you feeling?"

"Good. Really good. Amazing, actually," I admit.

"When did it happen?" he asks, his brow crinkled with confusion, probably wondering why during all of our texts I never mentioned it.

I hesitate for a moment before saying, "The end of May."

"Ah." Clarity enters his eyes, and for a moment I worry it's too much clarity. "Now I know why you didn't tell me. I wish you would've, it would've been some good news to counteract the bad."

I breathe a sigh of relief, that at least for the moment, he hasn't put two and two together.

Meredith cheers and we all look up to see she's managed to get a spare.

She starts doing a victory dance that includes a lot of booty shaking.

"Bow down to me, bitches. I am the bowling master," she chants, causing a couple with their two small children to glare at us.

"Actually" —I stifle a laugh— "Spencer is still winning."

"Logistics," she argues. "Of course he's winning, the race is to be number two. None of us have a chance of beating him. This is between the three of us." She flicks her fingers between herself, Harlow, and me.

"I'm just here to have fun," Harlow pipes in.

Meredith glares at her as she sits down. "This is war and there will be a clear victor."

"Which will be Spencer," I interject.

Meredith whips her head toward me, her eyes narrowed.

"You better sleep with your eyes open, Hansen."

I shake my head, laughing easily.

"On that note" —Harlow stands— "it's my turn."

Harlow grabs her lime-green ball and steps up to the lane. She holds the ball up, her tongue sticking out slightly between her lips as she concentrates. She swings her arm back and lets the ball fly.

Right.

Down.

The.

Middle.

"Oh, game on," Meredith yells, when Harlow gets a strike.

Harlow turns around and faces us, taking a bow.

She reaches the table and Spencer holds both his hands up to her for a high five. I swear her cheeks flush, but then her hair falls forward, hiding her face, and I can't be sure.

We finish the first game, Spencer winning, of course, with Harlow coming in second, and order some food.

When the order comes up, Spencer carries the two trays over to our table.

I sip at my Sprite I got from the vending machine as Spencer passes the food around.

I take a hot dog, squirting ketchup and mustard on it.

Before the transplant, a hot dog was a big no-no. I mean, hot dogs aren't good for anyone, but sometimes you just want a damn hot dog. I always had to avoid them, but today's my birthday, I'm post-transplant, and I'm going to enjoy one as well as crisp bowling alley fries. I've always loved their fries here. I don't know if it's necessarily that they're good or they just fill me with a feeling of nostalgia.

We eat our food happily, talking and laughing. Spencer fits easily into our little group, almost like he's always been here.

Sadness stays in his eyes, but he starts to smile more, and I can tell it's genuine. It makes me feel good that he seems to be enjoying himself somewhat. I know I haven't been there for him like I should. Maybe it's selfish of me, but it's been too hard knowing the kidney I got is more than likely T.J's. It seems wrong, almost gross, to comfort Spencer right now with that knowledge.

We finish eating and Spencer gets rid of our trash before we set up another game.

This time we divide into teams, Meredith and Harlow versus Spencer and me.

This ought to be interesting.

Meredith goes first, slinging her ball like she's performing shot put, very badly, might I add, for the Olympics.

"What was that?" I tease her as her ball flies straight into the gutter.

She shrugs. "Bowling is not my sport."

"Nothing is your sport," I remind her.

"True," she concedes, waiting for the ball to come back.

When it does, she grabs it and cradles it in both hands as she steps up to the lane.

She spreads her legs and swings the ball in both hands before releasing it. It flies down the lane and knocks down all but two pins. She turns to us and curtseys.

I shake my head as we all clap.

It's my turn next. I take a deep breath before grabbing my ball, concentrating.

"You got this, Willa," Spencer cheers behind me.

I swing my arm back and let the ball fly.

Squishing my eyes closed, I barely peek and gasp when all the pins are knocked down.

"Oh, my God," I scream, and turn around to find Spencer running toward me.

He opens his arms and I jump into them as he spins me.

"That was amazing," he says, setting me down.

We high five before sitting down to let Harlow take her turn.

When the game ends, Spencer and I winning—and we perform an epic winning dance just to rub it in their faces further—the four of us pile in my tiny car to head back to my house where Meredith and Spencer met us and where cake now waits for us. I didn't want to have my cake at the bowling alley since my parents weren't going there with us.

I pull my car into the driveway and Spencer tumbles out of the front passenger seat, stretching his legs.

"I'm sorry," I apologize with a laugh as I get out. "I know it's a small car."

"It's a clown car," he declares, wagging a finger at me.

I shrug. "Yeah, you're right," I concede.

It *is* small, but I love it.

I lead the way inside and kick off my shoes.

"Mom? Dad? We're back," I call out.

"In here," my mom answers back from the area of the kitchen.

I smile when I spot them both in the kitchen, my dad's arms around her. My giant chocolate cake with chocolate icing sits on the island, HAPPY 18th BIRTHDAY WILLA in cursive letters on top with yellow and pink flowers. Candles are already stuck in it, waiting to be lit.

My dad releases my mom and she grabs the lighter. "I assume you're ready for cake?"

I'd only eyed the cake all morning. There was a teeny tiny dent in the icing where I snuck a taste. I couldn't help myself—and it was just as yummy as I'd hoped.

Harlow slides onto a stool; Meredith and Spencer following suit.

My mom lights the candles and then Dad turns off the lights, plunging the room into darkness, the only light the flickering candle flames.

"Happy birthday to you. Happy birthday to you. Happy birthday, dear Willa. Happy birthday to yooou."

"Make a wish," my mom whispers.

I close my eyes, make a wish, and blow out the candles.

It's my first birthday in four years where I haven't wished for a kidney.

Instead, this time, I wish for a change. Maybe some option other than transplant that would give people a better life. I read once about a bionic kidney that's being made. There are too many people on dialysis, having their lives ruled by something unnatural. And sadly, if people aren't in your shoes, they don't care. They might think they do but they *can't*, because it's easy to ignore how bad it is.

The lights flick back on and my mom starts cutting the cake, handing me the first corner piece because she knows I'm an icing fiend.

My friends, sister, and I take our plates outside onto the small deck to sit on the steps and eat.

"Killer view," Spencer declares.

"Where do you live?" I ask him.

"My mom is a single mom so we live in a condo. It has a decent, though distant view, of the ocean. It's not the same thing as walking out your back door and having it right there."

"Definitely not," I agree.

Even though I've never been into water sports, and don't spend much time in the ocean, I've always appreciated living right on the beach. It's like waking up to a special miracle right outside your door every day. It's not something everyone gets to enjoy on a daily basis, so I'm determined to soak it up.

"Thanks for coming today, guys," I say, licking icing off my fork.

Meredith bumps her shoulder against mine. "You know there's no place I'd rather be, even if you did want to go bowling of all things," she teases with a laugh.

"Yeah, it's your birthday," Spencer agrees. "There's nowhere else we'd be."

"And I don't have a choice, I'm your sister," Harlow jokes, and I glare at her, both of us dissolving into laughter.

"I'm glad I have you guys in my life, truly, all of you."

There are a lot of people in the world who will get to know you to try to bring you down or undermine you, but I'm lucky to have friends, and a sister, who are the rare kind of friend. The one that's there no matter what, who you can be at your happiest or your angriest with, who doesn't care how ugly you can be because they know your heart is made of gold.

Spencer might be new to my friend group, but he rounds it out perfectly.

And while I technically don't have many friends, you only need a few good people in your life. The number of friends you have doesn't equate to how loved you are. In fact, the more friends you have, the less they know the real you and you with them.

"Aww, look at you getting all sappy." Meredith wraps her arms around me and, before I know it, Harlow and Spencer are getting in on the group hug action.

I smile beneath their embrace and, for the first time in years, I can say I'm truly happy.

CHAPTER FOURTEEN

It's probably dumb, but I honestly thought turning eighteen would make me feel different, more grown up and ready to take on the world.

But instead, three days later, I feel like the same old Willa.

I guess that's a good thing—at least I haven't fallen off the deep end and started balancing checkbooks and talking about taxes and the stock market.

"Are you seriously going to sit there and read the whole day?" Meredith asks, applying more sunscreen to her body.

We've come to the beach by the pier. I want to sneak off and go see Julio, to tell him about my transplant, but Harlow and Meredith haven't left my side and I know if I tell them where I'm going they'll want to follow. Sometimes, I want to do things by myself.

When I first got diagnosed with kidney disease everyone around me treated me like a delicate, breakable flower and a lot of that overprotectiveness hasn't left them.

They don't understand I just want my freedom to be a normal person.

"Yeah, probably," I answer her.

"Ugh," she groans. "You can be so boring. Do you not see how many hot guys are here today? How can you be surrounded by this man meat and care more about your book?"

"For your information, there's man meat in my book and he's my future book husband."

"But he's not real," she reasons.

"To you," I mutter under my breath.

Non-readers don't get how real characters become to us bookworms. They have no idea what they're missing out on.

She huffs. "You're weird, but I love you."

I crack a smile. "Love you too, Merebitch."

She grins at the nickname.

I peek over the top of my sunglasses at this so-called man meat. The beach is covered in scantily-clad women and men in board shorts. Out in the water there's the usual grouping of surfers.

My eyes are drawn to them, like usual, and envy runs through my veins.

Envy at their ease in the water, and how fearless they are when they catch a wave. I'd be afraid I'd crack my skull on the surfboard when I inevitably had an accident.

My eyes zero in on a guy in a wetsuit. He's with a group of four other guys, all bobbing on their boards. While the others laugh, his eyes are focused straight ahead on the water, like he sees something they don't.

He starts paddling, though I can't see an approaching wave.

The other guys stop chatting and watch him too.

He keeps paddling and paddling.

And then the wave starts to form.

He turns his board around and I watch in awe as he catches the large wave, possibly the best one all day, though I haven't been watching, and rides it out.

There's something about him that's magic on water.

He rides the wave like he owns it, not like it's a creation of Mother Nature that could crush him at any moment.

When he successfully catches the wave and rejoins his friends they exchange clasped hands and fist bumps.

I return my eyes to the pages of my book but I can't help but peek up every now and then and find him.

An hour passes, and Meredith stretches beside me.

"I'm going to grab a smoothie, you guys coming?"

She looks at me and Harlow on my other side.

Harlow puts down her magazine. "Yeah, I'm starving."

Meredith stands and brushes the sand off her body. Even with each of us sitting on a towel it's impossible not to get sand on yourself.

"I'm good," I tell them.

"Are you sure?" Harlow asks. "You don't want a water? Maybe coffee?"

"Yeah grab me a water, thank you," I tell her.

I watch them disappear into the distance, turning into tiny specks as they head off to get drinks and food.

My eyes return to the ocean and my throat catches when I see the guy I was watching get out. He sticks his board in the sand and unzips his wetsuit, tugging it harshly off his arms and letting it hang down to expose his chest.

Tucking his board back under his arm, he starts up the beach.

He doesn't seem to be looking anywhere at first, but then somehow his eyes land on me, and I gasp.

"Oh, shit," I mutter. "It's *him*."

The guy Perry almost mowed over, the guy who opened the door at T.J's parents' house. This can't be happening.

Nope.

I watch his face switch from curiosity to recognition.

I jump up, dropping my book. I pick it up hastily—never leave a soldier behind, or a book—and try to make a run for it.

Well not quite a run, but I do speed walk in the opposite direction.

"Hey!" I hear him call out.

He's not talking to you. He's not. Keep walking.

"Wait up!"

Nope, no, he's definitely not talking to you.

A hand closes around my elbow and I cringe, because he was *definitely* calling out to me, and now he's caught me.

Kill me now.

I turn around and face him, but he doesn't release me like he's afraid if he does I might run away again.

"I remember you, you showed up at my house." I flinch, because it sounds stalkerish, and redness rushes to my face. "Were you a friend of T.J.'s?" he asks, which wasn't what I was expecting, but suddenly it's the most logical explanation and I feel stupid for not realizing that'd be his reason for stopping me.

"Um … yeah … something like that," I stutter.

"I don't remember seeing you at the funeral." His green eyes sear into me, like he can see much more than I want him to.

"Yeah, I was … uh … sick," I finish lamely. I mean, it's kind of true. Not a total lie.

He nods and tilts his head. "I feel like I know you from somewhere else too."

"Uh … my dog kinda ran into you and knocked your coffee down," I remind him.

"Oh," he laughs, his laughter easy but with a slight edge like he hasn't laughed in a while. "I remember now. You haven't knocked down any more unsuspecting guys, have you?"

"Nope, not that I know of." My heart eases a bit at the easiness of conversation.

"But you have shown up at their house and played ding dong ditch," he jokes. "You know," he whispers conspiratorially, and a tiny dimple appears in his right cheek, "you're supposed to run away *before* the person opens the door."

"I'll remember that next time," I quip, and he grins. I pale. "Not that there will be a next time."

His smile grows impossibly wider. "How'd you know T.J.?" Before I can answer, he blurts, "You weren't an ex-girlfriend or something, were you?"

"No, why?"

He looks at me and my belly does somersaults. "No reason." He shrugs. "You know," he starts, "if we're going to keep running into each other like this you might as well give me your number."

I snort and then instantly want to punch myself for being the awkward human being I am.

But I'm freaking out on the inside, because even though I don't know this guy, it's like I do. It's weird the way my body seems to recognize him. I've never been interested in dating or anything of the sort, but I know I'm interested in *him*.

"I don't even know your name," I remind him.

"I don't know yours, either," he counters.

"I'm Willa." I smile.

Is this flirting? Are we flirting? Am I good at it? Bad? I'm going to throw up.

DON'T THROW UP ON HIS FEET!

"Jasper." He grins, his smile is easy, his teeth are white but not perfect unlike almost everyone else around here. His front two teeth overlap slightly giving him a quirky, almost boyish smile. It suits him. "You know," he begins, quirking his head and squinting from the sun so he can see me better, "I think it's funny we keep running into each other. First the coffee shop, then you show up at my house, now here we are."

"Or, it could be the fact we live in the same town."

He shakes his head. "This place is large enough, with a big enough population, that you don't meet someone and then continue to see them like we have. That has to mean something it has to be …"

"Has to be what?" I prompt when he bites his tongue.

He lets out a breath. "You're going to think I'm weird."

I shake my head. "Trust me, I won't."

He shakes his shoulders like he's shaking away his thoughts. "It's like maybe T.J. is pushing us together. Maybe we're meant to know each other."

My heart accelerates, beating so fast I'm surprised it doesn't fall out and roll around on the sandy beach.

He's right, it *is* a bit odd the way we'd never seen each other until that day outside the coffee shop and then here we are again and again.

It has to mean something.

"How did you know T.J.?" I ask.

"He's my little brother," he answers without thought. "Was," he corrects, his face drawing into sadness. "He *was* my brother." He swallows past a lump in his throat, his eyes darkening with seriousness. "Have you ever lost someone?"

"Yes," I answer without thought. *Myself.*

After my diagnosis, I literally mourned *myself.* I mourned for the life I had before, for the *normal* that no longer existed. It was gone, and I had to accept from here on out that Willa was gone, and a new Willa existed.

I think anyone who's gone through any kind of trauma or been diagnosed with a disease does that. It's the only healthy way to continue.

If you don't grieve, you stay stagnant.

"Then you get it," he continues.

My heart pangs realizing I'm standing in front of my donor's *brother.*

The guy I've secretly been crushing on, for no good reason other than the way I felt the first time I met him, is my donor's brother.

It's like some being out there is mocking me.

Ha! Willa finally starts crushing, so we're going to make him her kidney donor's brother! Let's see how she handles this one!

"Yeah, I get it."

"Why'd you run away? That day you came to the house," he clarifies.

Panic seizes my body, and I know I can't tell him why I was there. "I … uh … just wanted to share my condolences."

He nods and looks away out toward the water. "I need to grab a bite to eat. You want to join me?"

"I'm here with my friend and sister," I hedge.

His green eyes meet mine and my breath catches. I don't know this guy, I only just learned his name, but I can't deny how I'm drawn to him.

He runs his fingers through the short strands of his hair, which in the summer sun is almost dry already.

"Yeah, well maybe I'll see you around then." He gets a small grin, that dimple flashing for a millisecond on his cheek. "You know, since we keep running into each other, I doubt this will be the last time."

He starts to walk away, where in the distance I know there are food stands.

I war with myself, my normal reserved self telling me to go back to our towels and where the girls will be meeting me.

But the other part of me, the one who just got a kidney and whole new life, says to take a fucking chance and go after the guy.

For the first time in my life, I don't make the safe choice.

I turn around and jog to catch up to him.

"Wait up," I call out.

He looks over his shoulder at the sound of my voice, his lips quirking up in surprise.

"Decide to join me after all?"

"Yeah, yeah I did." I stop beside him. I'm slightly out of breath, having had to run farther than I anticipated since his long legs had already carried him so far away.

"Good. You hungry?"

"Not really," I admit.

He makes a sound.

We trudge through the sand to the stands, passing Meredith and my sister.

Meredith stops, her jaw dropping, and my sister grabs her arm, yanking her. Meredith gives me a look that tells me I'm going to owe her a major explanation with lots of details.

Jasper steps into line at one of the sandwich shacks and orders two wraps and two waters.

He hands them a card that he pulls from a zippered part of his wetsuit. Taking back his card and food he nods for me to follow him to one of the tables.

He chooses a small red table that sits crookedly in the sand with two chairs that do the same.

He hands me a bottle of water and a wrap.

"I didn't want anything," I remind him.

He shakes his head, tearing into his. "EatWhatchaCan," he slurs around the large bite he took.

I shake my head and remove the paper from around the wrap. It looks good. It's not something I'd normally I get.

I take a bite, chew and swallow. "This is delicious," I tell him.

"See, you were hungry and didn't know it." He chuckles as I take another bite. "How'd you know T.J.?" he asks.

"Oh … um, I'm friends with Spencer, that's how."

He nods. "Yeah, him and Spencer were best friends. I haven't seen him since the funeral. I told him he could talk to me, and he's practically like family. It's weird not having them both around."

"Are you in college?" I ask.

God this whole small talk thing is super weird and awkward.

"Just finished my second year." A look crosses over his face.

"What is it?" I prompt.

"I've been doing a lot of thinking since T.J. passed. It's nearing two months now, and I just … I don't see myself going back to college, at least not this year. I need time," he admits. "That probably makes me sound like a wimp, but I'd only been home a couple of weeks when we got the call he was dead. I'd just seen him that night, laughing and happy, and *alive.* Hearing he was gone was a wake-up call that I need to figure out what I want to do with my life."

"I'm the last person who's going to judge you," I admit, taking a sip of water. "I was diagnosed with kidney disease at fourteen. I only recently got a transplant." I pause, taking a breath, part of me wanting to tell him his brother's kidney is inside me, but I can't. *I can't*, because for whatever reason, I'm drawn to this guy and I know that the truth will only send him running away. "And I've decided not to go to college this year, like all my friends are. I'm taking a year off for myself, just to live. I want to do all the things I haven't gotten to do."

I haven't told my parents my decision yet. I'm positive they already know since nobody has brought up college.

"Whoa," he whispers. "I … I can't even imagine that." He runs a hand over his short hair. "But you're okay now?"

"Yeah, I'm doing great. The last few years haven't been easy, and it's kept me from doing a lot of things. Fear, mostly. Dialysis sucks, but it's not entirely debilitating."

"So," he starts, and waits until he finishes chewing to continue, "what are things you want to do?"

"I don't know," I answer honestly. "I don't have like a bucket list or anything like that, and I don't have a desire to do anything crazy, I just want to remember what it's like to feel normal."

"What is normal?" he muses with a shake of his head. "I thought I knew what that was, but then T.J. died and I just … I feel like I don't know anything anymore."

"I feel that way, every day of my life," I admit with a small laugh.

With a shrug of his shoulders, he says, "I believe normal is overrated anyway." Changing the subject, he asks, "No dog today?"

I shake my head. "He wanted to come, but we left him home. He's still a puppy so he's a handful."

"He's a big puppy."

"He *is* a Golden Retriever."

"True," he agrees, wadding up his trash.

I take another bite of the wrap, surprised to find that it's almost gone.

"What were you studying at college?" I ask.

He crossed his arms on the table. "I was studying to be a personal trainer and nutritionist. I still want to do that, but I need a break."

"Believe me, I understand that."

He stares at me quietly for a moment. It's like those sea-green eyes are seeing past my flesh and into the inner workings of my mind. I've never felt like someone's my kindred spirit before, but it's like my body recognizes that this guy is made up of the same things I am.

"I want to take you somewhere," he confesses.

"Now?" I question.

"No, tomorrow morning if you're free."

"What time?" I ask.

He makes a face like he's unsure of how I'm going to like this—which never bodes well.

"I'd have to pick you up at five."

"In the morning? Not night?" I blurt, appalled.

He chuckles. "Yeah. Just trust me, it's worth it."

I think for a moment, remembering how it felt watching him walk away from me, and my ultimate decision to be brave.

Be brave.

"Yeah, okay. I'm in."

Selfishly, I just want to spend more time with him. Being around him makes me feel comfortable. I'm also insanely curious about what he'd want to show me that I have to get up at five in the morning for.

We exchange phone numbers before he heads to his car, and I leave to rejoin Meredith and Harlow.

My butt barely plops on the towel when Meredith grabs my arm, lowering her sunglasses to peer at me. "Spill, girl."

I fill them in on Jasper, how we met that day months ago when Perry got loose, and I gloss over my next encounter with him, not wanting to tell them he's T.J.'s brother. I know Harlow will give me a lecture on that fiasco, and I don't want to hear it. I *know* it was a bad idea. I know it's a bad idea to see Jasper again too, now that I know he's T.J.'s brother, but I can't help it. I want to get to know him. I like the way I feel around him. I feel more like my old self, but also like I'm around someone who *gets* it. Losing a loved one is totally different than having a disease, but it's still a life experience we're both too young to have to go through. That experience binds us together.

I guess you could argue the same is true for Spencer and me then, but I only feel friendship with him, and I think that's all he feels for me and *has* felt. Before T.J. died I was beginning to think he had a crush on Harlow. She might be younger than him, but not by much.

"You *like* him," Meredith declares, excitement in her voice.

This is a *big* deal for her, since she's boy crazy and I'm not.

"Yeah, I think I do," I admit. "But I don't know him well," I add.

"Not yet," she reminds me.

"He's cute," Harlow pipes in.

I don't tell them, but I know I can't have anything real with Jasper, not until I tell him the truth of where the kidney I got came from. The thought of telling him is frightening. It was scary enough showing up at his parents' house that day and I don't know if I'm brave enough to do it again. The wind seems to have left my sails.

It's awkward to tell the guy you maybe sort of like, even though you've only seen him three times and basically ran away two of those times, that his dead brother's kidney is in your body.

I have the greatest luck EVER.

CHAPTER FIFTEEN

Since Jasper said he'd pick me up at five, I get up at four to get ready.

I spend way more time than I normally would, which makes me slightly frustrated with myself that I'm trying to impress this guy. I leave my hair to hang down in its natural waves. On my eyes I add eyeshadow in light brown colors, making my hazel eyes stand out more. I don't bother with foundation, that's never been my thing, but I do put a moisturizer on my face with some sunscreen protection in it. I swipe some gloss on my lips that has a pink tint and decide that part of getting ready is done.

I raid my closet, unsure what to wear.

This isn't a date, not by a long shot, I know, but I still want to look nice.

I hold a dress up to myself and shake my head.

Definitely not a dress.

Finally, I decide on a pair of high waisted jean shorts and a white tank top, topping it all off with a red and blue plaid shirt which I roll up the sleeves on and then tie in the front.

I spray a bit of my favorite perfume, not enough to be suffocating during a car ride, but enough that hopefully I'll smell nice.

I assess my appearance in my floor-length mirror. It's still strange to see the flush in my cheeks, the symbol of healthy blood from my working kidney, and the healthy glow beneath my eyes where dark circles used to linger. I can't help but smile while my eyes shimmer with tears I dam back.

Even two months later I'm incredibly thankful for the gift of a healthy kidney. I'm sure I'll *always* feel that way. It's impossible to describe the thankfulness I feel for my donor, for T.J., and his family's selfless decision to donate his organs. I get to live a healthy, full, vibrant life because of that. It's like this immense weight has been lifted off my shoulders, I've been suffocating for years and I didn't even know it. Now, I can finally breathe again.

I look at the time and grab my bag, heading downstairs.

I lied to my parents last night and told them Meredith was picking me up early and we were heading to Santa Barbara for the day. It's nearly a two-hour drive from here, so I made it seem like we were getting a head start on our day. Five in the morning is still a little early for that, but I haven't lied to them before so they believed me. I hated to do it, but I couldn't tell them about Jasper. Selfishly, I want to keep him to myself, and I knew my dad would suddenly go into overprotective mode, and I didn't want to deal with it.

While I lied to them, Harlow watched with a little smirk but didn't rat me out. She knows I never lie to them, and besides, sisterhood bonds us. I'd keep my mouth shut for her and she knows it. But don't get me wrong, neither of us would stand idly by if the other was doing something seriously wrong.

I write a quick note, saying I love them, and check my phone.

Almost as if he knew I was going to look, a text comes through.

Jasper: Just pulled up.

Willa: Be out in a minute.

"Be cool," I tell myself, taking a deep breath. "Don't make a fool of yourself."

Perry raises his head from his cushion. "What are you looking at? I'm fine," I tell him, though I'm the farthest thing from fine.

It's just hit me—I'm about to get in a car with a guy, a guy I barely know, and go who knows where.

"What have I done?" I mutter and head outside.

I approach the car waiting outside—a yellow Jeep with the roof taken off—and stop outside the passenger door. I don't have to wait for him to roll down the car window since there isn't one.

"What are you waiting for?" he asks with a laugh.

I tilt my head. "I've been thinking, how do I know you're not going to kidnap me? You could be a murderer for all I know."

"Do I *look* like a murderer to you?" he scoffs, mildly offended.

I shrug. "Most murderers are good looking. It's how they kill so easily, women go with them willingly."

He grins. I don't find this a grinning matter. "You think I'm good looking?"

I roll my eyes. "Oh, my God, after what I said that's *all* you got from it?"

"Well, I mean, it's a backwards compliment, but a compliment is a compliment."

I shake my head. "I've decided you're too dumb to be a killer," I say, and open the door.

He makes a sound. "Now I feel like I shouldn't be offended, but I definitely am."

"Hey, if the shoe fits . . .," I joke.

He shakes his head. "You're something else."

He pulls away from the curb—it's my last chance to jump out, but I don't.

"Where are we going?" I ask.

"I can't tell you that, it sucks the fun out of it," he protests. "All I'll say is, it's one of my favorite places in the world. I . . . uh . . . haven't shared it with anyone before, but after talking to you yesterday, you . . . you *get* things, and I think you'll appreciate this."

"Wow," I say, slightly shocked.

"We have a fairly long drive ahead of us," he warns. "I'm going to swing by McDonalds's for some breakfast. Is that cool with you?"

"Yeah, that's fine."

After a quick detour where I order an Egg McMuffin and he orders a bagel egg sandwich, we're back on the road.

"Tell me something about yourself," Jasper says around a mouthful.

"Um … I mean, I'm boring. I read a lot. I used to dance before my kidneys failed. I want to get back into it; I miss it."

"What do you like to read?" he asks.

"Romances, mostly," I admit and blush. I don't know why I'm embarrassed by it. There's nothing wrong with a little smut. Smut makes the world go around. "Contemporary, paranormal, and some fantasy now and then."

"That's cool. I like fantasy and thrillers. The occasional biography now and then depending on who it's about."

"Really?" I ask, shocked.

He chuckles. "What? Since I'm a guy I can't read?"

"No, no, it just … surprised me, that's all."

"Don't get me wrong, surfing is my passion. If I could've gone professional, I would have."

"Why didn't you?" I question, curiosity getting the better of me.

He shrugs and shifts in his seat. "There are a lot of guys out there way better. Liam Wade for example. That guy *kills* it every time. He's a legend and he's just up and coming. I can't compete with that, and frankly, I don't want to. I want it to remain fun. To try to make a career out of it would suck the fun out of it. I want to love it for the rest of my life."

"I can understand that," I admit. "I used to dance before … before the kidney failure. It was my passion. I didn't care that it was hard work because I *loved* it. But I never wanted to try to pursue it professionally. I didn't want to lose my love for it because I *had* to do it."

"What kind of dance?" he asks.

"Ballet mostly, and jazz. I did a little bit of hip-hop too."

"I have such a hard time seeing you do ballet." He shakes his head.

"Really?" I laugh. "Why?"

"I don't know … you have that wild, carefree, can't hold me down vibe about you. Dance seems very rigid."

"It's the opposite," I disagree. "Yeah, it has rules, but everything does. But learning to be in tune with your body and flow with the music, there's nothing else like it."

He nods. "That makes sense."

"How old are you?" I ask him.

He chuckles. "I'm twenty. What about you?"

"I turned eighteen on the fourteenth."

"Happy belated birthday then." He grins in my direction.

"Thanks."

My hair whips around my shoulders as he speeds down the highway, heading south. I still can't believe I'm in a car with Jasper, headed who knows where, and I'm *excited.*

I'm excited to be doing something I never normally would do.

I'm taking a leap of faith and seeing if it pays off.

"How old were you when you started dancing?"

"Around four—and before you ask, no, my parents didn't push me into it. I was *always* dancing. Spinning, twirling, I couldn't sit still. My mom enrolled me in dance and it was a natural fit."

"That's cool."

"What's your favorite color?" I ask him and wince. "I'm sorry, that's a lame question."

He chuckles. "No, no. I think a person's favorite color is very telling about them. Mine's yellow, I do like orange too. What's yours?"

"Purple," I answer immediately. "But that funny kind of purple you only see as the sun is going down."

He laughs heartily. "That is … very specific."

I shrug. "Without specifics life would be one giant what if."

"That's true," he agrees. He taps his fingers against the steering wheel, a song by The Fray plays through the speakers from a playlist on his phone. "If you could go anywhere in the world, money wasn't an issue, where would you go?"

"The Kawachi Fuji Gardens in Japan."

"The what-a-what?" he says, taken aback. "No offense, but I was expecting Paris or London. Maybe Rome."

"Don't get me wrong, I'd love to see those places one day too, but you asked where I wanted to go most and that's where."

"I've never heard of it."

"It's this magical garden with these flowers making arches in all these bright colors, it doesn't look like it belongs on this planet. It's magical," I gush. "Here, I'll show you."

I grab my phone and do a quick image search. Pulling up a graphic, I show him.

He glances over. "Whoa, you weren't kidding. That's amazing."

I smile, pleased he agrees.

"How on earth did you ever discover that place?"

"I had to do a research paper on a country and I chose Japan. Where would you go?"

"Mine seems so boring and dull in comparison," he admits with a mock wince.

"Oh, come on." I bump his shoulder playfully with mine. "Now you have to tell me."

He chuckles. "I want to go to Vancouver, Canada to snowboard."

"Oh, you snowboard too?" I inquire.

"No, but I want to."

"You're quite the sports guy, huh?"

He flashes a grin at me, his dimple winking from his cheek. "Yeah, I guess. I played baseball in high school and I was on the swim team."

He changes lanes and takes the next exit.

Nothing looks familiar and grasslands stretch on either side of us, with an intermittent cow or two.

"You know, I'm still not convinced you're not planning to kill me."

He laughs. "Think what you want, but I'm not planning to kill you."

We drive for another twenty minutes, the scenery changing to more mountainous, before he turns on to a dirt road and drives some more.

Eventually, he stops and parks the Jeep. Light is beginning to creep into the sky.

"Where are we?" I ask.

From what I can tell, we're in the middle of nowhere. There's no trail, no more road, no other cars, and just trees.

He hops out and the door closes with a creaking noise. "This isn't it. We have to go on foot from here."

I look down at my feet, thankful I wore my sneakers; they might not be cute but at least they're comfy.

I hop out and fumble with my bag.

"Leave it," he tells me.

"Um …"

"Trust me, no one comes out here, it'll be safe."

I decide to listen but tuck it under the seat just in case.

"It's not a long walk, I promise."

We fall into step beside each other. His arm bumps into my shoulder as we walk, reminding me how much taller he is than me.

I have no idea what he could possibly want to show me way out here, but I'm curious.

The trees begin to thin and, suddenly, we find ourselves on the edge of a cliff overlooking the whole world—or so it feels like.

"Oh, my God," I breathe, watching the sun rise over the ocean. Below us the shore is rocky and dangerous, not the kind that's safe for the public. The rays of the sun seem to stretch out infinitely, hugging the globe. I look up at him and find he's watching me instead of the magic that's happening in front of us. "How did you ever find this place?" I ask.

"My grandparents own all the land here; it's on their property. I was out exploring one day and found it. I've never shared this spot with anyone, not even my brother," he says significantly. He shoves his hands into the pockets of his board shorts. "I've spent a lot of time out here since we heard about T.J." He shakes his head. "It's the only place I feel truly at peace. Even the water isn't entirely my safe place anymore, because it was something I shared with T.J. since we both liked to surf."

"Why would you share this with me then?"

"Because when I look into your eyes, I see something I see in myself. Sadness, but a fighter too. But every fighter has weak moments, and when I feel weak I come here and let it out."

"Let it out?"

He turns away from me, walks to the edge, throws his arm out and screams.

His scream echoes around us, and I swear some birds take flight somewhere behind me.

Suddenly, he stops and looks over his shoulder. "Come on, you do it too."

I shake my head.

"You'll feel better if you let it out."

He holds out a hand coaxingly to me. I shove my fear aside and place my hand in his. He pulls me forward gently, entwining our fingers.

I look down at our joined hands, surprised by how easily our hands fit together, his tan and freckled, mine pale and slender.

He bends his head and my breath stutters when I feel his lips touch the shell of my ear.

"Let it out, Willa. Let the world swallow your pain so you don't have to."

I look into his eyes, and in my gut, I trust him, I trust him to let my guard down, to allow myself to feel vulnerable.

Turning back to the water, I do what he says—I let it out.

I scream.

He screams.

And the world swallows it whole.

The sun has fully risen, and even though it's early it's already grown hot enough that I've taken off my plaid shirt and tied it around my waist.

We sit on the edge, our feet dangling beneath us.

"What was it like?" he asks, breaking the quiet that surrounds us. "Being told your kidneys had failed?"

"Honestly?" I think for a moment how best to explain. "I didn't think or feel anything at first. I was too sick, I guess. I mean, I knew that was *bad*, but I couldn't comprehend how bad. I didn't understand I was close to death because I didn't *feel* sick. Yeah, I had symptoms, but they were weird so I brushed it off. I don't think it hit me until almost a year later, when I couldn't find a living donor match, just how bad the reality was. Dialysis sucks. It's hard on the body, and don't let anyone tell you otherwise. It's not *natural.* Your body isn't meant to go through what it puts you through. It's draining on your body and your mind. I started to give up hope then, for a while." I swallow thickly, remembering how I felt then, how alone and desolate my thoughts were. A tear falls down my cheek and I brush it away. "There were a lot of nights I laid in bed, the anxiety suffocating me, the stress of the dialysis, school, a life I didn't want to live, and I thought about ending it all. About how easy it would be, and peaceful compared to everything else. I didn't fear death anymore, I still don't. I snuck downstairs one night and emptied a palm full of my pills into my hand. I stared at them for a long time. I thought about my parents, my sister, my friends, and a future that at the moment seemed to hold no hope. But, suddenly, I saw a small glimpse of light, of what I might get if I could be patient enough to wait for a transplant, and all the things I could do after. But only if I was strong enough to fight to live." I grow quiet and look at him for the first time since I started talking. I expect to see judgment on his face, but I'm shocked to find respect instead, and maybe awe. "I haven't felt suicidal since that day," I add. "And now, here I am, post-transplant." I spread my arms wide. "That small light I saw then is a blazing sky today."

He continues to stare at me some more, and then in a whisper so soft it's almost as if he doesn't mean to say it aloud at all, "You are amazing."

"I'm nothing special," I argue. "I'm just someone who got dealt a bad card, and I'm doing what I have to do. I don't have a choice."

"But you did, you just said it yourself. You thought about killing yourself. You could've ended it all, avoided it all, but you haven't."

"That doesn't make me special."

He blinks at me, his eyes scanning my features. "I think it does."

He stares at me so intensely I swear I can feel it all the way inside straight down to my core. I feel like I'm being x-rayed and he can see every good and bad thought I've ever had plainly laid out. But he doesn't look afraid, in fact, he almost looks like he likes me *more* because of it.

"When you said you'd lost someone …," he starts and clears his throat. "You were talking about yourself, weren't you?"

I crack a smile. "Perceptive, aren't you? Yeah. Yeah, I was."

He nods. "I thought so."

"I was fourteen when it happened. I had to mourn for a life that I no longer had. I can never get that naivety back, of not even considering the fact my body might fail me one day."

He takes my hand again, fitting our palms together. Both of us look down at them.

"I think you're the strongest person I know."

"You don't know me," I protest.

His eyes meet mine. "I know enough, and I want to know more."

I think back to that day where Perry ran into him outside the coffee shop, how he made me feel with one glance, and I think about all our encounters since.

I became a big believer in signs after my diagnosis, and once you start looking for them and pay attention, they're everywhere. I don't believe everything is by chance, I do think sometimes the world places things in your path for a purpose.

For some reason, I'm supposed to get to know Jasper.

He's supposed to be in my life.

Of that, I am certain.

"I'd like that," I admit.

"Good." He stands and hauls me up.

He holds onto my hands, looking at me as my hair swirls around my shoulders from the breeze.

"I need to stop in at the house before we head back, is that okay?"

"At your grandparents'?" I ask stupidly, and he cracks a grin.

"Yeah."

"That's fine," I agree.

We walk back to the Jeep and a part of me is sad to leave this place behind. I can't help but hope I get to come again.

The drive up to his grandparents' house is longer than I expected. They must own *a lot* of land. Eventually, we turn up a gravel drive and bump along until we come across a decent sized house covered in blue siding with a red front door and red shutters. To the right, I can see a stable, and out in the field cows roam freely with no fencing. This place is so different compared to the beachy fun time vibe of Santa Monica.

Jasper parks the Jeep in front of the house and hops out. He starts up the steps and looks back at me.

"Are you coming?"

"N-No, I'll just sit here."

He comes back down the steps and opens the car door.

"You're coming," he says stubbornly.

I laugh. "You don't take no for an answer, do you?"

"Never," he quips.

I shake my head at him and slide my legs out of the Jeep. When my feet hit the ground, a small cloud of dust from the gravel and dirt billows up.

Five steps lead up to a porch with two rocking chairs by the front door.

Jasper doesn't bother to knock, he doesn't even pull out a key. He just puts his hand on the knob and twists and it opens right up.

"Granddaddy?" he calls out. "Grandma?"

"In here, sweetums," a lady's voice calls from the kitchen.

I snort. "Sweetums?" I question him.

He shrugs, clearly not bothered by the endearment. "My grandma grew up in the South," he says like that explains it.

We enter the kitchen and the first thing I notice is the explosion of cupcake and brownie pans everywhere.

Then I notice a tiny woman, barely five feet, standing on a stool at the island stirring yet another bowl of goodness. Her gray hair is clipped back, with several strands falling forward. An apron sits around her tiny waist.

"What are you up to today?" she asks him.

"Just swung by for a visit. This is Willa."

"Willa?" Her head whips up. "A girl?" she questions as her brown eyes collide with mine.

Jasper and I laugh.

"Yeah, I'm a girl."

"Wow," she says. "Interesting," she adds. She looks me over. "Can you bake?"

"Yes," I reply.

"Good, you can help me. I need to make five hundred brownies and five hundred cupcakes for the local bake sale tomorrow. I didn't realize it'd be this much work when I signed up. Honestly, I should know by now. I *always* do this to myself. *Put that down, Jasper,*" she scolds, and Jasper drops the brownie that was halfway to his mouth. "The sale of these is to benefit *needy* people, unless you're paying up, keep your grubby paws off of them."

Jasper raises his hands in surrender.

"Go help your granddaddy; he's out back doing lord knows what that he's not supposed to do. I don't bother scolding him anymore. It's a waste of breath. Stubborn old man."

Jasper whispers, "Good luck with this one," in my ear and disappears.

Suddenly, I feel unsure about being left alone with this lady I don't know. But I don't have time to dwell on it because she puts me to work making icing and then frosting the cupcakes while she makes more batter.

"How do you know Jasper?" she asks.

"It's complicated," I mumble, because it *is*.

"We have time, dear."

I guess she's right.

"We just keep running into each other," I explain. "He asked me to hang out today and here I am."

"That doesn't seem very complicated, but I'm guessing it's more than that." She gives me a knowing smile.

I instantly feel at ease with her. She's very comfortable to be around and kind.

"How'd you guys come to live here?" I ask her. "It seems so remote."

She stirs the batter vigorously—despite the fact that I notice a state-of-the-art Kitchen Aid mixer on her counter.

"My husband inherited it from his father and so on."

I add some sprinkles to a cupcake I just frosted. "Do you like living here?"

"I love it. It's … peaceful."

"It's definitely that," I agree. "Like another world."

She smiles. "That's how I've always seen it too."

She finishes stirring and begins to scoop out the batter into clean cupcake tins.

"Do you like my Jasper?" she asks suddenly, taking me off guard. "He's a good boy. Kind, and smart too, he deserves to be happy. He's been too sad since …"

"Since T.J.?" I leave out the part where I want to tell her she just described her grandson as having the same attributes as my Golden Retriever.

"Yeah." She nods sadly and takes a shaky breath. "It's hit us all hard, but especially him. They were close. He blames himself."

"He didn't tell me that."

She reaches over and places her hand on top of mine. "I'm sure he'll open up more. Give him time."

I realize I've basically spilled my guts to him, opened myself up and put myself out there, and I don't know him at all.

I don't feel angry, because his pain is fresh, and mine is old and that makes a difference. It's easier for me to talk about now, but if I was in his situation and all this was two months ago, my lips would be sealed. I feel thankful that he feels like talking to me at all. I know he makes *me* feel better, not so alone, and I only hope I can do the same for him.

"We all tend to blame ourselves for things that are out of our control," she continues. "It's human nature, I think, to want to find some source to direct our pain even if it's our self."

"Wise words," I murmur, carefully frosting yet another cupcake.

She chuckles. "I have my moments."

She finishes scooping the batter in and slides the pan in the oven—taking another out to cool before setting the timer.

"That should do it," she mutters, hands on her hips as she looks around at the mess and all the cupcakes waiting to be frosted and brownies to be cut into squares. "For the baking part, at least," she sighs, blowing out a breath that fans her loose hair around her face.

She grabs up another bag already filled with icing and begins to pipe it on.

We work quietly and as quickly as we can. There are *a lot* of cupcakes to frost, and it seems that no matter how many we do, there's more.

When the last batch comes out of the oven she sets it down to cool and turns to me.

"Let's take a break and have some lunch."

My stomach rumbles. I hadn't even realized it was lunchtime. I was so busy frosting the cupcakes I lost track of time.

I help her make enough sandwiches for four, and then we set the table on an enclosed patio out back.

"Can you grab the lemon water from inside?" she asks.

"Sure thing."

I head back in and open the refrigerator, finding a large pitcher of fresh water with ice and lemon slices.

I carry it back out, careful not to let it slosh over the sides. I set it in the center of the table and Jasper's grandma, I realize I don't even know her name, opens a door on the side of the enclosed porch and steps outside.

"Boys!" she calls out, her hands cupped around her mouth. "Time for lunch!"

It isn't long until I see Jasper and his grandpa emerging from a copse of trees.

"Oh, God," I squeak, when I realize Jasper is shirtless and dripping with sweat.

Sweet baby Jesus, why is he so hot? It's not fair.

The three step onto the porch and I quickly take a seat. Jasper pulls out the chair beside me and his grandpa takes the one across from me.

"You must be Willa," he greets me, holding out his hand. I shake it, and his grip is firm. "Jasper has been telling me all about you. I'm Leo."

"Oh," his wife pipes in. "How rude of me, I never gave you my name. I'm Mary Beth."

"Thank you, guys, for welcoming me into your home."

"Any friend of Jasper's is a friend of ours."

I pile some of the sides on the plate with my sandwich. Mary Beth had pulled homemade macaroni salad from the refrigerator as well as some sort of casserole that I wasn't entirely sure what it was made of, but it looked delicious.

"Did you get done with the cupcakes?" Jasper asks.

I shake my head. "We have a lot more to go."

"She's been a great help," Mary Beth tells him, and I smile at her praise. "I'm definitely much farther along than I would've been on my own."

"What have you been doing?" I ask him.

I'm surprised by how comfortable I feel with him, with his family too. Normally I'm uncomfortable around people I don't know, it's a fallacy of being shy, but something about these people makes me feel warm and at home.

"Are you in college with Jasper?" Leo asks me.

I shake my head. "No, I've been homeschooled, I graduated high school in December. I … uh … I'm planning to take the next year off before going to college. I've had a lot of health issues, and I kind of just want a break to live for a little while and figure out who I am before I start school."

Willa, you have got to tell Mom and Dad what you've decided. They might've figured it out on their own already, but they still deserve to hear it from you.

I resolve to sit them down tomorrow and tell them. I know they'll understand, I'm not worried about that, but I still can't help feeling like maybe I've failed them in some way.

Leo nods. "I think you're making a smart decision."

"Really?" I blurt.

He nods, chewing his food and swallows. "Yes, I think it's better to understand your heart before you make such a big decision. You should know what you *truly* want to do. It's not fair for anyone to be stuck in a job that makes them miserable because of a decision they made when they were young."

We finish eating and, afterward, Jasper says we have to leave.

"But there are more cupcakes to frost," I protest, and he chuckles.

"Grandma can handle it, can't you?" He looks at her over my shoulder.

"I'll be fine. You two go on, but promise you'll come back, Willa."

I glance at Jasper. "Only if he wants me to."

He stares at me for a moment, actually, it's probably less than a second, but that look makes me shiver. "I want you to." His voice is husky, and I swear it turns my stomach to jelly.

"I'll be back then."

I exchange hugs with Mary Beth and Leo and then we're back in the Jeep and on our way home.

"I wish we could hang out longer," Jasper says, turning into my neighborhood, "but I coach the boy's eighth-grade swim team."

Can he get any more perfect? He freaking coaches a kids' swim team and all I can say for myself is I grocery shop and make dinner.

He parks the Jeep in front of my house and turns to me, resting his arm around the seat, his fingers dangling dangerously close to my shoulder.

"I want to see you again."

"I'd like that too."

I'd like that too? How formal can you be? Surely you could've said something better? You are sooooo bad at this whole dating thing. Read a freaking Cosmo magazine already, Willa.

He grins. "Cool. I'll text you."

"I'll see you then."

I unbuckle and slip out of the Jeep.

"Bye," I call, and my cheeks heat as I walk away. "I am the most awkward human being on the planet," I hiss to myself.

I hear him laugh behind me and the redness in my cheeks burns even hotter.

"I think you're the most adorable human being on the planet."

I turn around and he catches my gaze, flashing me a wink, and then he pulls away and is gone.

CHAPTER SIXTEEN

It's later that night, after midnight, and I can't sleep.

Instead, I lie awake staring at my ceiling. I can't read the words glued to my ceiling, but I pretend I can.

Beside me, the table is now empty, has been for some time, of my dialysis machine.

It's strange that I kind of miss it. I guess sometime in the years we spent together I grew rather fond of it in a way.

I clasp my hands over my chest, tapping my fingers. I've been lying here since ten o' clock. Two hours of sleep evading me.

Two hours of my mind going round and round, replaying the day over and over again, wondering if I could've done or said anything differently. I'm always convinced I've made a fool of myself, even when I haven't.

What can I say, anxiety is a bitch and makes you think stupid things.

I wouldn't say I used to be an anxious person, but my disease definitely made it develop. Certain things, small things, suddenly became mountains I felt like I had to climb.

My phone vibrates and momentarily lights up my room.

Who's texting me this late?

I roll over and pick it up. It takes my eyes a moment to adjust to the sudden brightness.

Jasper: Are you awake?

Willa: Yeah.

Jasper: Come outside.

Willa: Outside?

Jasper: Yeah, that's what I said.

Willa: ...You're here?

Jasper: Yeah.

Willa: Be there in a sec.

I slip out of bed and throw on a sweatshirt over my pajamas. The sweatshirt is so loose it almost covers my sleep shorts, making it look like I'm not wearing anything.

I shove my feet in some flip-flops and hurry downstairs as quickly and quietly as I can.

Opening the front door, I find Jasper leaning against the doorway.

Gone is his carefree smile, and in its place is a frown and red-rimmed eyes.

My heart aches for him, for the pain so plainly reflected on his face.

I close the door behind me.

"Follow me," I whisper, like we might be overheard.

I've never in my life done anything like this, sneaking around with a boy in the middle of the night. But I don't feel afraid of him, and I know he needs me. For whatever reason, he just does.

Like me, he appears to be in sleep clothes. A pair of loose gray shorts made of sweatpants material and a plain tee with a faded logo and the sleeves cut off.

I lead him around the side of the house and into the back onto the beach. We sit down in the sand, side by side, looking at the dark ocean. You can barely see it, even with the stars glittering above, but you can hear it, and the sound always calms me when I'm feeling down.

We sit quietly. I don't want to pressure him to talk, I want him to do it in his own time.

"I couldn't sleep," he finally whispers. "Every time I closed my eyes I saw that truck slamming into T.J.'s car. They said he died instantly, but I can't help thinking what if they're wrong. What if he sat in that car, suffering, knowing he was dying? What if he was all alone, knowing it was the end?"

"The end isn't as scary as you think," I whisper.

I don't look but I feel him look at me. "How?"

I shrug. "There's something quite comforting about it … like you're going home."

"I miss him," he confesses, his voice pain-filled and full of longing. "We fought like brothers do, but we also loved each other. He was my best friend."

"I feel the same way about my sister. Living without her would be like living without part of my heart."

He nods, bending his knees and draping his arms over the top.

"We had this game we used to play, only the two of us, it was stupid." He shakes his head. "We'd slap these stickers on each other, each one had instructions like *jump off the pier* or *eat a raw fish*. Stupid stuff," he reiterates. "But I can't stop thinking about how, even though we haven't played it in years, we'll never get to do it again."

"You're always going to miss him."

"I know," his voice catches, "but I'm scared for the day when it doesn't hurt so much and is just *normal*. Or when he's been dead longer than he was alive. My chest literally seizes up when I think about it." He holds up a clenched fist to demonstrate. "And my parents … *fuck*." He rubs his hand over his hair. "I can't imagine how they feel. I lost my brother but they lost a son. My mom starts crying over everything and I can't blame her. She found a baseball mitt stuffed under the couch the other day and started sobbing. I don't even know how to comfort her because I'm so broken myself, but I hate seeing her fall apart. She's always been strong and now she's just … *sad*. We all are. The house seems empty without him. And I might be taking the next year off, but what happens when

I *do* go back to college and the house is empty of the both of us? How will she take it then?"

I don't know what to tell him. I'm afraid to say the wrong thing but don't want to say nothing at all, either.

"You can't think that far ahead. The now is complicated enough as it is."

He looks over at me. "You're right. Why were you up?"

I sigh, letting out the heavy breath that's been weighing down my chest. "Lots of reasons."

Like the fact that I have your brother's kidney—that I need to tell my parents I'm not going to college—that I'm unsure about life and I feel like I can't breathe.

"I know I don't know you that well yet, but I feel like I can talk to you," he admits. "I want you to know it's okay to talk to me."

I nod and pick up some sand, playing with it in my hands. I'll have to take a shower when I go in, but I don't care. This is way better than staring at my ceiling, unable to fall asleep.

"My life has been focused on my disease and dialysis the last three years, it's weird to not have my life revolve around that now. I feel … off balance. Don't get me wrong, I'm incredibly thankful for this transplant, more than you can ever understand, but it's an adjustment."

"I can't imagine what you've been through."

"I can't imagine what you're going through."

He shakes his head. "It might be different, but I think you have a better grasp on my situation than I do yours."

I look at him, my hair blowing in the breeze. He stares back at me, his gaze intense. The sadness still lingers in his eyes, but he seems more peaceful now than when he first showed up.

The urge to lean over and kiss him is so strong my heart speeds up in my chest.

I've never kissed a guy before.

Literally, never.

I haven't had the desire to. This is a new feeling, a strange one, but a good one too.

I swallow thickly, scared but slightly exhilarated.

Maybe it's the cover of the night sky, or maybe it's the symphony of the ocean, or maybe it's just *him*, but somehow, I find the courage to lean a little closer.

His eyes flick down to my lips and his tongue flicks out the tiniest bit, like he knows what I'm thinking and anticipates it.

Be brave.

Those two words send me over the edge, hurtling my body into uncharted territory.

I close the distance and press my lips to his.

It feels weird at first, and I wonder why people like kissing so much, but then his mouth moves beneath mine and my whole body goes *oh*.

Now I get what the fuss is about.

He cups my face in one large hand, angling his lips over mine. The kiss is soft, sweet, but I feel it all the way down to my toes.

My heart shivers. I didn't know it could do that, but it does.

He nibbles my bottom lip and I let out a soft sigh.

If I'd ever thought to imagine my first kiss, *nothing* could've ever compared to the reality.

Jasper pulls away, his hand still on my cheek with his fingers slightly grasping my hair, and presses his forehead to mine.

"I knew the moment I saw you you'd wreck me, but I honestly thought I'd never see you again."

"Huh?" I whisper through my kiss-induced haze.

"I kind of lied to you. I remembered you from the coffee shop. I didn't want to seem like a weirdo for remembering you, but I did. You're kind of unforgettable."

I'd never had anyone say anything like that to me before, and my heart leaps, grabbing onto his words so it can cradle it within its depths for all eternity.

"Do you …" I start and clear my throat, my cheeks heating with embarrassment. "Do you think there are people in this world you're already connected to before you even know them?"

He stares at me significantly. "I do now."

CHAPTER SEVENTEEN

I stir my bowl of yogurt and granola, staring into its depths like it holds the answer to every question in the world.

Unfortunately, it doesn't.

It's just a plain ole boring bowl of yogurt and granola no matter how hard I stare at it.

I don't know why I'm scared to tell them. It's mid-July, so they *have* to know I'm not starting college. But no matter how much I comfort myself with this information I can't help feeling like a disappointment and a complete and utter failure.

I set my spoon down. "Mom? Dad?"

Dad looks up from his newspaper and my mom stops eating her cereal.

"Yes?" my dad prompts, raising a brow inquiringly over the top of his reading glasses.

Beside me, Harlow stops eating to listen to the conversation.

"I've been doing a lot of thinking and I've decided not to go to college this year. I want to focus on recovery and get through this year of many doctor's appointments, and hopefully figure out what I want to do, before I start next year."

They stare at me and my mom finally picks up her coffee cup, cradling it in her hands. "I think that's an excellent decision. We didn't want to pressure you into going this year, either, and if you said you wanted to go, we were going to let you know how we felt but we would've still helped with late enrollment if it's truly what you wanted."

I breathe a very audible sigh of relief. "Thanks, guys."

Their support means a lot to me, more than I think I even realized.

Beside me, Harlow shakes her head stifling a laugh. "You look like you just dodged a bullet."

"I feel like I did," I admit, and laugh too.

My dad lays down his newspaper. "You've been through more in the last three years than most people go through in a lifetime. I think it's only right to want a break. You deserve it."

My lip quivers. "Thanks, Dad."

I can't help it. The tears begin to fall. Having my parents behind me means more than they can possibly know.

"We're proud of the woman you've become," he continues, which only makes me cry harder. "Your mother and I have watched you handle everything with such grace. You're incredibly strong, Willa, and we know we've raised a brilliant young lady. We couldn't be more proud."

I get up from the table and go to hug him. He hugs me back, his grip bear tight.

"I love you," I whisper into the scruff of his neck.

"I love you too, Willa."

He lets me go and I hug my mom. She too squeezes me like she never wants to let go.

I know when this happened they wished they could wrap me in bubble wrap and make it all go away, but they couldn't, and while they didn't go through what I did, they had to experience their own unique pain over the situation.

My mom releases me but holds onto my elbows, forcing me to look at her.

"Remember, always, that you're a vibrant ray of light. No demon is too big or tough for that light not to squash it." She reaches up and wipes a tear from my cheek. "You're beautiful, smart, and kind. We're always here for you. *Always.*"

I hug her again, not wanting to let go.

Eventually, I have to.

I sit back down and finish my yogurt.

My parents leave for work, each of them kissing me on the cheek and doing the same to Harlow who squeals like she's grossed out by all the affection.

The house grows quiet and Perry sits at my feet while I rest on the couch with a book.

"How'd it go yesterday?" Harlow asks, hanging upside down in the chair. I don't even bother asking her why exactly she's upside down. Harlow does what she wants.

"It was good. He took me to his grandparents' place. They have a farm, and it's gorgeous."

"A farm?" she muses. "That's cool. Do you still like him?"

I blush, thinking of the kiss last night. "Yes."

"Oh, my God," she shrieks and suddenly flips upright. How she doesn't get whiplash is beyond me. "You *really* like him."

"Maybe," I squeak.

She shakes her head. "I never thought I'd see the day. Did he kiss you?"

"Harlow!" I cry, dropping my book. My cheeks burn even brighter.

"You *so* kissed." She claps her hands giddily.

"I saw him again last night," I admit.

"What?" Her mouth pops open and she tucks her legs under her body, leaning over the arm of the chair. "Do tell."

I shrug like it's no big deal. "He texted me and he was here. I couldn't sleep, he couldn't sleep, we ended up hanging outside and … talked."

"*And* kissed?" she prompts.

I can't hide my smile as I relive the kiss. The best, and only, kiss of my life. But I don't need another to know it was special.

"And yes, we kissed," I admit.

Harlow shrieks and whoops with joy. "This is *the* most exciting thing to ever happen around here, you little hussy. I can't believe you weren't going to tell me."

"I still can't believe it happened," I admit.

"This is better than the Korean dramas I watch," she squeals, kicking her legs out.

I stare at her incredulously. "You don't speak Korean."

She waves a hand dismissively. "I know a little. Besides, there are subtitles."

"Wait, is that weird music I hear you play in your room Korean?"

She rolls her eyes. "It's *K-Pop*," she emphasizes the word like I'm an idiot. "And if you listened to it, you'd love it too. BTS gives me life, but don't even think about coming after my bias. I will cut you."

"Your what-a-what?"

"My bias—my favorite member. Don't get me wrong, I love them all, I do, but Jungkook makes my legs quiver."

I shift my eyes around. "Junghook? Is that even a real name?"

She rolls her eyes again and I'm surprised they don't fall out of her head. "It's Jung*k*ook, and he's my future husband. You better learn how to say his name right."

I snort.

She glares.

"Oh, you're serious."

"I take my hot K-Pop husband very seriously."

"Boy, this escalated quickly."

"When you insult my spouse I become defensive," she reasons, and I laugh.

"Now I know why you've spent so much time in your room this summer."

"K-Pop all day every day, bro," she quips and we both laugh.

"Do you want to go to the pier today?" I ask her. I selfishly want to visit Julio.

"Only if I can introduce you to the wonders of K-Pop on the way."

"Knock yourself out."

She squeals and runs up the stairs to get ready. "I low you!" she calls over her shoulder.

I set my book down to do the same, Perry loping behind me like an ever-present shadow. He follows me into my room and plops on my bed as I close the door behind us. Opening my closet, I scan my clothes, looking for something to wear. I pull out a pair of shorts I forgot I owned. They're high waisted and black with a yellow and peach floral print. I pair them with a cropped short sleeve white shirt and a hat. Forgoing my usual sneakers or flip-flops I put on a pair of strappy black sandals I've worn maybe once.

I glance at my reflection in the mirror and smile. I'm not wearing any makeup, but I think I look cute. I don't normally dress nice and it feels good.

Grabbing my bag, I meet Harlow downstairs and we get in the car, taking Perry with us because he suckers me into feeling sorry for him.

He sits in the back, wagging his tail. I swear he smiles.

"If you do anything bad," I warn him, pointing a finger, "I'll never speak to you again."

He just pants in response. Apparently, I'm not very threatening.

Whatever.

At least I tried.

Harlow wastes no time hooking her phone up and blasting her K-Pop. It isn't that bad, actually. In fact, it's catchy, and soon I'm bobbing my head along as we drive to the pier.

"Good, right?" she asks, while I maneuver the car into a parking spot.

"I like it," I admit.

She claps her hands giddily. "I have converted you to the dark side."

"I wouldn't go *that* far."

"You just wait," she warns. "You've been sucked into the K-Pop black hole and you're not coming back."

I can't help but laugh at her.

Getting out, I grab Perry's leash and ease open the back door, grabbing his collar before he can jump out. I wrestle with him to attach the leash and then I let him hop out.

I lock up behind us as Perry drags me along. You can't walk this dog. He walks you.

Harlow bounces along beside me in a bright and cheery mood. But when is she not? If I could bottle her energy and attitude then shake it across the world like a pepper shaker, the world would be a much happier, brighter place.

"I want cotton candy," Harlow declares, walking backward to face me. "You want any?"

"No." I shake my head. "You go on. I'll meet back up with you."

"Sure." She turns and scurries off.

I guide Perry, as best I can since he's stubborn, into Julio's shop.

The bell dings above the door and Perry lifts his head sniffing the air.

"I detect a shift in the air. Is that my Ms. Willa?" Juilo calls from the corner and I find him in his swinging chair smoking a blunt.

I laugh. "It's me, Julio."

"You *said* you wouldn't wait long to come back," he tsks.

Perry sniffs Julio's bare dangling feet.

"I had a good reason."

"Mmm, is that so?" He lets out a cloud of smoke. "Did my prediction come true?"

I smile, bending to pull Perry back. "It did."

"And who is this delightful creature with you?"

"This is Perry, our dog." I pet him on his head and he looks up at me.

"He is very fond of you," Julio comments, taking a drag of the blunt. "I sense a strong connection."

"And I think you're baked out of your mind." I laugh.

He chuckles. "Nonsense. Tell me, how do you feel?"

I shrug, even though he can't see. "I feel like a person again. I don't have to rely on a machine to live anymore. I feel *amazing*. Like, I literally didn't know it was possible to feel this good."

"I am very happy for you," he says in his raspy voice. "You deserve this."

"Not more than anyone else," I whisper, still petting Perry. "There are many people on the transplant waiting list. They all deserve it."

"That is so," he agrees. "But this was your turn. Don't be sorry for it."

"So many people die waiting." My voice cracks. "It's not fair."

"Your concern for others is beautiful, m'dear Willa, but the tides of Earth ebb and flow. Death is a natural part of the cycle. When it's your time, it's your time, and nothing can stop that."

"I suppose you're right."

"I might be a blind pothead, but I'm right."

I snort. "Julio, you are one of a kind."

"Everyone's one of a kind, but most people try to become like someone else because being unique is looked down upon."

I shake my head.

"Do you still have your bracelet?" he asks.

"Of course." I hold out my wrist with the bracelet and he grabs it, his fingers lightly touching the dangling sun charm. He releases it and my arm drops back to my side.

"I think of you often, my flower. I say to the gods above, watch over this sweet girl, give her strength for she must battle things no one her age should ever have to contend with."

"What about you?" I ask. "You lost your eyesight."

"And I fought my own kind of battle. Just because you have to fight, doesn't mean you should have to do it alone. The people around you are there to help, if you let them, and the spirits. The spirits will tell you things if you open yourself up to listen, but most people think that's nonsense."

The bell on the door chimes and I jump, realizing I need to find Harlow.

"I have to go, Julio." I grab his hand and squeeze it. "I'll see you next time."

I slip out of the store, Perry sniffing everything as he goes.

I find Harlow sitting on the railing eating her cotton candy with Spencer leaning beside her. They laugh at something he said, and he reaches up, swiping some cotton candy from her lip.

"Hey, guys."

"Hey!" Harlow jumps down from the railing.

Spencer jumps away like he got caught doing something he shouldn't, and I suppress a smile.

Meredith might've called dibs on Spencer, but I think Spencer already had his sights set on Harlow. She might be younger than us, but not by much, and while she's always been upbeat and peppy there's a part of her that's like me and very much an old soul.

"Hey," Spencer echoes, his voice gruff. "I was just here to get out for a while and spotted Harlow." He tosses his thumb in Harlow's direction.

"Cool," I reply, for a lack of anything better to say.

Harlow pinches off a piece of cotton candy and shoves it in her mouth.

"What do you want to do?" she asks me.

Perry watches her, waiting and hoping she'll drop a bit of the sweet treat.

"I want to get a smoothie. I haven't had one in *forever* and I'm craving one."

"Ooh! A smoothie would be yummy," she agrees.

The three of us, Perry pulling me along, head down the boardwalk to the smoothie stand.

Finally, I order a pineapple coconut smoothie and Harlow gets a strawberry one. We move to the side and let Spender place his order, then the three of us wait together.

I can't help but study Spencer as we wait, noting the fact that he looks like he's lost weight. Despite everything I've been through I still don't know how to comfort someone who's hurting. It's all too easy to say the wrong thing by mistake and then you can't take it back.

Once we have our smoothies, we continue to walk along the pier.

"This is delicious," Harlow gushes, slurping her smoothie. "Here, try mine." She holds her drink out to Spencer.

He takes a sip and makes a disgusted face. "Mine's better."

"Not a chance." He holds hers out to try.

"Okay, that is good."

"What'd you get?" I ask.

"Blueberry with kiwi."

"Interesting," I comment. Thinking that combination sounds absolutely disgusting.

He laughs, picking up on my tone. "Here, try it." He holds it out to me and I take a sip.

"Okay, okay," I relinquish. "You were right, it's good."

He grins, a little bit of light flashing in his eyes. "See."

Eventually, the three of us find a spot and sit down on the wood-planked pier, letting our legs dangle over the edge and using the fence to drape our arms over.

"This summer is nothing like what I thought it would be," Spencer admits. "I thought it'd be fun, a last hoorah before college, and now it's just … T.J.'s gone." He looks at Harlow and then me. "We should cherish every day, because you never know when it'll be your last."

"True dat." Harlow lifts her smoothie cup in salute.

Perry's head perks up, thinking he's about to get some.

Spencer's words hit home with me. It's something I've given a lot of thought to, my own mortality. There's an endless list of things I want to do before I die, most fairly mundane, but it scares me to think I might not get the chance do them.

But I did cross off one very important thing.

My first kiss.

CHAPTER EIGHTEEN

Jasper texts me again that night, unable to sleep just like me, and I meet him outside. Once again, I lead him to the back on to the beach where we sit side by side.

Tonight, we sit close enough that our legs touch.

My skin prickles with his nearness.

"I haven't felt … *right* since T.J. died. Like I'm lost. I feel like I don't know who I am anymore and then …" He looks at me and I look back. "And then I'm with you and I feel like me again, and I know that's crazy, we don't know each other yet but I can't help it."

"I feel it too," I whisper.

I knew from the first time I saw him many months ago that he was different. I honestly never believed I'd see him again, and yet here we are. That has to mean something.

"Yeah?" he murmurs, almost surprised.

"Yeah," I echo.

"The night is the hardest," he admits. "I don't know if it's because he died at night or because when I lay down to sleep all I can think about is his body in that mangled car. Then my chest gets tight and it's like I can't—"

"Breathe," I finish for him.

He snaps his fingers. "Exactly."

I know what he's talking about. I feel it too, but for an entirely different reason.

The emotions of receiving a transplant are off the charts, especially when you're convinced you're falling for the guy whose brother died to give it to you.

Life has a fucked-up way of mocking us.

I'm, sadly, getting used to it.

Sometimes I think I'm not meant to be happy.

But then I tell myself I'm being pathetic and to stop complaining.

Things aren't always happy. They aren't always easy. They just *are*.

You either roll with the punches or get run over.

"I'm glad I stopped you the other day at the beach," he admits, his green eyes flashing with an emotion I can't quite decipher. "You're the first person I've been able to talk to about it since it happened. My friends … they don't get it. I mean, they feel sorry for me, but that's pity not sympathy. And my parents are grieving too, I don't want to add to their pain, same with my grandparents. But you? You get it. You let me talk. I'm afraid if I don't I'm going to suffocate. I feel like before I met you I was a balloon floating away, and then you grabbed the string and you're slowly pulling me back to Earth, reminding me that I'm not lost I'm just figuring out how to live *after*."

"You see it too?" I question softly, my eyes flashing from his down to the sand in nervousness.

"See what?"

"The distinct line between before and after when bad things happen? How it changes your life so distinctly that it's never the same again."

"Yeah," he whispers, drawing something on my hand. Goosebumps prickle my skin and it's not from the night air. "Yeah, I see it."

He suddenly curls his fingers into mine and those sea-green eyes look up at me. "Is this okay?"

I nod. "It's okay."

It's more than okay. His hand feels good in mine, solid, like we fit together.

"Thank you for coming out here with me. I swear I'll stop dragging you out in the middle of the night." He chuckles, looking at the waves as they crash against the sand with a soft roar.

My heart seizes at his words. "Don't stop," I gasp. "Please. I … I can't sleep a lot too. And this … this is nice. It reminds me I'm not alone."

"Are you hungry?" he asks suddenly.

I hadn't realized it but, at his words, I suddenly notice I am.

"It's after one in the morning, nothing is open, and I can't sneak you into the house and cook for you."

He grins. "You would cook for me?"

I bump his shoulder with mine, our hands still clasped. "Oh, shut up. I do like to cook."

"I was actually suggesting we go to this diner I know. It's not far and it's open twenty-four hours."

"Um, okay." I bite my lip nervously. "But I'm in my pajamas."

"You can change if you want. Or I have a sweatshirt in my car you can use."

I may or may not be having heart palpitations over the fact he said I can wear his sweatshirt. Excuse me while I die a little inside.

"Yeah, that'd be great," I say.

He smiles and my stomach flips but I notice it doesn't quite reach his eyes.

Even here, even now in this moment, his sadness about his brother lingers in the air. I don't blame him. Losing a loved one isn't easy. You can't be expected to get over it in the blink of an eye. Grief may suck but in a lot of ways it's like a warm coat, keeping you cozy as you remember the person, refusing to let go and believe they're gone. But eventually you get too hot and have to remove that coat, and that's when the real pain comes because there is no protection to soften the blow anymore.

He stands and helps me up, both of us dusting the sand off of our bodies. He towers above my five-foot-two frame, tall and lean I'd say he's six-foot-three. I feel like a tiny little doll in his presence. If he picked me up my toes would dangle in the air.

He leads me around the side of my house, holding back some of the overgrown plants for me. We need to either trim or get rid of some stuff. They're starting to look more like weeds than actual plants.

Jasper stops at his Jeep and reaches into the back, pulling out a sweatshirt with the mascot of his college, an eagle.

"Hands up," he commands.

I do as he says and he slips the sweatshirt down over my body. It hangs past my pajama shorts and I have to roll the sleeves four times to be able to use my hands.

He looks me up and down. "I dig it."

"I look like I'm naked." I look down at my bare legs.

His eyes glimmer. "Tuck that part up too then."

"That would look dumb."

"Then just pretend you're wearing an oversized dress." He shrugs and opens the passenger door for me.

"M'lady."

I shake my head at him and climb inside the giant Jeep. A giant Jeep for a giant guy.

I can't believe I'm doing this. I think to myself as he jogs around the front and climbs in the driver's side. I look to my right at my house, the windows darkened as they all sleep, and here I am with a guy.

It almost feels like I'm living someone else's life—like nothing this exciting should possibly be happening to me.

"Ready for an adventure?" Jasper asks me, starting the Jeep and turning up the heat to stave off the chilly beach night air.

I nod and smile. "I'm ready."

I don't feel scared, or even worried, instead I feel exhilarated.

More than that I feel alive which is all I've wanted since all this happened.

To feel alive again is the greatest gift anyone could ever give me.

Jasper smiles back at me and, for a brief moment, his grief doesn't exist and neither does my transplant.

He's just a guy and I'm just a girl and we're going to get something to eat. Something perfectly normal and innocuous and yet it feels like the world.

As we drive it amazes me how quiet the night is. There's a peacefulness that exists while everyone else is sleeping. It's like stepping into an alternate universe, one where only the two of us exist. Part of me wants to stay in this little bubble for as long as I can.

Jasper glances at me, but I continue to look out the passenger side, my hair blowing around my shoulders from the open Jeep. The heat he put on seems pointless but a little manages to seep into my bones.

I can't help but wonder what he thinks when he looks at me.

Does he see in me what I see in him?

I cross my arms and lean out the window.

Occasionally we pass a house with a light on and I wonder why that person is up.

Maybe they're taking care of a crying baby. Or they could be working. Perhaps, like us, sleep evades them.

I wouldn't say I have insomnia, not in the normal sense, my guilt keeps me up at times, my guilt at being alive while someone else had to die, but sometimes I'm up because it's like I'm afraid if I fall asleep I might miss something. With my transplant, I have so much life to live now. I don't want to miss a single moment.

Within ten minutes of leaving my house, he pulls into the lot of a small diner. I'm sure I've passed this place thousands of times, but it's never caught my attention.

The front is rather plain, with two large windows, the name of the diner stenciled on both in large bold letters.

MEL'S it reads.

Jasper parks and I follow him inside.

The place only boasts one customer, but it's one more than I expected at this hour.

Jasper leads me to a booth beside one of the windows. The seats are black with white piping and the floors are checkered black and white title. The walls boast black and white photos of the owners and patrons through the years, along with other random memorabilia like a signed baseball glove and dominos glued to the wall in a floral pattern. On our right is a long black counter with round stools covered in blue vinyl upholstery. It's weird and quirky and utterly perfect.

"I can't believe I've never been here before," I say, my voice full of awe.

"It seems to exist in its own little world."

He grabs two menus off the table and slides one to me.

"What's good?" I ask him.

"Everything," he replies. "You can't beat the pancakes."

I look over the menu but decide pancakes sound good.

The lone waitress appears. "What can I get you guys to eat and drink?"

Jasper points at me to go first. "A water and chocolate chip pancakes."

"Good choice." She smiles. "And for you?"

"A Sprite and blueberry pancakes."

"That shouldn't be long." She taps her pen against her notepad and goes to put our order in.

"How are you feeling?" he asks me. "I mean, it hasn't been that long since your surgery, right?"

"No, it hasn't been long. I feel great. Still a little sore at times, depending on what I do, but other than that it's been smooth sailing. I can't complain. I still have to go to the hospital a lot, but again I can't complain. They're making sure the kidney works and that's all that matters. Gotta make sure I don't end up back on dialysis. That would … Well, that would suck."

"What's dialysis like?" he asks.

I shrug. "I was on hemo-dialysis in the beginning since I had to start immediately. I was on it for a good year, actually, while we were trying to find a living donor match. It was hard on my body. I felt sick and tired all the time. I hate feeling like I just wanted to sleep and stay in my bed all day. Plus, everybody in there is sick. I hated seeing that and not being able to do anything about it. I'm a doer. When I was little I always wanted to save any sick or injured animal I ran across. That hasn't changed." I pause and gather my hair into a ponytail, securing it with a band from around my wrist. Talking about this always makes me hot as my temperature rises, so getting my hair off my shoulders helps. "I finally switched to peritoneal dialysis. It's done through a tube in your stomach at home every night. I could do it myself and I felt a lot better doing it. That's not the case for other people. I believe you have to find the right fit for you and that's what worked for me. It wasn't ideal, none of it is, but it gave me a sense of normalcy again."

"Wow," he whispers, letting out a breath. "I never realized it was like that."

"A lot of people don't."

I offer a smile to the waitress as she drops off our drinks.

I rip off the paper from around the straw and dunk the straw in my drink.

"And what about transplant? What's that like?"

I sigh heavily. "Exhausting. Mentally and emotionally *exhausting*. The doctors and hospitals are great, they are, but the process is slow. When we were doing living donor workups it was taking months and then eventually everyone got weeded out. And I … I didn't want to keep feeling like I was begging, you know? It's a big deal to ask someone for an organ, and I was beginning to feel like a broken record, I resigned myself to the fact that I was just going to have to wait for someone to die. Which wasn't easy either, to come to terms with the fact that I was waiting for someone to die so I had the gift of living. Do you know that *one* person donating their organs when they die can save around eight lives? Maybe even more? It's a beautiful thing, but a lot of people freak out when you bring up the topic of organ donation, but wouldn't you rather save lives?"

"We donated my brother's organs," he says softly.

I gasp, for a moment I forgot where I suspect my kidney came from.

"We thought if … if T.J. had to die, others should get to live. We didn't want his death to be in vain. We wanted something good to come out of it."

My heart clenches and my throat closes up with the threat of tears.

Maybe he won't be mad. Maybe … maybe he'll be grateful you got his brother's kidney.

I'm saved from saying anything by the arrival of our food. Pancakes stacked five high rest on each plate.

"Enjoy, guys."

I drench my pancakes in syrup and for a brief second my heart stops in panic that I don't have my binders to take with my food, but then just as quickly I realize I don't need them anymore.

"I think that's … beautiful," I tell him finally.

He gives a small smile but there's sadness in his eyes. I hate that his brother is gone, and I hate that I might finally be able to live because of it.

I decide to change the subject in the hopes of getting the sadness out of his pretty blue-green eyes.

"Do you think you could teach me to surf?"

He chews and swallows a bite. "Of course."

"Even if I'm really—like I mean, *really*—bad?"

He chuckles. "Even if you're the worst I think I can handle it."

We smile at each other and warmth spears my body. I love spending time with him. A few short days and I'm becoming addicted to it—to being around someone who I can be myself with, who gets it, who's incredibly easy to talk to.

I want to get to know him more. I never want to lose this feeling.

I take a bite of chocolate chip pancake and cover my mouth to stifle my moan.

"Good?" He chuckles, clearly amused.

"This is the best damn pancake I've ever had."

"Maybe that's how we should advertise them," our waitress jokes, refilling my water glass.

I blush.

She winks and heads away.

"Besides surfing what do you like to do?"

He thinks for a moment, a tiny bit of blueberry clinging to his lip. I don't tell him, because he looks adorable.

"I like to build things. Mostly, I just like to keep my hands busy. I get restless if I'm not doing anything."

"What kind of things do you build?"

"Last summer I helped my dad redo the deck to our house. And I built a tree house for our neighbors. Usually it's smaller stuff, like birdhouses and shelves, a bookcase. Stuff like that."

"I always wanted a tree house growing up," I say wistfully.

He gets this look in his eyes. "I can build you one."

"You're not serious. We don't have a tree you could even build one in."

"We do."

"You would build a tree house for me at your parents?" I raise a brow.

"Why not? They wouldn't care. They're cool. I always wanted one too growing up. So did T.J. It could be for the three of us."

"Well, if you're serious, that'd be amazing but I want to help."

He smiles. "I'd like that."

My stomach flips. It seems to do that constantly around Jasper.

I don't know if I'll ever get used to the feeling. I'm not sure I want to.

We finish our meal, making small talk.

The more I get to know him the more I like him. He's easy to talk to, nice, and he makes me feel like me. Not the old me, or even the new me, but a version of me who's happy and strong and excited about living.

He drops me off and kisses me on the cheek.

My cheek tingles all the way into the house and up to my room, and when I wake up there's still a pleasant warmth.

CHAPTER NINETEEN

I sleep in, my night excursion having worn me out. The smile won't wipe off my face. I feel giddy, something I *never* feel.

When I get downstairs my parents are already gone for work and Harlow lies on the couch, the TV on for background noise, with her nose buried in her summer reading. It must not be very good because she wears a look of intense concentration and her lip is curled in distaste.

"Good morning," I sing-song, dancing into the kitchen and doing a dip as I open the refrigerator door.

"Good dream?" she asks.

"Yes, and even better reality."

She slaps her book closed and sits up. Her hair is in a messy ponytail, some of the loose blonde strands fluffing around her head. "Do tell."

"Jasper and I hung out again last night," I tell her, biting my lip to try to damper my blinding smile.

"What?" she gasps, her jaw dropping.

She swings her legs over the couch and hops up, running into the kitchen.

I nod excitedly. "He took me to eat at this diner. I'd never even noticed it before. It was delicious."

"You're like … *glowing*."

I fix myself a bowl of Fruity Pebbles cereal—the breakfast of champions.

I lean a hip against the counter and my spoon clangs against the glass bowl when I dip it in.

"I like hanging out with him."

She grins and sits on one of the stools. "I think you more than like him."

"Maybe … but I'm just getting to know him. I don't want to rush anything just because this is new and exciting. I have to keep my head."

She snorts. "For a guy that hot, he can have whatever he wants, my head, my hand, my underwear. Just take it."

"Harlow!" I screech and flick my spoon at her.

She dodges the flying milk and cereal. Perry skids on the floor, excited to lap it up.

She shrugs. "What? He's seriously good looking. Like an Abercrombie model."

"He's not that … Okay, he kind of is, but in a real way, not a stone cold let me smolder at you way."

She snorts. "I low you."

I shrug. "What can I say? I'm very lowable," I joke. "Anyway" —I take a bite of cereal— "he's teaching me to surf today. You wanna go?"

She crinkles her nose. "And be your third wheel? I don't think so." She shakes her head. "Besides, I *have* to finish this book today and start my summer essay. Remind me again *why* I decided to take all honors classes?"

I laugh. "Because you're a smarty pants."

She groans. "Yeah, well apparently not smart enough to realize this was a very bad decision."

"You've done it the last two years too," I remind her, pointing my spoon in her direction.

"It just keeps getting harder and harder," she complains.

I shrug. "It'll be worth it."

"I suppose you're right." She sighs. "Still, I'd rather be learning to surf with my hotty pants potential boyfriend."

I snort. "We're nowhere *near* that point, and might never get there, besides if you want a hotty pants boyfriend I'm sure Spencer would jump at the chance."

She blushes and mumbles something before hurrying from the kitchen back to the family room and her waiting book.

I could tease her about it, we're sisters after all, but we've always had a little bit more respect for each other than that. Maybe it's because I got sick, or maybe it's just how we are, but if she likes him I can't mock her feelings. That'd be wrong of me.

I clean my bowl and head back upstairs to shower and get ready. I don't know what time Jasper will want to meet, but I figure I should be ready to go when the time comes.

Perry follows me to my room and sits on my bed while I go to shower.

When I come out he's lying on his back with all his paws in the air. I shake my head.

"Perry, you silly boy."

I rifle through my drawers and find my floral, black and white, one-piece swimsuit. Most girls my age would be wearing bikinis, but my scars aren't something I like to show off. I'm not ashamed of them, not at all, they show how hard I've fought, but the questions are something I can avoid by keeping them covered so I do. I have a couple round scars from my peritoneal catheter and then my scar from transplant surgery is about six inches but crescent shaped. The scars on my chest are impossible to hide. They're from the catheter in my chest when I first started dialysis, since it was an emergency situation.

I slip on a pair of jean shorts and a loose sweater. I choose to leave my hair down, knowing it's going to end up wet.

Flopping down on my bed beside Perry, the dog turns to me and smears a wet kiss on my cheek.

"Ew, Perry, that's gross." I wipe my face on my sleeve.

Perry gives me a lopsided smile.

I grab my book off my night table and read for a little bit. It isn't long until my phone is buzzing.

Jasper: Look outside.

I stand and rush to my bedroom window, a smile immediately lighting up my face when I see Jasper's yellow Jeep parked out front. He leans against the passenger door, his arms crossed over his chest and his legs crossed at the ankles.

I raise my hand to the window and the movement causes his head to rise.

He smiles, his eyes hidden behind a pair of dark sunglasses.

Turning back around I slip my feet into a pair of flip-flops and rush downstairs.

"I'll be back later!" I call to Harlow, sprinting out the door before I can hear her reply.

Jasper chuckles as I come to stand in front of him.

"Eager, are we?"

I blush. "I'm excited about surfing."

I am, but I'm more excited about being with him and he knows it.

"Mhmm. I'm sure that's all it is." His dimple winks from his cheek.

He opens the passenger door with a sweep of his hand.

I climb inside, still not used to the height of the Jeep. With my short stature, it's akin to climbing a damn mountain.

I flop into the seat and he closes the door, shaking with silent laughter.

I can't even feel embarrassed, because I'm sure it was funny.

When he slides behind the steering wheel, I say, "I figured I'd meet you at the beach. I didn't expect you to pick me up."

He shrugs and looks in his mirrors before pulling out onto the street. "This is more fun. I like being with you."

He smiles over at me and my heart grabs onto his words, cradling them close like they're precious, because they *are*.

"Were you able to get some sleep?" I ask him.

He shrugs, his smile falling. "A little."

I frown.

"What about you?"

"I slept in."

"Is there anything you want to talk about?" I hedge.

He shakes his head, staring resolutely ahead. We stop at a stoplight and he finally looks at me.

"His room is right across from mine. It's still the same, but it's *not*. There's this emptiness there. This lack of *life*. It's disturbing, how he's gone but everything is left the same but not at the same time. Like how can that be? He ceases to exist but there are reminders of him all around. They're painful to see, but I don't want them to go away, either. Does that make me weak?"

I shake my head as the light turns green and he drives forward.

"No, I think it makes you human," I reason. "It's human nature not to want to let go, but that part that's trying to protect you urges you to hide from it."

"Is this ever not going to hurt?" he asks softly, almost pleadingly.

I shake my head. "No, I'm sorry, but it's always going to hurt. Just like I'm always going to be affected by my disease. Yeah, it gets better, the pain dulls, some days you don't even think about it. But it's always *there*. It still exists."

He works his jaw back and forth. "He was too young to die. It's not fair."

"Life *isn't* fair. As cliché as it sounds, it's true. People die too young, animals get run over, kids get shot, cancer eats people alive, but you have to get up, brush yourself off, and move on. Because where bad exists, so does good, and it's up to us to remember that—to find it and use it to bring light to others."

He parks the Jeep and I look around, realizing we've already made it to the beach before I know it.

"You're far too wise for your age," he whispers sadly, looking me over. I'm sure he's imagining all I've been through, I'm sure his ideas of it are bad but I have news for him, whatever he's thinking, it's been *worse*.

"That's what happens when life deals you a bad card. But it's one bad card out of my entire hand. I can still live a happy life. I can still run, and talk, and smile, and *live*. Living is the greatest gift of all, no matter how it's done. Each breath is a tiny little miracle."

He shakes his head. "You amaze me."

"I'm nothing amazing," I argue. "I'm just being honest."

He smiles. It's a soft, hesitant smile. "I still think you're the most remarkable person I've ever met. Now" —he claps his hands— "no more serious talk. It's time to surf."

He hops out of the Jeep and leans the front seat forward, pulling out two wetsuits. "This one should fit you." He tosses it to me.

I stare at it like it's completely foreign to me, because it is. I might've grown up at the beach, but I've never spent much time in the water so I had no need for a wetsuit.

Jasper slips his on easily and I climb out, fumbling and nearly tripping.

"How did you make that look so simple?" I gripe, nearly falling on the ground.

He chuckles and comes to help me. Like that day at the beach, he has the front hanging down, and his shirt is gone giving me a nice glimpse of his tan, bronzed chest.

"Lots and lots of practice." He chuckles. "I'll help."

Even with his help, it takes me ten minutes to get in the wetsuit. By the time we're done I'm out of breath and questioning my life choices.

"You okay there?"

"I'm not sure," I pant.

He chuckles. "Think you're going to live?"

Again, I answer, "I'm not sure."

He grins slowly. "I mean, I could always give you mouth to mouth."

My cheeks flood with brilliant color. "I'm good," I answer in a squeaky voice.

We haven't kissed again since that first night on the beach, and while I've dreamed of doing it again, I don't feel quite as bold or as sure of myself as I did then. Maybe it was the cover of night that made me take a risk and kiss him, or maybe it was the magical bubble that seems to cocoon us on those nightly meet-ups, but whatever it is I don't feel it now. In fact, on the busy public beach, in broad daylight, with hundreds of people around is not where I want to have my second kiss. I can already see that turning into a disaster.

He laughs at me and goes to remove two surfboards off the top of his Jeep, leaning them both against the back.

"This one's mine." He points to the orange and cerulean blue one with some kind of swirling design. "And you can use this one." He indicates the other, bright yellow with a floral design. "It's my mom's. It should work well for you."

I reach out a hesitant hand, touching the shiny board.

"Think you're ready?" he asks me, crossing his muscular arms over his chest.

"No," I answer honestly, and my eyes flick up to meet his steady gaze. "But when are we ever ready for anything? You just have to get out there and do it."

He nods and grabs his board. "Then let's do it."

I grab the other board and struggle to carry it, even under my arm.

"Here, let me get it," Jasper says, taking mercy on me.

We walk side by side, our feet sinking into the sand. The sun shines brightly upon us, my skin already warming. I'm sure by the end of the day my freckles will be darker than normal.

Jasper sets the surfboards in the sand near the water.

"Okay, a couple of things to go over."

"I'm listening."

"First" —he ticks it off on his finger— "you're going to fall, a lot. You might even get bruised or hurt but get back out there and try again. Don't let it scare you away. Secondly, you might not catch a wave today but we're going to keep at this until you do—and not like a baby wave, either, I mean a real wave." I gulp at the idea.

"Third, just have fun. That's what surfing is all about. Having fun and being a part of the ocean."

"Okay." I nod. "I can do that."

He smiles. "Good. Now grab your board and let's go."

I grab it and carry it the short distance to the water. I mimic him, walking until the water is about waist height on me and climbing on top of the board. Then we paddle out and wait.

He sits up, his legs dangling over the side, and I do the same.

"Now, we're going to start with those baby waves first. Don't chicken out on me, okay?"

"I won't."

"When you see one start to rise, paddle toward it and then quickly turn around so it can carry you. That's when you stand up. It'll be hard to get your balance at first, but you just have to get used to the feel."

I nod. I'm nervous, of course, but I've wanted to do this forever and Jasper seems like the best person to teach me.

It isn't long until a small wave forms.

"Paddle, paddle, paddle," Jasper chants, and I do just that.

I turn the board around, already out of breath and my arms shaking.

I am seriously out of shape.

I used to run a couple of times a week but haven't at all since my surgery and I can definitely tell a difference in my strength and energy level.

Like an awkward baby gazelle, I try to stand on the board, and promptly fall into the water with a small scream.

Surfacing for air, I push my wet hair out of my eyes, the surfboard bobbing like an obedient puppy waiting for praise and attention.

Jasper laughs heartily. "Good try."

"I didn't even stand up for one second," I groan, swinging my body back onto the board. I'm glad now for the wetsuit. Even in July the water is chilly and in only my swimsuit I would've frozen to death.

"Hey, you tried, and that's all that matters."

"Yeah, yeah."

He chuckles. "Next one's mine." He winks.

"You're going to ride a baby wave?" I scoff.

He shrugs, smiling cockily. "Someone's got to show you how it's done."

"Maybe I want someone else to show me," I mock, fighting laughter.

He raises one dark brow—a talent I've never been able to master. "Is that so? I'm sure I could find someone willing to help you." He waves his hand in the direction of other surfers.

I pretend to think about it. "Nah, I'll stick with you."

"Good choice. I *am* the best."

"Cocky much?" I joke.

"Hey, I know what I'm good at and I own it. I don't think that makes me cocky." He pauses and tilts his head. "Okay, maybe a little bit cocky," he relents.

A few minutes later, another small wave comes along and he talks me through everything he does as I watch.

He makes it seem easy, completely effortless. He rides the wave until it ends and then jumps into the water and back on his board.

We spend several hours in the water and I only manage to ride a small wave once, and only for about five seconds. Jasper swears it's longer, but I know he's only trying to make me feel better.

We drag the boards out of the water and collapse onto the sand with them.

"I'm tired," I declare, removing the clasp around my ankle.

He chuckles. "Your body will get used to it."

"Used to it?"

"I told you, we're not quitting until you ride a *real* wave."

I crinkle my nose and mutter, "Slave driver."

"I heard that." He sits down beside me, draping his arms over his knees.

"I meant for you to." I laugh.

"We'll take a break tomorrow," he says, squinting from the bright sun. "Give your body a chance to recover." I doubt my body will recover in one day, but I'm not about to argue or I know he'll make me do it again tomorrow. "There's somewhere I'd like to take you tomorrow night."

"Where?" I ask, trying to breathe normally and not like I've just run twenty miles.

"It's a club," he hedges, waiting for my reaction.

"Uh …"

"It's not at all like you're thinking," he says. "It's for dancing, but like real dancing, not that grinding stuff."

"Don't act like you've never grinded on a chick before." I bump his shoulder.

"Maybe once or twice." His eyes sparkle with laughter.

"Mhmm." I press my lips together and look at him like a scolding mother.

He laughs and rubs his stubbled jaw like he's embarrassed. "Will you go with me?"

"Sure. I'll make a fool of myself, but why not." I shrug, reminding myself of my vow to get out of my comfort zone.

He smiles, his white teeth sparkling in the sunlight. "You're going to love it."

"If you say so. Now" —I stand up and brush as much sand off the wetsuit as I can— "can we *please* get something to eat. I'm starving."

"Sure. I'll go grab my wallet from the Jeep and put these away." He indicates the surfboards. "Why don't you go get in line somewhere and I'll catch up with you?"

"Sounds good."

I head off in search of the food stands while he leaves in the direction the Jeep is parked.

My stomach rumbles as I walk. I worked up an appetite while I was out there.

There are several stands to choose from but I end up going with the sandwich one, since I usually always get a hamburger when I'm at the beach.

Several people are ahead of me, by the time it's my turn to order Jasper has appeared.

I order a turkey sandwich with lettuce, tomato, and avocado. Jasper gets the one with practically everything on it. I'm not even surprised. And then he also orders a cup of fries for us to share and two waters.

After we have our food we sit down at a table to eat. I'd love to sit in the sand and eat but without towels, there's about a hundred percent chance sand would end up in our food and I don't want a literal *sand*wich.

Jasper unscrews the cap on his water bottle and downs about half of it in one gulp.

I give him a skeptical look and he laughs, wiping the dampness off his lips with the back of his hand.

"I was thirsty," he reasons.

Unwrapping my sandwich, my stomach grumbles yet again in desperation for food. I take a bite and it settles, somewhat.

Jasper chews a bit of fry and clears his throat. "If you don't mind, could you tell me what it was like … in the beginning … when you were first diagnosed."

"I don't mind," I reply, and wipe my hands on a napkin, wondering where I should begin. "For starters, I was naïve. We all were. We didn't understand what my diagnosis meant and just assumed transplant would happen easily and quickly. It didn't. It's a long, hard process. I was only fourteen at the time, but I had to grow up quick and deal with my reality. The first couple of months after I was diagnosed were the hardest. I spent a lot of time in the hospital then, having to go back for one thing or the other. I had to have a catheter in my chest and that sucked balls. It hurt and itched like crazy, but with it being an open hole to my heart I couldn't scratch it. Do you have any idea what it's like to itch twenty-four seven? I started to feel like I was losing my mind." I pause and shake my head as I catch my breath. "Then I had to have a fistula put in my arm, since I was on hemo-dialysis to start." I hold out my left arm and point to the inch-and-a-half long scar on my wrist. "Here, feel my arm."

He places his hand on my arm and his eyes grow wide with shock.

"Whoa, what the fuck is that thing?"

"They attached an artery to a vein—the artery pushes extra blood into the vein, making it grow bigger so it can withstand the pushing and pulling of blood so quickly during dialysis. That's why it feels like it's buzzing—it's all the extra blood. I can hear it at night," I admit. "It's like my body is humming."

"That's some weird shit."

"The weirdest," I agree. "I call it my Hulk vein." I laugh. "See the difference in the size of my arms?" I hold them both out together. "It looks like it's swollen, but it's not, it's because the vein is big."

"That boggles my mind," he whispers, reaching out tentatively to rub my arm. I hold myself still as he touches me. My arm isn't nearly as sensitive as it used to be, but sometimes it still bothers me when someone touches it. "Is this okay?" he asks, either picking up on my stiffness, or maybe he's just that in tune with me.

"It's okay." I nod for him to continue.

He moves his hand lower, to where the thrill is stronger.

He holds it there, feeling it, feeling not only the flow of blood but how it beats in time with my heart. I'm sure, with as strong as it is, he can feel it speed up as my body reacts to his touch.

"And this never goes away?" he asks.

I shake my head. "They can tie it off, but they usually leave it if it's working. Transplant doesn't last forever—and the peritoneal dialysis doesn't work long term, either. That's what I ended up doing after about the first year. My mom did it for me in the beginning and then I ended up taking over. That one was done through a tube in my stomach. I'm just glad my arm doesn't look *too* crazy. That was one of my biggest worries."

"What do you mean?" he asks.

"Well," I begin to explain, "the longer you use the vein for dialysis the bigger it gets until it literally surfaces and looks like a snake living under your skin." He stares at me. "I'm not kidding. Do you have your phone? I left mine in your Jeep."

"Yeah, I grabbed it when I got my wallet." He hands it to me.

I open the web browser and type in *dialysis fistula* and click on images before sliding it back over.

His jaw drops. "That's fucking crazy."

"That pretty much explains it."

"It looks . . ."

"Gross?" I supply.

"I was going to go with gnarly." He shrugs.

"Well, now if you see someone with an arm that looks like that you'll know they're on dialysis. You know, before this, I *never* noticed anyone with an arm that looked like that. Now I see it all the time. I guess I didn't know to look for it, or maybe I didn't care to see it since it didn't matter to me. But it does now. Matter, I mean."

"I feel like a prick complaining about losing my brother when you've literally been through hell and back."

"So have you," I argue. "Just because it's a different path to hell doesn't mean it hurts any more or less or is any worse. It's just *different* that's all."

"Not many fourteen year olds could go through what you have. I mean, I'm almost twenty-one and I'm man enough to admit I don't think I could do everything you have. I passed out when I was twelve getting my blood drawn. I'm not quite that bad now, but you've been through more than anyone should ever have to go through."

"What's sad is there are a lot of kids suffering with this disease, I mean, I was a kid too, but I'm talking like *young* kids. Anywhere from five to eight years old. They don't even know what a normal life is. They'll never have a normal childhood. How is that fair? Our time as a child is already so short, and to be saddled with something like this?" I shake my head. "It's just wrong."

"Is there anything we can do?" he asks, finishing his sandwich. I've completely forgotten about eating mine.

I shrug. "Beyond talking about it and raising awareness I don't know of anything."

"Let's do that then. You should go around and talk to people about it."

"Harlow wanted me to talk to her high school," I admit. "I didn't want to, and then I got my transplant so there was no way it was happening before the year ended."

"She's right. You should. People need to hear about this. They need to hear your story, to understand."

"There are so many other people out there that are probably better to do this," I hedge.

"I don't see them standing up and making noise, Willa. People tend to sit back and wait for someone else to take that first step, to raise their voice, you have to decide if you're going to be a follower or a leader."

"I don't know what I am," I whisper.

"I know what I see in you, but the question is, do you see it in yourself?"

CHAPTER TWENTY

"Sit still," Meredith declares, pushing me back down into the chair in front of my bathroom mirror.

"You're going to make me look like a porn star," I groan, trying to tilt my head away from the daring red lipstick she's trying to put on me.

She grabs my chin, forcing me still. "You are not going to look like a porn star. Maybe a classy hooker, but not a porn star."

"How is that any better?" I argue.

She shrugs. "I don't know. Now hold still. This goes with your smoky eye look and besides, you're going to a *club*, Willa. I can't exactly put a nude lip on you. You need to be bold."

"I'm regretting calling you."

"Oh, codswallop."

"Are you a hundred years old now?" I fight laughter.

She smirks. "If it'll get you to hold still, then yes, I am."

Harlow sits on the bathroom counter watching us battle back and forth. "Let her put it on, Willa. I think it'll look nice."

"Traitor," I mumble, and then reluctantly hold still for Meredith.

She finishes my makeup and moves on to my hair. She braids it on the side, but not like a normal braid, it's something complicated that I know I could never recreate. Stepping back, she appraises her handiwork and then douses me in a can of hairspray.

Coughing, I ask, "Are you trying to kill me?"

"Never," she scoffs. "But this needs to last through not only the night but sweat and dancing. I can't have you looking like you rolled in bed all night." I blush at her words. "Now, it's dress time." She claps her hands and runs into my room and back, carrying a garment bag. "I bought this because it was to die for, but I haven't had anywhere to wear it yet. But I think you deserve to wear it tonight."

She removes the dress from the garment bag and my jaw drops.

"Mere, I can't wear that. I might not have a lot going on in the boob area but what I do have is going to fall out. I don't think my nipple popping out on a kind of sort of first date is the best idea."

She rolls her eyes. "Men love a little nip slip. Besides," she continues when I open my mouth to protest, "I brought tape."

She reaches into her makeup bag on my counter and shows me the tape.

"Fine," I grumble.

"Strip, girl."

I shake my head and she helps me into the dress. It's skintight and I have trouble shimmying it up over my hips.

Meredith zips the back and helps guide me on where to place the tape.

"One last thing," she declares, and adds a black choker around my neck. Grabbing my shoulders, she turns me toward the mirror. "What do you think?"

"You look beautiful," Harlow breathes.

I gape at my appearance. I look like a goddess. My skin is glowing and bronzed, but not overly so, and contrasts nicely with the smoky gray eyeshadow and bold red lip. I might've blanched when she pulled out the red lipstick, but the girl knew what she was talking about.

A few loose pieces of hair frame my face, softening the look.

"Okay, you did good," I admit grudgingly.

Meredith smirks, crossing her arms over her chest. "Always trust me, I know what I'm doing."

Even the dress, while far more daring than anything I would pick for myself, is perfect.

It's black and ends higher above my knees than I'm used to, but it's not short enough for me to feel insecure in. The front dips low, with crisscrossing straps. It definitely exposes way more skin up there than I'm comfortable with, but I know I own nothing in my closet that would be appropriate to wear. I turn to the side.

"Whoa, I have a butt."

Meredith laughs and pinches my butt. "Of course you do, girl, show it off."

"You look pretty," Harlow says.

"Thank you," I reply.

The girl in the mirror seems like a stranger, but when I poke my cheek she does too. I guess it's definitely me after all.

"You're next," Meredith tells Harlow.

"But we're not going anywhere."

When I called Meredith to help me get ready for tonight she agreed on one condition—that she get to stay the night so she can hear all about it after.

Meredith shrugs. "Who cares? You can still watch a movie in a full face of makeup. It's called being fabulous."

I turn to Meredith. "I changed my mind. I'd rather stay here with you guys and watch movies."

She grabs my shoulders, looking at me dead on. "Don't make Merebitch come out to play. You're going out with this boy and you're going to have the time of your life. You've literally barely left the house since you were fourteen. Now's your time."

I take a breath. "What if I make a fool of myself?"

"What's life without a little laughter? If you can't laugh at yourself then you're kind of a sucky human being. Just remember, you're beautiful and smart, don't let your insecurities tell you otherwise."

I hug her to me. "I love you."

"Stop getting all mushy on me," she jokes. "But I love you too."

"Oh, let me in on this lovin'." Harlow wraps her arms around us.

"I don't know what I'd do without you guys," I tell them honestly.

"You'd be awfully lonely," Meredith says.

Harlow adds, "It'd also be creepily quiet."

Meredith picks up a black sparkly clutch she brought with her, slips in the lipstick, a pack of makeup wipes, my phone, and …

"Is that pepper spray?"

She shrugs. "Just in case hottie gets handsy."

I don't argue with her because having it does make me feel a little better. Not that I think Jasper will try anything, but I don't know where he's taking me and who might be there.

"I think we should put a cardigan on her," Harlow tells Meredith.

Meredith scoffs. "And ruin my masterpiece?"

"Well, I mean, she told Mom and Dad she's going on a date, so they know she's going out, but I'm sure my dad will flip his lid if he sees her like that."

I look down at myself and then at Meredith. "She's right."

"Ugh, fine, but as soon as you're in homeboy's car take it off—preferably in a sexy striptease sort of way."

"Don't push your luck," I warn with a laugh.

She groans and mumbles to herself all the way out of my bathroom and into my closet as she searches for something for me to cover up with.

"What is this?" she holds out a large sweatshirt and I blush.

"Nothing," I answer automatically, as she holds up Jasper's sweatshirt that I should give back but haven't yet.

"Mhmm," she hums with a twinkle in her eyes, shoving it back into my closet. "Aha, this will do." She pulls out a jean jacket with a hoodie attached.

I shrug it on and zip it up so only the bottom half of the dress is exposed.

"One last thing, I promise," she says, grabbing a pair of black heels off my bed.

I stare at them. "Do you want me to break a leg?"

"Willa," she groans, "you cannot wear a dress like that with sneakers. You just can't."

I take them from her and slip them on, gaining at least three inches, if not more, in height. I wobble a bit and hold my hands out to balance myself.

"Look at our little girl," Meredith says to Harlow, wiping away a pretend tear. "She's all grown up."

"Oh, shut up," I groan.

My phone vibrates inside the clutch and I check it.

"He's here," I say, and swallow thickly as fear threatens to strangle me. I'm miles out of my comfort zone with this.

"Showtime. Let's go, let's go." Meredith pushes me out of my room and then has to help me down the steps because … *heels*.

"Wow, you look beautiful," my mom says, unloading the dishwasher.

"Thank you."

"Don't be home too late," Dad says. "In fact, I think I'm going to go talk to this guy."

"Dad, no." I blanch at the idea of him meeting Jasper.

"Why not?" He narrows his eyes.

"I-I don't want you to scare him away."

He chuckles in only the way my father can—husky, but with an edge that lets you know he means business. "I won't scare him … too much," he mutters.

"Jake," my mother scolds, swatting him with a dishtowel.

My dad follows me to the door and I swing it open to find Jasper already standing there. I stumble back into my dad's chest in surprise.

Jasper stands there dressed in a pair of khaki pants that sit snuggly on his hips with a white button-down shirt tucked into them, the sleeves rolled up his tanned muscular forearms. He looks like a damn snack—no scratch that, he's the whole meal.

"These are for you." He holds out a bouquet of assorted flowers. I spot a lily and inhale its fragrant scent.

"Thank you."

"I'm Willa's dad." My dad holds his hand out to Jasper and when Jasper takes it he gives it a rough shake.

"Dad," I hiss under my breath.

Jasper flashes me a smile and shakes his head, telling me it's okay.

"You look old," Dad states.

I bury my face in my hands.

Jasper chuckles. "I'm twenty, sir."

My dad makes a noise in his throat. I'm tempted to step on his foot with my heel.

"I have my reservations, but Willa seems to like you, and …" He pauses and looks at me sadly but with pride. "And I trust her judgment. If she likes you I'll give you a chance."

"Thanks, Dad." I hug him, and he wraps his arm around my side.

"Have her home by midnight," my dad warns him.

"I can do that, sir."

"Good. Now have fun, but not too much fun."

"*Dad*," I cry. "Stop it."

He chuckles and heads back toward the kitchen.

I spot Harlow and Meredith peeking around the corner and give them a small wave before stepping outside with Jasper.

I close the door behind us and look up at him. "I'm sorry about that."

He chuckles. "I wouldn't have expected anything less."

I look down at the flowers in my hands. "Oh, let me take these back in. I'll be right back."

Upon opening the door, two forms fall to the floor. "Really, guys?" I glare at my sister and best friend.

"Again, wouldn't expect anything less," Jasper pipes in with a laugh.

"Here, take these and make yourself useful." I hand the flowers to Meredith and promptly close the door again.

"Let's get out of here before we have two, maybe three, stowaways.

"I like the way you think."

We walk side by side to his Jeep and he opens the passenger door for me.

"You look beautiful, by the way. You always are." He brushes his fingers over my cheek and then tucks one of the loose strands of hair behind my ear.

"Thank you," I whisper, glowing beneath his praise. I don't need him, or any guy, to tell me I'm beautiful. Even though some days I feel like a troll, I know in my heart I'm pretty, everybody is. But that doesn't mean it doesn't feel good to hear it.

Climbing up into the Jeep is normally difficult—in heels, it's impossible.

"Let me help," Jasper says. Before I can protest, his hands are on my waist and he lifts me up into the seat. "Need me to buckle you in too?" he jokes, smiling crookedly.

"No, I'm good," I squeak, and reach for the seatbelt before he can get any ideas.

Jasper climbs in and looks at me. "Are you ready?"

"As I'll ever be," I shrug.

I feel apprehensive about what he has planned, but I keep reminding myself I can't be that scared little girl who sits at home by herself anymore. Going somewhere like this is completely out of my comfort zone and that's exactly why I need to do it. Complacency is okay for a bit, but after a while it's stifling. Being nervous or afraid is a natural emotion—you can't avoid it, you might as well embrace it. I want to be able to say I *lived*, that I *did*, I don't want to say I sat by idly and watched it happen. I want to be a part of things.

"You're going to have fun, I promise you," he assures me.

It's weird being with him like this, I don't think this is an actual date, however maybe it is since I'm clueless when it comes to this kind of thing, but it's nice too. I haven't known him long, but he's easy to be around and he *gets* me. It's rare to find someone like that I think.

"Just don't let me make a fool of myself." I laugh lightly, the sound twinkling with the hesitation of my nerves.

I haven't danced in so long, and never this kind of dancing, but as I sit in his Jeep my body vibrates with the need to move, to flow, to get lost in the music. Giving up on dance might've been one of the worst decisions of my life, but at the time it was what I had to do. I was so tired and weak, not myself at all, that I had no energy or passion left to give it. The dialysis seemed to suck the literal life out of my bones and then, when I did feel better, it felt like too much time had passed to bother going back. It was easier to stay away than to fight my way back into dance.

Jasper doesn't drive for long before he turns into a lot outside a building I'd probably never normally notice during the day. The outside is a gray color, blending in with the other similarly shaped buildings around it. This one, however, in the growing darkness, is lit up with a sign on the outside. It's not a word, but a simple wave design. It's large, taking up most of the wall facing us. There's a line of people outside waiting to get in.

"Are you sure I'm going to be allowed in there?" I ask, undoing my belt as he parks the Jeep. "I *am* underage," I remind him.

"Willa," he laughs. "So am I, remember?"

"Oh, right." I feel silly for my total lapse; besides, I should know by now Jasper isn't the type to try to get me into trouble.

He hops out and is there to help me before I can blink. I'm thankful for his help, considering the death traps Meredith forced me to wear. I stumble a little when I get out, falling into his chest.

Our gazes connect, and for a moment everything around us disappears.

If I concentrate even the slightest I can recall the feel of his lips on mine that night at the beach. I'm desperate to kiss him again, my body aches with the need, but tonight I don't feel as bold as I did then. Beneath the pulsing neon blue light radiating from the outside of the club, there's no hiding, not like there is beneath a blanket of darkness and the crashing of the waves.

I look away first, down at our feet, mine clad in heels I'd never normally wear and his in a pair of brown leather oxfords that match nicely with his fitted khaki colored pants.

I remove my jacket and toss it back into the Jeep before he closes the door.

When I turn to face Jasper his jaw is slack as he gawks at me. His eyes trail slowly up my legs, over my hips, up my breasts—lingering a little longer there—until finally his gaze meets mine. I never knew someone could caress you with their eyes but I know now.

He swallows thickly. "I … um … *wow*. You look amazing."

I smile from ear to ear, silently reminding myself I owe Meredith thanks later. I love that for once Jasper is the speechless one.

"Thank you," I say, smoothing my hands down the front of the dress.

He shakes his head as if trying to rid himself of a fog.

"We better head in," Jasper says, trying to act as if he didn't just blatantly check me out. I love the affect I seem to have over him.

He places his hand on the small of my back, and my body instantly reacts to the feel of his touch. He guides me into the line and we wait for our turn. To my surprise, we get right in.

Inside, I'm pleasantly surprised and look around in awe.

There's a bar on one side, a screen behind it playing a video of a beach at night. Tables line the perimeter of the room, leaving the center open for dancing. Different colored lights flash, reflecting off bubbles that float through the room. There's a distinct smell too, one of the ocean, that seems to be pumping throughout the room.

A remix of a Lana Del Rey song plays through the speakers, bodies swaying and shimmying in time to the music.

Watching them, my body itches to join in.

"Dance with me?" Jasper asks, holding out a hand to me.

I nod, my throat too tight to speak.

He leads me out onto the dance floor and faces me.

Bending his head low, so his lips graze my ear, he whispers, "Don't think, just be."

Just be.

I place my hands on his chest, the muscles hard and solid, and behind them the steady beat of his heart pulses, centering me, reminding me that it's okay to let go. I don't have to be afraid of making a fool of myself—we're all fools, after all.

I take a breath, and when I let it out my body begins to move. Jasper's lips quirk, pleased that I'm giving in to my need to dance.

His body begins to move with mine. We move together easily, like our bodies were made for each other, both of us seeming to anticipate the other's moves and counteract them with something to match.

The blue and purple lights glimmer over his face and to the small exposed bit of his collarbone. They then reflect off of his bright white shirt, making him glow like some paranormal fairy prince or something.

He smiles at me, encouraging me to let go and be free.

I close my eyes and do just that. I feel his hands at my waist. He doesn't guide me. Instead, he follows.

I wasn't looking forward to this, didn't think it was my thing, but suddenly I'm glad he brought me here.

For the moment, I'm not the girl who needed a transplant and he's not the guy who lost his brother. We're just Willa and Jasper, existing as we always should have.

The music changes and our bodies adjust to the new beat.

I feel his lips at my ear.

"Open your eyes," he whispers.

I do, slowly, and feel as if I'm looking upon a whole new world.

The rainbow hue of lights reflects in his eyes as he lowers his head toward me.

"I want to kiss you," he confesses.

Boldly, I say, "Then why don't you?"

His lips tilt up in the smallest of grins before they're pressed against mine. My eyes flutter closed and a tiny sound, completely muffled by the thundering music, escapes me. My whole body melts into him, my arms wrapping around his neck and my chest pressed to his.

The ever-changing hue of lights flash behind my closed lids, making me feel as if I've been transported to another dimension. Maybe I have for all I know.

His lips coax against mine and my lips part.

This is how people are kissed in movies. Passionately with all the air being stolen from the room. It's never how I imagined I'd be kissed, but here I am living it because I took a leap of faith.

Our lips break apart and he rests his forehead against mine, breathing heavily. My hips move to the song, his hands still there following my movements.

"Who are you?" he whispers so low I can barely hear him.

"What do you mean?" I take a deep breath, trying to get enough oxygen to my brain.

"I've never met anyone like you … someone that … that makes me *feel* like this." He removes one hand from my waist and presses it to his chest.

"I know what you mean," I admit, blinking up at him.

"It's strange," he continues. "But it's right."

"It's right," I echo, because it *is*.

So much about us doesn't make sense, but there's no denying the connection that's there. It's more than my transplant, and his brother, there's something about us that has always clicked since that very first time I saw him. Since before I knew his name.

We dance to several more songs before we decide to stop for a break.

Jasper guides me to a round barstool table and I hop up onto one of the chairs.

"I'll get us some water," he says, before disappearing into the crowd.

I take a moment to catch my breath while he's gone. Sweat dampens my brow, and I worry about the state of the makeup Meredith applied—but not enough to go check.

It isn't long until Jasper returns with a glass of water for the both of us.

I slurp it down greedily and he chuckles.

"Remind me to hydrate you more often." He winks, sliding his own glass toward me.

I blush. "I'm supposed to drink loads of water, because … you know … *transplant*, but I find I want to drink all the time now anyway." I shrug and finish off his water while he crunches on a piece of ice from mine.

"How are you liking it?" he asks, motioning to the club.

"I love it," I admit, tucking a loose hair behind my ear. "I never imagined myself liking a place like this, but I do."

His answering smile is blinding. As much as he insisted I'd like this he was still unsure.

"Do you want to dance some more?" he asks.

I nod, and he stands, holding out a hand to me. I slip my hand into his marveling at the contrast of his tanned skin against my pale one.

Back on the dance floor we fall into the rhythm.

All too soon, our night has to come to an end since my dad insisted I be home by midnight like some masquerading Cinderella.

Jasper leads me out of the club and I shiver when the breezy night air hits my heated skin. He tosses his arm around me, drawing me close to his warm body.

I curl against him.

Safe.

Secure.

I could get used to this.

He unlocks the Jeep and helps me inside.

When he gets inside he doesn't start it right away. Instead, he leans across the center console. Our eyes meet like stars crossing paths in the night sky.

He reaches up, his hand cupping my cheek. It's funny how much larger his hand is than my face. His eyes flick down to my lips and my heart skips a beat. It picks up speed when he kisses me.

If I get to kiss him for the rest of my life, I hope it's always like this.

When he pulls away, I breathe, "What was that for?"

"Because I wanted to." He grins. "And," he begins with a shrug, "because I figure your father will be watching with his face pressed to the window when I drop you off."

I smile. "That's a very good reason."

He starts the car and puts it in drive before holding out his hand to me.

I look at it stupidly for a moment before I take it. His hand curls around mine, making me feel small and protected.

The drive home is too short, and I find myself sad when he parks outside the front walk.

Sure enough, I can see my dad's shadow hanging near the windows by the front door. I glance at the dashboard; the vivid green lights shine back a resounding 11:56pm.

"Will I see you tonight? On the beach?" I add unnecessarily.

He shakes his head.

"Why not?"

He smiles, tucking that stubborn piece of hair behind my ear. "Because, tonight I'll be able to sleep."

"Why tonight?"

"Because right now, only you fill my thoughts and nothing bad can bring me down from this high."

"Oh," I whisper into the darkness.

"I'll walk you to the door." He undoes his seatbelt and gets out.

He helps me out, which is unnecessary since I ditched the heels the second I was in the Jeep and now clasp them in my hands. I quickly shrug into the jacket, hoping my dad hasn't spied what I'm wearing from the window.

We walk side by side up the walkway, careful not to touch since we have an audience—an audience I'm sure that thinks they can't be seen, since I also spy my sister and Meredith watching from upstairs.

Jasper kisses my cheek. "Thank you for coming tonight."

"Thank you for asking me."

Thank you for asking me? God, Willa, that sounds pathetic. Could you be any more helpless when it comes to dating? Read a book on it or something.

"I'll see you back on the beach tomorrow, right?" he asks. "No offense, but you need *a lot* more surf lessons."

I snort—so attractive, I know. "Am I that bad or do you just want to spend time with me?"

His lips tilt up on one corner. "A little bit of both."

I smile back. "Well, I'll take that. Goodnight."

I give him a small wave and then I open the door, stepping into my house.

"Hi, Dad."

"What? Who? Me? Hi." He peeks back around the wall that separates the foyer.

I shake my head and laugh before starting up the stairs. My feet are sore, but I don't even care.

I barely cross the threshold of my room when Meredith and Harlow inundate me with questions.

But I answer them all with a smile because I can safely say this was the best night of my life.

CHAPTER TWENTY-ONE

I roll over and get a face full of blonde hair. Opening my eyes, I spot Harlow passed out beside me, sleeping like nothing in the world could possibly wake her up.

Rolling to the other side I smile when I see Meredith on the floor in a sleeping bag, her red hair fanned around her. When we were little I was convinced she was Ariel from *The Little Mermaid* and kept waiting for her to grow fins. Unfortunately, she never did.

Beside Meredith, curled on his side, is Perry—snoring like a grown man.

I can't help but smile. I love my sister and best friend so much and even that crazy dog.

Easing up my sheet and blanket I slip from the bed and tiptoe across the room to my bathroom. I freshen up and, when I come out, the girls are stirring.

"Morning," Harlow says, sitting up and stretching her arms.

"Ugh, can we sleep all day?" Meredith asks, rolling over in her sleeping bag and clutching her pillow to her chest.

"Well," I begin, heading to my closet, "Jasper invited me to surf again today, that's what I'm doing. Do you guys want to go?"

"I'm in," Harlow says, rolling out of my bed. "Spencer said he's going to be at the beach today, I can hang with him."

"And what am I? Chopped liver?" Meredith scoffs. "So much for hanging with my girls this summer. You both go and get boyfriends and I turn out to be the single one. What kind of stupidness is this? I'm hot, I deserve love too."

"He's not my boyfriend," Harlow and I say together and both laugh.

"Whatever, they're close enough to it. But fine, I'll go too."

"I can ask Jasper if his friends are going?" I suggest.

Meredith perks up. "Hot college boys? Um, *yas*, girl."

I shake my head and grab a swimsuit, shorts, and a tank to change into. Harlow heads to her room to change and Meredith takes over my bathroom.

After I'm dressed, Perry follows me downstairs to make breakfast.

My dad sits in his chair drinking his coffee and reading the newspaper. I told him once that he could get the newspaper on his iPad and he looked at me like I just killed all his hopes and dreams.

"You girls going out today?" he asks, not bothering to look up from behind the newspaper.

"Yeah, to the beach," I say, pulling out the carton of eggs. "Are you hungry?" I ask.

"Yeah, what are you making?" he asks.

"I was going to do omelets."

"That sounds good."

I pull my phone from my pocket and turn my music on so that it's not completely quiet while I make breakfast.

I make an omelet for me and the girls, my dad, and my mom.

"That smells delicious," my mom says, coming down the stairs, the girls behind her. Everybody greedily grabs a plate. My mom sits down at the kitchen table and we all join her, even Dad who reluctantly puts down his newspaper.

"Willa, I wanted to remind you," my mom begins, "you have a doctor's appointment at the hospital Tuesday. I took off to take you."

I nod—I haven't forgotten. I'm down to the monthly checks right now, and while everything has been looking good I still can't help but worry. I'm not sure the fear will ever go away, especially with knowing it's inevitable that this kidney fails too. I know I have to live in the moment, and right now everything is great, but sometimes I can't help but go to that dark place.

"Maybe we can get lunch together while we're out?" she suggests. "Harlow, you can come too if you want."

"Sounds good to me," I agree, and Harlow nods, her mouth full of food.

We finish breakfast and the girls and I clean up. Once everything is clean I send Jasper a text letting him know Meredith and my sister are coming—and I hint that it'd be much appreciated if he invited a friend so Meredith is occupied.

Since it's still early, I rope the girls into helping me clean my room since *most* of the mess is their cause.

Meredith grumbles the whole time, as per usual. I'm used to her whining at this point that once she starts I tune her out.

Harlow turns on some music while we clean—and you guessed it, it's her K-pop boys. The songs are catchy, and I'm afraid she's going to suck me fully down the rabbit hole.

Once my room is clean, Meredith insists on redoing her makeup.

"You do realize we're going to be outside. In the sun. Where it's hot. And you sweat," I deadpan.

She rolls her eyes. "That doesn't mean I can't attempt to look my best. Plus, have you ever heard of the word *waterproof*?"

With a swish of her hips she disappears into my bathroom once more while I shake my head.

Harlow flops onto my bed and Perry joins her. He looks up at me with his big brown eyes, giving me a sad look. He's already figured out that we're leaving and he wants us to stay or take him with us.

"Sorry, Perry, you have to stay here today. I'll take you for ice cream tomorrow."

He perks up at that, wagging his tongue.

Out of the corner of my eye I see movement and jump. Calming back down, I mutter, "It's your stupid cat," to Harlow.

"Aw, Webber, come here. Did you miss Mommy?" Harlow coos at the cat as he sneaks into my room, looking this way and that like he's being followed.

Weirdest cat ever.

She picks up the cat, who glares at Perry. Perry just pants and wags his tail, not at all bothered by the mutant cat.

I watch in astonishment as the cat's tiny pink tongue flicks out and licks the side of Harlow's face. She giggles and hugs him closer. The cat's eyes land on me and I swear he looks at me like he wants to murder me. I shiver in response. It's silly, but I'm afraid of my sister's cat. He's abnormal.

When Meredith is finally done getting ready we head to the beach. It's still a little early, but this way we can sit and have some more girl time before the guys show up.

Meredith and Harlow fight over who gets shotgun—I don't know why it matters. My car is so small that the backseat is practically in the front. Meredith ends up winning and Harlow slides glumly into the backseat.

"Can we get coffee first?" Meredith asks, slipping on her sunglasses—some designer monstrosity I think looks stupid but she insists is in fashion. She should know; she's way more into that stuff than I am.

"Yeah, sure. I wouldn't mind one myself."

I head to our favorite place, Cool Beans, because when you want coffee there's nowhere else to go.

I park on the street since there's an open spot and we head inside. Meredith places her order first and then Harlow and I follow.

Since we're not staying we don't sit down at a table and instead stand off to the side to wait for our orders.

I feel someone step up behind me and I can't help but look.

I gasp, and Jasper smiles down on me. "Are you following me?" he asks, his smile turning mischievous.

"N-No of course not," I stutter, shaking my head.

"I'm kidding," he says, putting me out of my misery.

"What are you doing here?" I ask.

"It's the best coffee in town." He shrugs, shoving his hands in the pockets of his cargo shorts. "*And* my parents kind of own the place," he adds.

"Oh," I mouth. "I forgot."

He chuckles. "Are you guys already headed to the beach?" I nod in answer to his question. "I have to help out here for a bit, but I'll text you when I'm on my way there. And …" He lowers his voice and crouches down so his mouth is level with my ear. "I promise one of my friends will be there to entertain your friend."

"Thank you."

He smiles and tips his head at Meredith and Harlow before heading toward the back of the shop and around the counter.

Meredith bumps my shoulder with hers. "He is so hot, seriously. I'm proud of you, girl."

I shake my head. "That's not why I like him, you know."

She rolls her eyes. "Of course I know you're all about *substance*, but it doesn't hurt that he looks like a Calvin Klein model, either. I mean, those biceps? *Damn.*"

I'm saved from replying by our drinks being ready. I grab my iced coffee and stick a straw into the cup before taking a sip. Like always, it tastes like heaven. I wonder what they do that makes it so good.

We head out and pile back into my car to go to the beach.

Once there we gather our stuff—the usual, towels, magazines for Meredith, my book, our drinks, and totes we have pre-filled with things like sunscreen, hats, lotion, and a change of clothes if need be.

We walk along the beach, scouting for the best place. It's busy, but not as crazy as it can be at times. We eventually find a spot and lay out our things. On my one side, Meredith stretches out on her stomach, flipping through a Cosmopolitan magazine. On the other, Harlow lies on her side, facing me but looking at her phone. I wiggle around and get comfortable, lying on my back with my book held above me.

I have a little trouble focusing on the book, and if I'm honest it's because my mind is preoccupied with thoughts of Jasper. While I *do* want to learn to surf, I honestly just want to spend more time with him. With him I'm myself—a self I didn't even know existed, but who has been there all along begging to break free.

"Is that book not any good?" Harlow asks from beside me, her brow raised.

I jolt and look over at her. "It's not the book, it's me," I admit.

Meredith sits up, tilting her sunglasses down so we can see her eyes. "You're thinking about lover boy, aren't you?"

"Don't call him that," I scoff.

She gives me a patronizing look. "You might be blind to it, but I've seen the way he looks at you. I don't know what kind of freaky voodoo love spell you've put him under but it must be strong as hell."

"You know I haven't put him under a love spell," I grumble.

She lifts a brow. "You barely know the guy and yet you both act like you've been in love for ages."

"We're not in love," I defend. "But …"

"But what?" she prompts.

"He's different."

"Ugh." She rolls onto her back and sits up. "How would you know? He's the first guy you've ever taken interest in."

My cheeks heat at her condescending tone. Like somehow because I haven't been around a few times I don't know what I'm talking about.

"That's not fair and you know it," I grit out through clenched teeth. "Besides, I'd hardly count you as qualified. Losing your virginity to our junior year fill-in math teacher doesn't mean you know any more than me. In fact, I think it means less, because you're always looking for *love* in the wrong places."

She breathes out heavily, her eyes brimming with hurt.

"Meredith," I breathe out, instantly feeling bad for all the words that spilled out of my mouth. Words that have hurt and cut her deeper than any others, words that I cannot take back now that they're out there. "I'm so sorry."

She stands. "I'm going to get ice cream."

Her hair swishes over her shoulders as she walks away from us.

Harlow lets out a low whistle. "That was harsh."

"I know." I frown, hurting as deeply as my friend. I can't believe I said that to her. She'd gotten under my ski and the venom had come spewing out. Why is it that the ones we love the most are the ones we invariably hurt the most?

"She'll get over it," Harlow promises.

"I know," I say again.

As best friends we fight, we make up, we move on. It's what we do. But that doesn't mean it hurts any less when we're on the outs.

"I'm going to go walk for a bit," I tell Harlow, standing and brushing sand off my shorts. Even with a towel spread out, it still manages to get on my butt.

"Okay," she agrees, knowing I want to be alone.

I head toward the ocean and then walk along it, watching how my shoes get stuck in the wet sand. My long blonde hair swirls around my shoulders from the breeze. I bat it away like it's a nuisance. My stomach feels like a heavy pit as I play over what I said to Meredith. I could smack myself in the head for my stupidity. Meredith might not readily air her insecurities, but as her best friend, I've taken notice. And when it comes to guys, she always picks the wrong, most unavailable guy, like she's purposely looking for heartbreak. I know she sees what she does to herself, but she also seems helpless to stop it. I know I'm not in love with Jasper, not yet at least, but I wish Meredith could find someone she connects with like I do with him. I wish she'd realize *that's* more special than someone showering you with gifts so they can get in your pants.

But some things you just can't tell a person and they have to eventually learn it for themselves.

I've been walking for at least ten minutes when a voice calls out to me.

"Willa! Hey, Willa!" I look around wildly expecting to see Jasper and instead my eyes land on Spencer, waving as he jogs toward me.

"Hey," he says, falling into step beside me, not a bit out of breath.

"Hi," I say, my voice rather glum.

"Are you okay?" he inquires, picking up on my tone.

"Fight with Meredith," I supply with a shrug that says *whatcha gonna do?*

"Ah, I see." He nods, his shaggy hair blowing away from his forehead. "I was looking for Harlow," he admits.

"She's back that way." I point behind us. "She's got on a yellow shirt and by now she's probably blasting K-pop. You can't miss her."

He chuckles. "You guys will make up. You and Meredith."

"I know. That doesn't mean I don't feel like a colossal idiot for what I said."

"We're all idiots now and then. It's human nature."

"Thanks."

"Anytime." He grins boyishly and heads off in search of my sister.

I suck in a lungful of air, thankful to be alone once more. I walk a little further and find a less busy part of the beach. Sitting down, I kick off my shoes and dig my bare feet into the sand, draping my arms over my knees. I watch the ocean, like I do often, and it fills me with calm. The ocean is one of the steadiest constants in my life. I can always count on it to be there when I need it.

The sun shines brightly, glimmering on the blue-gray water like a bunch of glitter. It isn't long until I start to feel better—not perfect, but better.

My phone buzzes in my pocket and I'm not surprised to see it's Jasper telling me he's here. He tells me where he parked and I get up to meet him there so I can change into a wetsuit.

I hadn't realized just how far I'd walked from the main crowd so it takes me a little while to get to where he's parked. When I do, he's already unloaded the surfboards and has them leaning against his Jeep. His wetsuit hangs on his hips, ready to be put on fully and zipped up.

He smiles when he sees me but that smile quickly turns to a frown.

"Are you okay? What happened?"

I wave a dismissive hand. "Meredith and I got into a little fight. It's not a big deal."

"Your face says different."

"You notice everything, don't you?"

He shrugs. "It's hard not to when you wear your emotions openly on your face—that's not a bad thing," he adds when I pull a disgusted face. He leans against the Jeep and tilts his head. "What happened?"

I sigh. "I don't want to talk about it."

"Okay," he agrees, and straightens.

My mouth parts in stunned silence. "That's it? You're not going to press me to talk about it?"

"No." He shakes his head. "Sometimes we all need time to process things through our own mind in our own way. If you want to talk about it with me, you will. And if you don't that's okay too."

I stare at him in wonder.

How on Earth did I get so lucky to have someone like this come into my life?

My conscience then reminds me, *you were very unlucky before it was time something good came along. You deserve to be happy even if you don't feel like it.*

"Heath—my friend—already went to find her, I told him what she looks like, maybe he can cheer her up." He shrugs and then holds up a wetsuit. "Ready to suit up?"

I nod and take it from him. I step out of my shorts and take off my tank, laying them on the seat of his Jeep for safekeeping. It's a struggle to get into the wetsuit, but I manage with Jasper's help. I'm not sure I'll ever get used to the way they literally suction to your skin.

"Ready?" he asks with a smile.

"Ready," I echo.

He carries both boards—Lord knows I'm too small to manage one—and I walk along beside him. I struggle to keep up with his long-legged strides.

When we near the water, he stops and finally gives me the board.

"Remember what to do?"

"Yeah, I got this part down." I laugh. "It's catching and riding a wave that I'm not sure I'll ever master."

He chuckles warmly. "You've only been out *one* time before today. Give yourself a break. I didn't learn overnight, and neither will you. The best things take time and effort. If something is easy that feeling of being proud of your accomplishment doesn't last nearly as long."

"That's true," I agree, because he's right.

We carry our boards out into the water and when it's about waist deep on me I lay down my board and climb on top, paddling out.

Jasper goes over his same instructions and then we wait for a small wave to come around.

"I had fun last night," I tell him as we bob in the water.

He grins over at me. "Good."

"It was … different for me, but I'm glad I stepped out of my comfort zone. You make me brave even when I'm not."

His turquoise-colored eyes darken like storm clouds are covering them and I can't help but shiver.

"You make me brave too, you know," he confesses as people around us holler. Somehow, even with all the chaos, it feels like only the two of us exist right here in this moment. "You make me realize it's okay to hurt, but I don't have to hurt all the time. It's okay to miss my brother, and while he's gone in the physical sense, he's not *gone*. He'll always be with me." He touches a hand to his heart. "I know it'll probably be a long time before I'm my normal self all the time, but here, with you, I feel like me and that means more than you can ever know. I don't know what it is about you that's so right for me, but you are, right for me, that is. I know it's crazy, we don't know each other that well yet, but we will. I know it."

"I get what you mean," I whisper, feeling choked up because he's expressed everything I feel and now I don't feel so crazy.

This isn't a case of love at first sight.

It's more than that.

Deeper.

It doesn't mean we're crazy, or that this is that dreaded insta-love I hate reading about, it just means we have a connection that transcends the rational. When you think about it and pay attention, there's nothing much that's rational about *anything* in this world. We just delude ourselves into believing it is.

"I think this is your wave," Jasper says, his words breaking into my thoughts.

I watch the small swell about to form and start paddling.

Jasper yells out directions to me and I only half listen. I let my body guide me. I know what to do even if I haven't accomplished it yet.

You can do this, Willa. You can and when you do it'll feel amazing.

I take a slow breath and let it out, turning the board and feeling the ocean swell behind me. I slowly come to stand on the board, my arms held out at my sides for balance. My legs are wobbly, and it's definitely not graceful, but I somehow manage to remain upright on the wave for ten seconds before I lose my balance and plunge into the chilly water.

I surface, pushing my wet hair from my eyes.

"Did you see that?" I scream at Jasper, the biggest smile ever on my face.

He dives off his board, swimming toward me. It bobs behind him, connected to his ankle.

He pops up right in front of me, smiling as big as I am.

"You're amazing."

I startle when he grabs my face and kisses me.

He pulls back, still smiling. "I'm so proud of you. Now it's time to prep you for a bigger wave."

My smile falls. "A bigger wave?" I mumble hesitantly. "I was only on this baby wave for a few seconds."

"A few seconds is more than enough to change everything."

My heart catches at his words.

"What do you mean?"

He shrugs, and I notice the way the water clings to his long lashes. "You can learn a lot in a few seconds. I know it doesn't seem that way, but you can. Your body learns."

"All right." I nod, grabbing my board and resting my arms on it. "Let's get back to it, Sensei."

Hours later we emerge from the water, tired, but unable to stop smiling. I walk with Jasper back to his Jeep so I can change from the wetsuit back into my clothes.

His friend waits near the Jeep texting on his phone. His sandy blond hair is on the longer side, hanging past his ears, and a couple days' worth of scruff covers his cheeks. He seems like the kind of guy Meredith would be all over so I hope he was able to find her and when I get back to where we laid out our towels maybe she'll feel like talking. I hate knowing she's mad at me.

Jasper loads the surfboards onto the Jeep and I watch—you know, in case he needs help, it's not like I'm staring at his biceps or anything.

When he finishes loading them I decide to broach something. "How are you doing? With … everything."

His smile disappears and his eyes grow sad. "It still sucks. Every time I think about him my chest gets tight and I can't breathe." He grabs at his chest to demonstrate. "Some days, I wake up and for a split second I forget he's dead, but then it all comes rushing back and it hurts like hell. I've accepted that I'm not going to get over his death easily, if ever, but I am learning that I can have moments where everything is okay and I'm happy and I can have moments where I'm sad and angry too."

My body feels heavy with the burden of the truth I've yet to tell. A truth that feels impossible to let slip the more time passes.

"I wish I'd known him better," I whisper.

Although, if I had known T.J. better that would make this all the more difficult.

He nods. "I wish you had too. You should come over one day—I can show you our old family albums and tell you about him. Only … only if you want," he stutters.

"I'd like that."

As much as it'll feel like torture, I can tell Jasper needs this, and I think I do too.

"Good." He smiles, but it's not carefree and happy like it was moments before when we were walking up to the Jeep. I felt like I had to bring T.J. up. Since yesterday and today we had so much fun I didn't want him to forget that I'm here for him to talk to if he needs to.

I change into my clothes and place my wetsuit with his in the back seat.

"I better get going," he says.

"Yeah, I better find Harlow … and Meredith."

"I'll see you." Before I can blink he bends and kisses me.

I can't get over how simple and easy it is kissing him. I always thought it must be weird in a new relationship, not knowing when or if you should kiss the other person, but with him, it's always right.

Heath laughs. "Gonna kiss your girl but not introduce me? Shame on you, Werth."

Jasper punches him in the shoulder. "Shut up," he growls. "This is Willa."

"Nice to meet you, Willa." Heath holds out a hand and I shake it. He smiles, his teeth bright, white, and even.

"Nice to meet you," I echo, blushing. I'd completely forgotten he was there.

"Don't let him rattle you," Jasper tells me. "He likes to embarrass people."

"Mhmm," I hum. "Well, I better go."

I walk away, waving over my shoulder, and head to where I left Harlow much earlier, hoping my embarrassment stays behind.

Our towels are still here, but nobody else is. I look around and spot Harlow running away from Spencer, her laughter echoing around her like music.

He catches up to her and loops one arm around her torso, picking her up. She kicks her legs wildly, both of them laughing, and they fall into the sand, her on top of him.

I can't help but smile. They're cute together.

My jaw drops when Spencer tucks a piece of hair behind her ear and then leans up, kissing her.

I think I just saw my little sister get her first kiss.

I can't help feeling a little giddy.

Quickly, before they can spot me, I plop on my towel and grab my book.

Pretending to read I finally put it down when their shadows approach.

"You're back," Harlow says, slightly out of breath.

I close my book and look up. "I'm back."

Spencer smiles sheepishly and I swear his cheeks are flushed—probably figuring I caught them.

"Where's Meredith?" I ask.

Harlow's face falls. "She called her mom to pick her up so she went home."

"Oh." My body is suddenly seized by a piercing pain. "She was upset, wasn't she?" I mumble.

"Yeah," Harlow admits with a sad look.

I exhale a sigh. "I hate it when we fuck up."

"We all do it now and then," Spencer says. "We're only human."

"We better head home," I tell Harlow.

She glances at Spencer, her cheeks tinged pink, and then she looks back at me. "Yeah, you're right. It's getting late. I'll … uh … see you later."

He chuckles and bends, kissing her cheek. "Later." He winks at her and walks away.

I look up at Harlow and see she's watching him go.

"Spill," I tell her.

She plops down beside me, unable to get rid of her smile. "I don't know what it is about him, but we … click."

"I get that, believe me."

"Did you … uh … see what happened?" she hedges.

"*Yes*," I draw out, urging her to tell me more.

She lets out a dreamy sigh. "I didn't expect him to kiss me, but oh, my God, Willa, it was everything I could've ever hoped for in a first kiss. It … it scares me, you know. I'm only going to be a junior in high school and he's going off to college. Where can this go?"

I shrug. "Don't overthink it right now. He's a good guy. See where things go and then decide what you want to do."

She lays her head on my shoulder. "You're right."

"Of course I am," I joke. "Big sisters are bestowed with a wealth of knowledge."

We gather up our stuff to head home, and I spend the entire time thinking about how I can apologize to Meredith.

CHAPTER TWENTY-TWO

I have a fitful night of sleep—due in part to my own anxieties and the fact that Meredith currently hates my guts.

At seven in the morning, I finally get up and shower, knowing sleep is a lost cause at this point. I dress in a pair of ripped jeans with the bottoms rolled up, a striped top, and my white Converse sneakers. The house is quiet, no one else up yet, so I write a note and head out.

I drive around for a little while, my windows rolled down with my hair whipping around my shoulders, and allow myself to think.

Eventually, I stop at one of Meredith and my favorite breakfast joints and order us each an egg and cheese sandwich on a croissant as well as coffee. I grab the paper bag when it's ready and place our coffees in a drink carrier so I don't have to worry about spilling them on the way to my car.

I reach my car and set everything inside, making sure there's no chance it can go flying.

On the drive to Meredith's house, I think about what I should say or do, but nothing sounds good enough and in the end, I decide to roll with it and hope for the best.

Twenty minutes later I park outside her Spanish-style house. The landscaping is pristine thanks to the company who comes once a week to mow and maintain everything.

I take a breath, bracing myself for her possible wrath. I'd deserve it.

I grab the coffee and bag of food, walking slowly up the walkway to the front door.

Pressing my finger to the doorbell, I wait.

Normally, I'd walk right on in—I have a key.

But not today. I don't have any right to let myself in uninvited.

The door swings open and Meredith stands there in a fluffy white robe cinched at the waist overtop a pale pink tank and her favorite pair of pajama bottoms with eggs on them.

She sighs and leans against the doorway. "Come to belittle me some more?"

Shaking my head, I hold out the bag of food. "No, just swinging by with a peace offering." I give the bag a small shake.

She presses her lips together for a second before stepping aside to allow me inside.

Well, at least that's a good sign.

I follow her through the house and up the curved staircase to her room.

Meredith's room looks like something straight out of a Pottery Barn magazine. Shiny dark wood floors, gray walls that shimmer when the sunlight hits it, and mismatched furniture that somehow looks cohesive with a Parisian style.

She plops on her unmade bed, leaning back against the tufted headboard.

"Give me the food and coffee and start talking. I expect lots of 'I'm sorrys' followed by 'I love you, Merebitch, and from now on I'll remember you're the only bad bitch in this group who can say rude things.'"

I hand her the sandwich and the coffee before sitting on the end of her bed and getting my own food.

"I am sorry," I begin. "So sorry. I don't know why I said that, I never should have. I know how awful you felt after that and I *never* should've brought it up."

She looks at me sadly and nods. "Thank you. And … I have a confession to make."

"What?" I tilt my head.

"I haven't had sex since then."

My jaw drops. "Wait … *what?*"

She shakes her head. "It wasn't exactly pleasant and made me feel dirty and used, so I haven't had sex since then." She shrugs like it's no big deal, but I can see the depth of emotion in her eyes and understand that this is a very big deal

"But you always have all these crazy stories."

She shrugs. "In school, it was the cool thing. It's stupid, but it's true. And I know you're not like that, but it was easy to keep the charade going. The truth is, I'm not like that at all. Especially after what happened. I realize now what an intimate part of myself I shared with someone who didn't matter, and I can never take that back. I'm not saying you have to be twenty-five before you lose your virginity, but no matter when it is, it should be with someone you care about. There are no take backs. No do-overs. Once it's done it's done."

"Oh, Meredith," I breathe.

"Don't feel sorry for me, seriously don't. I made a bad choice, but I learned from it. It hurt when you brought it up yesterday because I could see the judgment in your eyes because you believed all the lies I'd told. But even if I had done all that, I still shouldn't be judged for it."

"You're right," I admit.

She holds out her coffee cup. "We're good now."

"We're good," I echo, and bump my cup against hers.

Somehow, I guess to make up for my being a bitch, I let Meredith talk me into going to the mall.

It's not that I mind shopping, I like it *sometimes*, but with Meredith it usually turns into an all-day excursion where I fall into bed dead tired at the end of it.

We walk into the mall and Meredith stops dead in her tracks inhaling a big breath.

"Do you smell that?"

"Um … no?"

She smirks. "It's the smell of the smoke that's going to be coming off of my credit card when I'm done here."

I shake my head. "Your parents were so dumb to add you to their account."

She shrugs. "They haven't regretted it yet, so let's put it to good use."

She grabs my hand and begins dragging me around from store to store, dressing me like I'm some sort of project of hers—which I have to face it, *I am.* Meredith has been trying to style me a whole new wardrobe for years. I guess now she's decided she'll have to buy it for me.

She holds up a white shirt with a yellow daisy print.

"This would be cute on you." She piles it into my arms with the other garments she's deemed worthy.

"Meredith, seriously, stop it. I can't afford this and you don't need to be buying it for me on your parents' credit card."

"Oh, shush," she hushes me, already perusing another rack.

"Meredith—" I start again.

She glares at me. "This is still you making up for yesterday so zip your lips."

"How is you buying me stuff a part of me making up to you? I'm lost."

She sighs, clearly exasperated. "Because you're my Barbie doll for the day."

"Oh no, no, no, *no*," I chant.

She glares, her eyes narrowed. I'm sure if she had laser vision I'd be fried right about now.

"You owe me," is all she says, before turning back to the rack.

I whimper. I'm in for it. I know it.

An hour later we leave that store, laden down with bags. Thankfully, it's not all for me and she did splurge on herself some. Unfortunately, I know she's far from done shopping, so I brace myself for the rest of the day.

"Come on, Meredith. My arms are killing me," I whine, dragging bags along the ground since I'm too weak to carry them.

"I'm done, I'm done," she declares, "but we have to eat first."

I perk up at the mention of food. We skipped lunch and it's now dinnertime so my body is begging for sustenance.

"And, since you've been *so* good today, I'm taking you to the Cheesecake Factory."

"Mmm, cheesecake," I hum in delight.

Thankfully, the Cheesecake Factory is attached to the mall so we don't have to go far. Plus, sitting down and eating will give my arms and legs a break. After a small wait we're seated—we have to pile all the bags on one side of the booth and sit side by side.

I grab the menu, which feels like it's about a hundred pages long. I don't know why they give so many choices for indecisive people like me. It's like they're asking us to sit here for an hour before we finally give up, go eenie meenie minnie mo, and pick something random off the menu.

Maybe that is *what they want.*

When the waiter stops by we both ask for a water and he drops off some bread—which I immediately devour. Meredith might want some but I don't care. If I don't get food in me now she's going to have to explain why I'm dead to my parents and I don't think after what I've been through that *shopped till she dropped* would be a good enough excuse.

Meredith reaches for a piece of bread and I swat her hand away.

"Mine," I growl.

"Fine." She rolls her eyes. "You sure turn into a she-beast when you're hungry. I'm the one with red hair, shouldn't that be me?"

"Mine," I say again, guarding the bread.

She sighs and our waiter drops off our drinks, taking our order while he's there.

As he walks away, Meredith says, "Don't judge me, but I sure do love those tight white pants they wear. Is it a requirement for the people who work here to have buns of steel?"

I snort and pieces of bread go flying out of my mouth.

"Ick," she clucks her tongue. "That was gross."

"Then don't make me laugh when food is in my mouth," I retort, wiping my mouth on a napkin. "It's not like I enjoy spitting my food everywhere."

I grab for another piece of bread and slather it with butter.

Oh, butter, how I love thee.

Meredith chats about some of the different clothes she picked out for me and how I need to style them—I'm only half listening, but she doesn't seem to notice as I interject the necessary "hmm" and "I see" as needed.

"Here you ladies go," our waiter says, setting down our plates of food.

I inhale the smell of my salmon and my mouth waters at the sight of the mashed potatoes and asparagus. You'd think after all the bread I gorged myself on I'd be stuffed, but I'm still hungry—I'll definitely be taking my cheesecake home for later.

"So," Meredith begins, twirling her pasta around her fork, "admit it, you've had fun today."

"I have—but you seriously didn't need to buy me anything, you're flat out nuts."

She shrugs. "Actually, I'm flat out awesome." She sticks her tongue out at me.

"That too," I agree.

"I think I've decided that's what I'm passionate about—styling," she clarifies. "I love shopping for people and putting things together you might not otherwise think to put together."

"Well, you're pretty great at that," I praise, and she smiles.

"You're really not starting college in the fall?" she asks.

Growing up, before my disease, we always dreamed of going to college together and living in a tiny apartment that was all our own.

I shake my head. "I need time to figure everything out. I know the first year is basic classes, but … it doesn't feel right to go yet," I explain.

She nods. "I understand. Still, it'll be weird without you."

"Oh, please." I roll my eyes. "You'll be home every weekend because you miss me so much."

She laughs and points her fork at me. "Only in your dreams."

I toss my napkin at her and we both can't help laughing.

I think we both needed today. It's been too long since we've hung out with only the two of us.

We finish our meal, order our cheesecake to go, and head back to her house.

"Why don't you stay the night?" she suggests as she pulls her car into the driveway. "You can borrow some of my pajamas."

"Let me double check with my mom, but I don't see why not."

After a quick call to my mom where I get the okay—I may be eighteen but I have respect for my parents and I'm not going to stay gone all day and night and not ask for permission—Meredith and I unload the bags into her room.

I take a quick shower and change into a pair of her pajamas. When I step back into her room, all the bags of clothes have exploded all over her bed and floor.

She immediately begins going over, yet again, what pairs with what.

"Why don't you come over and dress me every day?" I joke, rubbing my damp hair with a towel.

"That's a good idea," she replies, dead serious.

"I was kidding."

"And I wasn't," she retorts, her tongue sticking out slightly between her lips as she thinks.

"Forget the clothes," I beg. "Let's put a movie on and relax. My feet are killing me."

"Fine," she agrees reluctantly and starts putting the clothes back in the bags.

After she showers and changes we put a movie on and pile into her bed, lying on our stomachs clutching pillows.

Meredith lays her head on her arms and tilts her head over to the side to see me. "I love that you're my best friend. We fight, we make up, and we move on. It's not the end of the world."

"I love that you're my best friend too."

I reach out my arms and hug her.

Sometimes it's the people you choose to love that are the best kind to have around.

CHAPTER TWENTY-THREE

I rush around my room, nearly falling over as I wiggle into a pair of jean shorts.

"Come on, girls, we have to go! We're going to be late!" my mom yells up the stairs, her tone showing her irritation.

"Coming," Harlow hollers back, and I hear her footsteps thunder down the hallway to the stairs.

I quickly button my shorts and grab a black and white striped cropped T-shirt—courtesy of Meredith.

Normally, I'm always ready to go and never running late, but I started a new book, got sucked in, and completely forgot to pay attention to the time. Before I knew it, my mom was yelling at us to hurry up.

I glance in the mirror and frown at my messy hair. It's beyond help and I hope I can play off the whole messy bohemian look or something. Shoving my feet into a pair of white Converse I grab my purse, the book that got me in trouble, and dash down the stairs nearly tripping on my untied shoelaces.

"Let's go, let's go, let's go," my mom chants, clapping her hands for good measure and ushering the two of us to her car.

Harlow darts past me and screams, "Shotgun."

"Fine by me." I slide into the back of the car and stretch my legs out on the black leather seats. I open my book and hold onto my bookmark, planning to read on the drive.

My mom slides into the driver's seat, grumbling about our lateness, traffic, and God knows what else.

Harlow and I wisely choose to stay quiet.

Twenty minutes into the drive my phone buzzes and I grab it from my purse, finding a text from Jasper.

Jasper: Working at the coffee shop this morning—surfing later?

Willa: Can't, sorry. I have a doc appt. today. We'll be gone most of the day.

Jasper: Everything ok?

Willa: Yeah, they keep a close check.

Jasper: How about this weekend? Let's go to the pier.

Willa: Sounds fun.

Jasper: It's a date.

My cheeks flush with his last three words. It feels weird the way he so casually uses the word *date*. I guess with my inexperience it feels like such a big thing, and mostly, I never in a million years believed a guy like him would be interested in someone like me. That's probably everyone's biggest mistake—we always undervalue our own worth.

I put my phone back and return to reading my book while my mom grumbles about traffic, the weather, and probably aliens but at this point I'm not listening to her. Even Harlow has stuck her earphones in and is currently bobbing her head along to whatever she's listening to.

When we arrive at the hospital my mom parks in the parking garage and then ushers us quickly inside like we're small unruly children holding onto her legs and begging not to go.

I sign in and answer the same questions I always do about insurance, employment, and all that fun stuff. You'd think when you're here practically all the time they wouldn't have to ask these same questions, but they do.

Once the question and answer session is done I sit down with my mom and Harlow in the waiting room.

Looking around at the periwinkle blue walls, navy plastic couches and chairs, and numerous magazines littering the laminate coffee tables, I can't help but remember back to the first time I had to come here for a consultation to apply for the deceased donor waiting list.

I remember the way my heart beat too fast but too slow at the same time. How my palms grew damp and sweat prickled my forehead. I remember the fear, the fear of the doctors I'd yet to meet, the fear of the process, but mostly the fear of the unknown. I'd been thrust into this strange new reality where nothing made sense but was suddenly my whole life. I felt swallowed by it, completely suffocated; everywhere I looked there was a reminder of my failure. Of my body's failure to sustain my life, and how from now on my life would never be the same, and neither would my family's since I'd unwittingly dragged them into this with me. I didn't ask for this to happen, who would *want* this to happen, but I couldn't help feeling guilty that they were sucked into this with me. By the time they called my name at that first appointment, I was nearly ready to faint. I remember going through the whole appointment, meeting the nurse, social worker, dietician, surgeon—the whole team—and feeling like I was in a daze. I was there, processing information and asking questions, but it was also like I was watching it play out from someone else's perspective. As if, by detaching myself, I could somehow pretend this wasn't happening to me—that maybe I was watching a movie, because surely this wasn't real life. But it was real then, and it's real now, and it'll be real twenty years from now. This stuff happens *all* the time. To your friend, to your neighbor, to that person suffering silently in the grocery store that you pass by and don't even know how much they're hurting.

"Willa Hansen?"

The call of my name breaks me out of my thoughts and the three of us stand, heading to the door that leads us into the hallway.

After getting my blood pressure and weight, we're taken to a room with a table, four chairs, and your standard doctor's examination table.

I sit at the table, refusing to get on the exam table until I have to.

Even now, I always choose to have a few moments, sometimes even seconds, to pretend I'm normal—to pretend I'm not the one here to sit on that table, that I don't have someone else's organ in my body.

"You've been feeling okay, right?" my mom asks. "Taking your medicine like you're supposed to?" She licks her top lip, a habit I've learned she only does when she's nervous.

"Yes, of course," I say, mildly offended she'd assume otherwise, but I also know she gets like this every time we're here, panicking that something is going to be seriously wrong with me. I'm sure, for her, having witnessed how sick I was in the beginning, it's got to be scary thinking about me being like that again.

She rifles through her purse and pulls out a piece of gum—another sign she's nervous. She pops it into her mouth and chews madly, staring at the diagram on the wall showing how a kidney is transplanted.

Harlow's eyes connect with mine and she gives a small shake of her head as if to say, "She's crazy."

Minutes that feel like hours pass and my nurse comes in, asking the same standard questions they always do.

"How are you feeling?"

"How much are you feeling?"

"What's your activity level?"

"Are you eating? How's your diet?"

Over and over they go, and I shoot out my answers sounding like a robot as she enters each answer into her handy dandy iPad. She finishes up with me, saying the doctor will be in soon.

I let out a breath, relieved this visit is almost over.

Before my transplant, I didn't have to come often which was nice, but now, the checks are frequent and while I understand the need for that, and am even thankful for it, that doesn't mean it's fun being here.

There's a knock on the door and Dr. Marks enters, spinning his pen between his fingers, which he quickly tucks behind his ear. He's dressed in a pair of tan slacks and a button-down shirt paired with bright red Converse.

"New shoes?" I joke, and he grins, pulling out the rolling stool.

"I decided I needed more than yellow." He shrugs and pushes his black-framed glasses further up his nose.

"How are you feeling?" he asks me, and I sigh loudly. He chuckles. "I'm sure you're sick of that question."

"I'm feeling great," I tell him. Which is true. "I have way more energy, I don't feel tired like I did or achy. I feel . . . alive. I'm sure that sounds weird, because of course I'm alive, I was alive then and I'm alive now, but . . . I don't know, I finally feel like for the first time ever I'm *living* and I believe there's a huge difference between being alive and living."

Dr. Marks stares at me for a moment, a slow smile forming on his face. "Willa, you are far wiser than your eighteen years and I don't know whether to be proud or afraid." He chuckles warmly. "You've been through more at your age than most people deal with in a lifetime. That's changed you—for some people they take that and change for the worse, being angry at the world for the cards they've been dealt, but not you. No, not you." He shakes his head. "You're quite remarkable."

"Thank you, I think," I laugh, and he does too.

"Hop up on the table and I'll take a look so you can be on your way."

I sigh and do as he says, unbuttoning my shorts so he can peek at my incision and feel around.

"Everything looks great. I'm happy with everything and your last blood work was excellent. We'll have you stop at the lab before you go to do a draw today and when I get the results I'll call you. If everything looks great I'll want you back in another month, if everything is still holding steady then we'll move it to every other month. Sound good?"

I nod, more than happy to agree to that.

"Good, good," he chants and holds out his hands to help my short ass down from the exam table. "Let me go write up your orders and I'll be right back with that—but first, any questions for me?" He looks from me, to my mom, and even my sister.

"She's all right then? The kidney is doing great?"

He nods. "Everything seems to be as we like to see it. The kidney has taken to her body amazingly well." He swivels his gaze to me. "But do not get any ideas and stop taking your anti-rejection medicine. If you stop, it *will* fail. Your body will attack and kill the organ."

"Trust me, that won't be happening."

He nods and smiles. "I know, but I have to remind everybody. Some people assume it won't happen to them."

I shrug. "Doc, if it wasn't going to happen to me my kidneys wouldn't have failed in the first place."

He laughs outright. "That's true. I'll be right back."

We're all silent as we wait. I don't know what it is but there's something about this place that always seems to rob us of our voice. Like if we speak the whole place might come crashing down around us.

Dr. Marks returns and hands me the slip of printed paper.

"I'm sure you know where the lab is." He winks.

"You aren't taking seventeen vials of blood from me today, are you?" I joke. That's happened before. I nearly fell flat on the floor when it was over.

He laughs. "No, not today, sorry."

"Thank God," I mumble.

"I'll call you with the results," he reminds me before leaving.

My mom picks up her bag and the three of us head out to the lab across the building.

There's a line of people waiting, so I get in the back of the line while Harlow and our mom try to find a place to sit.

As per usual, the line moves at a snail's pace. Hospitals are severely understaffed. It's ridiculous.

By the time it's my turn, the lady working the front looks ready to cry.

I smile pleasantly at her and try to, hopefully, brighten her day a little. I get irritated having to wait, but I also realize it's usually not the staff's fault. But that's not always the case.

Once she has my information entered into the system I'm instructed to wait my turn again.

I sit down between my mom and sister, who are both occupied on their phones. I choose to read my book while I wait. Reading, for me, always passes the time way faster.

Of course, I've reached one of the best parts when my name is called. It always happens, without fail.

Slipping my bookmark into my book, I stand and follow the lady back to the small closed off room with the lone gray chair and loads of vials for blood.

She consults her paperwork and begins printing off the labels and sticking them on the vials.

When she finishes with that she gets everything ready to stick me, tying a tourniquet around my arm and disinfecting the area.

"This is going to hurt a bit," she warns.

"Trust me, I'm a pro at this."

I look away as she sticks me. It's not that I'll pass out if I see the needle go in, but I don't like to see it.

I hear the telltale popping of the vials going in and out. It always makes me cringe. I think it's one of the worst sounds in the world.

She finishes up and sticks a Band-Aid on my arm.

"You can head out the way you came," she says, gathering up my blood and placing it in a holder.

I make my way through the hallway back out into the waiting lobby.

"I'm done," I announce.

"We're done? Ready to go?" Mom asks.

"Yep, all done."

"Thank God, I'm starving," Harlow says, rubbing her stomach dramatically.

"I guess you should've thought about that before you overslept," my mom grumbles, heading for the exit.

It takes us a little while to get back to the parking garage—since it was near the transplant center and we ended up at the lab but, finally, we reach the car.

"What do you girls want to eat?" she asks, starting the car.

"Food," Harlow jokes.

"Well, I'd deduced that much," my mom laughs.

"Honestly, I don't care," Harlow says. "I'm so hungry I'll eat anything."

"What about you?" she asks me, looking in the rearview mirror at me. "Do you want anything in particular?"

I shake my head. "I'm good with whatever."

She sighs. "I swear to God if I pull in somewhere and you guys say you don't want it I'm going to strangle you both," she jokes, pulling out of the garage and into the lane to get out of the hospital.

Twenty minutes later she pulls into the lot of a restaurant. It's one of those chains that has an assortment of all types of food, so I know exactly why she's chosen it.

"Sustenance!" Harlow cries and leaps from the car, running for the entrance as the two of us trail behind her.

My mom shakes her head and mutters to me, "If I could only have a quarter of her energy I could take over the world."

I snort.

"Come on," Harlow cries, holding open the door and waving for us to hurry up. "I'm starving. Let's eat."

We step inside and get led to a table in the back. The lights are muted and sports memorabilia hangs on the walls and from the ceiling.

Harlow buries herself behind the menu, moaning and groaning about how everything sounds good and she's so hungry she knows she could eat it all.

By the time our waitress appears we're all able to place our drink and food orders. My mom might not have been complaining but I know she's hungry too. It took much longer at the hospital than we anticipated, not to mention the drive there.

My mom laces her fingers together and places her elbows on the table, looking across at me.

"Have you thought any more about dancing?" she asks me.

I shrug and let out a sigh. "Three years is a long time to be gone from dance and I'm eighteen now. I honestly . . ." I struggle to find the right words. "I don't feel like it's my passion anymore like it once was. Don't get me wrong, I still love it and enjoy doing it for fun, but I want to do other things."

"Like what?"

"I don't know," I answer honestly. "Nothing major, I'm still planning to go to college next year. But I want to save up some money and travel."

As soon as the words leave my mouth I realize how true they are. I want to see more of the world than my four bedroom walls and the ocean outside them. Now, thanks to this kidney, I have the opportunity to see the world and do things I couldn't have done before. I don't want people to say, "Poor Willa, her kidneys failed and she had to have a transplant." Instead, I want them to say, "Wow, Willa saw, she conquered, and she soared." I want to be remembered for living, not for hiding.

"Travel? Travel where?" she asks, her brows knitting together with worry.

I'm sure this revelation is a shock for her. I've been so dependent on my parents since this happened, needing their support to keep me from giving up, that I'm sure the thought of me leaving is scary for her.

"Yeah," I say, smiling at the waitress as she drops our drinks off. "I don't know where exactly. Maybe Japan," I muse.

"Japan?" she blurts. "Why on Earth would you want to go there?"

"I want to see the Kawachi Fuji Gardens," I explain. "They look magical. I figure it can be like my present to myself for finally getting a kidney. After everything I've been through I think I deserve a vacation, don't you?" I joke.

She sighs but smiles slowly. "Yes, I suppose if anyone in the world deserves a vacation it's you. Your dad and I would pay."

"Thank you, that means a lot. But I only want you guys to help. I want to pay for some of it."

She nods. "I can respect that."

"You should take me with you," Harlow says jokingly.

"You're not setting foot out of this country, young lady. Don't even think about it," our mom warns with a pointed finger.

"Why does she get to leave?" Harlow grumbles.

"Because she's eighteen and legally an adult so I can't stop her—but believe me that won't stop me from worrying myself senseless."

"Oh, Mom, it's not like I'm leaving today. Calm yourself. I don't even have a job yet."

"Well, that's a small comfort."

We're saved from more conversation by the arrival of our food, and since we're all starving we dig in and have no time to talk. It's nice, being with my mom and sister. We don't get times like this often enough and I miss it. So I choose to enjoy the moment, because moments like these are always gone too soon.

Ping.

Ping.

Ping.

I roll from my stomach to my back and immediately flop onto the floor with a small thunk. Thank God my mattress is on the floor or else that would've been loud and I'd probably have hurt myself.

Ping.

I hurry over to my window and lift it up, looking down at Jasper below with a small handful of pebbles cradled in his palm. He looks distraught, and if I didn't know better I'd say he's been crying.

"Are you okay?" I whisper-yell down to him.

He shakes his head. "I need you."

I need you.

Not I need to *talk* to you.

No.

I need you.

I nod. "I'll be right down."

I throw on a sweatshirt—I still haven't returned his and I don't plan on it—and shove my feet into a pair of flip-flops.

Meeting Jasper at the front of the house, we make our same path around the side to the back, finding a seat in the sand.

He draws his knees up, draping his arms over them, and lets out a heavy sigh weighted with pain and worry.

I don't say anything, not wanting to push him.

It's been a few days since we've met like this, and I've missed it, but I know he's not here just to see me. He's sad, visibly shaken.

Placing a hand on his shoulder I rub it softly, feeling the muscle flex and pulse beneath my hand.

He sniffles and looks at me with red-rimmed eyes.

"My mom started cleaning out T.J.'s room today." He lets out a heavy breath and looks away. "I didn't think it would bother me this much, I knew it had to happen eventually, his room couldn't sit there like some sad tomb but … this sucks. It's like seeing the last of him erased right before my eyes. And it got me thinking," he pauses, swallowing thickly. "I can't remember the sound of his laugh. He's only been gone a few months and I already can't remember his laugh. I called his phone today, to hear his voicemail to make sure I at least still remembered the sound of his voice."

"Jasper," I breathe.

The words *I'm sorry* are on the tip of my tongue, and while I *am* sorry I know those aren't the words he wants to hear right now. I know I wouldn't. Sorry doesn't change anything.

"Am I being stupid?" he asks, his voice cracking. "It's only a room."

I shake my head. "You're not stupid and it's more than a room. A person's room is a reflection of their soul, of who they are, it can't be easy to see it disappear."

He clears his throat. "She says she's not getting rid of anything yet, except clothes she's going to donate, but the rest she's packing away so even though it'll be in the house it won't be *there*."

"I can't imagine how you feel, so I won't pretend like I do, but I can tell you if this was Harlow, my soul would be crushed. She's more than my sister, she's my best friend."

He nods, looking back at the ocean.

He grows quiet, so I do too, not wanting to urge him to speak if he doesn't want to. Sometimes, we need a moment to ourselves but we don't want to be alone, either. So, I stay by his side, giving him that comfort and quiet.

CHAPTER TWENTY-FOUR

I jolt awake suddenly and my eyes blink rapidly against the blinding sun.

Why is it so bright?

I place my hands on my bed … no, no that's not my bed, that's definitely a chest.

Why is Jasper in my bed?

As my eyes adjust I see that I'm not in my bed, instead I'm on the beach. Jasper and I clearly fell asleep and now are bodies are entirely entwined together. Beside me he begins to stir awake, his hands tightening against me. He pauses, like I did, wondering why things aren't right.

He blinks his eyes open and looks at me. Up this close I see a small smattering of lightly colored freckles on his nose.

"Hi," he says, his voice husky with sleep.

"Hi," says another voice, but it's not mine.

Both of our heads jerk up and he look up to find my dad standing over us, his mug of coffee in one and the newspaper in the other.

"I was on my way back from getting the paper and I wondered why the gate was open. Now I know."

Jasper jumps up, brushing sand off his clothes and then holds out a hand to help me up.

"I'm so sorry, sir," he rattles. "We lost track of time and must've fallen asleep."

"Sure seems that way, but why were you even here?" My dad tilts his head before slowly bringing his coffee mug to his lips. "Hmm?" he hums when Jasper doesn't reply immediately.

Jasper looks from Dad to me and back again. "Um … I needed to talk to Willa."

"And this conversation was so important it needed to take place in the middle of the night on the beach? Interesting. Care to enlighten me?"

"Dad," I hiss. "Please. It's obvious nothing happened, let it go."

"I'm not going to *let it go,* Willa. This isn't okay with me."

I feel anger bubble up inside me. "Dad," I say again, this time sterner. "I think over the years I've proven I have my head on straight and that I'm a good kid. It's not like I'm out dancing on tables or getting drunk. But I am allowed to have a life. I haven't had one in three years, not a real one anyway, I was too scared and held myself back when I shouldn't have, but now that I am getting out there you have to let me go. I'm not a little girl anymore."

He sighs, his face softening. "But, Willa, you'll be my little girl until the day I die."

"I know that, but it doesn't mean I *am* one. I have to grow up and spread my wings."

He looks over at Jasper and back at me, his jaw tight. "Okay, fine, but this better not happen again."

I nod, because if I open my mouth I'll have to lie. I can't make that promise to him.

He sighs, shaking his head as if he can't believe he has to deal with this kind of stuff and heads back around the side of the house, leaving the two of us alone once more.

"I didn't mean to get you in trouble," Jasper says sadly.

"Don't worry about him. I'm not."

He pulls his phone from his pocket and looks at the time. "I have to go. I'm working at the coffee shop today," he grumbles, stuffing the phone back in his pocket and then running his fingers roughly through the short strands of his hair.

"That reminds me," I sigh. "I need to get a job. I got to thinking—I want to save up and go see those gardens I told you about. The one in Japan."

His smile is blinding. "Really? I think that's awesome. Good for you. And as for the job, I can help."

"Seriously?" I raise a brow. "How?"

"My parents are looking to hire a couple more baristas. I'll put in a good word for you. Swing by the shop this afternoon and my mom will probably interview you."

"That would be awesome. Thank you."

Working at a coffee shop sounds hectic, but fun, especially with Jasper there.

He pulls out his phone and looks at it again. "I don't have to be there for another two hours—think your dad would let you go to breakfast?"

I shrug. "I can ask. The worst he can say is no."

Jasper and I make our way to the front of the house and he sits on the steps while I go inside.

"Dad?" I call out and hear a grunt from the direction of his chair.

I tentatively step in front of him and he lowers the newspaper, looking at me over it.

"Yes?" he prompts.

"I was wondering if I could go to breakfast with Jasper."

He lets out a gruff sigh and I give him a look. Softening, he asks, "Just breakfast?"

"Just breakfast."

He nods. "I don't see anything wrong with that."

"Thank you, thank you, thank you," I cry, bending to hug him.

He squeezes me tight. "Stop growing up."

I laugh. "Sorry, no can do."

He shakes his head. "You girls will be the death of me."

I have no doubt we will be.

I rush up the stairs and into my room, changing quickly out of my pajamas and into a loose T-shirt style dress and tie a plaid shirt around the waist before ditching my flip-flops for my white Converse—although, at this point they're far from white, but that's okay, they tell a story.

Tumbling back down the stairs I call out a last thank you to my dad and dash out the door completely out of breath.

Jasper stands chuckling. "You okay?"

"Yeah," I pant. "Totally fine, why would you ask?" I joke, and he cracks a grin.

"Come on." He holds out a hand to me.

"Where's your car?" I ask, noting the bright yellow Jeep isn't in front of my house.

"I parked down the block in case one of your parents woke up and looked out the window. I didn't think we were going to fall asleep on the beach and give ourselves away anyway."

I laugh, leaning into him as we walk down the sidewalk. Sure enough, I can see the Jeep in the distance.

"That was smart," I say. "The parking thing, not the falling asleep thing."

"I can't believe your dad's letting you go to breakfast." He opens the passenger door of the Jeep for me and I climb inside. It's seriously a workout considering the height of this thing.

When Jasper slides in the driver's side, I say, "Yeah, I'm surprised too if I'm honest, but he must've listened to what I said. Besides, it is only breakfast."

"You good with Mel's again?" he asks, starting the Jeep.

"Absolutely."

I can't help smiling to myself. I love that we seem to have these things that are entirely ours now.

The drive is short, but even still my stomach is growling obnoxiously by the time we arrive.

I follow Jasper to the door and he pulls it open, letting me go in first.

The same booth we sat in before is empty, so I choose it, my butt sliding along the black vinyl.

The same waitress as before appears a few moments later, and Jasper and I both place the same orders we got last time. Him, chocolate chip pancakes and a water and for me blueberry pancakes with a Sprite.

The waitress taps her pen against the pad and smiles at me.

"You know, I have to say how nice it is to see this one here with a girl. He's normally always by himself."

"I have a hard time believing that." I laugh.

Jasper's not only good looking, but kind and smart, he's the kind of guy who cares deeply about his family and friends. I highly doubt there's never been a girl in the picture before.

"Well, if there ever was one she wasn't important enough to come here." She shrugs and disappears.

I look across the table at Jasper and raise a brow. "Is this the time when we have a conversation about former lovers?"

He shakes his head. "I'd rather not."

"For the record, I've never had a boyfriend," I admit. "Just you—not that you're my boyfriend or anything you're … the closest thing I've had I guess."

"I'd like to be," he says quietly. "But I worry I'm not good enough for you."

I snort. "You? *You* not good enough for me? Why?"

"After losing T.J. I'm … not broken, but I'm less than whole and you deserve everything."

"Jasper," I blurt, "you do realize I'm the girl who lost her kidneys. If anyone's not technically whole then it's me—but, honestly, no one's perfect. We all have emotional scars. Anyone that says they don't is a big fat liar."

He smiles slowly. "You're right—and I like you, a lot, and I think you like me, so I'd like to see where this thing goes. Do you want that?"

"I do." I nod. "But I feel like I suck at this whole thing."

"You don't," he promises. "Not by a long shot."

"So ...," I prompt again. "You've never brought another girl here before?"

He shakes his head. "Nope. I dated now and then in high school, but nothing serious. I didn't have the time between school, swimming, and baseball. Besides, no one caught my eye. And last year, college was not what I expected and there was barely time to take a breath let alone go out. People partied and hooked up for sure, but those were the ones not going to class and flunking out. That's not me."

"I think it's awesome you've put your future and passions first. Not enough people do that."

"No, they don't," he agrees. "But I think most people don't know what they want from life. I've always had a good understanding of what I want. Now, with losing T.J. it makes me realize how important it is to be there for the people you care about. When I was gone at college it wasn't like I could come home every weekend, but now I wish I had come back more than I did." He shrugs sadly. "Hindsight sucks, and it is what it is. I know T.J. knew I loved him, and it's not like we didn't talk on the phone or text but ... you should still *see* people. Being there is more important."

"It is," I agree, feeling a pit form in my stomach.

The pit that always rears its ugly head when I think about the fact that I probably have T.J.'s kidney, and here I am sitting right across the table from his brother, too afraid to tell him. Terrified, because I'm falling for this guy. Falling hard, and fast, and I'm more afraid of losing him than I am of the lie, and I think that scares me the most—that I already care so much. The guilt weighs heavily on me too, that even if it wasn't T.J. someone died that night in order for me to live.

The waitress drops off our drinks and I rip the paper off my straw. I dunk the straw into the clear soda and then take the paper, twirling it around my finger.

I'm a liar.

I'm a fraud.

I'm a flat-out terrible person for not telling him, but I can't now, not yet. Not when things are this good. I know that makes me selfish, but I need to enjoy these moments with him for a little while longer before he hates me forever.

"You okay?" he asks, setting his water down after having a sip.

"Yeah." I drop the paper onto the table, now wrinkled and hardly recognizable.

"You got quiet," he comments, raising a brow.

"Just thinking."

He nods. "I get that way sometimes too." Smiling, he leans toward me from across the table. "By the way, my grandparents are begging me to bring you back. They like you."

I blush. "I like them too."

"They're coming up to my parents' house for a cookout at the end of the month. It's like a family tradition. You should come."

"That sounds fun," I agree. "I'd like that."

I know it'll be hard for me being around his family, in fact I can already feel my body seizing up with anxiety at the thought, but his happiness means more than my fear and if he wants me there then I'm going to be there. I can't believe it'll be the end of August already. This summer is passing by faster than I ever expected. It's like I blinked and it's over.

"Here you go, kids." Our waitress places our plates of pancakes on the table.

Both of us drench them in syrup and I dig in like I haven't eaten in a week.

"These are seriously the best pancakes I've ever eaten in my life. How did I never come here before I met you?" I wonder aloud.

Jasper shrugs. "I guess you were meant to find me first, pancakes second." He winks, and I can't help but laugh.

We finish eating, pay, and then Jasper drops me at home reminding me he's going to talk to his parents and he'll let me know if they want me to come in for an interview.

My heart beats erratically as I leave him, because if they say yes then that means I'm possibly meeting my donor's parents.

I wanted to meet them from the start, to thank them for giving me my life back, but as time has gone on the fear grows bigger and bigger. I'm afraid of them hating me for the very gift they gave me, because my life means T.J.'s death.

Receiving an organ is a big deal. Whether it's from someone you know who gives it to you in life out of the goodness of their heart, or someone who passed and had the forethought to think to save others in their absence. It's not something that's taken lightly on anyone's part. I understand what responsibility I have to take care off myself and this organ, because it's a *gift* and every day it thrives inside me is a blessing. It's one more day I get to live like a normal person.

"Have a good breakfast?" Harlow calls out from her room as I top the stairs. Perry pokes his head out from her room and runs toward me, rubbing himself against my legs.

I lean into her doorway. "It was delicious."

"And so was the company?" She wiggles her brows

I laugh. "Yeah, yeah, he's not so bad."

"Do you want to go to the pier?" she asks, setting her laptop onto her bed.

I shake my head. "Jasper is going to see if I can get a job at Cool Beans since his parents own the place. I'm going to shower and get ready in case they call for an interview."

"Oh, okay. I might see if Spencer wants to hang out?" She frames it as a question, biting her lip.

"Doesn't matter to me. I won't tell." I mime, zipping my lips, and she laughs.

"Do you think I'm crazy?" she asks. "For liking him?"

I think for a moment. "No, because if I look back, that first day Spencer spoke to me on the beach … when he mentioned your name his face lit up. I think he's liked you for a long time."

"But he's older than me—he's going to college."

"Jasper is older than me," I reason. "Besides, it's not like you have to marry the guy. You're young. See where it goes."

"You're right. I'm going to text him."

She picks up her phone and I leave her to it.

I take a shower, making sure to shave and lather my body until I smell head to toe of coconut. Then, I spend way more time than usual making sure my hair looks decent and not like a wild chaotic mess. I even put on a little makeup, but I only bother with mascara, some blush, and a pink tinted gloss. As much as I want to wear my usual shorts and tank I decide to put on a dress. If I'm going to get a job I need to look decent.

By the time I'm done Harlow is gone and there's a text on my phone from her explaining Spencer picked her up and they're gone to the movies.

Perry follows me around the house as I tidy things up in an effort to calm my racing nerves. I hate feeling unhinged like this.

Around noon my phone rings and my heart jolts when I see it's Jasper.

"Hey," he says when I answer. "I'm on my lunch break and Mom said for you to come on in. Honestly, I think she wants to meet you. She berated me for not inviting you to dinner one night, but I told her I didn't want you scared away." He laughs warmly.

"Oh, I'm sure she wouldn't scare me away," I breathe with a hint of wary laughter. "I can head in now."

"Cool, I'll be here. The hot tall guy in a lime green baseball cap and black smock."

"Hmm, seems to me like I've seen a lot of guys matching that description at the coffee shop," I joke.

"Better not have," he growls playfully, and I hang up.

"Well, Perry …" I look down at the dog and he looks up at me with his big brown eyes, tilting his head as he listens. "Wish me luck. I'm going to need it."

When I park on the side lot of Cool Beans I take a moment to catch my breath and calm my racing nerves.

Even though I've never interviewed for a job before that's not what has my stomach in knots.

I stretch my fingers in an effort to rid them of the slight tremor they've developed on the ride over here. I can't have them thinking I'm a complete basket case.

There's a knock on my driver's window and I scream, jolting in my seat hard enough that the seatbelt locks.

Jasper busts out laughing as I roll down the window and undo my seatbelt.

"Stop laughing," I groan. "It's not funny. You scared me."

"It's not my fault you're jumpy." He bends down, the brim of his hat shielding his eyes from the sun. "You don't have anything to be nervous about, you know?"

I give him a look that says I hardly believe him. Motioning for him to back up, I roll the window up and shut off the car before stepping outside.

He looks me up and down. "Nice dress."

"If you're being sarcastic I might kick you," I warn him.

He chuckles. "No, you look nice."

I let out a breath. "I wanted to make a good first impression."

He takes my hand and looks down at them, rubbing his thumb against my fingers. "You have nothing to be nervous about." His striking blue-green eyes make contact with mine. "I know you don't believe me, but they'll love you. Besides, Dad's not here, so you only have to meet my mom."

I swallow past the lump in my throat, surprised I don't choke on it.

"We'll go in the back," he says, leading me around the lot and to a door painted the same color lime green as his hat. The door leads to a small back area with a love seat and a table with two chairs. "Wait here." He points to the couch. "I'll grab my mom from the front."

As he walks away my heart beats out of control and my palms sweat.

I'm about to meet T.J.'s mom.

Right now, I can't even think of her as Jasper's mom. All I see in my mind is T.J. The boy I only saw briefly at the beach one day. The boy I never knew. The boy who might've saved my life.

The swinging door across from me opens and a woman around my mom's age steps into the room. She's taller and curvy with long brown hair with lighter streaks from so much time in the sun—I can tell it's natural and not from a hair salon. She's dressed in a Cool Beans black shirt with the logo across the chest, jeans, and a smock tied around her waist.

"You must be Willa." She smiles, holding out a hand. Her eyes crinkle at the corner, and she has this warm presence. Looking at her like this you wouldn't know that she's only recently suffered an incredible loss. "I'm Tessa."

"Y-Yeah, I'm Willa," I stutter, shaking her hand and hoping she can't feel the slight dampness. "It's nice to meet you, Tessa."

"Sit down." She indicates the couch, and I realize after Jasper left I froze and never sat down.

I do as she says, and she pulls one of the chairs up to sit across from me.

"Jasper says you're looking for a job?"

"Yeah—I'm taking the next year off before I go to college and I wanted to work and save money."

"Awesome." She nods. "Have you worked in a coffee shop before?"

I shake my head. "This would be my first job. I've been … sick the last few years and working wasn't an option."

"I see. I'm sorry about that. Well, I see no reason not to hire you. You seem nice and a little shy. Jasper can teach you everything you need to know, and frankly we need the help desperately. I have one last question for you. Are you dating my son?"

I open and close my mouth. "Um … yeah … I think so?" It stupidly comes out as a question

She smiles. "You've been good for him. It hasn't been that long since he lost his brother, but I see a huge difference in him since he met you. At least, I'm assuming it's you."

"I really like him," I say in response. "He's an amazing guy."

She smiles the way only a mother can when thinking of her child. "He is. Anyway, can you start now?"

"Like right now?" She nods. "Um … yeah."

"Great. Come to my office and we'll fill out paperwork."

I follow her to a small side room and thirty minutes later I'm a brand-new employee wearing a shirt over my dress and a hat on my head.

Thankfully, when I enter the coffee shop—behind the counter for the first time ever—it's not busy and no one is in line waiting at the moment. Jasper grins at me in my clothes—I'm sure I look goofy wearing this with a dress—and immediately starts telling me what everything is and showing me how to use the machines.

"There's a book with all the drink recipes, so use that to start but eventually you'll have it all memorized. It doesn't take long I promise."

"You make an awful lot of promises," I joke, bumping his hip with mine as we work side by side.

The rest of the day passes by in a busy blur and by the time Jasper and I are closing the place down I'm exhausted, all in all I had fun.

Jasper flips the sign on the door to CLOSED and I collapse into a chair.

"No, no, no," he chides, "we have to clean first."

"I can't go on," I cry dramatically and then laugh.

He turns up the music on the Bluetooth speaker and moves toward me slyly like a lion stalking its prey.

He holds out his hands to me. "I promise to make it fun."

"There you go again with those promises." I cluck my tongue. "Oh." I jolt when he places a hand at my waist and pulls me flush with his body. Guiding my other hand up, we begin to sway. "What are we doing?" I ask with a laugh.

"Dancing," he says with a tone that implies *obviously*.

"But why? Aren't we supposed to be cleaning?"

He takes my baseball cap off and tosses it on the table. Brushing a hair behind my ear that's come loose from my ponytail, he says, "I decided this was more important."

He lowers his head and presses his lips softly to mine.

"I like this way more than cleaning," I joke as we continue to sway to the song.

He spins me out and then twirls me toward him until my back is to his front. His arms wrap around me and he rests his head on my shoulder. We rock back and forth. I decide to commit every bit of this to my memories because this moment, while simple on the outside, is something I never want to forget.

He spins me again and this time when I come back I'm facing him. I reach up, wrapping my arms around his neck. He dips me down and lingers there for a moment before he presses his lips to my throat. Pulling me upright, he whispers in my ear, "I don't know what conspired to bring you into my life, but I believe we were destined to meet."

I smile at him, my heart leaping. "I think that too."

Something, somewhere, somehow, and someway made sure our paths crossed before T.J. even died. If that's not destiny I don't know what is.

CHAPTER TWENTY-FIVE

Saturday comes, and even though I haven't even worked a full week, I'm exhausted. Cool Beans stays busy almost the whole day with little time to breathe in between customers. It's fun. I love working with Jasper; he makes me laugh and it's more time I get to spend with him. His mom is great too and I quickly find myself feeling like a part of their family.

The problem is I know this feeling can't last. I have to tell him eventually that I think I got T.J.'s kidney. Each day that passes makes it that much harder and I grow more conflicted.

At the end of the summer I'll tell him. That's only a few weeks away. You can do it, Willa. He deserves to know.

I nod with resolve, knowing I have to do this before I suffocate from the stress and worry of what he'll think of me.

As much as I don't want him to hate me for keeping this a secret I mostly don't want him to look at me differently because a part of his brother might live inside me.

"Can I come in?" Harlow asks, poking her head into my room.

"Yeah, yeah," I chant, setting my book aside. I haven't even turned a page in twenty minutes I got so lost in my thoughts.

"You're going out with Jasper tonight, right?" she asks.

"Yeah."

"Do you guys mind giving me a ride? Spencer asked if I could meet him at the beach and you know if I ask Mom or Dad they'll ask too many questions and Dad will have a conniption that I'm hanging out with a boy."

"I'm sure Jasper won't mind, and you know I don't care. We're going to the pier so it's not like it's out of our way."

"Thank you so much," she sighs in relief.

She turns to leave and I call her back. "Harlow?"

"Yeah?" She steps back into my room and I motion for her to sit on my bed with me.

I take a breath, giving myself time to think about how to frame my question.

"Do you think it's wrong that I haven't told Jasper yet that I might have T.J.'s kidney?"

She considers my question, pressing her lips together.

"Yes and no. You've been spending a lot of time with him and you both seem to like each other a lot., On that hand it feels like you should be honest with him. On the other, you haven't known each other *that* long, and you waited over three years for this kidney. That's a long time, and you have every right to be protective over your feelings and emotions because of it. I can see how conflicted you feel. You needed that kidney but you didn't want someone to have to die for you to get it. Unfortunately, that's how the process works, and it's amazing that people and families are generous enough to give others life when they lose a loved one. I honestly think you have every right to protect your feelings and emotions on this. I don't think Jasper's the type to do this, but some people might make you feel guilty for it, because people can be shitty when they're grieving. But at the end of the day, no matter whose kidney that is, you deserve it. You deserve to be happy. You deserve to live."

I can't help it, I start crying.

"Thank you," I say, choked up, and wrap my arms around her. "I low you."

"I low you too." She hugs me back tight. "So much."

I don't know what I did to deserve a sister like Harlow, but I will never take it for granted.

Later that evening, Harlow and I are dressed to go out.

I opt for a pair of ripped blue jeans, a loose tan sweater that falls over my shoulders, and my trusty pair of white Converse. I leave my hair down and wavy and swipe some mascara on my lashes. Harlow wears a flowered romper with her hair pulled back in a low bun. A few stray blonde hairs frame her face.

"How do I look?" she asks, spinning in the hallway.

"Beautiful." I can't believe how much my little sister has grown up. It seems like only yesterday we were playing on the school playgrounds and now here we are.

"You too," she says with a smile.

We say goodbye to our parents and meet Jasper outside.

"Evening, ladies," he says with a bow, dressed in jeans and a loose gray t-shirt. He opens the car door for each of us.

We park beside Spencer's car and Jasper promptly locks the doors so Harlow can't get out.

Looking at her in the rearview mirror, he says, "No funny business. Don't do anything stupid that you'll regret later."

She laughs. "Thanks for the advice *Dad*."

"Just looking out for you." He cracks a grin and unlocks the door.

"See you guys later."

She slips from the car and Spencer greets her with a hug. We watch the two of them disappear onto the beach. Jasper shuts off the Jeep and the two of us head to the pier.

"There's someone I want you to meet," I tell him, tugging on his hand and pulling him in the direction of Julio's shop.

"Should I be jealous?" he jokes.

"Maybe." *Two can play this game.*

The sun is beginning to set, and it bathes the boardwalk in a warm orange glow. The lights glitter and sparkle, reflecting off the ocean below as it laps against the frames.

We reach Julio's shop, the friendly bell chiming above the door.

"Julio?" I call out.

"Ah, my Ms. Willa has come to see me," I hear him speak, and shuffling.

He moves forward slowly, moving around boxes and display cases easily despite his blindness. Julio is not the type to let a handicap stop him from anything.

"There's someone I want you to meet, Julio."

"I sense a strong male presence," he hums. "A warrior. Your protector. Two souls written in the stars destined to cross paths. A tale foretold since the beginning of time, waiting for the right souls to enter this world."

I look up at Jasper and shrug. "This is Julio," I say, like this explains everything. Which it kind of does because Julio is one of a kind.

"I'm Jasper," Jasper introduces himself.

"Jasper," Julio muses. "Jasper and Willa." He clucks his tongue. "I have something for the two of you." He shuffles behind a counter and bends, pulling out a basket. He grabs several items, feeling them until finally he holds them out to us.

"For my friends," he says, and we each take a green leather bracelet. It's braided and smooth.

"Let me pay for these," Jasper says, pulling out his wallet.

"No, no." Julio waves him away. "I cannot charge friends. Friends are family and family does not pay Julio."

"Julio …," I begin, and he tilts his head. "This is green, and green is the color of kidney disease awareness."

"Julio knows," he answers with a gummy smile, the smell of pot clinging to his skin.

"But … *how?* You can't … um … see."

"I don't need my eyes to see, Ms. Willa. Only my heart." He touches his chest.

"You're amazing," I whisper.

"I'm not any more remarkable than the next person," he argues. "I happen to be more aware of my surroundings. I sense things. Most people have their noses buried in their phones. I don't have that so I *see* even if I can't."

"I've missed hanging out with you, Julio."

He chuckles. "Why would you miss an old man like me?"

"You're not old," I argue.

"Oh, I am," he declares. "My spirit is young, but my shell is old."

"Well," I reason, "the spirit is the most important part."

"You have a point, Ms. Willa."

"We better get going," I say. "Give me a hug before I leave."

He chuckles and gives me a hug. "Come back now. Don't forget about me."

"Never." I smile.

"It was nice to meet you," Jasper tells him.

Julio's face suddenly grows serious. "Young man, remember anger is a fleeting emotion, but love? Love is forever. And forgiveness is the greatest gift you can give not only yourself, but the one you love as well."

"Um … thanks," Jasper gives me a quizzical look and I shrug in response.

We leave, the door squeaking shut behind us.

"That was ... uh … interesting," he supplies.

"That's Julio. He's one of a kind."

"That's one way of putting it." He takes my hand and we walk along the boardwalk. It's the weekend so it's busy.

Normally, that would bother me, but with Jasper I don't mind. "What do you want to do first?" he asks.

My eyes get wide and I grin from ear to ear. *"Ice cream."*

He groans playfully. "I should've known."

"Ice cream and coffee are the two most important food groups."

"That they are," he agrees.

I pull him along to my favorite ice cream stand. There are a few people in line so we have to wait.

"What's your favorite ice cream?" I ask him. "This is a very important question and if you say you hate ice cream I'm going to have to reevaluate our relationship."

He chuckles. "No, I love ice cream, believe me. My favorite is chocolate. What's yours?"

"Banana and strawberry." I hum at the very thought of the delicious combination. "And this place has the best."

We move up in line and when it's our turn I order one scoop of banana and one of strawberry on a sugar cone. Jasper gets a cup with two scoops of chocolate.

With our ice cream in hand we move further down the pier and take a seat on an empty bench overlooking the ocean.

"Oh no," I cry, giggling as ice cream drips onto my fingers. I lick it up quickly, determined not to miss out on a delicious drop. "God, I've missed ice cream."

"Why couldn't you have it?" he inquires.

"When your kidneys fail your parathyroid gets out of whack so you have to limit dairy products, plus at room temperature ice cream is liquid so it counts as a fluid."

"I can't imagine," he says, his eyes sad.

"It wasn't so bad. Sometimes I'd crave something bad and it would be hard. That's usually when I'd cheat a bit. I didn't feel bad about it as long as it was only once in a while and I followed my diet in the meantime. I remember one birthday sobbing because all I wanted was a chocolate cake, and chocolate is a no-no. I think I broke my mom's heart because she had to say no. She knew I wouldn't be satisfied with only one piece of birthday cake."

He shakes his head. "I don't know how you've done it. It would be hard to go to sleep one day thinking everything is normal and then wake up the next and have your whole life overturned."

"It wasn't easy. It'll never be easy, but you learn to adapt." I lick another swipe of ice cream as it drips down the cone.

"You inspire me," he confesses, his voice soft. "I wish more people could be like you. You're not … angry about this, and you have every right to be if you wanted. But instead you … I don't know … it's like you handle it all so gracefully. When I found out T.J. died I wanted to destroy everything in my path. But you? You're not like that."

I shrug. "I already lost my kidneys, I lost a chance at a perfectly normal life, but it could be worse. It could *always* be worse. And I'm alive, that's what matters most. And while things will always be different at least I get to live a healthy life. But, most importantly, after this took so much from me I refused to let it take anything else—especially my happiness. If I lose my ability to be happy then I have lost everything."

Before I can blink, his lips are pressed to mine, the taste of chocolate clinging to them.

"What was that for?" I ask breathlessly.

"I had to kiss you."

I feel myself blush and turn my attention back to my ice cream. His fingers brush against my cheek and curl under my chin, gently guiding my head up to look at him.

"Don't get shy on me now." His lips quirk at the corners.

"I can't help it."

"I want to be able to kiss you without you trying to hide from me after."

"I'm sorry," I whisper. "It's … you make me feel things I've never felt before and it scares me too."

"It scares me too," he admits. "But that fear is what tells me how good and right this is."

Boldly, I lean forward and kiss him this time. I let my lips linger against his, savoring the moment. When the kiss breaks our eyes connect and I refuse to look away.

"Better?" I ask.

"Much."

I smile and turn my attention back to my ice cream cone. If I'm being honest, kissing Jasper *might* be better than ice cream. *Might.* Ice cream is damn hard to beat.

We finish our ice cream and continue our trek down the pier, ending up in front of the Ferris wheel. The sky has darkened to a deep purple color with the moon rising and stars twinkling. The lights on the Ferris wheel twinkle, illuminating the area around us. When I look at Jasper, his face glows red and blue as the wheel turns.

He feels my gaze and looks down at me. "You want to get on?"

"Of course," I cry, bouncing the balls of my feet. "I haven't done this in forever. I got kind of afraid of it, but I don't feel scared now. There are far scarier things to be afraid of."

"This has always been one of my favorite places. Up there … nothing else exists. It's you and the whole world spread out before you. There's a peace up there I find nowhere else. I haven't been here since the day after T.J. died. I came here and rode it three times. It sounds dumb but looking out over the ocean and the city helped me see how much beauty is in the world. Even when bad, truly awful things happen, there's still beauty around us if you allow yourself to look. I won't lie, it made me angry at first. Angry that I could see this, experience this, while he couldn't. Some days I still feel that way. I think, thanks to you, I've accepted that bad days will happen but I can't focus on them. I'm allowed to feel angry or sad as long as I don't let it consume me."

"Sometimes you need to scream," I add, and we both smile remembering that first day when he took me to his grandparents' property and we screamed, letting it all out on the edge of a cliff. That moment is one I'll never forget. I literally felt the anger, sadness, fear, and frustration poor out of me in that moment like a faucet of water being turned on.

When it's our turn we sit down and the bar goes across our laps. As we start to ascend the Ferris wheel jolts and I quickly grab Jasper's hand, holding on tight. I know realistically if I fell to my death his hand would do little to help me, but it makes me feel better so that's all that matters.

The higher we go, the more my fear disappears. You'd think it'd be the opposite, but I find there's nothing to be afraid of. Fear is objective anyway. Some people are afraid of a mouse, others fear death, but being scared doesn't conquer anything. You have to shove it away and force yourself out of your comfort zone, and once you do that's usually when you experience something unbelievable.

"It's so amazing up here," I whisper, looking down at the tiny people below. My stomach dips a little, but not enough for me to look up right away. In the distance I see people strolling the beach, couples holding hands, and even lines at food stands.

"It is."

I look over at him and our eyes meet. As we near the top he cups my cheeks and slowly pulls me in until our lips meet. This kiss starts slow, but that small spark soon ignites a fire and by the time we reach the top I think I might spontaneously combust on the spot.

He rests his forehead against mine, his breath tickling my skin. "In the short time I've known you, you've completely unhinged me. I'll never be the same because of you and I mean that in the best possible way. You make me see things in a different light. I find myself being grateful for the simplest things, because each day is a gift and I can find something good in it, because if T.J. has to be gone his life should be celebrated and being depressed about it isn't going to bring him back."

"But you're allowed to be sad sometimes," I remind him.

"Sometimes," he repeats. "But not all the time."

"And if you need to scream, or talk about it, or whatever, I'm here for you."

"And I'm here for you."

As we both turn away, at the same time and completely unplanned, we scream.

It's not a scream like we had that day on the cliff.

That scream was filled with pain, and anger, and pure sorrow.

Not this.

No, this is a cry of a joy.

"Slow down!" I scream, clinging to Jasper's back as he runs on the beach, the pier now behind us as we go in search of Harlow and Spencer. "You're going to drop me," I giggle.

"I'm not going to drop you," he scoffs.

I squeeze my arms around his neck and tighten my legs around his waist.

"But you might choke me to death," he squeaks out.

"Oh, sorry." I loosen my hold and kiss his cheek. "I won't do it again."

He chuckles. "Why do I doubt that?" He continues down the beach, now walking. "Did she say where they were?"

"Just that they were sitting on the beach."

He groans. "Because it's not like the beach is miles long or anything."

"Hey, at least this is fun."

"For me or you?" he jokes.

"Me, of course. But you're strong. You'll survive."

"Yeah, yeah, yeah," he chimes, and I know he's smiling even if I can't see him.

"Ooh, I think that's them." I point in the distance to a couple sitting on the beach, side by side. It's dark enough out now, even with the light from the streets, that I can't be positive.

"Willa!" Harlow waves.

"Yep, that's them."

"Thanks for the confirmation," he jokes. "I didn't gather that when she called out your name."

"You're welcome," I say sassily and hop down from his back.

Harlow and Spencer stand, dusting sand off their butts.

"Hey, Willa. Jasper." Spencer greets us with a tip of his head.

I hug Spencer and turn to Harlow. "Are you ready to go?"

She nods. "Yeah, we better get home before Dad kills us." She rolls her eyes playfully and we both laugh.

Honestly, our dad has lucked out that the two of us haven't been interested in boys until now. I guess it sucks that it's both of us at the same time. Though, he doesn't *actually* know about Spencer.

"Did you guys have fun tonight?" Spencer asks.

Jasper and I exchange a look. I think of the ice cream and our kiss on the Ferris wheel.

"Yeah," we both say at the same time.

Tonight has been fun, but I always have fun with him no matter what we're doing. He's shown me that it's not what you're doing, but the person you're with that makes things the most worthwhile.

We say our goodbyes and Harlow, Jasper, and I walk back to his Jeep.

He drops us off without a minute to spare, and we head up to go to bed.

When I climb into bed I fall asleep almost immediately and sleep deeply. No text or ping of a rock on my window comes, and I know that Jasper too has been able to sleep tonight.

CHAPTER TWENTY-SIX

"Watch out." Jasper passes me buy, three coffees balanced precariously in his hands as he rushes to get them out to customers.

Cool Beans is packed with customers and we can't seem to get things done quick enough. Tessa, Jasper's mom, covers the register and the two of us, along with another employee, Kate, scramble to take care of the orders.

I feel like I'm running around like a crazy person. I'm sure I look deranged. But as quick as I get one drink made there are five others needing to be made.

Jasper, Kate, and I seem to do a dance around each other as we do our best to keep up.

"Please tell me it's going to slow down soon," I beg of Jasper as I scoop ice into a cup.

"We can hope."

"Ugh," I groan.

The only good thing is at least the tip jar is getting full. We all split it evenly, but anything extra is something I can put toward my trip. I get giddy thinking about it. I've never been out of the state, let alone the country, so this is a big deal for me.

I fill the cup with our house blend coffee, add a pump of caramel, and slap a lid on it before calling out the customer's name.

Brushing an escaped hair behind my ear I pick up the next cup and start the order. It didn't take me more than a week to learn the drinks. It felt overwhelming at first but now it's a piece of cake.

An hour later things begin to slow enough that Tessa lets Jasper and me take our lunch break.

We head down the street to Monsterwiches, order our food, and sit outside.

"You know," I begin, unable to stop myself from smiling, "this is where Harlow and I were the day Perry got loose. The first day I met you."

"Everything's come full circle. It's funny, isn't it?"

"Life's weird." I shrug and pick up my sandwich, taking a bite. "This place has the best sandwiches. Seriously, nothing tops it," I say around a mouthful.

So ladylike.

"You're right," he agrees.

"I can't thank you enough for getting me a job, but I did not realize how chaotic a coffee shop is."

"It's nuts, but it makes the day go by faster."

"That's true."

"Well, well, well look who we have here." Meredith pulls up a chair from another table and sits down.

"Hey, Mere," I greet her with a smile, and then swat her hand when she makes a grab for the other half of my sandwich.

"Haven't you heard of sharing?" she jokes.

"I'm starving. Get your own."

"I was *actually* going to get coffee, but then I spotted you two losers here. Shouldn't you be working?"

"We're on our lunch break."

"Right, of course. I knew that." She waves a dismissive hand.

"Do you want to get something to eat?" I ask her.

She shakes her head. "No, I better get my coffee. I'm on my way to the beach. Too bad you guys can't come."

"I know." I frown. "I need more surfing lessons."

Jasper chuckles. "That can be arranged."

"Text me if you guys come to the beach after work. If I'm still there we can hang out." Meredith stands and puts the chair back before hugging me. "Bye." She waves over her shoulder as she heads down the street.

"We can swing by my house after work to get the boards, if you want?" he suggests. "Then I can drop you off back at the shop to get your car after we're done surfing."

"I'm good with that. I have my swimsuit in my car so I can grab it before we go."

We finish our lunch and head back to finish our shift. It's after three when we're done and I grab my beach bag from my car before getting into Jasper's Jeep.

The drive to his house is familiar since I took it nearly three months ago on my quest to meet the potential family of my donor. Looking back, I don't know what possessed me to do that. Now, I feel the furthest thing from brave when it comes to thinking about telling Jasper. But back then I didn't know he was T.J.'s brother.

He pulls in the driveway of his parents' house and pushes a button for the garage door to go up.

"You can come inside to change. No one's home so don't worry, but you can change in my room. It's upstairs, third door on the left. I'll load the boards while you change."

I follow him into the garage and he points me to the door into the house.

Inside it's painted in warm neutral colors with dark rustic hardwood floors. I head toward the front of the house and find a Spanish-style staircase with intricate wrought iron work. I take the stairs up and push the door open on the third door on the left.

It's my first look at Jasper's room and somehow, it's everything I expected and completely different at the same time.

The bed sits against the left wall—which is done in some kind of weathered wood while the rest of the walls are painted a deep blue. The headboard is a dark wood color that contrasts nicely with the gray of his comforter. There's a dresser across from the bed and above it are posters of surfers and pictures with his friends and family posted. There's a desk in the corner with a large iMac and several notebooks and pens littering the top. Overall, it's super clean and neat. Somehow, I expected it to be messier. On the contrary, my room is *far* messier than his and I feel like I need to go home and clean it now.

I turn around and close the door so I can change. Knowing I've probably spent five minutes gawking already and he's bound to come looking for me if I don't get with it.

I change into a red one-piece swimsuit with black piping on it and stuff my discarded clothes into my bag. Heading back downstairs I hear someone in the kitchen and head that way.

"All set?" Jasper asks, pulling two water bottles from the refrigerator.

"Yep." I look around the kitchen that's as warm as the rest of the house with dark cabinets and a cream-colored granite countertop. A row of windows overlooks the backyard, which is surprisingly large with bright green grass, a pergola, and outdoor furniture, set up around a fire pit.

He hands me a water bottle and I follow him back into the garage. We both change into a wetsuit before getting in the Jeep to drive to the beach.

I lean out the window with my arms crossed, my hair blowing in the wind. I can't stop myself from smiling. When I was fourteen and my whole life imploded I always pictured this day. A day when I finally had a kidney and I'd feel better than I ever had. At the time, it was hard believing this day would come true. I knew it had to, that dialysis wasn't forever, and each day was a step closer to transplant, but it wasn't easy. The first few months I cried myself to sleep every night. Not because I was sad, but because I was in mourning. Like I told Jasper, I grieved for the loss of the life I'd never have again. I had to put it to rest and accept that life would always be different, but because it's different doesn't mean it's *bad.* If anything, my life is better because of what I've gone through. I understand things most people don't even begin to grasp even if they live to be one-hundred. While this hasn't been easy, not by a long shot, if you told me that it could be taken all away and it never would've happened … I'd say don't do that. Because the person I am now is stronger, kinder, and more compassionate than I ever could've been if I didn't go through this. Life's full of trials and tribulations, tests to see how we respond; do we become stronger or weaker for it? Sometimes we think we have no choice in the matter, but we do. We always have a choice in how we *react.*

I turn to Jasper as we reach the beach. "I'm going to catch a big wave today and I'm not going to fall down, either."

He chuckles. "You think?"

"I know. If I will it, it'll be." I stick out my tongue and laugh.

He shakes his head. "Whatever you say. But I believe in you. You almost had it last time."

I feel eager to get out on the board and see what I can do. I know I'll never be Jasper's level of good at surfing, but I find that when I'm out there with him I can't think of anything else and that's nice. I like having my mind emptied of all other thoughts.

Gathering the boards, we head for the water. When we reach the ocean Jasper hands me my board and I carry it into the water, setting it down when I'm waist deep and climbing on top. Jasper, with his height, has to wade further into the ocean before he can get on his board. Together we paddle out to wait for a wave.

While we sit on our boards, legs in the water and bobbing up and down from the current, Jasper goes over instructions again. Even though I remember most of what he's taught me, I appreciate the refresher.

"All right, here comes a good one. Paddle, paddle, paddle," he chants.

My arms work hard to propel me through the water. I'm sure this would be easier if I had longer arms, but hey you work with what you got it. It doesn't mean I can't do it, just that it might be more challenging.

I rise up on my board, feeling the wave swell below me.

My legs shake, and I hold my arms out, exclaiming, "Whoa," as I try to maintain my balance.

"You've got this!" Jasper calls out.

I take a breath and find my balance, riding the rest of the wave.

I hear Jasper cheering and I smile so big I'm surprised my face doesn't split into two.

I did it. I actually did it.

A year ago, I never could've imagined this happening, but here we are.

I drop into the water and climb back onto the board, paddling over to Jasper.

"I did it," I exclaim, slightly breathless.

"You did it," he echoes and reaches over, taking my face in his hands so he can kiss me.

I smile against his lips. "Thank you," I breathe. "This is all thanks to you."

He rests his forehead against mine. "No, *you* did this. That was all you. I only helped."

I place my hand over one of his, still pressed to my cheek. In that moment I can only look at him because there aren't words to describe how I feel in this moment. But the way he looks back at me … he knows.

Letting me go, he says, "Next one is mine."

Two hours later we tumble from the water, laughing and unable to stop smiling. My fingers are crinkled and shriveled from the water but I don't care. I managed to catch two more waves but wiped out on most. I'm so happy to have caught *one*, let alone three, that the times I fell don't matter.

We head back to his Jeep and he loads the boards before we take off the wetsuits and pull on our clothes over our swimsuits.

"I'm going to text Meredith and see if she's still here," I tell him.

He nods, wiping his hair with a towel.

Willa: Hey are you still at the beach?

Meredith: Yep. We're setting up a bonfire.

Willa: Where?

Meredith: I'll come find you guys. Where are you parked?

Willa: The usual spot.

Meredith: Be there in 5.

"She still here?" he asks when I put my phone down.

"Yeah—she says they're setting up a bonfire and she'll come find us. I have no idea who she's with, so knowing Meredith this could be a total bust."

He chuckles. "Hey, it's worth checking out. The worst that can happen is we eat some s'mores and I can never say no to that."

"I don't like them."

His jaw drops. "You don't like *s'mores?* Who are you? I went nuts when my mom had a limited time s'mores coffee drink at the shop. I drank that thing every day."

"They gross me out."

"How? It's chocolate? And marshmallows? And graham crackers? Nothing gross there."

"Marshmallows," I shudder.

"Marshmallows? You don't like marshmallows? But … they're marshmallows."

I shrug. "They get all gooey and stretchy and it freaks me out." I nearly gag at the thought.

He shakes his head. "That's it, I need a new girlfriend."

I frown.

"I'm kidding—but seriously, you don't like marshmallows? That's wrong."

"I know it's weird but I don't like them. I like the chocolate, though."

"Well, at least there's that." He cracks a smile.

"Oh, there's Meredith." I point to the red head stumbling through the sand. The sun is beginning to set and the deep orange of it seems to make her glow.

Jasper locks the Jeep and reaches for my hand as we go to meet her.

"My friends," she cries, when we reach her throwing her arms around us in the most awkward three-person hug known to man.

"Meredith," I say in my best Mom voice, "have you been drinking?"

"No … yes … maybe. Just one. Don't judge me," she says holding up three fingers.

I shake my head.

"Don't worry—one of them was for you since you can't drink, and I'll be sure to have one for you later too." She latches onto my free arm, pulling on my slightly to lead me in the right direction too. "I've been thinking too. If one day you two want to have kids, I'll *totally* be your surrogate. I won't even charge you a penny."

I force a laugh and my eyes dart to Jasper in panic. He seems merely amused.

"Thanks for the offer, Meredith, but since I just turned eighteen and all babies aren't a high priority on my list."

"I'm just sayin' when the day comes, I'm your girl."

"Okay, thanks—you're seriously wasted and it's not even dark yet."

"I want to let loose and have some fun," she whines. "So that's what I'm doing."

"Well . . . good."

We finally reach the bonfire and Meredith nearly rips off my arm when she starts to run toward it.

"Oh, sorry. I forgot I was holding on to you." She releases my arm and I rub it.

"That much was obvious," I grumble, already wanting to leave but I refuse to be a Debbie Downer.

Now free of me, she takes off for the bonfire, which is surrounded by people she went to school with. People, that once upon a time, I went to school with too. I recognize a few people from middle school, but none that I knew too well so I don't dare say hi for fear of not being recognized. Talk about embarrassing. So, instead, I cling to Jasper like a life raft.

"I hate things like this," I admit. "I'm way too socially awkward for this."

"We'll have fun," he promises.

"If you say so," I grumble, not believing him.

Music plays and some people dance, but it's not like the dancing Jasper and I did when we went out. No, this is the kind of dancing I fear the most—raunchy grinding of pelvises that looks about as close to sex with your clothes on as you can get.

"Looks like there's drinks over here." Jasper leads me to some coolers. One is filled entirely with different types of beer. Another has water—I guess you have to stay hydrated if you're going to get wasted—and the third has sodas.

Jasper grabs us each a water.

"You can have a beer if you want," I tell him. "I won't get offended."

"Firstly, I have to drive you back to your car so I won't be drinking. Secondly," he pauses, letting out a breath. "I haven't even wanted to look at a beer since T.J. died. If it wasn't for that asshole being wasted out of his mind he wouldn't have killed my brother."

"What happened to the guy?"

"He's in prison. Apparently, T.J. wasn't the first time he's had an accident while drunk. It happened to be the first time he killed someone. You know, sometimes I wonder if he thinks about my brother. If he regrets what he did, ending a kid's life before it ever really started."

I press my lips together. "I hope he does. If he doesn't … well, that's bad and he doesn't deserve to live."

Jasper and I find a place to sit a little way from the chaos but close enough to see the bonfire.

"I always wonder, why so often it's the person that's drunk that walks away from the accident. I mean, they're the one doing something wrong. Not that I want anyone to die, but … it seems unfair that the person doing what they're supposed to, minding their own business, is the one who dies while the drunk walks away unscathed. He was a kid, Willa. This shouldn't have happened. He should be over there with those kids" —he points to the people dancing and those lingering around the fire— "living up his life before he goes to college. Instead, he's gone."

"Things don't seem fair most of the time." I sigh.

"No, they don't."

I could say something about how everything happens for a reason and life goes on, but Jasper knows that already and, in this moment, he needs to feel sad and angry so I let him have that. It's the best gift I can give him.

He looks over at me suddenly, a strange look in his eyes. "Can I take you somewhere?"

"Right now?"

"Yeah."

"But … don't you want s'mores?" I ask, confused

He shakes his head. "Not anymore."

"Um … yeah, okay."

He stands and holds out his hands to help me up. I pick up our water bottles from the sand, not wanting them to get left behind.

I spot Meredith and run over to say goodbye. "If you need a ride home, call me," I whisper in her ear.

She nods and says thanks before beginning to dance once more.

Jasper is waiting for me and the two of us make the trek back to the Jeep.

I don't ask him where we're going as he drives a little way out of the main city of Santa Monica. I'm not afraid, either. Jasper has never done anything that would make me not trust him. I seem to understand that right now he doesn't need to talk.

When he pulls up to a quiet street and parks against the curb I look across and know the reason for everything now.

The cemetery is surrounded by tall wrought iron gates done in what I'd assume is a gothic style. They're imposing but quite beautiful.

Jasper hops out and I follow his lead, meeting him at the front of the Jeep. Taking my hand, we cross the quiet street and stop in front of the gates.

He takes an audible breath and looks at me before pushing open the gate. It squeaks loudly, an ominous echo through the otherwise quiet street.

"It's this way," he says, guiding me to the right.

The cemetery is large and it takes us a couple of minutes of walking before he begins to slow.

He stops in front of a simple headstone.

Thomas James Werth

October 11th, 2000 – May 22nd, 2018

Beloved son and brother.

I look at Jasper and find him working his jaw back and forth.

"You can let it out," I tell him. "Don't hold it in. That only makes it worse."

His lower lip begins to tremble. "Before I met you I would've traded places with him in an instant. Now, sometimes I hate myself for being grateful that I am alive and I got the chance to meet you."

"You shouldn't feel that way. You can't change what happened any more than I can change my situation."

"You're right." He nods, rubbing a tear from his cheek. "Still, he's not here and I am, and that hardly seems fair."

He lets out a scream that's full of anger and pure mourning before dropping to his knees.

"Oh, Jasper," I breathe, my heart breaking for a million different reasons, but mostly because if his brother hadn't died I wouldn't be standing here whole right now.

I sink down beside him, wrapping my arms around his shoulders. He turns to me, his own arms twining around my torso. He rests his head on my shoulder and I feel the dampness of his tears on my bare skin.

It feels wrong to comfort him right now, like I'm doing something dirty while this lie clings to me like a soiled towel. My fingers dig into his shirt, grasping at the material like it's a lifeline.

I begin to cry too, but for different reasons.

I have to tell him, and when I do, I'm going to lose him.

CHAPTER TWENTY-SEVEN

"Today is the day, Willa," I tell my reflection.

My eyes look sad, glazed with the tears that threaten to fall. Taking several deep breaths, I attempt to get myself under control. That day at the cemetery I made up my mind that I'd tell him at the end of the summer—the day of his family's barbeque. I can't let this drag out any longer. The truth hangs like a guillotine over my neck, threatening to fall any second and I can't take the stress and worry any longer.

In hindsight, today probably wasn't the best day to choose to tell him since I'm going to be at his family's house, but I refuse to talk myself out of it now.

This has to end.

Shaking myself free of my thoughts, I finish getting ready. I twist two front pieces of hair into braids and secure them in the back with bobby pins. The rest hangs down in loose waves. For makeup I opt to add a little shimmer to my lids, mascara, and some pink gloss on my lips.

I flick off the light and then move to stand in front of my closet, contemplating what to wear.

I hold a couple of options up to my chest, finally settling on a long mustard-yellow dress with a floral design. It's, once again, a piece of clothing in my closet that is thanks to Meredith.

I slip the dress on and assess my appearance in the mirror, deciding it's perfect.

Dropping to my knees, I rifle through my shoes on the floor, locating an old pair of brown sandals that will pair much better with my dress than my normal pair of flip flops or Converse.

Slipping the shoes on and buckling them at the ankles, I stand and smooth my hands down the front of the dress.

I feel sick at my stomach, knowing what I have to do.

I don't want Jasper to look at me differently. Like I'm a leech, stealing his brother's life. Mostly, I don't want him to hate me, but how can he not? I kept this from him for months while he spoke to me of mourning his brother.

Throwing a hand over my mouth, I run to the toilet and heave into it, but nothing comes out.

Standing, I straighten my rumpled clothing and take a few deep breaths.

I hear my phone chime from my bed and my heart drops.

Jasper is here.

"It's now or never, Willa."

I grab my clutch off my dresser and put my phone in it. My sandals clack on the stairs and I call out, "Bye, see you later."

"Wait, come here a second, Willa," my mom calls out.

I detour into the family room and find my mom and dad on the couch and Harlow lying on the floor on her stomach with Perry curled up beside her.

"Yeah?" I ask.

"Your dad and I have a surprise for you when you get home," my mom says with a smile.

"Oh, really?" I ask intrigued. "Do I get a hint?"

She shakes her head and laughs. "Nope, no hints."

"Do *I* get a surprise?" Harlow jokes, winking at me.

My mom glances at her. "In a couple of years … maybe."

Harlow shrugs and turns a page in her magazine. "I can live with that."

My phone chimes again. "I better go." I point in the direction of the front door. "Jasper's waiting."

"Have fun," Mom tells me.

Dad grunts.

"Dad," I say warningly.

"Have fun," he replies grudgingly.

I stifle a laugh, knowing it's the best I'm going to get.

I hurry outside and into Jasper's waiting Jeep.

"Sorry about that," I say, pulling the seatbelt across my chest. "My parents wanted to talk before I left."

"You're not in trouble, are you? Your dad's not planning to kill me and cut me up into a million pieces?" he jokes, pulling out onto the street.

"No," I laugh. "They told me they have a surprise for me when I get home."

I bite my lip, wondering what it can be.

Now, between that and what I have to do I'm certain I *am* going to be sick—and God that'd be beyond embarrassing and make this day for sure go down as one of the worst. Not *the* worst, certainly, but definitely up there.

"Any clue what it is?"

"Nope, no idea. In fact, I'm kind of worried, but my mom seemed excited so it can't be anything too bad."

We near his house and I notice some cars parked on the street.

"Don't worry," he begins, sensing my unease. "It's not too crowded, my parents, grandparents, and a few family friends."

He parks in the driveway and I follow him to the garage and into the house.

"Mom, I'm back," he calls out, heading for the kitchen.

Inside, I find a smorgasbord of food laid out. Everything from snacks like chips, to veggies and dip, beyond that there's mashed potatoes, hamburgers, hotdogs, grilled chicken, green beans, rolls, and more. How anybody is going to eat this much food is beyond me.

"Grab a plate, Willa," Tessa says with a smile, sticking something in the oven. "Everyone's out back."

Jasper and I load up plates with food—well, he does, mine looks naked next to his since I don't have much of an appetite.

He slides open the back door and we step out onto the patio. He's right, there are not many people.

"Willa," his grandmother cries, throwing her arms around me. I nearly drop my plate but somehow manage to hold on to it and not get any food on her or myself.

"Hey, how are you?"

"Good, good," she chimes, letting me go. "I keep telling Jasper to bring you back by and he hasn't."

"Grandma, I told you we've been busy."

She harrumphs. "Come sit by me, dear," she tells me. "This one can go eat by himself."

"Don't go stealing my girlfriend," he jokes.

I let her guide me over to the patio table where Jasper's grandpa also sits.

"Hey, Granddaddy, you remember Willa," Jasper says, sitting down to which his grandma glares at him. He simply smiles as I sit beside him and his grandma takes the other chair.

Some of their family friends sit on the outdoor couch eating and chatting, not paying us any mind.

"Of course I remember Willa. I'm old, not stupid."

Jasper laughs. "Sorry."

"How have you been?" she asks me.

I push some food around my plate pretending to eat. I feel bad, the food looks and smells delicious, but with the current turmoil rolling around in my stomach I know food is the last thing I need.

"I'm doing good. I got a job at Cool Beans."

"Oh, really?"

"Yeah, I needed a job and Jasper said they needed to hire someone so …" I trail off.

The sliding door opens, and a man steps out in a pair of cargo shorts and short sleeve white T-shirt. I know instantly he must be Jasper's dad. They have the same build and similar face shape—the same curve of their jaw.

"Is everything good?" the man asks. "You must be Willa." He smiles when he sees me. "I'm John." He holds out a hand and I shake it. "Jasper's dad."

"It's nice to finally meet you."

"Make yourself at home," he tells me, his eyes crinkling at the corners. "I'm glad Jasper invited you."

"Thanks. I'm happy to be here."

He goes over to his friends then and I return my attention to pushing my food around the plate.

"Are you not hungry?" Jasper asks, having already devoured half of his plate.

I shake my head. "I think I might be coming down with something," I lie.

He frowns. "You should've told me. You didn't have to come."

"No, no," I rush to reassure him. "I wanted to be here, and besides it's probably from too much sun."

It's a weak excuse, I know, but it's the best I can come up with on short notice. Lying isn't exactly my forte.

Jasper finishes eating and I do the best I can, which isn't much. I throw the rest away, feeling bad since I know his mom went to so much trouble to prepare the meal.

The radio plays and Jasper stands, holding out his hand to me with a smirk.

"Why do you always want to dance with me?"

"Because when I dance with you nothing else exists."

I shake my head and take his hand. He leads me to the center of the grassy area and we begin to dance.

"We look stupid. No one else is dancing."

He lowers his mouth to my ear. "The only time we ever truly look stupid is when we think that. As long as you're having fun and happy all other people see is joy, not stupidity."

The last thing I can feel is joy, not with knowing what I have to tell him. I never should've let it drag on this far. It was selfish of me, but … it's felt so good being with him, and I wanted to hold on to that for as long as I could. For years all I've had is my illness, dialysis, and doctor's appointments. For once, I wanted something that was just for me and Jasper was that for me.

I lay my head against Jasper's chest as we sway. His heart thumps steadily beneath my ear and tears threaten to fall because by the end of tonight that heart will be broken.

Mine too.

"You're shaking," he comments. "Are you sure you're okay? I can take you home?" I look up at him shaking my head. He cups my cheeks. "Willa? Why—"

"Everyone, we have an announcement to make," Jasper's mom says from the top of the patio, her husband beside her. I didn't even hear her come outside I'd been so lost in my thoughts.

Jasper quiets, looking at his parents and I can tell from his inquisitive look he doesn't know what this is about.

Once she has everyone's attention she continues.

"John and I were able to get information on some of T.J.'s organ recipients. Some people opt to be able to be contacted by the donor's family if they wish, and we've been talking about it for a few months, and we've decided we want to meet anyone who'd be interested in meeting us."

The blood in my veins runs cold.

No, no, no, noooo. This is not happening. This can't be happening. Why today of all days? I think I'm going to faint. Or throw up. Oh, God, don't throw up.

I remember so many years ago checking a box saying I'd be agreeable to being contacted by my donor's family. It's not something every hospital offers, because let's face it this is an emotional process, but I liked having the option if they wanted to reach out to me they could. I'd honestly forgotten about it, having filled out that paperwork years ago.

The people around us murmur and cheer, seemingly pleased by this news.

Against me, Jasper's hand flexes at my back. I don't dare look at him.

"We found out one of the recipients was a girl T.J.'s age from right here in Santa Monica."

"What organ?" Jasper asks, his hand falling from my waist and his voice tight with tension.

"I'm not sure—kidney, I think."

Why is this happening to me? Why let him find out like this? This isn't fair!

Jasper glares down at me. "Did you know?" he spits out, hurt and anger leaching into his words. His eyes scream his hurt at me and I hate that I'm the cause. All these months I'd been erasing that look from them and now it's back all because of me.

"Did she know what, sweetie?" his mom asks, clueless, not knowing I have a transplant.

"Did you know?" he asks me again, his voice cracking. "Did you know you had my brother's kidney?"

My lower lip trembles. "I didn't know," I answer honestly. "But I … I saw an article in the newspaper after he died and I … I assumed."

"This is unbelievable." He runs his fingers roughly over the short strands of his hair. "That's why you came here that day? When you ran away?"

I nod, sniffling. "I wanted to meet his family but then you were here and I recognized you from that day Perry ran you over and I … I panicked."

"How could you?"

"I'm sorry," I sob. "I'm so sorry, but I wasn't certain and then we ran into each other again and started hanging out and … I have so much fun with you and I love spending time with you and I got selfish. I didn't want to lose you."

His jaw ticks. "You should've told me, because maybe you wouldn't be losing me now." He pushes past me and bursts into his house.

My tears threaten to choke me. Everyone looks at me, completely shell shocked.

I take off running for the house and burst inside.

"Jasper!" I scream, running toward the stairs.

He pauses halfway up.

"Please, listen to me. You need to understand."

"I don't need to understand anything other than you lied to me. You *lied* to me, Willa. There's a piece of my brother in you and you didn't even tell me." His brows knit together. "Do you not see how messed up that is?"

"I understand if you're grossed out by it—"

"I'm not grossed out by it, but this is something you shouldn't have kept from me. I came to you so many nights and sat with you spilling my heart out, because I trusted you and I lo—well, that's not important now. But you clearly don't feel the same. Go home, Willa. Whatever this is between us … it never really existed in the first place since it was built on lies."

"Jasper," I breathe, my tone begging.

"Go."

He turns his back on me and continues up the rest of the stairs. A moment later I hear the soft click of his bedroom door, which somehow seems even louder than if he'd slammed it.

I stand there for I don't know how long before arms wrap around me.

"Come on, sweetums, let's get you home," his grandma says, guiding me to the door.

Her comforting presence only makes me cry harder.

Jasper's grandparents pull the car alongside the driveway to my house.

"Willa, dear?" his grandma inquires, and I pause with my hand on the knob. "He'll come around. Our Jasper … he's passionate. He loves hard and he hurts harder for it. But he'll see. He'll understand."

"Thank you," I whisper. "But I'm not so sure."

I slip from the car, waving goodbye under the assumption I'll never see them again.

In a matter of minutes, I've lost a whole part of myself I've recently discovered.

I'm resilient. I'll move on. And I'll be stronger for it.

That doesn't mean it doesn't hurt in the meantime.

I let myself into the house and immediately my parents pounce like a bunch of leopards on a defenseless gazelle.

Do leopards even eat gazelle?

"Surprise time," my mom cries, pulling me into the kitchen. She's overflowing with excitement and my dad too wears a huge smile he doesn't normally sport.

They direct me to sit on one of the barstools, totally oblivious to how upset I am.

Harlow sits up from the couch. "Is it time? I want to know what's in the box."

"Get over here then," my mom tells her.

Harlow scurries over, nearly slipping and falling in her sock feet. "I'm okay," she cries upon recovery.

"Here you go."

Mom hands me a small box wrapped neatly in white paper with rainbow polka dots. I shake it, trying to get an idea of what it is but I have no clue.

I tear off the paper finding a small white box. I lift off the lid, confused at what I'm looking at.

At first, I think it's a concert ticket, but I quickly realize that isn't right.

My eyes analyze the symbols and letters and my jaw drops.

"You got me a ticket to Japan?"

My mom claps her hands. "Two tickets. I thought Jasper could go with you."

Dad growls. "Or Meredith, or basically anyone else."

My mom swats him. "Be nice, she likes the boy." Turning to me where I sit in a complete state of shock, she says, "I know you wanted to do this on your own, but your dad and I talked about it and we wanted to do this for you. You deserve it, Willa. We're so proud of the woman you've become."

"Um, what am I?" Harlow points to herself. "Chopped liver?"

"You, young lady, are only about to be a junior in high school so cool your jets," Mom warns Harlow.

"All I'm saying is Paris looks like an awesome city." Harlow holds her hands up innocently.

"Thanks, you guys," I breathe. "I don't know what to say. I … I doubt Jasper will be going with me. He kind of hates me right now."

"Why?" My mom's jaw drops. I look at my dad and the asshole is grinning from ear to ear. If I wasn't so upset I might kick him in the shin.

"He found out, didn't he?" Harlow asks. "Did you tell him or—?"

"Found out what?" my mom asks, her head swiveling between Harlow and me.

"I got his brother's kidney."

"Wait, what?" my dad interjects. "This escalated quickly. How do you even know that?"

"Well, I assumed after I saw the write up in the newspaper that I got T.J.'s kidney. I didn't know at the time Jasper was his brother and then … things spiraled out of control and I fell for him, and it felt impossible to tell him. Then today, his mom announces at the cookout that they're going to be contacting some of the donors who signed up to be contacted if the donor's family wanted and …" I shrug. "I checked yes all those years ago, so here we are."

"Willa," my mom starts, but I can tell she doesn't know what to say.

"It's okay," I say, though it isn't. "Good things never last." I slip off the stool. "Thanks for these." I pick up the box with the tickets.

"They're for two weeks from now," she tells me. "A hotel is already booked too. Maybe it'll be good for you to get away. Just what you need."

"Yeah, maybe."

But we both know nothing, not even my dream trip, can erase this feeling.

CHAPTER TWENTY-EIGHT

Heartbroken doesn't even begin to cover how I feel.

"Cheer up, buttercup, the party has arrived," Meredith chirps, barging into my room.

I lift my head from my pillow, dried tears clinging to my face.

She stops and shakes her head. "Isn't this a pathetic sight? Come on, girl, get your shit together."

"Why are you here?" I ask, my voice cracking as I sit up.

My bed's a mess, the covers twisted around me, and my hair is a complete bird's nest. Perry lies cuddled beside me, always wanting to be close.

"Harlow called me," she supplies. "And I brought ice cream." She shakes the plastic bag she holds.

Harlow pops into my room next like the sound of her name was some sort of summons.

"I thought Meredith could cheer you up. Moping doesn't solve anything, and ice cream makes everything better."

"I do love ice cream. Give it here."

Meredith hands the bag to me and I dig in as the two of them pile on the bed. I hand them each a plastic spoon that Meredith has in the bag so we can share.

"What happened?" Meredith asks.

Tears well in my eyes for the thousandth time but I dam them back so I can fill her in on everything that happened.

"Wow," she says, sucking strawberry ice cream from the spoon. "That's tough. But I mean … he has a right to be angry, don't you think?"

"Of course," I scoff. "I'm not saying that me keeping it a secret was a good thing, but I think he could've tried to listen to where I was coming from. I've been dealing with this since I was fourteen and it hasn't exactly been easy."

"All I'm saying is Jasper's a good guy. He needs to wrap his head around this. Give him time. I'm sure he'll come groveling."

I shake my head, lip quivering. "You didn't see his face."

"I'm sure he was shocked, Willa. Can you honestly blame the guy?"

"I don't want to talk about this right now."

"Oh, come on." She rolls her eyes. "Stop feeling sorry for yourself. You have your *life* back and he lost his brother. I'm sure he feels super conflicted at the moment, so chill the fuck out. I can't deal with you being a Negative Nancy."

I glare at her. "Whose side are you on here?"

She huffs out a breath. "Neither of yours. I think you're both idiots."

"Well, gee thanks."

I eat a spoonful of ice cream and not even it makes me feel better.

That's got to be a first.

"I think we should put a movie on," Harlow suggests.

"Good idea," I mumble, thinking a distraction would be best before I smother my best friend with a pillow.

Harlow runs downstairs and comes up with a stack of movies.

"Which one?" she asks me.

"You pick. I don't care."

She purses her lips but doesn't press me further.

She puts the movie on and the three of us move to the beanbags strewn about my room.

I put the ice cream away, knowing I'll get sick if I eat any more.

Somehow the movie does seem to distract me. When it's over, Harlow puts on another one. I feel better having them here, but I know soon my thoughts will go racing back to what a disaster yesterday was and that look of disbelief, sadness, and anger in Jasper's eyes.

The next day I don't feel much better than I did the day before. But I have to go to work, which means I have to see Jasper, and I can't decide if that's a good thing or a bad thing. I want to make him understand, but I also don't know if I can handle the cold shoulder from him.

I head in the back and then through to the counter.

I stop when one of the baristas that normally works a later shift is there and Jasper is not.

"Where's Jasper?" I blurt before I can stop myself.

The guy looks up at me from where he's bent grabbing something from the mini refrigerator. "He asked to work a different shift so we swapped."

"Oh."

I shouldn't be offended, and yet I am. He's so mad at me he can't even work the same shift as me. I'm probably going to end up getting fired.

This is great.

Anger bubbles up inside me. I can't help but be mad. It's not like I asked for any of this to happen to me. I never wanted my body to fail me or to need someone else's kidney to survive, so why am I being punished for something I can't control?

Surely, he must understand that. I don't have any control over whose kidney I get or when. When the hospital called all I knew was a good kidney was waiting for me and I couldn't pass up the opportunity. It shouldn't make me a bad person for finally getting what my body needs.

I know keeping the fact that I might have his brother's kidney from him wasn't good. I could've handled things differently that's for sure. And he's entitled to want his space, but I don't think I deserve to be shoved to the side like I don't matter.

Because despite what he might believe now, what we've shared these summer months is a connection that can't be replicated. I think we were always meant to cross paths and fate kept shoving us together.

As much as I want to dwell on things, I can't; I have to work.

This is first time I'm not happy being here and I don't like the feeling.

But as they say, the show must go on.

I rap my knuckles against Tessa's office door before I go.

She looks up from her desk and smiles when she sees me, which shocks me. I figured she'd be mad at me too.

"Come in, Willa."

I step inside and take a seat in front of her desk.

"Are you okay?" she asks with motherly concern.

"No," I answer honestly. There's no point in lying.

"I'm so sorry about what happened. If I'd known I wouldn't have announced it like that."

"It's okay. It's not like I advertise the fact I have a transplant so I can't expect for you to have known." Taking a breath, I brace myself. "I wanted to give my two weeks' notice. My parents got me tickets to Japan for two weeks, and … well after all this I don't want to make things difficult for Jasper, so I decided I'll remove myself from the situation so he won't have to worry about avoiding me."

She shakes her head. "Willa, don't quit."

"I don't *want* to, but it's for the best. He hates me and … I can't bear to be around to see that hatred from him. Anyone but him."

She clucks her tongue. "He doesn't hate you, not by a long shot. But it's the ones we care about the most that have the deepest power to hurt us—and hurt is all he feels right now. Jasper is a passionate person. He'll come around."

"I'm not so sure." I can feel the sting of tears piercing my eyes.

"I've known Jasper for almost twenty-one years now." She smiles, her eyes crinkling at the corners. "So, believe me when I say, I know given time he'll see how much he overreacted."

"I hope you're right."

I want her to be right. I want to believe he'll come to me, let me explain, and we'll make up but I can't help but think I've hurt him too badly for that to happen.

"Still want to quit?" She tilts her head slightly to the side, like she's daring me to answer yes.

"No."

"Good girl." She winks. "I'll see you tomorrow."

"Tomorrow," I echo, and leave.

Normally, Jasper and I would be leaving at the same time, and usually instead of going home we'd hang out.

Not today.

Instead, I drive home fighting tears the whole way.

CHAPTER TWENTY-NINE

One solid week passes without me setting my eyes on Jasper.

I send a few texts, he reads them but never responds, so finally I give up on that. I refuse to be that psycho ex-girlfriend everyone talks about.

I spend my free time at the beach, not because I want to be there, but because I'm desperately hoping to catch a glimpse of him.

As much as I miss being with him, I want to speak my peace, and then I think I could move on. If he's going to hate me I should at least have the opportunity to explain myself.

But I never see him, and I think he's purposely avoiding places he thinks he might run into me.

It hurts to think he might be going through so much trouble not to see me.

A frustrated sigh leaves my lips and I clutch my pillow tighter.

I can't believe I'm lying in my bed in the middle of the day doing nothing. I don't even feel like reading. Feeling this lost and out of control isn't a feeling I like very much.

"Ugh," I groan, and throw myself off the bed in a dramatic fashion—although not *that* dramatic considering my bed is practically on the floor already.

I look up at the ceiling, the pages we so lovingly glued up there what feels like so long ago now, but in reality was only a few years ago. Time is a fickle beast like that—at times a minute seems to span a thousand years, and at others a year feels like no more than the blink of an eye.

I push up from the floor, deciding I can't sit around and mope a moment longer.

Changing into workout clothes, I slip on some tennis shoes and go for a run. I haven't run in so long. I've been busy with so many other things and on the go that I brushed it off.

Now, I'm wishing I hadn't.

I'm barely a mile in when my lungs start to burn.

I push past it.

My legs propel me forward, my feet thumping steadily beneath my feet. My breath rattles with each shaky breath I take, but still I push on.

I'm two miles in when I spot a familiar figure also running.

In a pair of shorts, sweat glistening on his back, he runs ahead of me with earphones.

"Jasper," I call out, spurning my legs to go faster so I can catch up. "Jasper!"

On my second yell, he stops and turns around, pulling out an earphone.

My heart drops.

It's not him.

This guy is clearly older now that I pay attention.

"I'm so sorry, I thought you were someone else." The guys gives me a disgruntled look, shoves his earphone back in, and starts running once more.

I stop, placing my hands on my knees as I breathe heavily trying to catch my breath. The ragged inhales and exhales sound scratchy and I berate myself for not keeping up with my exercise regime.

Turning around, I start the two-mile walk back to my house.

It gives me plenty of time to think, and by the time I reach the driveway I feel like my head is clearer. I decide that I can't wait around any longer and I have to try to see Jasper, since waiting around and hoping isn't working.

I don't bother changing, because I'm afraid if I give myself time I'll change my mind. Instead, I grab my keys from the house and get in my car, making the quick drive over to Jasper's.

When I get there, I park on the street and I'm relieved to see his Jeep in the driveway because it means he's home.

I turn the car off and take a second to catch my breath before I get out and slowly make my way to the front door.

I ring the doorbell and it echoes around the house.

I wait, but nothing.

I ring it again.

"Jasper, please!" I call out, knocking on the door. "I need to talk to you!"

I ring the doorbell repeatedly but there's no sign of life.

I squish my eyes closed as tears dampen my cheeks.

Suddenly, I hear movement and open my eyes to look inside the window beside the door. Jasper's silhouette stands imposingly there and I can't help but feel like a small cowering animal.

"Go away, Willa, I don't want to talk to you," he says through the glass.

"Jasper, I need to explain—"

He shakes his head roughly. "There's nothing you need to say. *Nothing.* And let's face it, you're good at saying nothing so why try to change now?"

"Jasper—" Before I can say anything more, he turns and walks away.

I stand there for several minutes waiting and hoping for him to come back, but he doesn't.

Closing my eyes, I decide he's going to hear what I have to say one way or the other.

I head home and take the steps two at a time as I bound up them to my room.

Sitting down at my laptop, I lift the lid and open my camera app, pressing record.

I take a breath, and I begin to speak.

"Um … Willa, have you seen this?" Harlow asks, carrying her laptop into my room.

"What?" I ask, setting my book aside. It takes me a solid five minutes to read one page, but at least I'm reading.

She flops down on my bed beside me, placing her laptop between us.

Immediately, I see my video on her screen and I laugh.

"Of course I've seen this, silly. I kind of recorded it myself."

"That's not what I meant." She rolls her eyes. "Look at the views. It's gone viral."

I look, finding over one million views on the video I posted two weeks ago in the hopes Jasper might see it. I thought maybe he'd be more likely to listen to what I have to say in a video than face to face.

The video starts to play automatically and both of us sit there watching it instead of turning it off.

On the screen I clear my throat, my lips twitching.

"Wow … um … this is awkward … I've never … uh … done this before. Recorded a video, I mean."

I glance at Harlow. "I am so cringy. Why have so many people watched this?"

"Shh," she hushes me.

"This video is for you: Jasper … if you're watching this I'm sure you already know that. You won't talk to me in person, so this was the best thing I could come up with. If you never watch this … well, then at least I know I tried my best. I want you to know that every minute I've spent with you the last three months have been some of the best of my entire life. With you, I felt like *me* again. When I was fourteen and I got the diagnosis of end-stage kidney disease I felt like I lost part of my identity. So much of my life suddenly revolved around my disease. But when I met you, even though you knew about my disease and transplant you never looked at me differently and that meant more to me than you can ever understand." In the video, I begin to cry and wipe away the tears. "A few days after I got my transplant, I saw the newspaper clipping about your brother's death and it said that your parents donated his kidneys. Based on what I knew when the hospital called me that night with a kidney for me I knew in my soul that I'd gotten his kidney. I was determined then to meet his family, to thank them for the selfless sacrifice they made in the face of such a tragic loss. While they lost a son, I gained a life from that."

Even now, watching this I feel myself getting choked up and Harlow lays her head on my shoulder offering me comfort.

"Thanks to the newspaper article I had names and … well, you know how the internet is. You can find anybody. I found out where his parents lived, and I went there to thank them. In hindsight, that probably wasn't very smart of me, but I'd just gotten a transplant and my feelings and emotions were very raw and all over the place. But when I got there … it was you who came to the door. The guy I'd run into before, almost literally, thanks to my silly dog." I shake my head, wetting my lips as the video continues to play. "You were standing there and I felt my heart race and I … I couldn't take it. I felt connected to you in a way I never have with another person and I couldn't face you and I certainly couldn't tell you I thought I had your brother's kidney., I ran away. Then as luck would have it, or maybe it's fate, you saw me on the beach. I tried to get away from you again, but you wouldn't let me. As I got to know you in those early days I kept telling myself I'd tell you whose kidney I thought I had, you deserved to know, but as the shock from the transplant wore off, my defense mechanisms kicked in. I was afraid for how you might judge me if you knew where my kidney came from. I didn't want you to think I was a monster, some sort of leech taking away a life that didn't belong to me. The more time that passed, the harder I fell for you, until now where I can say for certain I'm in love with you. I might be young, but I know what I feel for you is real. You might hate my guts for lying to you, but I only did it because I love you. God, Jasper, do I love you. I love the way you smile. I love the way you laugh. I love the way we can talk for hours and it feels as if no time has passed. I love the way you care about your family. I love everything about you. I love *you*. And I know it's probably too late to tell you all this, but I want you to know. I didn't do this on purpose to hurt you. I wish I'd told you right from the beginning, but I was scared, and surely you can understand that. I don't deserve your forgiveness, but I hope somehow you can find it in your heart to forgive me anyway." I let out a deep breath and I'm silent for a moment before I finish. "My parents got me two tickets to Japan for the following Tuesday. If, by then, you want to see me again, and can find it in your heart to forgive me, one of those tickets is yours. I'll be waiting and hoping at the gate for you—but if you don't show up, I'll never seek you out again and I'll understand that this is truly goodbye. Your mom has your ticket, so all you have to do is ask her for it. I made her promise not to pressure you." I look down, quiet once more. "The last thing I want to say just in case I never get to tell you in person, I love you."

"We're going to miss you so much." My mom squeezes me tight.

"Can't. Breathe," I bite out between squished lungs.

"Sorry." She lets me go and kisses my forehead. "Call us as soon as you land, okay? And when you get to your hotel. And—"

"I promise to give you an entire play by play of everything that happens." I hug her again.

"Be safe, kiddo." My dad hugs me next, the worry evident in his eyes.

I won't lie, I'm worried too. The idea of traveling to a foreign country all by myself is scary to say the least. There's the chance Jasper will show up, but I'm not counting on it. I've learned not to put all my eggs in one basket.

Harlow throws her arms around me next. "I low you," she whispers in my ear.

"I low you too."

I let her go, looking at my family one more time before I head into the airport and through security. Despite telling myself repeatedly not to, I continue to scan the crowd for Jasper. Every time I don't see him I want to kick myself.

I make it to the gate with two hours before my flight leaves.

I take a seat in the corner on purpose so I can kind of hide and it makes it harder to constantly search for Jasper.

Because, I have to face it, there's no chance he's coming.

As the time ticks closer to boarding, my stomach grows heavy. I almost call my parents, begging them to come back and get me, that I can't do this. But I don't give in. This is my dream trip and I'm going hell or high water.

The attendant comes over the intercom, calling everyone to line up to board.

He's not going.

Deep down, I always believed he'd show up, and the fact that he's not here makes my heart shatter all over again.

I thought I hurt before but this is worse, knowing this is it.

I stand up, shrugging my carry-on bag over my shoulder. With my head bowed, fighting tears, I head toward the line.

A steady *thump-thump-thump* echoes and at first, I think it's my heart, but then I realize it's someone running.

My head whips up and my heart stops.

"Wait! I'm coming! Wait!"

With his backpack thumping against his back, Jasper runs to the gate as everyone waiting to board watches with curiosity.

Toward us.

Toward *me.*

"Willa," he calls out.

The way he says my name makes hope bloom in my chest.

He stops in front of me and the two of us stare at each other, neither of us knowing what to say.

"I'm sorry," he whispers. "I'm so sorry. I was so hurt that you didn't confide in me, not when I'd shared so much with you, and I … I snapped. You asked if I could forgive you, but can you forgive me?"

I nod, fighting tears, but for the first time in two weeks, it's happy tears.

"Of course." It's not even a question I could possibly answer no to. While I was hurt and upset, I'm not stupid enough to not see why he felt the way he did.

He cups my cheeks in his large hands and presses his lips to mine. My arms twine around his neck and I kiss him back, standing on my tiptoes.

Cheers and claps reverberate around us from the passengers waiting to board. Jasper smiles against my lips and I can't help but laugh.

I lay my head against his chest, hiding my face as I blush from all the attention.

"I love you," he whispers, pressing his lips lightly against mine again.

Hearing those words leave his lips sends my heart soaring up into the heavens.

"I love you too."

Though, he already knew that. And if I'm honest, I knew he loved me too, because it's love that makes us react in the most irrational of ways, since the one's who we love the most can hurt us the most.

As I cling to him, I can't help but smile. Once upon a time I dreamed of making it to the other side of tomorrow, a time when I'd finally have a transplant and life would truly begin, and now it's here.

EPILOGUE

Eight Months Later.

"Given enough time, things start to make sense.

"Like the whys of why certain things happen.

"The whose of who's most important to you.

"Everything clicks into place like pieces of a puzzle, forming a picture you couldn't see at first, one that creates the image of your life.

"Decisions become easier, and you find yourself growing and changing in unexpected ways.

"A year ago, I was lost. I didn't know who I was or where I was going in life. Not much made sense. I'd been through more in the three years before than most people go through in a lifetime, and it changed me. Sometimes, I thought it changed me for the worst, but I was wrong. It changed me for the better. It taught me more about myself than I ever would've learned otherwise. I got know people who lit up my life and impacted me in unexpected way.

People who I would've never met if my kidneys hadn't failed.

"You see, I've always believed everything happens for a reason.

"This … this was no different.

"Even if you can't understand something at a time, even if you're angry, that's okay because one day it'll all make sense.

"That's why I'm up here speaking to you guys today. I want you to understand it's okay to be afraid. It's okay to fight for what you want. It's okay to follow your dreams no matter what they may be. And it's always—*always* okay to be true to yourself."

Clapping echoes around the high school auditorium and I press my lips together fighting back tears as my first motivational speech comes to a close.

When Jasper and I went to Japan, I did a lot of soul searching and I finally decided I wanted to talk to people about what happened to me, to give them hope, because you don't have to have gone through the same thing to need hope. But more than that, I finally figured out what I'm most meant to do in this world. I think I knew all along but I was scared. Come the fall, I'll start medical school and several years down the road I'll be a transplant surgeon, giving people a second chance at life just like I got.

"Thank you, guys." I wave to the high school students, my heart filled with happiness and pride as I exit to stage right where my family and Jasper wait.

Jasper wraps his arms around me, grinning from ear to ear. "I'm so proud of you."

"You were so good," Harlow takes my hand and squeezes it.

I smile at her, pleased to have her up here with me when she's been going through so much herself the last few months. Getting pregnant her junior year *definitely* wasn't a part of her plans, but she's handling it like a champ. Her belly is still small, barely noticeable, but it's there and soon I'll have a niece or nephew.

"We're so proud of you." My parents pull me into a hug—well, as best as they can with Jasper still holding on tight.

Looking back up at Jasper, he says, "You did it."

I did it.

And you can too.

Spencer and Harlow's story continuing in the standalone The Infiniteness of Yesterday coming soon.

AUTHOR'S END NOTE

Willa's story has been such a labor of love. I loved experiencing how she grew and changed, becoming the person she always was to start with but she refused to see.

Like Willa, I have my good and bad days dealing with my diagnosis. Thankfully, most days are good. I think it's important when going through something like this to not let it consume you. Willa definitely struggled with that and I think it comes from so much time spent alone—I notice when I'm alone is when the bad thoughts get to me the most.

As of writing this it's been over a year since my diagnosis.

When I was in the ER being told my kidneys failed I naively thought transplant would happen quickly.

I never in a million years thought I'd make it to a year without a kidney.

But the truth is the search for a living donor match takes a long time and it's not a guarantee. Even with the people I have testing now nothing is set in stone. In fact, we got the great news my aunt is a perfect blood match (which is AMAZING because trust me they don't use the word perfect often) but with her liver numbers not where they want them they keep checking that to see if it's something treatable where she'll be able to donate and not be affected later in life. The last thing any of us wants is for her to give me a kidney out of the goodness of her heart and end up in kidney failure herself down the road. So now it's a waiting game to see if she is a good candidate to donate or if I have to wait for someone else to step up to the plate … OR if like Willa I have to wait for a deceased donor.

In which case I'd be waiting another three years or so, which, if I'm being honest, is terrifying.

While I switched to peritoneal dialysis a little over a month ago, and I'm truly so happy with this decision, it's not ideal. It's still not as good as having a real working kidney. But it's so much better for me than hemo-dialysis. I hate to say this, but I truly had gotten to the point where I would rather die than continue with it. I hated how tired I was all the time—and not a tired anyone else can know unless they've done dialysis too. It's a strange tired. Bone deep. And you feel so weak all the time. That's due to the fact of how fast the hemo-dialysis pulls and returns the blood from your body as well as going from carrying approximately four pounds of fluid to none. It's HARD on your body. With the peritoneal dialysis it's slow (for me 9 hours every night) and more natural. Not everyone's a candidate for it and not everyone wants to do it and that's fine. I like that there's options though and this has definitely been the best for me. I love that I have energy again and what's crazy is my color is even different. People who saw me on hemo and then after on PD all said my skin color looks so much better.

But if you're someone reading this who's going through this too, I want you to know you're not alone. Don't be afraid to talk to other patients and voice your fears and concerns. Don't keep it bottled inside.

Also, do your research because YOU are your best advocate.

Through all of this I've continued to repeat my life motto to myself.

Everything happens for a reason.

This is something I've told myself since I was a little girl and it couldn't apply more now. Especially now as I wait and hope for a donor. As much as I want it to happen quickly so I can get off dialysis and FEEL like a normal person for the first time in my life (seriously, I didn't know how bad I'd felt for so long because it was normal to me and they tell me if I feel better on dialysis a transplant will change my life) I know it'll happen when the time is right and I have to trust the process. That doesn't mean it's easy, or even that I have to like it at times. But I know one day, I'll look back and this will be just a blip of time.

If anyone out there is going through this and would like to speak to me you can email me at msmeltzer9793@gmail.com or message me on any of my social media.

Unlike Willa, from the beginning I've wanted to be an advocate for education people on kidney disease, dialysis, organ donation, and transplant. A lot of patients are like Willa though and would prefer to pretend it never happened. And everyone's entitled to how they feel.

But for me, I can't get a transplant in the future and act like this never happened to me, because it DID. And I'm not ashamed of it. This has changed me, but for the better, and yes in an ideal world this never would've happened to me or anybody but it did and therefore I want to do what I can to raise awareness. If you're someone reading this that has it in your heart to be a living donor reach out to a transplant hospital near you and speak with them and see if you could be a donor. You'd literally be saving someone's life. There are thousands of people waiting for a kidney, and some will die before they get one. If you don't want to be a living donor, consider being a donor when you die. You can save around EIGHT lives by donating your organs when you die. That's eight people who get a second chance at life. By donating organs and tissue over a hundred people can benefit from it. Organ donation is a beautiful thing. And I'll be honest, I wasn't a donor before this happened to me, but after learning about it I made sure to change that. No one wants my kidneys but everything else seems to be in good working order so they can have that.

I also want to add that when someone in your life has something bad happen to them, be it kidney failure, or cancer, or a death, anything that's life changing try to be there for them. I think we all have the tendency to try to give people space, but by not acknowledging that something has happened you're doing more harm than good. When this happened to me I was amazed by the people who I considered friends who never said one word to me about this, and to this day haven't, while people I haven't spoken to in years were the first to reach out. Just a simple, "I'm thinking of you," let's someone know you care.

But for all the people who have been by my side through this I'll always be so grateful for your love and friendship. It's meant the world to me and without your support this would've been so much harder.

—XOXO Micalea

ACKNOWLEDGEMENTS

First off, thank you to each and every person who has picked up this book. This book is my passion project. It's the most personal book I've written to date. And like I said at the beginning, while this is Willa's story there is a lot of me in it too. I really enjoyed spending time with Willa and Jasper and this story was extremely cathartic to write. I was definitely having a rougher time when I started writing this and Willa and Jasper helped lift my spirit.

Thank you to Regina Wamba for the cover image. As soon as I saw it I had to have it. At the time I didn't know what I was going to use it for, but Willa kept whispering to me it was for her story and it was time to write it. So, I did.

Letitia Hasser, this is the first cover we've ever done together, and you nailed it on the first try. The colors, the emotions, the vibrancy is all exactly what I wanted. I didn't want people to think this book was sad. I meant for this book to be uplifting and I think the cover nails that.

To my Fab Four girls Wendi, Barbara, and Sara … Gah, I love you guys so much. You are my people. Thank you for all the laughs. I don't know what I did before you guys.

My many beta readers who read my books when they're in the roughest state imaginable … You guys ROCK and I love you to pieces. I love that you guys don't sugar coat things and let me know when something doesn't sound right. I trust your opinions so much because I know you love my book babies as much as I do.

Regina Bartley … girl … GIRL. You are my bestest author friend and this last year has been tough for me writing wise, but you're always there for me to talk things through or just to give me support if I need it. I say it all the time but I don't know what I'd do without you.

Emily Wittig—thanks for getting me addicted to K-pop so much so that I had to add it into this book, ha! You've known me since the very beginning of my career and I think back then neither of us could've imagined how the last year would go. I know having you on my side has made it easier. Every time I get a card from you or flowers or just a little something it brightens my day and it's like you always know when I'm in a funk because a little something always seems to show up then. I'd rather get to see you, though, haha! I wish we didn't live so far apart. After all this we need a joint vacation so we can relax and have some fun.

To my readers, it doesn't matter if this is the first book you've picked up of mine, the tenth, or the thirtieth,

I want to say thank you. Because of you guys I get to live my dreams. At a lot of times this past year I thought I was going to have to say goodbye to my dream for a little while. Feeling so exhausted every day made writing so slow and nearly impossible. But I pushed through because it's what I love and I love being able to connect with you guys too.

Shout out to my grandma who I don't thank enough in my books. You are my rock, my best friend, and I know without you I wouldn't have made it this far. I love you and you are my sunshine.

Janiece and David, the best aunt and uncle duo ever. I love you guys with all my heart and knowing you guys have my back through this has meant more to me than you know. And Janiece, the fact that you're still trying to be my donor makes me cry. They've put you through the ringer and a lot of people would've given up and said they didn't want to test anymore, but not you, that's how I know you love me unconditionally and I hope you know I feel the same for you. Even if it doesn't work out, I will ALWAYS remember this and cherish the fact that you care so much. It takes someone with a special heart to donate an organ—family, friend, or stranger. Right now, I'm keeping faith that this might work out. I know there's a chance they'll say you can't, but right now I have to be positive and believe, and I love that you're keeping the faith too. God came to me and told me you're my match. He said it wasn't time yet and soon this would all make sense, that I had to wait. I know He can be wrong, but I'm putting my trust in Him because I have to believe if He truly whispered those words to me (and I think he did after the feeling of peace and awe that settled over me when it happened) that it's going to happen. Who knows, maybe before my twenty-fifth birthday I'll have a kidney. Wouldn't that be awesome?!

Lastly, to anyone who's reading this that's struggling with any sort of illness, disability, loss, *anything*, remember you're not alone. We're all fighting something.

Excerpt from *The Road To Finding Me* by SM Broad

When Aayla can't escape her demons, she takes off for the one place that holds the happiest memories for her.

What she doesn't expect is for her car to break down and the emerald-eyed mechanic who just might be the one to help her believe there's more to her than the evil she fears lives inside.

Can Latham rescue Aayla from her nightmares and her past, or will she run from the best thing that's ever happened to her?

Prologue

The clock on my cable box reads 12:45 a.m.

"What the hell have I done?" I cry to the empty room.

Staring out the window at the dark, rainy May night, I contemplate how my life had come to this. This can't be happening. What started out as my happily-ever-after had turned into every woman's nightmare.

Over our three years together, Brant had turned into a despicable man, but did he really deserve to die? I feel the throb from my split lip and pain radiates in my eye where he backhanded me. I glance down at my torn shirt and sleep shorts, then at the bloody knife in my hand. Brant's body sits, slumped over, on the kitchen floor. I begin to hyperventilate, sucking in breath after breath, but it's no use. I can't pull the oxygen far enough into my lungs to calm myself.

I need to call the cops, they'll help me. They *have* to help me. It was self-defense; he attacked me. Kill or be killed.

That's the way it was, right?

Dropping the knife where I stand, it lands on the

floor with a clatter. I stare at my bloodstained hands in horror before wiping them over and over on my pink cotton shirt, ridding my skin of the red color. I back into the living room to search for my phone, inhaling a breath so deep I feel it in my toes.

Then I dial.

Printed in the USA
CPSIA information can be obtained
at www.ICGtesting.com
LVHW040921091123
763185LV00040B/249

9 781720 907916